PRAISE FOR
A Forever Man

"Readers of Mary Flinn's *The One* will be thrilled to be reacquainted with Kyle and Chelsea Davis in *A Forever Man*. Flinn has given the reader a rare glimpse into a marriage as it grows and changes as well as tests its boundaries. The struggles Kyle and Chelsea face will resonate with anyone who has ever loved or been loved. *A Forever Man* is Flinn's best novel to date."

~Donna Small, author of *Just Between Friends*

"Mary Flinn's *A Forever Man* is by far her most titillating work to date. When a sensuous new employee joins Kyle Davis' construction firm, her designing ways include more than just interiors. But Elise Masters has a secret that puts her in danger time and again. Will Kyle's protective nature force him to rescue her one too many times? Or will his enduring love for his wife, Chelsea, and sons be enough to hold him to his promise of forever? Seductive prose and tempting scenes urge Flinn's avid readers on to a satisfying conclusion for the Davis family saga."

~Laura S. Wharton, author of
Leaving Lukens and _The Pirate's Bastard_

"Just when I thought I would never see Kyle and Chelsea Davis again, Mary Flinn brings them back in *A Forever Man*; they returned like old friends you feel comfortable with no matter how much time has passed, only this time with eight-year-old twin boys, and a new set of life-complications to work through. In this novel, Flinn provides a deft look at marriage when potential infidelity threatens it. *A Forever Man* is Flinn's masterpiece to date, and no reader will be disappointed."

~Tyler R. Tichelaar, Ph.D., and author of
Spirit of the North: a paranormal romance

A Forever MAN

A Novel

Mary Flinn

ISBN: 978-0-9907197-4-8

Editor & Proofreader: Tyler R. Tichelaar, Ph.D.
Cover & About the Author Photo: Jessica Flinn
Back Cover Flap Photo (Fly Fisherman): Mimi Skerrett Williams
Cover Design/Interior Layout: Fusion Creative Works, www.fusioncw.com

Printed in the United States of America

Second Edition 2014

For additional copies, visit: www.TheOneNovel.com

DEDICATION

For Mike

"Oh, what a bitter thing it is to look into happiness with another man's eyes."

– WILLIAM SHAKESPEARE

ACKNOWLEDGMENTS

Many people, whether knowingly or not, play a part in the crafting of my novels. From the man at church whom I've modeled Frank's character after, to the details my daughter, Jessica Flinn, has provided me with about the daily dealings of an interior designer in our dinner table conversations, I am grateful for all of these fortunate beams of inspiration. *A Forever Man* is the result of the characters calling for one last story and the end of the saga, before we all part ways in my head. I think. For now.

Who would have thought that writing *The One* three years ago would lead to the four novels in this series? I certainly would not have called it. If you are reading this, you are probably one of the contributing people who have given me the encouragement and support along the way that I needed to keep the story going. It is gratifying to have a small following, and had I published with a publishing house, as opposed to self-publishing these books, I wonder whether I'd have the good fortune to know my readers as I do. It is a wonderful thing to create a world where a stranger can live as comfortably as I do. The bond between writer and reader breeds a unique intimacy for strangers.

Self-publishing has also given me the opportunity to work at my own pace without deadlines or other imposed pressures that thwart the muse, rather than let it flourish. I owe great thanks to my family for their patient indulgence with my imaginary friends.

Songs and lyrics have always taken me to another place, and I was especially inspired by several songs alluded to in *A Forever Man.* The Band Perry, Adele, Sarah McLachlan, and Eric Clapton's music and song lyrics provided some of the voice for Kyle, Chelsea, and Elise in this book. It is a shame that copyright laws prohibit the use of their lovely words, but hopefully, the ideas get across.

Thanks to fellow authors, editors, and friends, Laura S. Wharton, Jennifer Bateman, and Donna Small, for encouraging me and reading my manuscripts tirelessly, giving advice and support.

I am so grateful to Tyler Tichelaar for his continued wisdom, wit, and sound advice in the editing and proofreading of these pages. I have learned so much from him in the last three years! Shiloh Schroeder of Fusion Creative Works has done it again with her beautiful cover and artful interior layout of this book. Thanks to Jessica Flinn, who created the cover photograph that has captured the essence of my forever man. I could not ask for a better team to help make this book come alive. Thank you also to Patrick Snow, my coach who taught me how to navigate the waters of self-publishing, making my dreams come to reality four times over now.

CONTENTS

Chapter 1

LIFE IN THE FAST LANE

It was the best way possible to wake up, he thought: heavy rain pouring on the metal roof from a spring storm, as they made love before the dawn was even close to breaking. Warm still, Chelsea lay in the crook of his arm now, her hand descending from his chest, her lips at his throat, teasing him for more. Thunder rumbled as he groaned in response to her body's soft curves pressing against him. He needed to get up; his presence was required at work this morning. He stroked her hair, murmuring, "No, baby," and closed his eyes for one more surreal moment before he moved.

Again she moved against him and he rolled toward her, nudging his hip into hers.

"Okay…I want a *girl*," he whispered, letting his lips rest on the small half-moon scar on the crest of her cheek.

After a brief hesitation, she laughed. "*I'm* a girl," she said into his mouth, kissing him and draping her leg over his hip suggestively.

"You know what I mean," he said, catching her sleepy gaze in the darkness, but she closed her eyes intentionally.

"Seriously?" she moaned. "We just now started sleeping through the night. Are you really willing to give all that up again?"

He said nothing further. It was best just to enjoy the moment, this languid, delectable moment they weren't likely to repeat any time soon.

They hadn't had sex like this in what seemed like weeks. With both of them working, life with the twins was a blur at best, and the boys—well, they were boys—kept them busy with the expected and the unexpected.

Suddenly, a crack of thunder bolted Kyle out of the bed onto his feet, reaching for the boxers he'd thrown on the floor an hour ago. He watched as Chelsea did the same, snatching her robe from the foot of the bed, and he allowed himself to enjoy the view of her, dark auburn hair a tumble over her shoulders, and that amazing body…damn! She still had it at almost thirty-five. People said she didn't age, and he agreed with them; she got better.

Surely after that crack of thunder, it would only be moments before the boys would appear from their room downstairs with Foscoe in tow. The yellow lab usually spent the night between the boys' two beds. Only recently had the eight-year-olds been able to sleep through the night; a sleeping bag on the floor of their parents' bedroom was evidence that they'd not mastered it yet. Stu was the worst, always finding his way into one bad dream or another. Chelsea suspected his clock was just off, and that cat-naps were programmed into his sleep patterns, but Kyle was getting awfully tired of the whole thing. He thought of Chelsea's comment about wanting her own room at that age, far away from her sister; but the twins had not slept any better in separate bedrooms. Moments passed, but no sound came from below.

They sat together on her side of the bed, waiting. She glanced at him, listening, whispering, "This is too good to be true. Should we check on them?"

"I'll go, if you'll start the coffee."

She stopped him before he left the room, slipping her arm around his waist, stealing one more kiss. "Damn!" he said into her mouth. Unable to resist her, he pushed her back on the bed, untying the robe, kissing her back, finding her breasts and sucking hard on one for a moment, making her dissolve into laughter. She was so cute when she played like this. He backed off the bed and threw up his hands in defense.

"You'll have to answer to Frank if I'm late."

She propped herself up on her elbows, making no move to cover herself. "So? I can deal with Frank…and *you*," she laughed, tossing her hair. He rolled his eyes, leaving their bedroom, and padded downstairs to check on Ty and Stu. The door was cracked enough to let in the light from the stairway, as they'd always left it. Upon peeking through the doorway, he could make out Foscoe's pale shape on the floor at the end of one of the beds. His tail thumped on the floor; otherwise, he made no move, only regarded Kyle with dark eyes, half-open, settling his tongue audibly. The boys were piled together in Ty's bed, still sleeping soundlessly. Kyle said a silent prayer of thanks, combined with long-awaited relief that they were getting somewhere with this sleep dilemma. If the boys could make it through a thunderstorm, that had to be a victory of sorts.

As quietly as possible, he crept back upstairs, avoiding the two that creaked. Chelsea smiled, handing him a mug of bold, steaming coffee, and he followed her to the large window in the cabin's living room to watch the rain, falling softly now. She nestled herself into his warm arm, extended to welcome her once again. "I love you," he whispered into her hair, breathing deeply of her sweet scent.

"I love you, too," she said into his shoulder, kissing him there. "They can't be sleeping."

"Yes, they are, unbelievably."

"You should get your shower. But make it a quick one. I think it's safe now. I haven't seen any lightning, and it's been a few minutes since the thunder. Let's see if they make it until their alarm goes off."

"Okay," he said, reluctantly releasing her and walking through the bedroom into their bathroom.

"What's going on today at work? I guess you won't be out in this mess," she said, following him, brushing her hair as he started the shower.

"No. We're interviewing another designer this morning," he said, thinking sadly that Faith, Frank's wife and the interior designer of their design and build firm, would be leaving. She'd wanted to spend more time with their grandchildren, knowing how fast they would grow and not wanting to miss any of it. Frank and she were doing well enough that they'd agreed she should follow her passion. The firm could save money too, hiring someone younger with less experience, and plenty of candidates were out there with the economy in such a slump. He was happy for them, but still, it was like the family was dissolving.

He showered quickly, and then wrapped his towel around him, as Chelsea returned to the bathroom with her coffee cup. She would take her turn before waking the boys.

"There's an English muffin in the toaster oven for you. Should I pack you a lunch, or are you going out to lunch today with your new candidate?"

"Thanks, and yes, I think we are going out, with or without her. I'm meeting Glen after work too, for a quick beer, remember? But I promise to be back in time for dinner."

"Oh…right. I have fajitas marinating. They'll be quick to fix. We'll need to be at the theater at 7:30," she said, examining her eyes in the bathroom mirror, searching for the crow's feet she swore were there.

Flicking water from his hair, he grinned at her in the mirror. "Are you still feeling *dull and drab* after what we just did?" He teased her about her recent lament over her approaching thirty-fifth birthday. He knew she was as tired as he was, but he allowed no self-pitying talk from her. After almost ten years of marriage, he knew how to handle her.

She reached out and yanked off his towel, making him retaliate by pulling open her robe, scanning her body for the purple blotch he'd made on her left breast. It was then that Ty chose to make his entrance, shouting, "Mom!" Kyle pulled his towel back in place as the blond head appeared through the door, followed by Foscoe.

"You'd better knock, buddy, or you'll see something you don't want to see," his father warned.

"Ew! Thanks for the warning. Is Maddie coming tonight?" Ty meant their favorite babysitter, a college student who babysat them during the summer when Chelsea taught dance classes at the university.

"Yes," Chelsea said, tying her robe discreetly. "You need to get dressed for school, and you and Stu had better make your beds and pick up your rooms. Is Stu up yet?" Ty shook his head. "Oh, and *congratulations*! You guys slept through the night again. Two more nights in a row and we get to go out for pizza!"

Ty hugged her around the waist as she slipped her fingers through his hair. It was darkening from the tow-headed blond he'd had as a toddler. "That was the deal, right?" she reminded him.

"Yep," Ty said, apparently thinking about it while clinging to her a moment longer, making her smile. He was the reflective one, the lover, Kyle thought and ruffled his hair, too.

"All right, man, go get dressed, and do what Mom said," he added, going to the closet to get dressed.

"Hospital corners!" she reminded Ty; even Kyle made a face at her.

"What? If they don't learn these things now, they never will care to. And who is going to marry them if they're pigs?"

"Okay..." he said indulgently. Chelsea had taken on motherhood with all the tenacity of a lioness, and he had learned not to stand in her way. Occasionally, he felt left out by the thoroughness of her leadership, but he knew his boys were better for her efforts. When he'd married her, he'd had no idea how opinionated she was, or how seriously she took her values, but motherhood had brought all that to the forefront. In a strange way, he was relieved that she took the burden off him, never leveraging him against his sons, but commanding his support when it was needed. An independent woman was a blessing. Twins were tough!

It did no good to wash the car, Kyle thought ruefully, as muddy water splashed noisily under the Explorer's fender on the way in to work. Sighing, he reminded himself that this much rain would be good to fill the river for the best fly fishing. His sons were intrigued with his addiction to the sport, making him even more anxious to take them out to practice their casts the following day. *Saturday.* Saturday was his day with Stu and Ty; his day to bond with them and make a father's impression. The boys looked forward to these excursions as much as Kyle did. They might even catch something. After tonight, he knew Chelsea would want to sleep in, so he'd get up early and make chocolate chip pancakes for the boys and a big pot of coffee for himself, he thought. The windshield wipers flapped in time with his brain, building a cadence for the day, getting his head on for the encounter with the new candidate for the job of interior designer.

They'd had a few interviews already. Mostly, the applicants were girls ready to graduate from Appalachian State University's program, with no experience but plenty of enthusiasm and willingness to work for anything since jobs were scarce and anxieties were high. So far, they all seemed adequate, although no one had stood out as truly exceptional, making him dread the training he knew would fall to him, being the "people person" he was, the architect, and the only other person in the firm to do the job Frank would loathe.

"*Been there, done that*," he muttered, quoting Frank, as he pulled into the parking lot behind the Mountaineer Builders office on King Street. He'd remembered the phone conference they'd had with Professor McHugh the previous day about this girl. "*You don't want to let this one slip through your fingers. She's got a gift. With her experience, you'd be foolish to let her get away*," he'd said about his former student, who'd fallen prey to the tanking economy, a girl who'd lost her job in a downsizing move a company in Charlotte had made months before.

As usual, Faith was the first to arrive at work, already there, making coffee in the breakroom. He smelled her perfume before he heard the familiar bustling sounds of her in the kitchen.

"Hey, darlin'!" she called out as he closed the door behind him, shaking raindrops out of his hair.

"Hey, Faith!" he greeted her, grinning as she appeared, colorful as ever. Today, she wore the typical black pants with a brightly patterned jacket that reminded him of stained glass windows, doing what it could to minimize her stout figure. She rearranged her gray-blond hair, which curled softly around her round face, and removed the red reading glasses that hung on a beaded chain. Her ever-present smile warmed him instantly as she reached up to do the same to his hair.

"Is it still coming down out there?" she asked cheerfully, attempting to smooth down a stubborn lock.

"Oh, yeah," he said, used to her grooming him, as if he were one of her boys. He stepped into his office and logged into his computer, starting his music, and checking emails. "Where's Frank?" he asked as John Mayer began to play softly; morning music.

"He decided to stop by Stick Boys to pick up some pastries for this morning. Here, I made you a copy of Elise Masters' resume," Faith said, breezing into his office, handing him a sheet of paper. He'd seen it, of course, in preparation for the day, but he had not printed a copy. "Honey, this girl's going to run rings around what I can do with her knowledge of the new technologies. And unlike the others we've talked to, she's actually *used it* with real projects."

He smiled to himself as she swished out of the room. "I'm going to miss you, Faith," he said softly. The coffeepot beeped three times to signal it was finished brewing, so he followed her into the breakroom to pour himself a cup as the door chimed and Frank made a noisy entrance.

They greeted one another as Frank brought an assortment of Danishes and scones into the small kitchen to the appreciative moans of the others. "Are those bear claws?" Kyle asked hopefully. Frank nodded.

"You're trying to make me fat!" laughed Faith. Frank winked at her. They were both constantly battling their weight, and with these daily indulgences, it was a losing endeavor and they knew it. But they didn't care. Faith rummaged in the cabinets, setting out paper plates and napkins in the conference room for the upcoming interview. "Do you suppose she'll be dragging in all those display boards in this rain?" she muttered to no one in particular, wiping her hands on a towel from where she'd cleaned in the kitchen. Ledges were on the walls for just such a purpose, but lately, much of what they did was on a computer, so they had painted the wall a matte cream color to be used as a projection screen, which saved both labor and storage. Faith eyed the treats one last time before retreating to her own office.

Frank sat down across from Kyle's desk. "I talked to Ed Tarleton, Elise's former boss, yesterday," he said, fluffing his close-cropped white hair to expel the raindrops.

"Yeah? What's the word on her?" Kyle asked.

"He said he hated to let her go. You know, last one hired, first one fired; that kind of thing. But he said she was the best designer he had and the hardest working. She's got a young daughter and no husband, so everything is on the line for her."

"That sucks," Kyle muttered.

"She's not like some of these young'uns that think they're entitled to everything on a silver platter for top pay. He said he'd highly recommend her, and that if he could take her back, he'd do it in a heartbeat."

"Hmmm. If she's that good, are you going to make her an offer today?"

Frank tossed a sheet of paper across the desk with a salary figure. Kyle raised his eyebrows and nodded, while studying Frank carefully.

"It's a partnership decision, my friend. We'll see," Frank said with a wink. "Okay? We'll do the coffee thing in the gathering room and head to the conference room when we get down to business."

Kyle nodded, watching Frank leave. He made a quick call to check on his subcontractors who were in the beginnings of a project, indoors, thankfully. Confident they could carry on without him, he looked over his emails, finally clicking open a file he'd been working on, a two-story house with a basement and an elevator for handicapped accessibility, perfect for a family with a lower level in-law suite that looked out over a small lake. He was distracted by a phone call he was expecting from the hotel concierge, and closed the file when he heard the front door chime at 10:00 on the dot, announcing the arrival of their candidate, and Faith's cheerful greeting. She had worn many hats in addition to interior designer—receptionist, coffee maker, and mother. She'd been the glue that had held them together. Faith Maynard had probably been instrumental in his own promotion to partner five years ago, which had endeared her to Kyle even more.

He stood, re-tucked his shirttail, and rearranged his tie as he stepped into the gathering room, taking in the tall, slender young woman who looked his way with interest.

"Elise, I'd like you to meet Kyle Davis," Faith was saying carefully, to make sure everyone got the names right. "Kyle is our architect. Kyle, this is Elise Masters," she said, smiling serenely, proud of this candidate she'd found, thanks to her continued relationship with Kenneth McHugh from the school of design at Appalachian State University.

Damn! He was unprepared for the woman who stood before him. Kyle extended his hand and took Elise's; her fingers were cold from the rain; otherwise, the handshake felt sure. Her hand fit his like a glove, as if they'd done this many times before. She met his gaze with cool green-brown eyes. They reminded him of the color of the river on a sunny day, sparkling, like the shallows where you could see flecks of small stones below the surface. Still, they were cool, tentative, taking him in without emotion.

"Hello. It's very nice to meet you, Elise," he said, remembering to release her hand, and swallowing, oddly thrown off by her appearance. The phrase "abundant hair" ran through his mind from novels he'd read in school. Hers was exactly the color of his, light brown with streaks of gold from the sun, not created in any hair salon, but real, and also like the river, swirling around her shoulders in layers. Her legs were long and shapely, and in her pumps, she was tall enough to look him straight in the eye. She wore a sharp-looking dress with a V-neck and a gold necklace that disappeared where he shouldn't look.

"Hello, Kyle," she said pleasantly, and he liked the sound of her voice, smooth and silky, not like the grating tone of the student they'd met on Tuesday with the nervous cackling laugh that distracted them all. "It's nice meeting you, too."

She did not smile until Frank appeared. Everyone smiled at the sight of Frank. He was tanned and prematurely white-haired, with the fun deep-set eyes and grin that made you think he was always up to something. Although short and stocky, he looked good in the sport coat and tie he'd gone to the trouble of wearing today. Kyle had only managed the tie. Sport coats were for big clients or business dinners, and this didn't count. They exchanged pleasantries, and then Faith began offering coffee and pastries. Elise accepted the coffee, looking reluctantly at the pastries, settling on a blueberry scone. Kyle refilled his cup and they seated themselves in the gathering room, chatting about the rain and Elise's slow drive up from Charlotte. Kyle noticed she came unencumbered by the usual portfolio of design boards that most of the others had brought. She took a sip of her coffee, sniffing just a bit, making him wonder whether she didn't like it; then she took a bite of the scone, wiping her fingers on the napkin in her lap. It wasn't fair to offer people food and then expect them to talk, he thought, watching her field the first of the questions.

"I worked for Tarleton Designs for about three years before they let me go. I designed everything from kitchens and bathrooms to custom homes and total renovations of older homes. I love renovations. They're the most challenging. Right now, I live at home with my parents in Charlotte. They help me out with my daughter, Lydia. She has special needs so I've needed their help. It's getting easier as she gets older, and I feel confident we can exist on our own at this point," she explained.

Exist, he thought.

"Oh? How old is Lydia?" Faith asked.

"She'll be seven in late October," she answered, making Kyle wonder how old Elise was. He had thought she was around twenty-five.

"So you'll be looking into schools for her if you relocate," Frank said, no doubt recalling all the discussions he'd had with his own children about the grandkids Kyle had heard about.

"Yes…it's somewhat of a concern. She doesn't need a special class, yet, but she requires therapies that are offered by the schools. They're offered in every school, but I've learned that some therapists are better than others, just like teachers," she said, her voice trailing off, leading Kyle to think she hadn't had the best experiences. "Lydia is very adaptable, but learning is hard for her. She has some developmental delays that hold her back from other kids her age."

"Well, I'm sure you'll be able to find the right fit here in Boone. Our school of education at ASU is excellent, as you probably know, and the trend has trickled into the schools here," Faith said, the warm smile reappearing. "When the weather is bad in the winter, we typically work from home. That way, you can stay with your daughter if school is cancelled."

"That's wonderful. So, tell me about what you do here," Elise said. "I've seen the website and some of the pictures of places you've built or renovated."

Interesting, he thought; none of the others had taken the upper hand at this point in the interview. Maybe she was shifting the attention from herself. She didn't appear to be needy, although she had every reason to be.

"Well," Kyle began as Frank gestured his way, "we do a mix of residential and commercial, although the commercial stuff is mostly inns, bed and breakfasts, and condos, sometimes office buildings. There are as many renovations as there are custom new builds, so we do it all. My specialty is historic restoration. There are some interesting buildings up here; lots of stone, which was a natural resource in a lot of the older homes. Then there are the places without plumbing that we've dealt with," he said, nodding to confirm his story at her incredulous look. "Oh, there's nothing more charming than a home with a matching privy!" he said, grinning, making her smile at him. It was unnerving, as beautiful as it was.

"We could tell you plenty of stories!" laughed Faith. "I guess you don't have much of that in Charlotte."

"No, I can honestly say I've never seen the inside of a privy!" Elise said, throwing her lovely smile toward Frank and Faith. Then, she said, "I brought some of my designs if you'd like to take a look."

When they nodded, she reached inside her large tote bag, producing a flat case, from which she drew out a computer tablet, opening the cover and touching the power button. "Is there somewhere we can plug this in to project some images?"

"Sure," Kyle said, getting to his feet and leading the way to the conference room, assisting her with her computer's operation. He dimmed the lights as her slide show began.

She narrated through drawings and photographs of various kitchens and baths in several houses. Total remodels appeared next, looking like pictures he had seen in *Architectural Digest*. They were impressive, reminding him that her clients must have had plenty of money for her to pull out all the stops as she had. He liked her subtle style. It was calming, alluding to his passion for sustainability and his love of Nature. And she was as talented as her references reported.

"We have clients with similar resources here as well," he murmured beside her. "But you'll find they desire an even more rustic look than what I'm seeing here, for the most part, that is. Your work is very impressive. It has a peaceful style about it...."

"Mmm-hmm," Frank agreed, while Faith looked on with an index finger at her mouth. "You'll have to readjust your style for some of our folks, maybe, but we have our share of high rollers too."

"How do you like this?" Elise asked, scrolling to another set of photographs. "These are from a house we did at Lake Norman, which shows a bit more of my rustic style."

"Nice," said Frank.

"These are lovely," commented Faith. "The art work is wonderful. The colors really blend with the water you can see from the window views."

"And remember, I went to school here, so I know what you're talking about. It wouldn't take long to switch back to my...*roots*, for lack of a better word," said Elise, a smile starting to form. Kyle glanced over at the resume on the table; she answered his unspoken question quickly. "I've been out of school for five years." So she was about twenty-seven and had a seven-year old daughter. She caught him making the calculations, and smiled, offering nothing. It was none of his business. She tossed the swirl of brown hair over her shoulder and addressed them. "Is there anything else you'd like to see?"

"Let's talk about how you handle difficult clients," Frank started. "We don't have any of those, of course, but what would you do if we did?" he asked, eyes twinkling. She shared his amusement.

"I try to de-escalate as much as possible. It's something I've learned from being a mom. The angrier they are, the more I let them talk. Sometimes, people just need to vent. When they're done, I affirm everything they've said, and I offer some reasonable solution, and if the situation is right, I throw in a little humor…self-deprecating, of course!"

Frank liked her response and continued playing devil's advocate. "So…what if you're the one who's pissed off?"

"Oh, that never happens," she said matter-of-factly, making them all laugh. She cast her eyes about for the answer. "Usually, the angrier I am, the softer I talk. It helps me de-escalate myself. And it works on them, too."

"Hmmm. Good to know!" Frank said, winking at her, then nodding to Kyle.

"Seriously, though, I think I'm a good listener. And the clients appreciate being heard. I get a lot of what they want by letting them talk about themselves. Often, they don't really know what they want, but their personalities come through in the conversation." The three of them mulled this over, nodding. It was the same approach Kyle used, too. They should get along well. Her eye contact was sincere and engaging. He felt a connection with her immediately. He thought Frank was getting the same vibe from her as well. Faith was glowing.

After a moment, Elise asked earnestly, "Who makes the coffee?"

Faith laughed. "I do," she said, crinkling up her nose. "My role has always been office manager, and keeping these two in line, aside from my design responsibilities. You have to keep an eye on Frank to make sure he's working, and then keep a watch on Kyle to make sure he remembers to go home!"

They laughed again, but Kyle detected a question in Elise's river eyes.

"I get over-focused when I'm on a project, I guess. I love going home, actually," he added to reassure her of his happiness at home. *Why was it necessary to throw that in?* he wondered.

"I can make coffee," she said, as if it were no big deal, letting his statement register. "And I like running things, so office manager sounds good to me," she said, directing her statement to Kyle.

Frank shoved his hands in his pockets. "So Elise, how long will you be staying in Boone?"

"Well, I'm heading back today. I don't know anyone up here anymore, so I'm going straight home."

"Oh, that makes for a long day. Hopefully, the rain will stop so you can have an easy trip back," Faith said.

Frank glanced at Kyle and they nodded slightly. "Would you like to join us for lunch? We haven't talked salary or benefits yet."

Elise looked infinitely relieved, saying, "Yes, that would be great."

Kyle unplugged her computer, which she took from him, placing it neatly back in its case, ready to go. He liked this low-maintenance style of hers; efficient without being fussy. He could definitely live with this, and Frank was looking as smitten as a kid with a new pup.

Faith clasped her hands together as she peeked out the window. "Oh look! It's stopped raining."

Chapter 2

CHIVALRY

At 4:45 p.m., as planned, Kyle wandered into the Mexican restaurant, looking around for Glen Dunham, his best friend since high school. This place had the coldest Dos Equis in town, so it was their favorite watering hole. As predicted, he found Glen in the back corner in a booth, facing the wall. Smiling inwardly, Kyle found it amusing that Glen was always lying low, trying to protect his reputation as a deputy sheriff.

"Hola, amigo. Is this a stakeout?" Kyle asked with brows raised as he slid into the booth opposite his friend.

"Hah! You found me. What's happenin'?" Glen exclaimed, clasping Kyle's hand in greeting.

"Oh, not much. It was a good day at the office. What about you?"

"It was my day off, so the kids and I had fun. When Abby got back from shopping, I worked out a little at the gym. Ready for our 'club meeting.'"

They'd gone from calling themselves "Dads with Doubles" to "Morons with Multiples" after Glen and Abby's triplets were born four years ago. After a few awkward years of desperately wanting children, Abby's fertility drugs had kicked in and she'd ironically scored three babies at one time. It had been awkward because Chelsea had never experienced difficulty getting pregnant, which had put a strain on her relationship with Abby. Now they had more children between the two families than any of them had bargained for. The friends had tried to stay in touch, but whenever they were together, there was always a crowd. Parks, hiking trails, and sledding parties were good venues for all of them. The best solution for the adults had been to divide their time into boys' nights and girls' nights so everyone stayed sane, and no one resented anyone. They had procured a harem of babysitters to share as well, and every now and then, they allowed themselves a night out for all four of them as a much needed respite.

"How's Abby?" Kyle asked, smiling back at an enthusiastic waitress who appeared to deliver a basket of chips and take his order.

Glen took note of the interaction, and rubbed a hand back and forth over his buzz-cut, shaking his head. "Ornery as ever. She was out shopping most of the day while I was home with the crew. All she does is spend money. You know how she always likes to shop and look nice. Well it's the same way—times *three* now. If she gets something for one kid, she has to get two more, you know? She's about to bust my balls, man," he said, taking a swig of his beer. "I'm not made of money, and since she hasn't been working, it's been tough."

"What happened to the budget idea?" Kyle asked, hoping not to hear yet another diatribe against Chelsea's friend. He realized, however, the point of these meetings was usually to vent to one another so they could retain their sanity in the face of their unusual odds.

"Pssh!" Glen commented, rolling his eyes. "She's out of control. I can't get detective status soon enough, you know? Just a few more months. The usual traffic stops and busting up parties like the ones we went to are getting old…and it will be a substantial raise in pay for me. You can imagine with two girls and a boy, I'll have three in college at once and then *weddings!* Jeez!"

"I'm happy for you, man, getting closer to what you want." Kyle nodded.

Then, perhaps realizing he was being a downer, Glen asked, "How's Chelsea? Is she ready for her big production tonight?"

"She's good. This should be a good show. She's choreographed a piece with the football players in it. She thinks it's hysterical, so we'll see."

"That's really cool, how she got the athletic director and the football coaches to get the players into dance classes. Maybe it helped. They had a good season again last fall."

"Yep. She usually gets what she wants." Kyle thought about the athletic director. He had certainly become a dance fan, or more like a *Chelsea Davis* fan, he thought irritably. She had that man eating out of her hand; no surprise there.

"Yeah, well tell her we said, 'Break a leg.'"

"I'll do that."

Glen looked distant as the beer arrived and Kyle thanked the lingering waitress, drinking down some of the cold liquid gratefully. "Aah!"

Glen shook his head, thinking. "Man! When's the last time you got lucky?"

Kyle licked foam from his lips. "Sex? This morning, actually." Then as Glen's face fell, he added, trying to mask his pleasure in the event he'd thought about off and on all day, "but it doesn't happen that often, you know, because the boys don't sleep too well."

"Well, all three of mine sleep just fine, but I'm still not gettin' any."

"Abby's tired, man. Three kids would wear anybody out," Kyle said in her defense.

"Ah...it's just not like it used to be, you know? Okay, so spill the details."

"What?"

"I want to hear what it was like. If I don't have a sex life, the next best thing would be hearing about yours. Hell, it might even be better than porn. So, who started it?"

"Uh…me, I guess. I mean, we woke up about five this morning and it just kind of happened."

"And?"

"Man, I'm not doing this. You're sick. Besides, you can't handle it."

"Okay, so I'll just fantasize about other women. Don't you ever do that? No. I guess you don't with a hot babe like Chelsea at home."

"Leave my wife out of this," Kyle joked.

"Seriously. You have women throwing themselves at you all the time, our waitress being just one example. How do you *not* think about them?"

"You're delusional." Kyle looked steadily at him, feeling at odds about several things. One, he didn't feel like sharing yet that he and Chelsea might be thinking about trying for a third child. With the triplets taking all his time and money, Glen would think they were nuts. When people knew you were trying, it put pressure on everyone. Glen would certainly get that, after the years Abby and he had spent trying to conceive. If Kyle and Chelsea didn't have another child, no one would ever give them any grief, especially with the obvious demands of their twins. And if no one knew about it, they could be disappointed all by themselves, without the communal sadness that tended to be inevitable.

The other nagging thought was that after today's meeting with Elise, Kyle had felt an attraction to her that he didn't want to admit. If he didn't talk about it, he could make it disappear, and he could push it out of his mind. Glen was right; women did pursue him, but he had always managed to ignore them. And Chelsea *was* one hot babe. Things were more than just good at home; he couldn't be happier. But something about what happened today had strangely rattled him. As professional as he had tried to be, he'd felt a connection between Elise and him, not exactly a sexual attraction, but that could happen if he allowed it, which was out of the question. To make matters worse, they'd hired Elise during lunch, so he was stuck with this problem for a long time to come. He could handle it without discussion.

Glen returned the stare, apparently unable to read Kyle's thoughts. "Okay, fine. Too much information. So what did you do at work today? I guess you weren't out breaking ground in this rain."

Kyle looked away for a moment and took another drink of the cold amber beer. "No. We hired a new interior designer. You remember I told you Faith is leaving? And you and Abby are invited to her going away party, by the way, since you guys hired us to remodel your kitchen."

"So we made the preferred clients list. Count us in," he said, shaking his head and laughing. "Faith is such a hoot. So, she's retiring?"

"Well, more like leaving. She's not really old enough to retire, but she wants to spend more time with their grandchildren, so she thinks now is the time. They've got a trip to Disney World planned in a few weeks when school is out, so we needed to get a jump on her replacement."

"So who did you hire…some young babe right out of school?" Glen asked, dipping a tortilla chip in the bowl of salsa the waitress had set before them.

"No. This woman is about twenty-seven, and she worked at a design firm in Charlotte before she got downsized. She does fantastic work and came with excellent references, so we hired her on the spot."

"So you'll be spending lots of time with her. Is she hot?"

Kyle shook his head and grinned. *Yeah, she's hot,* he thought. Instead, he said, "You're *so* messed up! This is professional. Faith and I spend lots of time together and you've seen her."

"So some hotness could really improve your day-to-day existence, *si?*"

"I guess you could see it that way. I think we'll get along fine," he said, thinking about Elise's word, *exist.* If all she could do were exist, then her life couldn't be too exciting, all alone with a child to raise, and one with exceptional needs at that. This North Carolina mountain town could be brutal in the winter, making the lonely that much lonelier. He remembered loneliness all too well.

"What?" Glen asked, again trying to tap into Kyle's thoughts.

"Nothing. I've got to run," he said, draining the rest of his beer. "We have to be at the theater by 7:30, so I need to get a move on."

"The perfect husband."

"Yeah, that's me," muttered Kyle, dropping a few dollars with Glen's on the table and slapping him on the shoulder as they left their booth.

Chelsea glanced at the clock as she shook the pan of fajitas. It was almost six, and she smiled, hearing Kyle's car crunch up the drive.

"Stu, Ty? Will you set the table? Daddy's home," she called across the room, where Stu was watching TV and Ty sat reading a rather large book for someone his age. Ty turned the book over, setting it on the coffee table and tugging at Stu before going to a kitchen drawer, reaching in for knives and forks. Stu eventually walked over and grabbed napkins, eyes still glued to the animal show he had been watching.

Chelsea was pouring four glasses of milk when Kyle came through the door, immediately wrapping a large hand around her waist, pulling her against his chest and breathing in her scent before kissing her hard on the neck. "Hey," he said, his mouth still at her face. "Am I late?" Foscoe rose from his spot near the fireplace and sauntered over to nose the backs of Kyle's legs in greeting. Kyle reached down to stroke the dog's ears. "Hey, buddy," he said to the dog, who settled in a soft heap whenever anyone touched his ears. Chelsea stepped around them in the small kitchen, adding items to the perpetual grocery list she kept on the counter before she forgot.

"No, you're right on time. We're just getting ready to sit down. Maddie cancelled. She's got a stomach bug, so the guys are going with us."

"Oh, too bad for her; good for us, right guys?" He glanced at the boys, watching Stu roll his eyes at the thought of spending an evening at a dance spectacle.

"How was Glen?" she asked as he squeezed the boys in greeting.

"Miserable as ever," he responded dully, making Chelsea frown. "Hey, guys. How was school?" he asked as the boys wandered over to give him hugs.

"Good," said Ty.

"Boring," said Stu.

"As I expected," Kyle murmured to Chelsea, taking from her the basket of warm tortillas and a bowl of sour cream to place on the table. "So are you excited about tonight?" he asked her.

"Yeah," she said, brightening at his interest. "It should be a good show. The rehearsal went well. I told you Meme Compton is dancing, right?"

"Yes, you did," he said, rolling up his sleeves and washing his hands at the kitchen sink. Meme was a student at ASU whom Chelsea had taught to dance as a child in a special program she'd started years ago. Meme still loved to dance and had landed a part in the Spring Dance Ensemble, a student/faculty choreographed show open by audition for anyone interested in dancing, including dance majors. They all sat at the table, holding hands as Kyle said the blessing.

"Meme's not in the football piece, is she?" Kyle asked as they started to pass plates.

"Oh, no, we didn't want to kill her! She's in a contemporary piece that one of my students choreographed with seven other girls. It's perfect for her. It's slow and lovely. She sparkles on the stage. You can just imagine…" she said, blinking, making Kyle aware that she was getting emotional about Meme's progress.

The boys were having their own conversation about the animal show as they passed their plates, while Chelsea, rolled the steak and chicken mixture into the soft tortillas for the boys. "How did the interview go?" she asked, handing Stu a plate, and beginning to work on Ty's, as Kyle prepared hers.

"It was good. We hired her today, in fact."

"Good! When will she start?"

"I guess right after school gets out. She has a seven-year-old daughter, and they'll have to find a place up here. She's from Charlotte."

"Single mom?" Chelsea asked, taking her plate from Kyle.

"Yeah," he said, placing a scoop of saffron rice onto his plate, and then serving the boys. She had thought twice about preparing their favorite black beans, out of respect for the others in the audience tonight!

She smiled at him. Not many men she knew would jump in and take over at the dinner table the easy way he did. She thought sadly about Abby and Glen and the tension that had built in their marriage over the years since the triplets had been born. There had been plenty of tension before that, actually, with the anxiety of wanting a family. Now that they had more than their share, it seemed things had gotten worse. Chelsea was lucky and she knew it, especially when Kyle offered to clean up after they ate so she could get dressed.

She heard him enlisting the boys' help loading the dishwasher and wiping down the counters as she slipped the short, lacy dress over her head, and she heard the discussion about what they'd wear. Of course, she had already laid out their clothes, Stu explained, as they scuttled downstairs. Kyle talked to Foscoe as he scooped food into his bowl. "Don't let him sucker you; he's already been fed!" she called out, then heard Kyle chuckle, letting the dog out to do his business one last time before they left. She would give Abby a call in the morning, she thought, pulling her hair into a low ponytail behind her right ear. Fastening her earrings, she walked out of the bathroom and met Kyle coming in to check on her.

"Does this look okay?" she asked, but the look on his face told her everything she needed to know.

"Damn! Baby, you're a knockout!" he said, a pained expression on his face, as if she were too much to take in. He slipped his hand across her cheek, pulling her in for a passionate kiss. "Would they really miss you if we just stayed here?" he asked, grinning, making her giggle.

"Well, I think I should make a *brief* appearance, at least," she joked back.

"So, I guess I just need a sport coat and I'm good to go?" he asked.

She ran her fingers through his longish hair a time or two and smiled; his hair was forever a tousle, the way she liked it. "Yes, you're perfect," she whispered, reaching her face up to kiss him. "Zip me?" she asked, turning around to show him the back of her dress, cut in a low scoop.

"Wow! This is getting better and better. You look like my kind of angel," he said, zipping the cream-colored dress and watching her adjust the three-quarter length sleeves, while stepping into heels.

The boys were back upstairs; he called to them to let Foscoe back in before they left.

"Whoa!" said Stu, as Chelsea came out into the kitchen, putting a lip gloss back in her clutch. "You look awesome, Mom!"

"Makes you want to be a dancer, doesn't it, son?"

"No way!" said Stu. "But I *do* wanna sit beside you!"

"That makes three of us," Kyle said, watching Ty's reaction as he came back in the front door with Foscoe.

Make that four or five, Kyle thought, amused, and proud of his wife, as they made their way through the crowd at the theater that night, coming upon the athletic director and the football coach and his staff, who'd boldly announced they'd saved Chelsea a seat. She looked back and forth from them to her family, apparently searching for the diplomatic way to decline their invitation. Some schmoozing was in order, so Kyle held back with the boys for a moment, while she greeted the men, waving over their heads to members of the dance faculty. Tim, the athletic director, shook her hand and then gave in to the sideways hug he wanted, knocking her slightly off-balance, which required her to steady herself by placing her hand on his stomach. They laughed and she glanced at Kyle, who did his best to control his eyebrows. The coach took her hand as well, as if to kiss it, but thought better of the move as he noticed Kyle continued to watch. *Did they all have to ogle her legs so openly? As if they were deprived.* Not that he blamed them, he thought, proudly.

"We should probably get seated," she said, then inclined her head toward her family. "I hope you can get through this without me. You remember my husband, Kyle? We're lucky to have our boys with us tonight, so I'll see you after the show. Thank you again for coming. The guys have done a great job, and I'm so glad so many of them agreed to participate. It might be a once in a lifetime event for all of us. I appreciate the opportunity!" she said, and again, Kyle noticed how they seemed to hang on her each and every word. Fortunately, at that moment, Meme's parents and her brother were making their way to their seats, attracting her attention. She waved to the men, winked at Kyle, and headed toward them, as he led them to four seats he'd spotted in the rapidly filling theater. After a quick word and a hug with Meme's family, she joined them in the seats as the lights flashed on and off, signaling five minutes to curtain.

"Mom, you're like a rock star," Stu commented on one side of her while Ty sat on the other, studying the program for her name.

"Thanks, honey. They're so excited backstage! I hope you'll like this," she said, unsure of their take on the experience. The twins had only recently been expected to attend her events, but they had been surprisingly well-behaved and tolerated them well.

"Look, there's Grandmommy and Granddaddy!" Ty said, spotting Chelsea's parents coming in at the last minute and looking around for seats.

"Oh! I wish I'd thought to save them seats! I wasn't sure they'd make it," she said, watching them find seats several rows below them. "We'll catch up with them at intermission."

Kyle thought back to his discussion with Liz and Tom from the previous day. He had secretly arranged for them to keep the boys while he planned to whisk Chelsea away to Martha's Vineyard for a long weekend in celebration of their tenth wedding anniversary. She had no idea any of this was in the works. She would be on vacation after the spring semester. He would tell her what to pack and the rest would be a surprise. She would figure it out after they boarded the plane. They had always wanted to visit Cape Cod, and this was a perfect opportunity. Again, it was something he couldn't share with Glen. Glen and Abby were strapped financially, but Chelsea and he were doing well, saving money, lots of money. And they deserved a break after all their hard work. They rarely got away by themselves. She glanced at him as the lights lowered; he winked, stretching his arm behind Stu to rub her shoulder.

Meme's dance was first. Kyle was amazed at the lovely young woman he saw on stage, moving easily with the music in some kind of fluid, ethereal costume. She couldn't be the same child who had struggled for balance ten years ago, but here she was, just like the rest of the dancers, only outstanding for the contagious smile on her face, and the exuberance of every move she made. He couldn't take his eyes off her. He watched Chelsea point her out to the boys, wiping tears from her cheeks as Ty patted her knee. What a rewarding experience this had to be. She had often said her students had taught her more than she taught them, and now he understood what she had meant. When the piece was over, several people in the audience stood to applaud, the four of them and Meme's family included.

She giggled as the music began for the football number. It was familiar upbeat classical music that he couldn't name, but the players were obvious among the other dancers. They moved well and did their parts comically, as was the plan, tossing about a tiny dancer dressed in a brown tutu that laced up the front, like a football. The twins hooted at some of the moves and the hilarious expressions on the men's faces as they hammed it up for the audience. When the "game" was over, there was another standing ovation, amid much laughter and crowing from the audience as the players bowed gallantly on stage. Kyle laughed to himself, wondering how he would have done in the same situation at the University of Virginia, where he'd started as a wide receiver in college. Surely with a teacher like Chelsea, he would have delivered a grand performance, as these men had done! He high-fived her over Stu's head, noticing the thumbs up she was getting from the football staff down in front.

Indigo mountains and lush rolling hills disappeared as the plane rose above the clouds. They toasted each other with Bloody Marys as they flew over Virginia on a sunny Saturday morning at the end of May. Chelsea sighed happily and sank back in her seat, looking out over the clouds, sipping her drink, savoring the flavor of freedom! She looked over at Kyle who watched her as if this were great entertainment.

"Okay, so I know we're going to Boston," she said, but it sounded like a question, which made him chuckle.

"Partly. We'll land there, and then you'll have to figure it out from there."

She thought about the bathing suits he'd made her pack and the casual clothes, sweaters and jeans; one nice dress. If she tried to guess, it might kill his fun, so she thought it best to keep her musing to herself, hoping her suspicions were right, while not imagining where she hoped they were going would ever happen. It was just wonderful to be away with him. Still, thoughts of the boys tugged at her heart. They hadn't left their sons very often. She would try to keep those thoughts to herself as well. He had tried hard to score this break for them. And the secretiveness of it all must have been hard for him to conceal.

"How did I get so lucky to marry you?" she asked, making him snort in return.

"I'm the lucky one. You know that," he said, and she knew he was referring to the awful times back in high school, before he'd come home and they'd reconnected as friends after his sister and father's deaths. Their feelings for each other had quickly intensified after that until she knew there would never be another man for her. They didn't speak of the sadness much anymore. They'd made a pact with each other only to mention the negative things once and be done with it, unless it was something that needed more discussion to work out. But all of that was water under the bridge, she thought, as he took her hand, lacing his fingers through hers. Besides, there was too much good in their lives these days to dwell in the past.

"Thank you for this trip," she said, "wherever it is you're taking me! I don't care. It's just great to be together this way," *without the boys* hanging in the balance of both their thoughts.

"Can you see anything down below?" he asked, making her look out the window again.

"Just clouds right now. It's like being in Heaven," she said, trying to pop her ears again.

"Can you believe it's been ten years?" he asked.

"No. It's gone by so fast. I guess when you're as busy as we are, it just seems to fly. Do you feel older?"

"Sometimes I think I do, because of all the responsibility, but basically, I feel stuck at twenty-five," he laughed.

"I want to feel like that, but I feel…*old!*" she laughed, thinking how the responsibilities of work and family had shrunk some of her old freedom.

"You won't feel like that once we get where we're going. And after I'm finished with you, you'll feel like you're twenty-*one* again," he promised with his scorching eyes as much as with the words. She felt herself slip into nonchalance, letting the stress from the semester, the show, and the boys' schedules slide away with another sip of her drink. She looked back at him, gazing past her, out the window, the sunlight from the window brightening his large blue eyes even further.

"God, we need this! How long have you been planning this?" she asked.

"For a while now. But that's really none of your business. No worries, okay? Just enjoy yourself."

She smiled and rubbed his arm. "I love you," she murmured, looking back out the window and finishing her drink.

Four hours later, they opened the door of their hotel suite in Martha's Vineyard, and the first thing Chelsea noticed was the four-poster bed sprinkled with rose petals, and another dozen red roses in a vase on a table accompanied by a bottle of champagne, chilling in a bucket with two antique crystal glasses waiting for them. Quickly, she took in the small fireplace on one wall and the view of the blue harbor from their French doors. She gasped as he lifted her, carrying her through the door, saying, "Happy anniversary," in her ear.

"Oh! Oh! My God! This is amazing! How did you do all this?" she asked as he carried her across the room and they collapsed together on the bed. Her fingers raked through his hair and she kissed him, feeling his strong arms around her, pulling her toward him, holding her, kissing her back eagerly.

"None of your business, Mrs. Davis. The best thing is, we won't have anyone bothering us for *three days*," he said, smiling into her cheek and kissing her again. "There will be so much to see and do, if you want, but I can promise you, it will be early to bed every night…if we choose to leave the room at all," he growled into her ear. "It's all up to you. I'm your slave for three days."

"Oh!….I can't believe you brought me here. And it's beautiful and warm!"

"The water will be cold, though."

"That's okay with me. There'll be no chance of getting stung by any jellyfish!" she said, remembering the unfortunate ending to their honeymoon ten years ago.

Eventually, they spent the afternoon wandering the streets of Edgartown, Kyle entranced with the architecture, taking multitudes of pictures. They visited the glassblower's shop, had clam chowder for lunch overlooking the harbor, and rented a tandem bicycle to tool around on. Their uncoordinated attempts at mastering the bike sent them into occasional fits of laughter. The shoreline was dramatic and rocky, like none Chelsea had ever seen. Back at the hotel, Chelsea wrapped her sweater around her, stepping out on their private balcony to join Kyle for a glass of champagne at sunset. She watched as the colors of the sky melted into the brilliant hues of turquoise and orange, giving his hair an extra golden tint and lighting his eyes dramatically. As usual, he waited for her before sitting down, handing her an empty glass. It had gotten chilly later in the afternoon. He looked so good in the fisherman's sweater she'd bought him in town. Deftly, he eased the cork from the bottle, saving it to remember the occasion, and poured her a glass of the cold bubbly, as she watched the froth disappear.

"You fit right in here," she said, sliding her arm around him, accepting the glass, and pressing a kiss into his chest. She liked the sweater's softness on her face and the scent of wind and ocean on him at the same time. His chest felt warm and hard, like the two smooth boulders she'd touched on the beach earlier in the day. He held her for a long moment, and then they sipped their champagne.

He took her glass and set both of them on the table, wrapping his arms around her and kissing her deeply. "Nothing's ever going to come between us, Chels…just so you know," he said softly, stroking her hair, making her head swim delightfully.

She laced her fingers behind his neck. "I know. You're my *forever man*," she said, reminding him of one of his favorite Eric Clapton songs. She looked up at him, but he turned his head slightly, toward the harbor, and she saw the seriousness in his eyes, wondering what was on his mind. "Is this because of all the trouble Glen and Abby are having?" she asked, recalling several conversations she'd had with her friend who was becoming more and more frustrated with Glen about their constant disagreements.

"No…they're just having the normal marital irritations everyone gets. He's working hard; she's not. With three kids at home and not much money, I get it. I just needed to remind you how special things are with us."

"Yes, they are. It's always been like this with us. People don't understand it," she laughed gently. He hugged her, reaching for the glasses again. "When we got married, did you ever think we'd still be this much in love in ten years?" she asked, stroking his arm, glad he had relaxed again.

"No. I guess I had no idea what was in store for us. The family just solidifies our bond even more, the larger it gets."

She loved hearing that from him. A large family had always been a part of her life, and Kyle had never had that. She remembered after his father's suicide during high school how adrift Kyle had been, how unsure of the world and all the people in it. He'd needed her to show him how life could be. But things had changed for them both. Now, he was the strong one, a major player in the group, taking on more and more in his roles as husband, father, and as son-in-law. It was easy for him to spend a couple of hours hauling wood for her dad, who'd had a heart attack years ago, or running the vacuum up and down her mother's stairs, and Kyle seemed to enjoy it as much as they appreciated it. He couldn't be a better father to the twins, who adored him. He respected Ty's reflective side while having the ultimate patience for restless Stu.

"So you know what I'm getting at?" he asked, turning to her suddenly.

His look penetrated her, making her body come alive from deep within, causing her skin to tingle at the definite possibility of his hands on her. It was dizzying, the effect he still had on her.

"Yes," she whispered. "You want another baby," she murmured, the emotion thick between them. He nodded, watching her for her reaction. She reached up and combed her fingers through his hair, suddenly sure of what she wanted. "I'll give you whatever you want," she said breathlessly, making him grin. He wrapped his arm around her again, burying his face in her neck.

"Oh, baby," he murmured into her hair. "Hold that thought, then," he said smiling. "I'm taking you to Henry's tonight for lobster. And then I'm having my way with you." He winked and downed the last of his champagne.

Chapter 3

THE NEW GIRL

Elise Masters was waiting at the door of Mountaineer Builders, holding a large box with a grocery bag over her arm, when Kyle rounded the corner onto King Street her first day on the job. *Damn*, he thought; she was the first one there. Frank and he had failed to give her a key.

"Good morning!" he said brightly.

"Good morning," she said, returning his greeting with a tolerant smile.

Great. He was already in trouble with the new girl.

"Sorry. I guess we forgot to give you a key," he said, making a mental note to run over to the hardware store at lunch to have one made. Or maybe Frank had Faith's key.

"That will be important since I'm the one making the coffee," she said, a hint of amusement in her river-colored eyes. He noticed the canvas grocery bag she carried.

"Uh, yeah…" he said, shifting his own package and opening the door, holding it for her to enter.

She set her box down in the gathering room and went directly to the kitchen; she set about unloading her bag, running water for the coffeepot, and setting low-fat creamer out on the counter. She'd brought a natural sugar substitute too, he noticed. There would be no donuts around here anymore, he thought. He placed his own parcel on the counter.

"These are from my wife," he said, removing a tin of blueberry muffins from the bag and opening it to show her Chelsea's gift.

"Oh! How nice of her," she said, registering true surprise.

"It's her way of welcoming you to the firm."

"Well, please thank her for me. This is my favorite breakfast. I have to confess, I didn't eat this morning," she said.

He could imagine how it might have been, hectic perhaps, getting out the door with her daughter in tow on the first day of a new job in a new town. Or maybe she was just nervous, he thought, watching her scoop coffee into the basket. She seemed young, and eager to make a good impression; still, she presented an air of confidence.

"Can I do anything?" he offered.

Her *just stay out of the way* look softened at his sincere expression. She smiled. "Show me your favorite coffee cup."

"It doesn't matter. Frank and I aren't that territorial."

"Okay," she said, brushing her hands together and folding her bag.

After an awkward moment, he turned to go to his office. "Okay. Well, *welcome.* Why don't we get settled in, and then we'll talk about the day," he said, wondering when Frank would make an appearance. Usually, they stopped by their building sites first thing in the morning, but he'd thought Frank would be here early today. He logged into his computer and turned on his music, checking his emails, all the while listening as Elise moved about in her office, probably setting out pictures, her favorite pens in a cup on her desk, turning on her own iPad, getting acclimated. The coffeepot beeped, and just as he was thinking about going in to get his cup of coffee, she was there, at the doorway, holding the brown and green pottery mug he'd used the day of her interview.

"Oh! Please, don't wait on me. I usually get my own," he said, standing quickly, accepting the mug. "Thanks…black…how'd you know?"

"I pay attention," she said, amused again.

He raised his cup to her and she returned the gesture. The coffee was rich and bold, a great improvement over the grocery store brand Faith used to buy. "Well, this is a major improvement," he said, gratefully.

"I thought I could be of some use in this department," she said, sipping hers from a tall ceramic mug he'd never seen before. He would need to start paying attention too. She was listening to his music.

"Is this Big Head Todd and the Monsters?" she asked, breaking into a smile.

"You know Big Head?" He grinned, pleased that her taste in music equaled her taste in coffee.

"Oh, yeah! My dad listens to them all the time," she said as his face fell. *Great*, now he was an old guy! He could switch it over to John Mayer, but that would be too obvious. *What was he thinking?* "Isn't that 'Forever Man' they're playing?" Kyle nodded. "The Clapton song. My dad likes him, too. You and my dad would probably get along really well," she said, and this time he thought it might be a compliment.

"How's that?"

"Oh…just an impression," she said, looking around the room, his photographs catching her eye. "The family shrine?"

"It is. Did you bring yours?"

"Yes. I'll show you. Is this your wife?" she asked, looking at a new photo of Chelsea and him at the harbor in Edgartown.

"Mm-hmm, that's Chelsea."

"Where was this taken?" she asked.

"That was at Martha's Vineyard. We went there for our tenth anniversary."

"Hmmm. That sounds romantic. Ten years...*congratulations*," she said, looking him over again, possibly trying to guess his age, as he'd done with her at her interview. "And these are your boys? Oh, how cute are they! Twins?"

"Yes, they are. This one is Ty, and that's Stu," he said, pointing to each boy, posed casually on a river rock during a hike they'd taken in the fall.

"How old are they?" she asked, clearly taken with them.

"They're eight."

"You must have your hands full," she said, moving on to a promotional shot of Chelsea in a tutu when she danced professionally.

"No way!" she said, looking back at the other photo. "You're married to Chelsea Davenport?"

"You know her?"

"No, but I've seen her dance! My grandmother always used to take me to the Carolina Ballet to see *The Nutcracker* when I was a kid. Chelsea was my favorite dancer...the Sugar Plum Fairy, you know? The ballet always made my Christmas."

"Really? Mine too," he said. *When I was a kid.* He was starting to feel old for sure now. "Does your grandmother live in Raleigh?"

"Yes."

"Then I guess you didn't know Chelsea's been teaching at App for the last ten years," he said, thinking it was a small world. She shook her head, giving the same kind of look. "Were you a dancer?"

"Hardly," she laughed. "I wasn't graceful enough. My grandmother would have loved it if I had been, though. She's quite the arts supporter.

But I played soccer and softball. I was a swimmer all through school. Hundred fly was my specialty."

That explained the trim figure and the broad shoulders, he thought. She looked elegant in her navy dress and patterned taupe pumps. She would make a good impression on their clients.

"How's your office coming along?"

"Come and see. I need another plant, and I have a picture I think I'll bring to hang, but it will be home soon enough," she said as he followed her to Faith's old office. Already, she had made her mark on the room, adding splashes of color, arranging her pictures here and there, with the desk adornments in place that he knew she'd have brought, and a small pot of irises. A lemony, flowery fragrance was there as well. "Here's Lydia," she said proudly, handing him a frame. Her daughter was lovely, with the same brown hair and eyes, though slightly vacant, and rosy full lips that weren't like her mother's.

"So how did it go leaving her this morning? Did you and Lydia get settled okay?"

She smiled. "Yes. It took me a while to find a first floor apartment. She doesn't handle stairs well. I was a little worried about getting her enrolled in day care, but everything worked out. Lydia was actually at the ASU day care program when she was a toddler. I was really lucky to get her in there. I put her name on the list the minute I left you guys after you hired me. She's been over there a few times, so she's gotten adjusted pretty well. The teachers there seem nice, and they understand her for the most part. Her speech is hard to understand, and she'll need help on the playground, but I think they'll have it under control. Some of the students who work there are training to be special education teachers."

He wanted to ask more but the phone rang. She picked it up promptly. "Good morning, Mountaineer Builders. This is Elise. May I help you?"

Kyle sipped his coffee, intrigued with her. She was definitely making a good impression on him. He watched as she frowned, sitting at her desk, and taking a pen to write something down.

"No, I'm sorry; Faith is no longer here, but I'm the designer. I can help you. What's the situation?" *Situation*, not problem; it was all in the wording, he thought, admiringly. Her calm tone of voice was right on par for the *situation* as well.

Kyle looked on, concerned. The tirade on the other end wasn't sounding good. She twirled the pen, nodding, looking at him with an expression of dread.

"Oh, no. That's not good….No, it's certainly not acceptable. Are you there now? Yes, I can certainly come over there and see what I can do. What's the address?" She wrote quickly on her notepad. "Yes, I know the street. I can re-measure everything and check it out….I know. I'm so sorry. Well…we'll do whatever we can to make it right. Is this number where you can be reached? Okay…let me check into it and I'll meet you there as soon as I can, in probably…thirty minutes?"

Kyle shook his head, wondering what this was all about as she listened some more.

"Okay. Great. I'll see you in just a bit then. Thank you, Mrs. Turner. Bye."

She replaced the handset and looked at Kyle. "Do you know anything about the Turner property? Mrs. Turner is over there and the installation of her kitchen cabinets isn't going well. They don't fit." She turned to the desktop computer, searching through files, and clicking on one before he could answer.

"Yeah, that's a remodel Faith and I were working on. It's here in Boone. You can make it in fifteen minutes, and that'll be mostly because of traffic."

"Yeah, I thought I recognized the street name."

"Do you want me to go with you? I'll be glad to…."

"Um…no, I should be fine. If it's only that they don't fit, I'll just re-measure," she said, looking at the cabinet specs. "Okay…I know this company. These are custom cabinets, so I should be able to fix it. Mrs. Turner is hopping mad, though. I'll call you if I need you. Thirty minutes will give her time to cool down," she said, programming the address into her phone, slipping it back into her purse. *Smooth.*

"And give you time to eat your breakfast?"

Elise grinned. "And here I thought Faith was the perfect designer."

"She is," he said, smiling. "Everybody's allowed one screw-up."

"I thought perfection was your expectation," she said, looking at him for affirmation. When he nodded, the gaze lingered, appraising him. "Well, I've had my screw-up already, and payback's been hell, so I'll be on my best behavior," she said seriously, heading to the kitchen for her muffin.

He followed her, going for a muffin himself, even though he'd eaten breakfast.

"Your screw-up couldn't have been that bad," he said, taking a bite, wanting to hear her story.

"Oh, it was. Someday maybe I'll tell you about it, but I don't want you to be too disappointed in me on my first day." She placed the muffin in a napkin, returned to her office, loaded the iPad back in its case, popped it into her purse, and was on her way out the door.

"All right. Good luck," he called after her. He sighed, frustrated with himself. Damn! He'd followed her around like a puppy, and this was her first day in *his* office. He thought about what needed to be done for the rest of the day, feeling flummoxed, as he thought he'd be spending the day training her, but here she was, off and running, putting out fires, and she hadn't been here an hour! He felt useless. *"You should be glad, idiot,"* he muttered to himself. *This is why we hired her.* He was glad she was competent. Still, he felt slightly off-kilter somehow, wondering why, and running a hand across the back of his neck. He'd have to get back in his groove.

At the computer, he found an email from his brother-in-law, Jay. Chelsea's brother operated the Davenport Winery he'd designed and Frank had built five years ago. They'd be having Faith's retirement party there, so Jay was requesting a headcount. That whole endeavor had gone well, except for his dislike of the investors Jay and Tom had gone in with. They were greedy suckers, the two of them, guys from New York, a father and son with money to burn. The son had little diplomacy, an irritating trait in one so young, Kyle thought. They were itching to get their hands on the Davenport family home, wanting to turn it into a bed and breakfast, which had everyone in a tailspin, especially his wife. Anyway, the wines were good and business was booming, so they had to tolerate the Gilmer men. Kyle had chalked it up as one more character-building experience, using the restraint and tact he'd found necessary to deal with them. Chelsea had chalked it up as a royal pain in her ass! It had been one of those one-session-discussions they didn't dwell on. He checked a file for the guest list Frank and Faith had compiled. He replied to the email, at the last moment, adding two more. Maybe Elise should be invited, plus one. He'd check with Frank. From what Faith had said about their transition time together, the two women had gotten along famously.

He spent the next hour working at his drafting table on his current project, a mountain A-frame remodel in Blowing Rock that would be part of the fall showcase of builders. Soon he would bring Elise in for the interior design, but today, he was finishing the elevations for a dramatic new family room and two upstairs bedrooms with breathtaking views of the Blue Ridges. He imagined applying her clean style to the scheme, much like what he thought he would do himself. Finally, immersed in his design, he was hardly aware of the door chiming. She was back. He waited a moment, but she did not report to his door, seeking praise or affirmation of a job well-done. He heard her in her office on the phone with the cabinetry company, alerting them to a reorder she was about to submit via email. He chuckled, pushing back from the table, waiting her out, listening to her finishing the call, then hearing her footsteps going into the kitchen for more coffee. He could stand it no longer, allowing himself to rise and check on her. But she was there in the doorway, holding the coffee cup against her hand, as if to warm it, a cool, but triumphant expression on her face.

"So…I take it you were victorious?"

"Evelyn Turner is a lovely person," she replied, her river eyes drawing him in. "What a cute little bungalow she has! That's what I want someday, a Craftsman bungalow. Anyway, we figured it all out and I just placed the reorder for the cabinet and the countertop. The installation crew was kind enough to wait for me, and they're going to return the cabinet that didn't fit. Faith wasn't too far off, but it wouldn't have worked."

"Congratulations. You just saved the day, and maybe our firm's reputation," he said, raising his coffee cup to her. The *situation* could have been a disaster.

"Thanks. So what's next? Or do you want me to leave you alone?"

No, he thought, hardly professional. *What?* "Well, let me show you your first project that I've got coming along." He led her to his computer to show her the pictures and the plans so far. She stepped around behind him to take a look at his screen, allowing him a pleasant breath of her fragrance, lemony with flowers, and a bit of her own scent. He breathed in again, slightly distracted, thinking about bungalows, and how much he liked them too.

Kyle showed her the plans he was working on. She nodded her approval, encouraged that soon she'd have a project to work on herself. Business had been good for them over the spring, but it would be summer this year when they really got rolling, he explained. At the moment, between projects like they were, there was not a lot for her to do, except to familiarize herself with the office, all the files, their calendars, the brochures, Faith's materials, and the advertising. She left him alone, getting settled in her office, and looking through the materials he'd given her.

An hour later, his stomach growled as he wondered where Frank was. A quick phone call let him know that Frank would be tied up at the work site all day. Elise's problem wasn't the only one they would have today. Frank told him definitely to include her and a friend for the party. Kyle debated what to do next, listening to her singing along to a song in her office. It was a song he'd heard before, a beautiful but melancholy folk ballad about a girl dying young, wishing to be sent away in a river to the words of a love song, and she sang it with feeling.

Sad, he thought, but maybe it was just a song. It might not necessarily be her anthem, but then, he listened to his own music for a reason. He wondered about hers. Perhaps he should suggest lunch, he thought, wondering about the bag he'd tossed in the refrigerator. It would have the same ham sandwich and apple that Chelsea usually packed, or maybe it would be roast beef and an orange, if she'd changed it up this morning. Normally, he would sit right here with a bottle of water, eating as he worked, but today seemed odd. Normally, Faith would be humming about, fielding phone calls, filling in his calendar, and tidying things up when she took a break from her own work every now and then. Sighing, he got to his feet and stretched. He had been distracted today, as if Elise's new presence in the office were equivalent to having a houseful of company whom he had to entertain. He'd stopped in the middle of his thoughts several times, wondering whether she was happy, or whether there was anything she'd need. Slowly, he wandered into the kitchen and rinsed out his coffee cup before sticking his head inside her doorway. She was oblivious to him, earbuds in place and humming along to the song, while her eyes roved over the company website.

He cleared his throat and she turned, letting the earbuds drop into her palm. She looked up with questioning eyes, lips parted, taking him in.

"I'm sorry. I didn't mean to startle you. I'm going to take a lunch break. Would you like to join me?"

"Oh. Sure. Do you bring your own lunch?"

"Usually. Did you bring anything? We could go out…."

"No. I brought mine, too. I wasn't sure how you and Frank rolled with that. I figured you'd be out or busy, or something, so I brought a sandwich," she said, looking tentative, the new employee, getting to know the territory.

"Good. Want to eat in the conference room? There's not room in the kitchen."

"Sure. Maybe I can redo that space so there is room," she said. "It's nice," she added quickly, "but it could be a little homier, more user-friendly."

She followed him into the conference room where they pulled out their lunches.

"So, do you like the updates on the website?" he asked.

"Yeah, I didn't expect my picture to be included yet, as well as the examples of my work. Who does your website?"

"I do," he said. "Frank had me replace the one he used when I came on board a while back."

She nodded. "It's nice…very manly and professional," she said, picking a green grape off the stem.

"Should it be manly?"

"You're an architect; he's a builder. It should be manly," she said, biting into the grape.

"Well, now that we have you in the firm, do you think it needs to be changed?"

She thought a moment, narrowing her eyes and chewing. *She's trying not to offend me*, he thought, attempting to read her look.

"No. I think it's perfect just the way it is," she said. He chuckled. "What?" she asked, tossing the swirl of brown hair away from her face, and wiping a crumb from her mouth with her fingertip.

"Do you have a thing about perfection?"

"No, but I believe you do," she said, a half-smile forming.

"Have I mentioned it?"

"No, you don't have to. You *exude* perfection."

He was surprised at her candor at this point, wondering what she meant.

"How is that?" he asked.

"Your work, for one thing. I've seen your stuff. The quality is amazing. I was so relieved when I saw it on the website before I came up here. You can't imagine what it's like, being out there, looking for work, and anything will do just to pay the bills. I thought I could be in for a really rude awakening with some companies, and I didn't know how yours would be. I had a good thing with Tarleton, and I didn't think I would be happy anywhere else, but then I saw your website. You and Frank are definitely the right fit for me. I can soften the edges a bit and bring the total package what it needs. So…it's perfect."

He watched her take another bite of her sandwich, hanging on her answer. *Who doesn't like being stroked?*

"Plus, you have the perfect family. How could everything in your life be so…*charming*?" she asked, searching for the word, and smiling this time. "Is it really that good?"

He smiled too, nodding. "Yes. It is that good. I don't know how I rated it. Maybe my number was up," he said, not meaning to be flippant, wondering about her life, and how she might think his circumstances were unfair. He thought about Chelsea and the boys and how thankful he was.

They ate in silence for several moments. As long as she was being so candid, he took a chance at what was on his own mind. "So, tell me about Lydia. You must have had her while you were in school?" he asked.

"I did," she said, looking away, then suddenly meeting his eyes. "After she was born, my parents kept her so I could go back to school....I missed a semester. We knew soon after she was born that she had some developmental delays. I'd go home on weekends to see her. The next year, I was able to bring her with me. The university let me have one of those apartments they usually give to married students, and I had a roommate who liked to babysit, so I kind of had it made," she said, her voice sounding matter-of-fact.

"What happened to Lydia's father?" Kyle asked, unable to contain his curiosity.

She sighed and crumpled her napkin, leaving the last of her tuna sandwich in its plastic container.

"Oh, he was sort of an afterthought....Now you're going to make me tell you about my screw-up."

"No, not if you don't want to. I'm sorry. I didn't mean to be so...."

She studied him carefully for a moment, making him regret asking. On her first day, this kind of question bordered on the inappropriate; he should have known better. Finally, she spoke. "No, it's okay. I like it that you're direct. I'm that way, too. I guess we might as well get it out in the open now, and that will be the end of it. I'm glad I was able to do something good today. As I told you, I'll have nowhere to go but up!" she laughed, running her hand through her hair, and searching the room, preparing to start her story.

"I met Lydia's father at a skiing party in the Catskills. I'd gone up there with some modeling friends after Christmas one year. There was a hot tub party after skiing, and he followed us there. We'd met him and his friend that day on the slopes. He was doing the same thing, staying with friends and having fun. So, without boring you with the details, I spent one evening with him and never heard from him again."

"And you were pregnant."

"Yes."

"Did you tell him?"

"No." She reddened, looking away. "I didn't know how to get in touch with him. I didn't remember his last name. Nobody knew him, and I couldn't track him down after I realized I was pregnant. That was before I was really into social networking, so, no, he's never known."

"But," he began, hoping to help her salvage her dignity, "you went ahead with the pregnancy."

Her eyes looked weary, making her appear older than she was. When she spoke, her voice was devoid of emotion, also making her seem older. "You would like to think that was my choice, wouldn't you? I didn't want to have a baby, and I wouldn't have continued the pregnancy, but I didn't have a choice. I was five months along before I even knew I was pregnant. I was doing some modeling at the time, and I had lost so much weight I thought that was why I was missing my periods. I was tired, but I wasn't sick, and it never occurred to me that I could be pregnant. I wasn't even dating anyone. Like most of the girls in my program, I spent most of my time in the design lab, so I didn't have much of a social life. I flew to New York for the modeling on weekends whenever I could. You can imagine everyone's surprise….I'm sorry; your opinion of me has probably gone down the toilet after hearing all this. But that's my story," she said, her face flushed and vulnerable.

"No. That's not at all what I was thinking."

"It's important to me that you know; that wasn't the kind of thing I normally did, I mean, just some random hook-up. I'm not like that. But, yeah, that's my screw-up, and I've been paying for it ever since," she said. He thought for a moment, wondering what to say.

"I love my daughter," she said softly. "Sometimes, I look at her, and I can't imagine that I ever could have ended her life. It hasn't been easy, and it's not the life that I'd have picked for myself, but who can choose, you know? You get what you get and you move on. I was lucky my parents were around to help me. It was hard on them, too. My mother had to quit her job. For a while, no one was happy with me….Lydia and I had finally gotten out on our own, and then I lost my job, so back to the nest I flew. But…now, it's time I moved on and made my own way. Lydia and I have our own life, and we're doing just fine. So, now you know how far from perfect I am!" she laughed.

"Well, perfection is probably overrated anyway; not that anyone is perfect," he said, thinking he might know just one person who was. He rubbed the back of his thumb across his lip.

She watched him thoughtfully.

"You can tell Frank if you want, and spare me this humiliation one more time."

"Sure, but don't worry about Frank. Nobody's judging you," he promised.

"Thank you. I had a feeling you might not…but still, I can't believe I've just unloaded all of this on you. In a way, it's a relief to get it all out, though. Some first day, huh?" she asked, her voice jittery with the weight of what she'd just told him.

He watched the nuances cross her face, making him want to put her at ease. There was no reason to prolong her agony. "How about taking a ride with me? We can get you a key to the office and I can show you the work we've done for real so you won't have to go by what you've seen on the website."

"Thank you. I'd like that," she said, breathing a long sigh of relief.

∞

They waited at the stoplight for what seemed like an eternity at the busiest intersection in Boone. He opened the sunroof in the Explorer, and she laid her head back on the headrest, letting the sun warm her face.

"Wow! The traffic here gets worse every time I come to town," she commented and he agreed.

"Yeah, but it's nothing like Charlotte," he said.

"That is something I do not miss," she laughed. "Are you from here?"

"Yeah. Actually, my family was from Charlotte, too, but I was born here. My grandparents still live there."

"Oh? Where?" she asked, turning toward him in her seat.

"They live in Myers Park. We keep trying to get them to move into something a little more manageable, but my grandparents are surprisingly healthy for their age, and they're afraid we'll stop coming to visit them if they move. How about your folks…where are they?"

"Not Myers Park," she said, referring to the wealthy neighborhood he'd mentioned. "My dad is a grocery store manager and my mother sells jewelry now. She started doing it after she quit her job and her friends have kept her in business. It's been fun for her. She deserves some fun."

He nodded, trying to imagine what they'd been through as a family. It reminded him of Chelsea's family and how they'd pulled together to help her grandmother when he'd come back to town in high school.

"So, how did you end up coming back here? I saw on your bio that you worked for a firm in Alexandria, Virginia. Did you get restructured too?"

"No, Frank offered me this job and I came back for Chelsea," he said as the traffic started to move. "Do you want to see Sugar Ridge first?"

"Actually, no. I've seen it already. I checked it out earlier, thinking there would be a condo there I could rent, and there was, except it was way out of my price range. But they're beautiful. I got the tour. You did a great job on them."

"Okay, then I'll take you to the winery," he said, thinking what a nice way this was to spend the day.

She smiled, going back to the original subject. "You and Chelsea were high school sweethearts? I still don't understand; how did she end up here when she was dancing in the Carolina Ballet?"

He chuckled, "She was doing the same thing I was, looking for me, I guess, wanting to be closer to her family. She never had a minute to herself in the company. But we were both doing what we thought we were supposed to do, getting the good jobs we thought we should have, but we lost each other in the process. She found the job at Appalachian and decided to come back."

"So you gave up everything to be together?"

"That's about it," he said.

"Huh," she said, fingering her necklace. "That's the most insane thing I've ever heard…or maybe it's the sweetest."

"Well, a lot of people thought we were both insane, but there have been no regrets, I can tell you."

"Did you build your own house?"

"No, we live in a cabin in Valle Crucis."

"Cool. Did Frank build it?"

"No, my dad built it."

"So he's a builder, too?" she asked, looking confused.

"He was. He passed away when I was in high school," he said, checking the rearview mirror and changing lanes.

"Oh, I'm sorry."

They rode in silence for a few moments, and he turned up his music a little. *Passing away* was an easier term for most people to digest than suicide; plus, it kept them from asking more questions; questions he did not care to answer.

"*Ugh!* You need a new playlist," she said, needling him after a moment.

"What? I thought you liked blues."

"It's fine; it's just *old*!"

"So who do you listen to?"

"Nobody you've ever heard of, apparently!" she said, laughing easily, a comfortable sound he'd never heard before. She held the charm on her necklace, absently sliding it back and forth on the chain, then let it drop on the side of her dress.

"A butterfly?" he noticed.

"Oh. Yes," she said, caught off guard. "My dad gave this to me when I turned eighteen. He said I was going through my own metamorphosis…." Her voice lost the laughter suddenly. He left her comment alone, considering the irony of her metamorphosis.

"I thought it was because you swam the butterfly…in high school?" he offered, trying to bring her back.

"Yes. I'm sure that's exactly what it was. This is so beautiful up here," she said as the road they'd turned onto wound around through pastures, quaint homes, and inns on the way to the winery. "I haven't been back here in ages. We used to go to the Mast General Store when I was in school. There's a park here now?" she said, as they passed the places that had become popular attractions.

"Yeah. Our cabin is down the road and up a ways, right on the river, but where I'm taking you now, Snowy Ridge, is where Chelsea grew up. Her family owned most of the mountain at one time. Her aunt and uncle operate the old Christmas tree farm at the top of the mountain. Years ago, her father started his own landscaping business on the property, and now, her brother has the winery. The bottom land was sold to pay the taxes on the farm, and then it was later developed into a golf community."

"They sound like busy people."

"They are. They're some of the hardest working people I know," he said, as the road wound tighter, the higher they climbed. First, the family home came into view, making Elise gasp with delight.

"Oh! Is that one of the inns you were talking about?"

"No. That's the Davenports' house…where Chelsea grew up. The winery is just down the road, beyond the White Horse Farm Nursery. That's her father's business. You'll be working with him. Tom's the landscape architect we use," he said, grinning at her awed expression. "He and my dad built the Snowy Ridge Country Club and most of the houses down at the bottom of the mountain where the golf course is."

"You work with her father…unbelievable!" she said. "I saw his picture on the website, but never made the connection to Chelsea."

"Well, more than that, he's been like a father to me since Chelsea and I got together."

When the winery came into view, she gasped again. "Oh, my God! It's like suddenly being in the French countryside with a little touch of our mountains thrown in. This is incredible! You did that?" she laughed again, her hand at her mouth. "Kyle, the photographs don't do it justice!" Pleased by her reaction, he drove into the parking lot and stopped the car, watching her stare at his creation.

"Wait until you see the inside. Faith outdid herself," he said proudly, wanting her opinion of Faith restored. They got out of the Explorer to walk down the stone walkway. He gestured toward the terrace beyond the building where she could see the vineyard. "They have weddings and parties here. It's especially beautiful at night. I can't take you inside today, though; they aren't open on Mondays. But you can see it if you'll come to Faith's retirement party next weekend," he said, watching her peer into a window. She turned suddenly.

"But I wasn't invited."

"I'm inviting you. Come, and bring someone."

She looked at him carefully. "I...haven't had a date in over seven years," she said, smoothing her skirt and her hair in a gust of wind.

This he found hard to believe.

"Well, just bring a friend."

"I don't even know anyone here."

"It doesn't matter. Just come. We'll take care of you," he said, making her swing her eyes toward him again, a question on her tongue. He looked away, realizing he might have given her the wrong idea. "Chelsea and Frank and I will introduce you to everyone. It'll be good for you to meet some of our clients, too. Lots of them are coming to see Faith off. Really, you should try to come." He looked at her again, hoping to convince her.

"I'll need to find a babysitter..." she whispered. "Thank you," she said, sweeping a strand of hair away from her face in the crisp breeze.

He smiled at the detail he was beginning to expect from her. "What's your cell number?" he asked, and she told him. Pulling his phone from his pocket, he texted Maddie's phone number to hers.

Chapter 4

A Party

He felt her walk up beside him and slip the empty beer bottle from his hand. Drowsing under the canopy of green trees on their porch, with the soft swoosh of the river in the background, had long been one of his favorite pastimes. Opening his eyes, he first saw the three pairs of chest waders draped over the railing, drying in the sun. Then her face appeared, her unusual pale aquamarine eyes gazing at him with amusement.

"Hello. I'm Chelsea," she said, extending her hand as if they'd never met. It was a game they played when one of them became so noticeably distracted that the other felt the need to bring him or her back to earth.

He extended his hand to hers, a wry smile plying his mouth. "Sorry," he said. "Was I in La-La Land?"

"Yeah, you were," she said, laughter in her eyes, seating herself on the edge of the Adirondack chair cornered next to his on the porch. "It's so warm and lovely out here that I don't blame you a bit," she said, stroking her hand along his forearm, large and dark under her slender fingers.

He closed his eyes at her touch and leaned forward, wanting her to kiss him. She did, and it was no disappointment. "Mmm," he whispered, wanting more. "Where are the boys?"

"Back down at the river with Thomas for a few minutes," she said, grinning, referring to the twins' fourteen year-old cousin who had come to babysit them for the evening.

"I never heard you all drive up," he said, searching for her mouth again.

She held his chin, kissing him softly. "I know. You tend to lose yourself in that river. Every spring, it's the same way. But I don't mind. Your addiction could be another woman," she laughed, making him remember what his mother had said about the cabin years ago, calling it *the other woman*. It had allured his father away in much the same way, but his mother *had* minded. "What were you thinking about?" she asked.

"Uh…I don't think I remember," he said, pulling her onto his lap. She giggled, sliding her fingers into his hair, still damp from his shower. She smelled incredible, fresh from her own bath before she'd left with the boys to collect Thomas for the evening. They were due at the winery in an hour for Faith's party. "Do we have time?" he asked, lips at her ear, making her giggle more.

"I don't think so," she said, and he knew they couldn't get away with what he wanted with the boys so close by. "Besides, I'd just have to take another shower."

"Oh, yes, you would!" he said, wrapping his arms around her and kissing her passionately.

She pulled herself away and stood, reaching for his hand, pulling him up with her. "Let's get dressed," she said, slipping away from him. But he lingered, looking down at the river, through the long fingers of the willow trees, catching a glimpse of the boys walking on the rocks with Thomas. The river was a dangerous yet compelling place, a fact he well knew from his childhood in this very spot. They were lucky that their part of the river was shallow and filled with large rocks, which made the best stepping stones, creating less of a water hazard for the twins, but still, it had always been a concern for Chelsea and Kyle when the boys began walking. Without Thomas there, he would never have allowed that kind of behavior, but Thomas was responsible and would watch them carefully. Jay had raised him right, he thought, taking one more look, then letting himself follow Chelsea into the bedroom.

She was slipping a red dress over her head; he watched it fall around her knees. It was her look all right, tasteful but sexy, not too revealing, alluring just the same. Every man in the place would take note of his wife tonight, he thought. Reaching for his shirt, he watched her shake out her hair, checking the diamond studs at her ears, the ones he'd given her when the twins were born. He remembered that day as if it were yesterday. How tiny they'd been! He had never felt so awed and vulnerable before that day. Their birth was one of those miracles that made him keenly aware of God in his life, and just how fragile they all were. Remembering the feelings of protectiveness that had been born in him that day, he reached for her when she stood close to him, buttoning his shirt. Questioning with her eyes, she let him hold her, hands pressed between them.

"I love you," he whispered, kissing the top of her head. She smiled at him, finishing the buttons and stepping away to put on her shoes.

"The boys had a great time fishing today," she said. "They told Thomas all about it on the way over. I think they're becoming as obsessed as you are."

"Is that a bad thing?"

"No…I'm glad you have that bond with them. It's so good for them to know this side of you. Now, when you start actually catching something, I might start to feel left out!"

"Hah!" he said, swatting her with a sock on her way out the door. "Maybe you should come with us sometime. The boys would love that, you know," he said after her. It had been years since she'd fished with him. He heard her greeting the boys as they tromped in the front door.

"Thomas, I've got spaghetti in this pot on the stove. It's all mixed together, so all you have to do is serve it up, okay? There's bread in the oven, and the salad is in the fridge."

"That sounds great, Aunt Chelsea. And it smells awesome!" he said, his voice deeper than Kyle remembered, and he had just seen Thomas last week. "You look real nice," he said to her as Kyle walked into the room.

"Thank you. Just rinse the dishes and put them in the dishwasher afterwards, if you would," she reminded him, not swayed from her instructions by his flattery.

"You bet," said Thomas. Kyle wondered whether he was as well-trained as he let on.

"Ty, Stu, go wash your hands. Thomas, they're really going to need baths tonight. They smell like little muskrats. After dinner, you promise?"

"Sure," he said to her indulgently.

"And we rented a movie for later. They got to pick it out, you know, because they've been sleeping through the night still. I'm doing everything I can to make that a new habit!" she said, crossing her fingers, making Thomas laugh. He probably wondered why it was a big deal, Kyle thought.

Kyle added, "And bedtime is eleven and no later…for them. You just lock the doors after we leave, okay?" Thomas nodded. "Hey, guys!" Kyle called downstairs. "Leave those wet shoes outside on the porch."

Thomas nodded again. "I have your cell numbers if there's a problem."

It *was* enchanting, like being transported to the French countryside, Kyle thought proudly as they walked up the drive to the winery, Chelsea warm and beautiful on his arm. What could be better than this? Shades of rose and mango tinted the clouds beyond the tiled roof as crickets sang; welcoming them, reminding him that summer was almost here. Torches guided them to the door where lights twinkled, warming the windows, inviting them in. They were not the first to arrive, as many people milled around among the barrels and displays of wines. Tables were set with hors d'oeuvres, cheeses and fruits, and a roast beef was being sliced by a server in a crisp white jacket. "Who else will be here that I haven't met?" asked Chelsea, eyes sparkling, as she pressed into him before they entered the doorway.

"Oh, I think you'll know just about everybody," he murmured as Frank greeted them at the door, pressing his hand into Kyle's and giving Chelsea a smooch on the cheek.

"Hi, Frank," she giggled, looking around for Faith. "Where is the guest of honor?"

"Hey, gorgeous! Here she is," said Frank, holding his arm out as Faith made her way toward them, dressed in hot pink silk with lips and nails to match.

"*Chelsea!*" she squealed, winking at Kyle, and wrapping Chelsea in a matronly hug.

"Faith! How have you been? Retirement definitely agrees with you!" said Chelsea.

"Oh, honey! I've been having such a wonderful time with the crew! We just got back from Disney yesterday, and I'm exhausted. I'm going to have to get a gym membership to be able to keep up with them! Oh, but I worry *so* about this man," she said, grasping Kyle by the arm and pulling them both into her space. "How are you holding up, dar-lin'? Frank says everything is fine at the office, and that Elise is doing a great job, but I worry that no one is taking care of you," she said with deploring eyes, patting his arm.

"Hey, Faith. I guess I'm hanging in there," Kyle said, kissing her chubby cheek, amused, playing along with her game. "The coffee sucks, but what can I do?" he said, winking at her.

"Seriously, I've heard that Elise is getting along very well. I didn't doubt for a second that she'd be an asset to the company."

"She is. It's fine. You have nothing to worry about, but I do miss you. You knew I would," Kyle said, catching a glimpse of others in the room who would be demanding his attention. Jay grinned and waved at him from the wine bar, across from Michael Gilmer, who turned and waved as well. Great, thought Kyle, the investors are here. Marcus, Michael's father, was deeply engrossed in a conversation with Michael's date. Or at least, he assumed it was Michael's date; with those two, you never knew. A glittering bracelet, dark hair be-ing tossed over a shoulder, and several different fragrances mingling among the crowd; all those sensations left a man swimming in a sea of estrogen, not that Kyle minded. He liked women.

Bri, Chelsea's cousin, who was approaching thirty, called out and waved to them from behind the bar next to Jay. She managed the winery these days, and with her open smile and streaming blond hair, added a certain mystique to the place; that is, if you were a man look-ing for a particular vibe. Jay was a smart man and he had placed his young cousin in a position that helped them both. Not only was Bri charming, according to the men in the place, but she had the knack with the women as well, with the brides-to-be who came in daily, shopping for the perfect wedding venue or the bachelorette party site. Jay had told Kyle that Bri was soon to be engaged herself, and he had worried that she'd leave, forcing him to find a suitable replacement, which was troubling, he thought. But more troubling was watching

Michael Gilmer eye her from his seat at the bar, sipping a red wine, casually watching her work, while his father flirted ridiculously with the twenty-something woman to his left.

Inwardly, Kyle seethed, knowing a man like Michael would be no good for Bri, or anyone else he knew, for that matter. Michael was a player, with his wiry light brown hair and impossibly red lips. He was the talk of the community, the new guy in town, with a different girl every weekend. He ran the new pub in Banner Elk that was getting all the press lately, and had done a bang-up job over the ski season at the foot of Sugar Mountain. No one from around here ever got that successful in one season, especially in this economy, and especially without the work Kyle was sure it would take to make it here. Michael was just lucky they'd had a record snowfall that year. People had come in droves to the mountain, and there had been numerous reviews in all the right magazines about his place, its food, and his wide variety of imported beers. There was no doubt in Kyle's mind that Marcus Gilmer was a masterful promoter and had created Michael's success. But what had disturbed him most of all about Michael was his audacious interest in the Davenports' house. *You've been inside; what would it take to bring it up to speed as a B and B?* he'd asked Kyle the last time they'd talked, as if Tom and Liz were the slightest bit interested in leaving the home where five generations of Davenports had lived. Michael's glance passed over Kyle, after acknowledging him only briefly, lingering on Chelsea for a moment, before settling on the dark-haired beauty at his side, who had taken his arm, a signal that she was bored with Michael's father.

"Hey, guys!" Abby Dunham cried, taking Chelsea's arm and whisking her to the side on her way to greet Faith while Glen raised a glass of red wine to Kyle, as they shook hands.

"Oh, hello, Abby! It's good to see you and Glen again! Are you all still enjoying your kitchen? And how are all those babies?" asked Faith.

"Well, the babies are four years old now. And the kitchen's still great. We absolutely love it. The extra room has come in really handy. There's always a crowd!" replied Abby. "I'm glad we did it when we did because there hasn't been a penny to spare since the triplets arrived!" Abby said, referring to the kitchen redesign she and Glen had hired Faith and Kyle to do for their modest little house in Boone before the triplets were born. Glen managed to raise his eyebrows so only Kyle could see, and Kyle clasped his shoulder in commiseration as the women took up the conversation.

"I guess you got Maddie tonight," Abby said to Chelsea.

"No, I thought you did," Chelsea replied. "When I talked to her about tonight, she said she already had a commitment, so I thought it was you," she went on.

Abby looked perplexed. "No, it wasn't me. Who else could be in on our secret weapon?" she asked, referring to the best babysitter they'd ever had. Kyle thought it best to avoid this conversation, knowing he'd be in trouble with both of the women for giving out Maddie's number, a move he was now regretting.

Kyle made his way to the bar with Glen to get a couple of glasses of wine. "Hey, Jay. Bri, hi, everything looks great tonight! And Jay, thanks for letting Thomas spend the night. He's sure been a hit with Ty and Stu. We might need his babysitting services more often if he likes it as well as they do. How about a couple of glasses of the Davenport Red?"

"Sure," Jay said, as Bri set two glasses on the bar and poured. "Well, Thomas is just as thrilled to have been asked. I'm sure it will be a nice change for him. Cleaning the barrel room after a bottling probably gets old when you're fourteen."

"Oh, you had a bottling today? Is that why the vultures are here? I didn't invite them," he said, giving Jay a look of displeasure.

"Hey, I didn't invite them either. Like I said, we bottled a new blend today, and they came out of curiosity and wanted to stay when they heard about the party. What could I say? They've been good investors, even though they might irritate you," said Jay, leveling a look at Kyle. "*Whoa!* Who's the goddess that just walked in?"

Kyle took the wine glasses, turning to see the focus of Jay's question. "That's our new designer, Elise Masters, Faith's replacement." Glen was looking that way, too, and giving Kyle a questioning and mischievous eye. Elise stood in the doorway, tall and willowy in a fluttery black dress, her brown hair flowing around her shoulders, looking poised for whatever awaited her—*like a model.* He felt drawn to her, an uncomfortable feeling in the presence of so many people, especially his wife, and after handing Chelsea her glass of wine and excusing himself, he walked over to take her arm, bringing her into the midst of the party.

Elise looked relieved to have found him, one of three people she would know in the room. "Hey," she said, a hint of nervousness in her voice.

"Hi," he said, making her smile. "I'm glad you made it."

"Elise, I'd like you to meet my wife, Chelsea," he said formally, watching Chelsea as her eyes grew large, nonetheless taking Elise's hand and looking up at her.

"Oh, Elise, I'm so pleased to meet you finally!" she said, shaking Elise's hand, glancing at Abby, introducing her friend and flicking her questioning eyes back at Kyle.

Kyle watched the interaction. Elise's cool green-brown eyes lingered for a split second on the crescent-shaped scar on Chelsea's cheek, the way it was with most people on first meeting her. He smiled, remembering Ty's comment when he was four, asking Chelsea if she'd carved her initial in her face. After all, it was common knowledge that she'd etched the letter C in the cabin window upon her engagement to his father! They had only told the boys that she'd been hurt in a car accident. But the fact that she'd almost lost her life in that accident had never been brought forth.

They were already talking. He knew they'd get along. If one woman in the world were like his wife, it was Elise Masters. Ballet was the topic.

"Oh, yes, I saw you dance many times," Elise was saying, as he watched Chelsea acknowledge the implications of how long ago it had been. "My grandmother is Helen Taylor."

"Of course! I remember Helen. She was a major benefactor with the Carolina Ballet. Is she still as involved as she was back then?"

"Yes, she still keeps up. I haven't been to a performance in a few years. I think my daughter would like to go…maybe this year," said Elise, her eyes giving away nothing.

"How old is she?" asked Chelsea, as Kyle watched the formidable Marcus Gilmer approaching.

"Kyle Davis! I should have known you'd have the two most beautiful women in the room on your arm!" he said loudly to Kyle, eyeing Chelsea and Elise with envy. Kyle shook his hand, as if squaring off for a duel. Marcus was ogling Elise, dying for an introduction.

"Marcus, how are you?" Kyle asked. He introduced Elise and reminded him that he'd met Chelsea. If Marcus started in again on turning the Davenport home into a bed and breakfast tonight, he would have to kick his ass to Tennessee, Kyle thought, smiling at him and pumping his hand, as Chelsea looked on, warily.

"Hey, Chelsea! It's good to see you again," said Marcus, taking Chelsea's hand, leaning in to kiss her cheek. "And Elise, what a pleasure!" he exclaimed, reaching for her hand as well.

"Elise is our new interior designer," Kyle explained, making Marcus' eyes light up even more.

Oddly enough, with all the ill-will surrounding the situation, Kyle had to admit that he really didn't *dislike* Marcus. He was a candid kind of guy, unlike Michael, whom he could never read. But Marcus was an up-front sort of man. He was brash, but honest. Faith had picked up whatever gossip she could learn on the man, and the word was that his wife had kicked him out of the Hamptons several years ago before he'd ended up in Blowing Rock, with Michael riding on his coattails, sucking up whatever he could.

Marcus was a large man, with the same wiry bronze-colored hair and patrician looks as Michael possessed. He was jovial in a sincere way, which was probably why he was so successful. Although he was from New York, his accent was Southern, leading Kyle to believe he must have been a transplant, although the same could not be said for his son.

Right now, Michael was making his way toward them, unencumbered by the attractive brunette he'd been cozy with at the bar, who was now chatting with Bri. As Kyle expected, he was on his way to make a move on Elise. He extended his hand to her, introducing himself. She tilted her head slightly, looked up at his tall frame, and shook his hand.

"Hello, Michael. I'm Elise Masters."

"*Elise*," he said, holding her hand too long. "An unforgettable name. So…you're with Kyle and Frank at Mountaineer Builders?" He'd apparently checked her out before coming over.

"Elise is our new designer," Kyle explained as if claiming her for his own. He watched Elise appraising Michael, probably unaware that moments ago he'd been bound to the brunette at the bar. Kyle felt himself heat up, as if he should protect Elise somehow. Chelsea looked on, undoubtedly wondering what he was thinking, and he turned away from Elise and Michael, trying to think of a way to extricate them all from the inevitable conversation with Marcus about the Davenports' house.

Marcus hovered, asking Chelsea about the family. He commented on Faith and how well she was looking, and asked Kyle about the business.

"I'd love to get together with you soon," he said to Kyle. Then lowering his voice, he continued, "I've got this property I just bought that I want you to see. It's a damn goldmine. It's a home I'm thinking about turning into a bed and breakfast, and I'd like to have your take on it," he said. Kyle stole a glance at Chelsea, who was watching with narrowed eyes. "Bring Elise. I'd love to see what you all can do with it."

"Sure; let's set something up. Call the office on Monday and we'll do it," Kyle said, trying to shake Marcus for the remainder of the evening. He'd spotted Tom and Liz Davenport walking in, at the same time as Chelsea, who excused herself eagerly to meet her parents.

At the same moment, Kyle heard a familiar voice greeting him from behind. Turning, he saw Lynn Schiffman's tiny figure approaching. Lynn, now in her mid-sixties, was still as fit and attractive as ever. "Kyle! It's so wonderful to see you!" she said, extending her arms for a welcome hug from him.

"Lynn!" he said, grinning and embracing her readily. "I'm so glad you were able to make it! Are you up here for good this summer?"

"I am!" she replied happily, her large hazel eyes bright. She would always be his favorite client, and without her influence, Mountaineer Builders might not have made it through the economic decline to which so many other builders had fallen prey. Lynn's glance shifted to Elise, and Kyle took her elbow, purposefully guiding her away from the Gilmer men and into a small space with Lynn.

"Lynn, I'd like you to meet our new interior designer in the firm. This is Elise Masters. Elise, this is Lynn Schiffman. She's the owner of Sugar Ridge," he said proudly, his hand at Elise's back, pulling her in closer to hear over the crowd.

"Hi, Elise. I hope we'll work together in the future. Kyle is my favorite architect, and Frank is a top-notch builder, so there's a good chance we'll get to know each other as well."

"Lynn, it's a pleasure to meet you too. Kyle's told me so much about Sugar Ridge. I think it might have been his favorite project as well. It certainly is a beautiful property."

"Thank you! You should come and see me in my house up here. Kyle's father built it, you know."

"Oh. I didn't know, but I'd love to see it. There's hardly enough time to see everything he and Kyle have built around here."

"Well, Kyle, you need to bring her by," Lynn said, smiling, glancing at his arm around Elise, which he dropped immediately. "Is Chelsea here?"

"Yes. There she is, talking with Tom and Liz, over by the bar," he said, aware that Chelsea was watching him as she conversed with her parents and Abby. He shifted his gaze to Elise, taking her by the elbow. "Come on over. You need to meet Chelsea's parents." He included Lynn in the statement, and they made their way through the crowd to the bar, listening to Faith's laughter as she greeted more guests.

Chelsea watched Abby sipping her wine; then she glanced across the room at Kyle, as Tom regaled them with a story about one of his landscaping clients. She could hardly listen, watching her husband's arm encircling his new colleague's waist. It was not lost on Abby either, as her friend shot her a warning glance. Kyle was coming toward them with Lynn and Elise to make more introductions, and by now, Tom and Liz were noticing the beautiful stranger in their midst as well. Chelsea's head swam as her parents greeted Lynn enthusiastically with hugs all around, and then Kyle introduced Elise, reaching for Chelsea's hand after he spoke. Realizing the two new arrivals didn't have drinks, however, he dropped her hand, leading them to the bar, resting his elbow on the leather ledge, waiting to get Bri's attention. Chelsea overheard him talking to Lynn and Elise in his smooth commanding voice. "Do you like red or white?" he asked Elise, already signaling Lynn's preference to Bri. When Elise replied that she preferred white, his eyes settled on hers. "Then you should try the *Moonlight*. It's a blend, like many of their wines," he said, giving her his most dazzling smile, as Bri poured a glass for Elise and a glass of cabernet for Lynn. Chelsea watched Elise breathe in the wine's bouquet, then sipped slowly and nodded. Kyle watched for her reaction, as if he'd made the wine himself. She sipped and swallowed slowly as he watched.

"Mmm…it's soft. It tastes like pears, or something. Thank you for suggesting it. I like it," she said, meeting his expectant eyes and smiling back at him. Lynn sipped hers as well as the three of them toasted each other.

"To new friends!" Lynn said, smiling.

Abby looked on and whispered to Chelsea, "*Girl!* You and I are going lingerie shopping tomorrow."

"What?" Chelsea whispered back, alarmed that Abby thought she was onto something.

"*Look at that girl!* If that's Kyle's new colleague, you're going to have to step up your game. She's a bombshell!" Abby whispered as loudly as she could for emphasis. "I'd say Kyle is rather spellbound!"

"Are you kidding? Kyle is just schmoozing with the clients. He's trying to showcase Elise so they'll know who they could be dealing with."

"I know that. And he certainly appears to enjoy his work."

"Abby…it's business. It's what you do," she said, sipping her wine, remembering Kyle's obvious displeasure at the dance ensemble when she had been required to pay homage to the football staff.

"I'm sure there's nothing to worry about, but it couldn't hurt to give him something to look forward to, you know? *Just saying.*…Look at her dress.…It's the perfect little black dress; not too dressy, but just dressy enough when you don't know what you're walking into. Elise is definitely sharp!" Abby whispered back. They watched Glen making his way toward them, wanting an introduction as well, Chelsea thought, giving Abby a smirk. They watched Kyle introduce her, and Glen shook her hand, exchanging a look with Kyle.

"You could use a new thong or something yourself, missy...*just saying*!" Chelsea said, catching Kyle's eye, as he made his way back to her through the large group. Abby ignored them, allowing them a moment of privacy so she could keep her eye on Glen and the new girl.

"You didn't tell me Elise was coming tonight," Chelsea commented quietly as he looked at her glass, almost empty. "And you failed to mention that she was drop-dead gorgeous," she added.

"I invited her at the last minute. As far as her looks are concerned, she was hired on the merits of her talent, so don't get the wrong idea; she's even more talented than she is beautiful...plus she's way too young for me," he added, making her laugh.

"You're so funny tonight! I just hope she's as professional as you're trying to be."

"Oh, she is, believe me," he said, making her raise her eyebrows. "I mean, it's not like *I've* been testing her."

She laughed, feeling his hand at her elbow as Elise looked around. There had been a time when this kind of situation would have worried her, but she knew not to go there again. Kyle's devotion to her had always been unshakable. Still, she was aware of the way he'd looked when Elise walked through the door, and of Abby's scrutiny of the whole spectacle, making her feel unusually defensive. Glen was certainly making a fool of himself, fawning over Elise as if she were the flavor of the week at the wine bar.

"You need another glass," Kyle offered, giving her a little wink.

"Yes, I do...make it *Moonlight*, please," she said, giving him a sweet smile. He eyed her, taking her glass and making his way back to the bar, where Elise appeared to be looking for a rescue from Glen. Kyle motioned his head toward Chelsea and Abby and Elise followed. So did Glen.

Handing Chelsea a second glass of wine, he made room for Elise in their circle. "Do you want something to eat?" he asked Chelsea.

"Not yet," she said, then addressed Elise. "Elise, you were telling me about your daughter. Did Kyle tell you we have twin boys?" she asked.

Elise glanced at Kyle, making Chelsea wonder what he knew that she didn't.

"Yes, he did. He showed me their picture. They're precious. My daughter's seven. Her name is Lydia. Oh, and by the way, Kyle, thanks for giving me Maddie's number. Lydia was already infatuated with her when I left," she said, smiling. Chelsea watched Abby's face ignite with color, as Abby threw Kyle an accusatory glance. He pressed his lips together, looking at both of them apologetically. Instinctively, his hand lifted to loosen the knot of his tie.

"You lucked out tonight," Abby said, jumping at the opportunity to set this intruder straight. "She's our top babysitter." Abby smiled broadly, making Elise look bemused.

"Oh, I'm sorry. I thought it was okay…" she said, glancing quickly at Kyle.

"Of course it was," Chelsea said, coming to the rescue, shooting Abby a look that said, *poor form.*

But all eyes were on Kyle. "Elise doesn't know anyone. This is kind of an important night for us," he said, glancing at Elise, as Chelsea saw Abby's brows ratchet up one more notch. "So, what do you think of the winery?" he asked suddenly, giving Elise a disarming smile, his blue eyes intent on hers.

Elise took a breath before answering, a flush appearing in her face. Could it be the wine, or was it Kyle's look that affected her? "It's as lovely as I thought it would be. When you brought me here last week,

I was dying to see the inside, and I'm definitely not disappointed. It makes a great venue for a party like this."

Now it was Chelsea's turn to raise her eyebrows, but she fought the urge. *When you brought me here last week?* And the look he was giving Elise was the same look that had made her own face flush thousands of times in the past. *Her look.* She ran her hand through her hair, wishing for a diversion.

Abby chortled openly. "Awkward," she whispered to Chelsea under her breath.

Kyle glanced at Chelsea. He had failed to mention a lot. Chelsea tried to regain the upper hand, circling her hand around Kyle's arm. "Why don't we get some of that food? I'm actually starving!" His business didn't involve her; however, she was used to hearing the humorous daily anecdotes of what was going on with Frank and Faith, and the progress on his various projects. However out of the loop she felt, she knew she wouldn't ask for explanations. There was nothing to it, she thought, but even then, Kyle and Elise were sharing glances she couldn't interpret.

Several of them sat outside enjoying the warm evening and the food, watching Faith open a few gifts. Elise chatted with Tom and Liz, and Frank and Faith. When Kyle stood to excuse himself to the restroom, he was aware that Elise had followed him.

"Kyle, thanks for including me tonight. This has been really nice, but I'm going to head on home."

"Oh, okay," he said, understanding that the babysitter was on the clock, something he'd considered himself. "I'm glad you came tonight. You were…certainly a hit with our clients. Let me walk you out."

"No, no, I'm good. I don't want to take you away from your family. They're all very nice. I did want to ask a favor though. Are you going to be busy tomorrow afternoon?"

He knew there were plans, but he was interested. "What did you have in mind?"

"I took Lydia antiquing today."

"Antiquing? Not Tweetsie?" he laughed, trying to imagine his boys bashing about in one of those kinds of shops.

"She's very tolerant for her age, and she's been to Tweetsie," she smiled, acknowledging his reference to the old steam engine train that was a necessary visit for those under the age of twelve. "Anyway, I bought a beautiful old bureau for her bedroom, and I have it in the back of my Jeep. I can't carry it in by myself, though. I was going to ask my neighbor to help me, but I think he's out of town. Would you mind stopping by and lending me a hand? It would only take a few minutes."

"Sure. No problem. What time?"

"Any time…whenever it suits you. We'll be around."

"Okay. I'll call you after lunch."

"That would be great. Thanks," she said, smiling, smoothing a strand of hair behind her ear. "Then I'll see you tomorrow."

"Yeah…have a nice night. Drive safely," he said, after she'd turned away.

She looked back one more time, smiling again. "Goodnight," she said.

"Goodnight…." He lingered a moment, watching her walk away, listening as she said her goodbyes to new acquaintances on the terrace. *Smooth*.

Chapter 5

QUESTIONS

An unusual silence accompanied them on the drive back to the cabin. There was no music. A veil of moonlight washed Kyle's face as he drove without speaking. His blue eyes focused on the road, but he was anywhere but in that car with her.

Unable to stand the silence any longer, Chelsea spoke. "It was a nice party."

"Yeah, it was," he said, as if surprised she were there. Normally, he would have reached for her hand, but his eyes swung back to the road; perhaps the effects of the wine were causing him to be extra careful. Still, she felt her heart quickening, yearning for his attention. How long would he ignore her if she continued to remain silent?

"I think Faith felt very flattered that so many of her clients and friends showed up. It was a nice tribute," she continued, sweeping her hair off her face in the breeze from the open window. He murmured his agreement. "Elise seems very nice," she commented, jolting him back to reality, making him turn to her.

"Did you like her?"

"Yes."

"I thought you would. She reminds me a lot of you," he said, making her wonder whether that was a good thing.

"I can't believe she saw me dance all those years ago...*when she was a kid*," she quoted Elise, laughing quietly, and he chuckled.

"Yeah...you had complained about feeling old. Now I get it. We're not the young people any more. She treats me like an old man."

She doubted that was the case. But he was right; they were no longer the center of attention. "Maybe she's just giving you a hard time."

"Yeah, that's kind of her personality. She has sort of a dry sense of humor."

He would like that.

"So what happened to her husband? Do you know her story?" Chelsea asked, curious, watching as his expression became guarded. His eyes remained on the road.

"She wasn't married," he said.

"Oh."

"She needs me to come over tomorrow and give her a hand bringing in an antique dresser she bought today."

"So she really doesn't know anyone here?"

"No. All her friends from college are gone. A neighbor she was hoping would help is out of town."

"Well, it was nice that you invited her tonight."

"It was good for her to meet our other clients. Lynn and Marcus showed an interest in working with us again. I won't be gone long tomorrow," he said, at last reaching for her hand, and giving her a reassuring glance, his eyes deep as water, stirring her. "It's Sunday after all, family day."

Silently relieved, she smiled. "Dad said something about us coming over in the afternoon."

"Yeah, he mentioned it to me too. He said he and Jay got that dead sweetgum tree down last weekend, so I promised him I'd bring the boys over and split some of it for him. Does that sound good to you?"

"That would be good. I really need to visit with Mom. She said my grandmother isn't doing well, and I can tell it's wearing on her. I think she needs my help, but she won't ask. You know how she is." She felt the tip of his thumb circling the back of her hand, thoughtfully. He was back with her.

"Then we'll make an afternoon of it," he promised, pulling her hand to his lips and kissing it. She sighed silently, not wanting him to discover she'd worried, or questioned. But she knew she hadn't imagined his pre-occupation. Instead, she turned his hand over, pressing her lips into his palm, making his eyes flicker toward her in the moonlight. "God, you're beautiful," he said, letting his knuckles brush her cheek, soft as a bird's wing.

Thomas was awake when they arrived home, with his feet propped up on the coffee table, texting on his phone and watching TV. After filling them in on their evening and the boys' baths, they all said goodnight and he excused himself to the downstairs guest bedroom.

Chelsea lay beside Kyle in the darkness, wondering why he seemed withdrawn, consoling herself that with Thomas in the house, he probably didn't want to make any noise that would make him feel uncomfortable. Kyle turned to her, patting her arm and murmuring, "Goodnight, angel." He kissed her and then rolled onto his side, away from her, his breathing becoming deep with slumber, as she lay there, as far from sleep as she had been an hour ago. Feeling his warmth with the sleep that came so easily to him, she turned toward his back, longing to reach for his broad shoulders, but not wanting to wake him just the same. Sighing, she curled her hands under her chin and closed her eyes, attempting to block out the exquisite face with the swirling brown hair that had distracted her all evening. It was not a problem that Elise was beautiful. What was a problem was the way she had managed to hold her husband's gaze, something Chelsea had never witnessed with a stranger. This woman was indeed a stranger, who had filtered her way into their lives, and it disturbed Chelsea that she had these feelings, these questions, especially when she believed her marriage to be so undeniably solid. It was possible she'd imagined all of it, but something didn't feel right. How life could change in an instant.

It was light when she heard the boys padding about in the kitchen. Their routine on the weekends was to fix bowls of cereal if they couldn't wait for breakfast, giving their parents a brief respite from the long week. Sleeping in was Chelsea's passion, and something that didn't happen often with twins. She felt Kyle stir, yawning and rubbing his face, and then rise to meet his sons for breakfast. She pretended to be asleep, knowing he'd tend to Foscoe and fix the coffee, giving her fifteen minutes of sloth before she had to emerge.

She heard them greeting each other, and chatting about the night before. It was expected that they'd go to church every Sunday, but with summer vacation here, it would be only the worship service and no Sunday school, which made the boys somewhat happier.

"Daddy, will you make us pancakes?" she heard Stu ask.

"You bet," Kyle said. "Why don't you go down and check on Thomas and see if he wants some."

Chelsea's eyes popped open; she had forgotten all about Thomas spending the night. They would meet Jay and Lauren at church and drop him off with them. Reluctantly, remembering she had company, she sat up, reaching for her robe. She would make herself useful, she thought, going to the kitchen, receiving morning hugs from all her guys. Taking in Kyle's progress with the breakfast, she set about assembling the necessary ingredients as he poured their coffee. Thomas appeared, with rumpled hair, in his clothes from last night.

"Good morning, Thomas," she said, grinning at him, as Kyle handed her a cup of coffee.

"Good morning," he said, his voice still thick with sleep.

"How about some pancakes?" Kyle asked, as he dumped mix from a box into a measuring cup.

As the morning progressed, her unsettling thoughts from last night melted away into the routine and conversations that comprised their life at home, and Kyle was himself again. The boys were excited to be visiting their grandparents today, and to be helping with a grown-up job like stacking the wood their father would split.

After church, as they walked up the cabin steps, Kyle hung back in the drive to make a phone call, reminding Chelsea that he had promised to help Elise unload a dresser at her apartment. She watched him walk to the shed to retrieve his axe, talking to Elise as he went, and she wondered why he couldn't talk to her in front of them all.

She made tuna salad as the boys and Kyle changed into their jeans and T-shirts. Her eyes drifted toward him as he emerged beside her, helping her set out plates and pour glasses of milk. It was her favorite look, an old white T-shirt and the jeans with the tear just above the knee. Could he look any sexier? And he was off to see a beautiful woman, a *single* woman dressed like this.

They ate without discussing his next errand, and he left as the boys were helping her place their dishes in the dishwasher. Wiping the milk from his mouth with his napkin, he kissed her and caught her around the waist. "I'll be back in two shakes," he promised with a wink. "Don't leave without me," he warned, making her laugh, alleviating her prior worries a bit.

Elise's Jeep was parked in front of apartment 1D as she had told him. He pulled in beside it, glad that she had four-wheel drive. She would need it up here, and it looked tested, plenty old enough to be the car she'd probably had in college. As he approached her door, it swung open and she was there, elegant even in her own jeans and a tank top, ready for work, as he was. He inspected her doorway, sturdy and metal with a deadbolt, as she greeted him, ushering him inside with a sweep of her hand.

"Hey," he said, noticing her smile. She didn't share that smile often, making him wonder how many people had even seen the inside of her place. It was more than he expected, but knowing her style, it wasn't surprising. The modest apartment was serene and welcoming, the furniture well-placed with inviting hues of muted greens, browns, and blues interspersed everywhere. The furniture was a mix of clean lined upholstered pieces and antiques. Lamps lent their warmth and an old walnut writing desk caught his eye under a watercolor of a morning garden. The smell of fresh paint hung in the air.

"Wow…this is much nicer than what I expected," he said, looking at her apprehensive expression.

"Really? That's kind of disappointing, given that you hired me for my particular skill set," she said, eyebrows raised, making him regret saying it. Then she laughed gently, watching him relax.

"No, I meant…did you paint?" he asked, noticing the warm green-gray color on the walls.

"I had to. This place was so depressing when I saw it for the first time."

"I didn't think they'd let you do that," he said.

"You don't think I asked them, do you?" she asked, and he laughed this time, shaking his head. "Oh, it's much easier to ask for forgiveness than for permission," she laughed again, the sound of it beginning to get under his skin. Another sound made him turn around. A tiny girl, almost a replica of Elise, but with rosy lips and soft wavy hair pulled back into a ponytail, appeared from around the kitchen cabinet.

"Kyle, this is Lydia," Elise said, taking her daughter's hand and sinking to her knees beside her. Kyle stepped forward and did the same. The child looked at him with the same river eyes her mother had, but her mouth seemed so different; yet she was familiar in a striking way. He extended his hand toward her, thinking at the same time it was ridiculous to expect a handshake, but she surprised him by taking his hand. He laughed quietly. "Lydia, this is Mr. Davis," Elise said, meeting his eyes with surprise.

"Hello, Lydia. It's very nice to meet you," he said, smiling, entranced by her beauty, like a storybook character. She smiled easily, unlike her mother, but she did not speak. He was aware of her hand still in his. How sweet a little girl was! She was so much smaller than Ty and Stu, he thought, feeling his thumb brush the back of her hand.

"She doesn't usually warm to men this way," Elise said, watching them. "I mean, not that she meets a lot of men…but my dad's friends usually scare her."

Kyle glanced at her, aware that Lydia was still holding his hand, and her eyes were locked onto his. "Who's this?" he asked Lydia, referring to the floppy-eared bunny she clung to in the crook of her other arm. Lydia did not answer.

"That's Pink Bunny. He came a couple of Easters ago, and he's been Lydia's best friend ever since. They were playing school before you got here."

"Oh," said Kyle with complete understanding. Lydia moved forward, resting her arm on Kyle's knee, a faint rustling making him aware that she wore a pull-up diaper still.

"I'm sorry; she's usually not this forward!" Elise said, pulling Lydia back as they stood. "I know you have things to do, so I won't keep you. We can go ahead and bring in the bureau, so you can be on your way," said Elise, tossing her brown hair over her shoulder, and reaching for her car keys.

Kyle followed her out as she instructed Lydia to stay inside, which seemed unnecessary as the little girl made no move to follow.

The bureau was a large oak piece with brass handles on the drawers and a detached mirror with an ornate scrolled frame that tilted on a metal rod. Kyle eased the mirror out of the back of the Jeep first, and Elise guided it into place on the pavement. Then he slid out the bureau, setting it carefully on the pavement. He removed the drawers and picked it up, carrying it inside, as she followed him with the mirror. She led the way into Lydia's bedroom, decorated with fairies, where two plastic tubs of her clothing had functioned as her dresser. He set his piece down, admiring the furniture, and giving her a nod. "This is a great piece. I can see why you wanted it. You have a lot of nice antiques," he said, running his hand over the oak, slightly rough to the touch, as he looked around.

"Thanks," she said, also spreading her fingers across the bureau's surface. "Don't you sometimes wonder what stories these pieces could tell? I wish I knew....My dad and I share a love for old things. He'd like this too," she said, her hand automatically going to the necklace. He looked away. "You know, the best thing about antiques is that they're cheaper than new furniture and so much better made, recycling in its finest form," she smiled, touching the dresser again, "*and* they're made in America!" He knew she would say that, and had mouthed it to himself as she spoke. She noticed, smiling at him in surprise. They brought in the drawers and slid them in place. Then she asked, "Would you mind helping me attach the mirror? It'll only take a second."

"Sure. I wish I'd brought my drill," he said, turning to see her lift a cordless drill off the kitchen counter. "Oh." Her self-help skills shouldn't continue to surprise him, but he shook his head all the same.

"If you'll hold it, I'll put the screws in," she said, ignoring his bemused look. He held the mirror in place, glancing at her bicep as she raised the drill. Holding the screw in position, she pressed the button, neatly locking one in, and then another. She repeated the process on the other side, and he stood, brushing his hands together; his services were no longer needed.

"Thanks for your help," she said, as he turned to go. Lydia reached up to him, and irresistibly, he lifted her in his arms, feeling her snuggle into his chest. Elise lowered her eyes, saying, "It looks like you've made a friend today."

"I'm flattered," he said. "She's a cutie. Well, I guess I should be going. My two boys are waiting on me to go split some wood at Tom's this afternoon," he said, setting Lydia back down, and they followed him to the door.

"Thanks again," she said, looking beyond him as a mud-splashed Jeep Wrangler roared up on the other side of Kyle's Explorer. "Well," she said. "Here's my neighbor…just a few minutes too late."

A short, dark-haired man about Elise's age hopped out of the Jeep, pulling a duffle bag out of the backseat, and shutting the door. He looked up, surprised, his eyes moving back and forth from Elise to Kyle. "Oh, hey, Elise! How're ya doin'?"

"Hi, Wyatt," she said, leaning against the doorjamb, folding her arms at her waist. His eyes still questioned as Kyle fished keys out of his pocket. "Wyatt, this is Kyle Davis," she said, as Kyle stepped forward to shake hands with her neighbor.

"Hey, Kyle. Wyatt Schmidt."

"Wyatt…how're you doing?" asked Kyle, eyeing him, interested in the misperception the young man appeared to be having, as Wyatt slung the bag over his shoulder and looked back at Elise. Elise seemed interested too, but said nothing to clear it up, as she watched him nod to them and head toward his apartment, two doors down. Kyle looked back at her. "Bye, Elise."

"See you tomorrow, Kyle," she said as he seated himself in the Explorer, chuckling.

Chelsea dawdled at the kitchen counter, adding pecans, strawberries, and goat cheese to the salad she'd made, after her mother had called, inviting them all for dinner. She sighed, listening to the boys' game of checkers on the sunporch; Stu must be cheating again, she thought, hearing Ty's complaint. She held her breath, listening to them work it out.

"Fine! I don't play with cheaters!" she heard him say, and then the sound of checkers scattering on the floor.

"Whatever. Help pick them up, then," said Stu, but Ty was having none of it.

"It's your problem. Pick them up yourself. And you can play by yourself, too," muttered Ty, stalking downstairs.

She left it alone, wondering what was keeping Kyle. It had been over an hour since he'd left for Elise's. She covered the salad bowl with plastic wrap, set it on the table, and sat down, pressing her fingers into the bridge of her nose. Her mother's voice had sounded weary, troubled almost, and Chelsea had thought about texting Kyle, telling him to meet them at her parents' house. But that would have sent the message that she was irritated with him, that she couldn't wait, that she was worried. Maybe she was. But the last thing she would allow herself to do was to let him see her insecurity. The sleepless night she'd spent was catching up with her. She pressed harder on her face. It was hard to watch her husband sharing private looks with someone new in his life, an associate, but nonetheless someone new. And someone so hauntingly beautiful it had everyone at the party talking. They would work together every day for the next twenty or thirty years. Elise Masters would spend forty hours or more a week with her husband and become a part of his family, the same way Frank and Faith had come to love him. It made her sick, the more she thought about it. Already, she could see Kyle's protective nature coming out to wrap Elise in the comforts Chelsea knew so well. His kindness extended to everyone, and she wondered how Elise would interpret this, and if Chelsea could stand to share him with someone like her.

Hearing Kyle's SUV rumble up the drive, Chelsea forced herself to breathe deeply, clearing her head, and called to the boys. She heard no movement from either of them. They must still be sulking, she thought, as she heard Kyle's work boots clunk across the front porch planks. She stood as he walked in the door, watching him glance at the canvas tote she'd packed with their bathing suits and towels for a swim in the lake, and then at the salad bowl on the table.

"Hey!" he said brightly, his arms going around her waist. He leaned in to kiss her, and she felt herself offer her cheek rather than her mouth, making him look at her with questions in his eyes. "Everything okay?"

"Sure. Just ready to go. Mom's asked us to stay for dinner," she explained, gesturing at the salad.

"Oh, that's nice of her. Where are the boys?"

"Sulking…self-imposed separation. Their checkers game didn't go well."

He nodded. "Ah, I see. Do I need to say anything…back you up or whatever?"

"No, but we need to get going," she said.

He gave the boys a shout, and stirring was heard from both points in the cabin.

"How's Elise?" she asked bravely, as if Elise were just a neighbor, just a business associate.

"She's good. We got her dresser all set up. Her little girl is adorable," he said as she tried to look only mildly interested. "We could have a little girl too, you know," he said, grinning at her, disarming any previously negative thoughts she'd had. She felt his hand circle her waist, pulling her close, and this time she gave him the kiss he wanted.

"Are we taking Foscoe?" Stu asked, as the boys and the dog made their entrance, suddenly filling the kitchen. She imagined what the room would feel like when the twins grew to be Kyle's size.

"Of course we are," said Kyle, lifting the tote bag. "Granddaddy would be mad at us if we left one of his best friends at home." Foscoe had made a name for himself over the past few years as Tom's buddy. Tom had come to love the dog as his own. It would be good for the boys to spend time at their grandparents' house. They could run around and play for hours without fear of falling in the river. Their own sloping lot was not well-suited to the recreation of little boys.

Chelsea smiled as they packed up to head out the door.

Her mother had lemonade and iced tea waiting on the stone terrace when they arrived. Her father took the boys to the lake to toss the retrieving dummy for Foscoe, while Kyle went to work, splitting the wood. The air was fresh and filled with the scent of summer roses and newly mown grass, mixed with the musky fragrance of the barn within view. Also within view was her husband, swinging the axe easily, the crack of it hewing the dead logs neatly in two. His broad shoulders worked fluidly, without effort, and both women watched with admiration.

Her mother sighed, pouring plastic tumblers of half-tea and half-lemonade, and adding mint leaves. "It's nice to see a young man work. Your dad really appreciates this, by the way. With Jay at the winery every Sunday, it's not as easy to get things done. You missed the plumbers this week. We had a broken water main on Friday, but it's fixed now. There's always something in this old place."

Chelsea nodded, accepting her tea, lulled into laziness by the warm sun embracing her shoulders. She remembered sitting here with her mother last summer, watching the new roof's installation.

"So, what was Kyle doing in town on a Sunday afternoon?" Liz asked.

"Oh, I thought I mentioned it," Chelsea said casually. "He was helping Elise Masters unload a chest of drawers she'd bought at an antique store." She had almost said, *he was helping Elise with her chest*, but thought better of it.

"Oh, that was nice of him. She and I had such a nice talk last night. I asked her to come over and take a look at the house. I'd love to see what she'd suggest doing to improve the looks of the place. Sometimes, I get tired of seeing the same old thing, you know?"

"Well…just don't let her change anything in the violet bedroom," Chelsea warned; memories of her old bedroom with the faded violets on the ancient wallpaper took her back to time spent with her grandmother, Kitty, a time she treasured in her heart. As a young child, it had been the room she'd spent the night in when she visited Kitty, and later, the room she'd lived in during high school. *Her room.*

"Of course, your old bedroom," said her mother. "I won't let her change it….She's an impressive girl, though. I enjoyed meeting her last night. And she said she had seen you dance."

"Mmm," Chelsea murmured, wishing her mother would change the topic. "Everyone liked her," she heard herself say with more sharpness in her tone than she intended, making her mother look at her.

"Well, I did hear several people comment about how stunning she is. She presents herself very well," said her mother, using a phrase Chelsea's other grandmother would have used. "Your dad told Frank he thought she was a class act."

"Now, Mom, you shouldn't be worried about Dad. He loves you very much," Chelsea said, giggling, knowing this was the turn the conversation would take.

Her mother shook her head, running a hand through her hair in the breeze, more pepper than salt now, but still at her age, she would not think of coloring it. Her dark eyes laughed with Chelsea. "Oh…honey, don't be silly about this. I'm sure it will be a fine working relationship with all of them and nothing more," she said with a wave of her hand. Then, "You know…I wanted to talk to you about your grandmother."

"I'm sorry, Mom, of course. I didn't mean to pour out my problems. I mean, they aren't problems, really," she said, watching Kyle swing the axe again, putting his finely muscled back into it, and toss the remains of the log to the side. She smiled, thinking he'd need ibuprofen tonight before he went to bed…and maybe a backrub.

Liz sighed, stroking her fingers down the back of her hand, seeming to examine her wedding rings. "Mother isn't doing well."

"You saw Grandmother last week?" Chelsea asked, aware that her mother had been to Greenville, South Carolina, where her mother lived, in her villa that was part of a retirement community.

"Yes," she said wistfully. She turned to Chelsea suddenly. "She thought I was you. She called me Chelsea twice."

"Oh, Mom! She's getting worse."

"Yes. I don't know how long she'll be able to stay in her place. I feel as if I should visit more. I'll probably go down again next week and see how it's going. I've asked the staff to check in on her more often."

"I'd be glad to go with you, if it would help. You know, I'm not teaching on Fridays at all this summer. Do you think you'll stay with her…for extended periods, I mean?"

"Like with Kitty?" her mother asked, looking back at Kyle, who was moving some of the logs he'd split out of his way, totally absorbed in what he was doing.

"No," her mother said definitively. "Not like with Kitty. Kitty was different. I'd have done anything for Kitty Davenport," she said, referring to Chelsea's father's mother. "Kitty was more like a mother to me than my own mother has been." It sounded harsh, but Chelsea had always known it was true. Tom, Liz, and Chelsea had moved into the family home when Chelsea was in high school, to take care of Kitty after she'd suffered a debilitating stroke. Liz had quit her job as the art teacher at her high school and concentrated all her efforts on Kitty's care, something her own mother had never understood. But the family hadn't talked about it.

"Why was it like that, Mom?" Chelsea asked, never fully having understood why her mother had always kept such a distance with her own mother.

"Well, we didn't always get along. I don't think we ever saw eye-to-eye on anything of real importance," her mother began. "When Tom asked me to marry him, she thought it was absurd. She wanted me to tell him no. She thought I'd be throwing my life away up here on the mountain." She gazed at the lake, watching the boys, but Chelsea was riveted to her mother's face. She had never heard this and couldn't imagine anything further from what her mother's life here had been. How could anyone think her father would not have been good enough for her mother? Being away from home during college and the years Chelsea danced with the ballet had made her realize how special their life was on this mountain. The Davenports' roots ran deep, compelling her to return with or without Kyle. But her grandmother had likely wanted a glamorous life for her daughter. She was the only woman Chelsea had ever known to wear a real fur coat. Being well-connected was the way to be happy in her grandmother's opinion, and Chelsea had gleaned that from her at a young age, thinking it a strange philosophy even then. She had been as different from Kitty as night was to day. Still, it was difficult to hear her mother acknowledge these feelings out loud.

"I know," said her mother, as if she knew what Chelsea were thinking. "I didn't tell you much about this. Why would I? As a child you didn't need to know what it was like. It would have made you feel differently about her when you were young. How could you have understood any of it, the way we lived? You idolized your father, and Kitty, too. Then, when Kitty got sick and we moved in with her, it was too much for Mother to stand. She withdrew further, out of jealousy, I think, and I didn't have the time to pacify her. For most of my life she wasn't very nice to me, so, no; I don't want to be spending a lot of time down there. That's a hard thing for me to admit, and it's even harder for me to tell you," she said, her voice taking on a new timbre. She blinked, suddenly looking away. "Besides, if she doesn't even know who I am, I can't destroy myself over worrying about it now, and what it could have been like for us. The relationship I've always wanted will never happen now. But...she's my mother, and she has no one else."

Chelsea ached for what her mother must feel. "Mom...I had no idea it was like that," she said, reaching for her mother's hand.

"Well, you can be sure it won't be that way for the two of us, sweetheart. You give me nothing but joy. I know whose granddaughter you are," she said, trying to smile, and holding tears that she willed not to fall. "You are so like Kitty. And it's not just that you have her eyes; you have her grace as well. And I'm so glad to see that you're loved the way you are. Kitty would be so happy to see the life you've made for yourself," she said, throwing a glance at Kyle again. The shirt was coming off, as his task was getting hot, and both of them laughed. He looked up and shook his head, draping the shirt over a log to dry.

Chelsea felt her heart swell being in the midst of all of them, seeing the boys coming up from the lake with her father, Stu swinging the plastic dummy by its cord, and Foscoe loping along beside them, his tail dripping water as it wagged back and forth. He stopped and shook, drenching the boys, and they jumped and hooted with laughter. Chelsea's father laughed with them, whistling his approval as he came upon the pile of wood in front of Kyle. "Lookin' good, son!" he said in his booming voice. Chelsea knew it was hard for him to watch Kyle doing work he wished he could do.

"'Bout time!" she heard Kyle say good-naturedly. "You guys have some logs to stack up here," he said, gesturing to the pile that had grown surprisingly high in the boys' absence. "Just think, Tom; no more gum balls to pick up," Kyle said, grinning at his father-in-law.

"And no more money to pay out to these little monkeys," Tom said, winking at Kyle. He'd often paid the boys to collect the pesky gum balls from out of the yard—five-dollars for every five gallon bucket they could fill. It had been a win-win situation, Chelsea thought, watching her sons bend to pick up the split logs, carrying them to the wheelbarrow to be stacked in a pile beside the porch. They would all sleep well tonight.

She turned to her mother again, touching her hand. There was something she could offer to comfort her. "Mom…Kyle wants another baby," she said, smiling, making her mother brighten in return.

"Oh! Are you sure? I'd almost given up hope for more grandchildren," she said, looking with surprise at her daughter. "I thought after the boys you all were finished. Twins are definitely enough, these days, that is."

"Well, the boys are sleeping through the night now. We've even put the sleeping bag away, so why not start all over?" Chelsea laughed. "He wants a girl," she added, thinking about his comment about Elise's daughter, her mood sinking slightly.

"Oh, honey, it would be wonderful to have a little girl. Do you think you'd stop working?"

"I don't know. This is all so new. We talked about it for the first time at Martha's Vineyard. But it's just between us for right now…I mean, you can tell Dad, but we don't want a lot of attention, you know what I mean?"

"Of course," said her mother, watching Kyle supervising the boys' work. "He loves you so very much. I understand him, you know—what it's like when you don't think you have love, and then you suddenly find it. It's something Kyle will never take for granted," her mother said, peering into Chelsea's eyes suddenly, as if delivering an important message.

"I know, Mom. I know what you're saying." Right here, right now, with her family around her and Kyle throwing his grin her way, it was impossible for her to doubt his love. She poured a cup of the tea mixture with mint leaves and carried it to him. She could feel the heat radiating off him. Wiping his forehead with the back of his hand, he accepted the drink gratefully, sweat glistening on him everywhere, and dripping from his sideburns. His arms were dusted brown with dirt.

"Thanks, angel," he said, letting the axe lean against his leg. "After a few more of these logs, I'll be ready for a swim with you in the lake." His blue eyes were like fire when he looked at her that way, erasing all the questions that had plagued her since the night before. She felt her heart skip a beat, realizing there was no need for new lingerie or whatever else she had thought she needed. Nothing, no one, not Elise Masters or anyone else, mattered right now, and she knew it. There were no more questions.

Chapter 6

DATING

Frank and Kyle dusted off their boots before entering the office on Tuesday morning. It was the first time this week Kyle had even been in, with the attention required at the new build on the Blair property they had started in Valle Crucis. Their meeting with the surveyor this morning had gone well, as they'd tromped around the property with Tom Davenport, confirming the terrain for the road entrance, the driveway, and the setting for the home. The day before, they'd met most of the day with the client at his office and at the site, going over the plans Kyle had drawn up, to make sure everything was set to go.

Elise was a pleasant sight, fresh and serene looking, in her pale green silk blouse and taupe slacks, arranging colorful plates and napkins with the coffee and bite-sized muffins and fruit for the conference with new clients they were expecting. He thought of Chelsea then, and the backrub she'd given him on Sunday night, and how he'd fallen dead asleep under her soothing hands. She'd made him blueberry muffins this morning too.

"Hi, strangers!" Elise said, greeting them with a warm smile. She seemed to be more and more comfortable in her new roles in the office, thought Kyle, as he noticed soft music playing in the background. The lamps she'd turned on added a nice ambience to the spread she'd set out, and he also noticed she'd rearranged the furniture in the gathering room, angling it to make it appear more inviting and warm.

"Hey!" they'd said in unison, taking in the scene. The place looked good even to the familiar eye, making Kyle feel proud, knowing the clients would feel at home here. Elise returned with mugs to set on the coffee table. She eyed him and looked at her watch.

"You do have a tie tucked away somewhere, don't you?" she asked Kyle.

"Do I look that bad?" He looked behind as she followed him into his office, grinning and tucking in his shirttail. "When are they coming?" he asked.

"Ten-thirty, so you both have about two minutes to make yourselves presentable."

He opened a drawer and pulled out two ties, sighing. "Which one?" he asked, holding them up, as she looked with a frown at his dusty work boots.

"The blue stripe," she said, studying his appearance.

"What is wrong?" he asked, uncomfortable under her scrutiny, slipping the tie under his collar and crossing one end over the other. She stepped closer and reached up to smooth his hair in place. Everyone seemed to do that to him, but oddly, when she touched his hair, it was like a lightning bolt had struck him, making him flinch involuntarily.

"Oh, I'm sorry!" she said, laughing, her hand going to her mouth. "I just figured you weren't planning on looking in a mirror."

"Oh…no, it's okay. Faith did that all the time. I should wash up, too. Don't you need to tend to Frank? He's a hell of a lot dirtier than I am," he muttered, watching her drop her eyes as he raked fingers through his windblown hair. Suddenly, he wished he'd had another shirt to change into. But he did have shoes. The jeans would have to do; after all, he was expected to be outdoors from time to time.

"I heard that!" Frank shouted from the bathroom, where they could hear the water running.

"Mr. and Mrs. Hayes called about ten minutes ago to let me know they're on the way. They're excited to see you again," Elise said, watching Kyle change shoes.

Kyle looked puzzled. "Do I know them?" he asked.

"Yeah," she said, squinting at him. "They said you would remember them. You went to college with their daughter."

"Oh! You mean Dr. Hayes? And his wife is Sara Lynn? Oh, my God! Emily's parents. Yeah, I knew her—knew them."

"Huh! A blast from the past?" Frank asked, wiping his face with a paper towel, as they traded places at the bathroom sink. Kyle washed his hands, checking his face for dirt. Elise handed Kyle's other tie to Frank.

"Sort of," Kyle mumbled. His last meeting with Emily Hayes had been on graduation day, and it wasn't a happy memory. A sharp image of her, crying into his shoulder in her graduation robe, as they'd hugged each other, cut him like a knife. He'd wondered why her parents had bothered to come here, and he wondered whether they knew the pain and suffering he'd caused their daughter. He hadn't meant for it ever to be that way, but the way she'd felt about him had been out of his control.

"An old girlfriend?" Elise asked, eyebrows raised, an impish smile playing at her lips.

"Not exactly. Just a friend."

"Right. Well, Sara Lynn is pretty stoked about seeing you again," Elise said, watching his reaction carefully. Frank watched, too.

"You should *never* play poker, my friend!" Frank laughed, tying on his tie, shaking his head at Kyle's face.

"Emily Hayes has been married for about eleven years. They have like, *four* kids, so there's nothing to talk about there."

Elise glanced at Frank as the door chimed, while Dr. Bruce Hayes and Sara Lynn walked through the door.

"Kyle!" Sara Lynn exclaimed, sweeping her blond hair back in place from the wind.

"Hello! Mrs. Hayes, Dr. Hayes, it's been forever! How are you?" he asked, shaking hands with Dr. Hayes, and accepting a hug from Sara Lynn, whose head came to the same place on his chest he remembered Emily's.

"Hello, Kyle!" Dr. Hayes said warmly, apparently no hostility implied, causing Kyle's guard to settle.

Sara Lynn's dark eyes danced as she began to reminisce. "Oh, Kyle, it's so good to see you again! This is *so* exciting! I couldn't believe this was your firm! We started researching builders in the area, and when I saw your picture on the website, Bruce and I said, 'Mountaineer Builders it is!' This was just meant to be!"

Kyle introduced Frank and Elise as they walked toward the gathering room.

"So, how's Emily?" he asked.

"She's doing well! She sends her love," said her mother as Kyle avoided making eye contact with Elise, whose brows were raised in amusement. "You know they have *four* children now!"

"Yes, I heard that. Well, we swap Christmas cards every year, but we haven't seen each other since graduation," Kyle said in an attempt to confirm his story for his colleagues.

"I know! She was so excited to hear that we'd stumbled onto your company. It's only a couple of hours' drive up from Greensboro for us. We've bought a lot up at Hunter's Ridge, and once our cabin is built, we're hoping to get them all to come here and join us as much as they can—well, Emily and the kids at least. You probably remember that she loves to ski."

"I do."

"Yes, her husband, Graham, is a trauma surgeon at UVA medical center, so you can imagine she's by herself a lot," Dr. Hayes added with a mix of pride and sadness maybe, it seemed to Kyle, and the men shared a look, letting the meaning sink in. Maybe her dad was the one who'd heard the story; Emily had been a Daddy's girl, he remembered, wondering whether she was happy with such a lonely life.

"I remember Graham. Well, this area is a great place to spend some R-and-R time," Kyle said, gesturing to the seating and the coffee. "Come on in, and make yourselves at home."

"Would you care for some coffee and a bite to eat after your trip?" asked Elise, coming to the rescue. As they nodded, she began serving. They seated themselves comfortably around the table and Sara Lynn continued the topic.

"Kyle was our favorite," she said winking at him, and checking her phone, setting it inside a pocket on her purse.

He took a deep breath. "Oh, those were some fun times we all had back in college."

"Kyle took good care of Emily, didn't he, Bruce?" she went on. "He escorted Emily to her debutante ball a million years ago."

"Yeah. You've heard of the DD? Well, I was the EE; *everybody's escort.*" They all laughed.

"You always played it well. How is Chelsea?"

"She's great. She's been teaching up here at Appalachian State in the dance department for the past ten years. Choreography's always been her thing and she's carved herself a nice niche here. We have eight-year-old boys…twins."

"That's what Emily told us!" Sara Lynn said wistfully, resting her chin in her hand and smiling.

"So, tell us about the house you'd like to build," Frank said, graciously changing the subject. Plans for a large rustic cabin with the mountain views most people wanted were presented, along with the usual pictures people brought to show. Kyle looked over the offerings, and they discussed the budget and square footage. It would be a typical project. Kyle knew the area well, and it was close to the place they'd just left. After the coffee, they'd adjourned to the conference room where they'd viewed other properties the team had built that were similar with what the Hayeses had in mind. They selected a couple of designs that might work, and Elise took over the conversation, talking with Sara Lynn about her style, and what she'd like to bring aesthetically to the home. Frank discussed the building process once the design was in place, and the Hayeses agreed to stay for lunch and then take the team on a tour of the property.

Frank stayed behind at the end of the day to make phone calls, while Kyle and Elise walked to their respective cars in the parking lot. He found her looking at him with amusement.

"What's so funny?"

"Oh…you must have edged out Graham as the top husband pick for Emily, from the way Sara Lynn went on and on about you today. Surely you were more than just her friend. Debutante ball escort? Come on!"

"No. I mean, Chelsea and I were trying to keep our long-distance relationship going and it got tough our senior year. But Emily was still just a friend."

"Ah, trying to help you through the pain. Was Chelsea dating other people?"

"We saw other people for a little while. It wasn't like what you're thinking," he said quickly, wondering why he was allowing this conversation.

"But still, Emily must have thought she had an opportunity."

"Maybe. You do realize this was a *long* time ago?"

"Sorry, I didn't mean to make you squirm. I'm just trying to figure out how the perfect couple came to be; that's all. I'm guessing this must have been your screw-up. You and Emily?" she asked, reminding him of several nights with Emily when he had kissed her, and he'd felt guilty later. He knew Chelsea was doing it too, so he'd let that absolve his feelings back then. It was college after all, and just a kiss here and there had meant so little at the time, or so he thought.

"Wow. Too much information, okay?" he said, attempting to speak like a twenty-seven year old, pointing the remote at his car, unlocking the door. For someone who didn't date, she was certainly interested in the topic, and boldly at that, razzing the boss this way.

"I'm sorry. That was inappropriate. I'm just giving you a hard time," she laughed, her comfortable tone with him adding to his discomfort.

He smiled politely at her. "Have a good night, Elise."

"You too, Kyle. See you tomorrow."

Later, after dinner, the boys were settled in front of the television, and Kyle poured Chelsea a glass of wine on the porch. The cicadas sang in soothing waves and the river's swooshing sound relaxed him further, as they sat in the Adirondack chairs, breathing in the pungent summer air. Kyle rested his head against the back of the chair, gazing at her as she sipped her wine, lovely in the simple short skirt and blouse she wore, feet bare and legs crossed. Foscoe stretched out at her feet, after giving her toes a brief lick. She twirled a strand of her hair around her finger, studying Kyle.

"Tell me about your day," she said.

"It was good. You'll never guess who our latest client is."

"Oh? Who is it?"

"Do you remember Emily Hayes? Her parents dug me up and came in today to sign a contract with us to build them a cabin up on Hunter's Ridge." He watched her reaction; surprise, nothing else.

"That's a surprise. What'd they say about Emily?"

"She's good. Graham, her husband, works all the time. He's a doc in the trauma center at UVA so he doesn't see his family much."

"That's too bad," she said, her sentiment warming him; she had always appreciated the way they spent time together as a family.

"I know. Anyway, they're hoping that she and the kids will come here as much as they can, probably in the summers and on winter vacations."

She nodded as if it were idle small talk. He let the topic die, glad she wasn't distressed.

"And your day?"

"Great. I started a new choreography piece with a new group of students today. It should be pretty special when it's done. It will be in the last summer program...."

He nodded; more small talk. "The one where you'll be dancing?"

She nodded, continuing to twirl her hair around her finger, thinking. "Can I ask you something?"

"Sure," he said, rolling his head to look at her.

"Why don't you ever say anything about Elise?"

"What do you mean?"

"I don't know. You always used to talk about Faith and Frank. It just seems that there must be more to Elise than meets the eye, and I think it's odd that you don't ever talk about her. What's up with her daughter? You said she wasn't married. I'd just like to know."

He looked away, collecting his thoughts. "It's just..." *none of your business* he wanted to say, but thought about how to phrase it. She *was* used to hearing everything, so he could understand her curiosity. Still, he felt as if he would betray a trust, telling her Elise's story. "She had a baby when she was in college, and her parents helped her raise Lydia. Lydia has special needs on top of all that, so it hasn't been easy. Elise is not helpless, though," he said.

The statement seemed to strike a nerve in Chelsea. She thought a moment. "What happened to Lydia's father?" Chelsea asked, resting her chin on her hand.

"He wasn't involved and never knew. It was a one-time thing."

"Oh. That must have been hard to go through. I can't imagine having a baby and trying to finish college."

"I don't think it was much fun for any of them. Her parents helped and her mother quit her job," he said, sipping the wine.

"You feel protective of her, don't you?" she asked, watching him carefully.

"I guess so, in a way. Since she's on her own and she works with us, I guess I feel like Frank and I are the people she'd go to if she needed help," he said, feeling a gut-wrenching sensation that Chelsea was dead-on about the way he felt concerning Elise. He had not even admitted it to himself.

"I guess she had to grow up really fast, then."

"Yeah, I'm sure she did," he said, thinking how scary it would be to be a parent when you were hardly a grown-up at all. How much of the carefree life she must have missed. For Elise Masters, college would have been all of the work, plus some, and none of the fun. He wondered whether she'd ever have many friends here. It was hard enough to meet people in a new place, but when you were tied to a child, and one with special needs, the possibilities would be even more limited. Elise seemed so young, yet so old at the same time. He wondered whether she had ever been in love, casting his eyes down to keep his wife from seeing his emotions. Life could be so unfair.

"Well, thanks for filling me in," she said. "Hey, I love you…for being the good guy." Suddenly, she set her glass on the porch and moved toward him in the chair. He pulled her into his lap, glancing in at the boys, whose faces were mesmerized by the movie they were watching. She kissed him, pushing her fingers into his hair.

"You owe me," she whispered.

"Yeah?" he asked, the image of Elise's face slipping from his mind.

"Yeah, for passing out on me on Sunday night."

He remembered how tired he had been that night; his back was still stiff from Sunday's woodcutting. "Sorry, but you give a mean massage, baby."

"You won't have that excuse tonight. If we're going to make a baby, we have to…do some things."

"Yes, we do," he agreed and kissed her again.

"Then it's a date."

On Friday morning, Kyle prepared for his meeting with Elise, to go over her plans for the Wilcox renovation project in Blowing Rock. Suddenly, all the business they were getting was making his head spin. Vacation was two weeks away, so he knew he'd be hitting the loft at home to work in the evenings to get things done so he could leave town with no worries. It was a sad thought, with the boys home and out of school, and Chelsea available with no homework to tend to since it was summer;

he felt as if he were cheating them somehow. His phone buzzed, signaling a message from Elise: *Running late; be there in thirty.* That seemed odd; she was never late. Frank had made the coffee that morning, and Kyle listened to him in his office, chuckling on the phone with one of the contractors, no doubt. He would be leaving in a little while to check on the work at the Blair cabin, where Kyle would join him after the meeting with Elise.

He pulled up the design for the Wilcox renovation on the computer-assisted design program, reviewing what he had done already, and determining his next steps with Elise, when the door chimed and fresh air blew in with her. He picked up his coffee cup and greeted her at the door.

"Hey! Everything all right?"

"Hi. Sorry for the delay. I had a dead battery in my car this morning. It took a while for my road service to get to me, but I've got a new battery and I'm good to go," she said with a sigh, and a sweep of her fingers through her hair, giving off her scent of lemons and flowers. She looked tired, but excited.

"No problem. Do you want coffee? Chelsea made banana bread…" he said, gesturing into the kitchen.

She looked relieved. "No, I don't want to hold you up. I know you're trying to get out the door."

"No, it's not a problem, really. You get ready and I'll bring it to you."

"Oh…" she whispered, uneasy with his waiting on her. She bustled about, setting up her iPad and setting design boards up on the ledges in the conference room.

"Boards?" he asked, returning with her breakfast, which she accepted graciously.

"Thanks! I didn't eat. I sent Lydia in to day care with a Pop-Tart this morning. They must think I'm a horrible mother," she said, taking a sip of the coffee he'd watched her make with a splash of creamer and a half-teaspoon of sugar substitute. "Yeah, the boards are for the Wilcoxes. They seem like the kind of people who might need to have more of a visual presentation. What do you think?" she asked, taking a bite of her bread, and watching his face intently for his reaction.

The work was highly professional and artistic. He looked at each board, renderings of the family room and the bedrooms, done in the earthy tones of the mountains, with splashes here and there of deep rose, purples, and indigo, the jewel tones of sunset that would set the rooms off beautifully with their outdoor views as a backdrop for what she had done. Black wrought iron lighting and fixtures contrasted nicely to the pale wood of the interior they'd planned. Her schemes had exceeded his expectations and he knew Mr. and Mrs. Wilcox would be delighted; he certainly was. He nodded as she continued to watch.

"Wow. These are excellent. This is exactly what I'd had in mind…but way better. They're going to love it. How much time did you spend with Jackie Wilcox? These look just like her, bold and earthy."

"Oh, not a lot of time, but you can get a feel for what people like by their personalities, the clothes they wear, and how they accessorize themselves. She showed me pictures of her house and the things she loves, and the things they have that she's dying to get rid of. We went shopping in Blowing Rock after lunch that day, and I noticed the things she pointed out."

"Kind of like being an interior design detective," he laughed.

"Sort of! Sometimes people can't put into words what they want, so you have to figure it out somehow."

"Cool," he said, looking at her admiringly, then feeling stupid. To cover for his gaff, he reached for the folder and pulled out his own plans to check her budget and other details they'd need to cover. "I think you should get the Wilcoxes in as soon as possible to meet with us, and let them see these."

"So, you wouldn't recommend any changes, then?"

"Hell, no. It's perfect," he said, watching a huge smile grow across her face, as she wiped the corner of her mouth with her napkin.

"You can't be this easy," she said, that shimmery tone in her voice that had gotten under his skin; it sounded almost intimate. He closed his eyes for a moment, trying to talk himself out of the feeling he had.

"Well, if you want, we could pick it apart and try to find something wrong with it, but I don't think that's happening. Or, we could let Frank see this and then you'd have a second opinion."

They heard the jingling of Frank's car keys as he collected his tube of plans, and his footsteps in the gathering room.

"Hey, Frank! Come take a look at this," called Kyle.

"Good morning, Elise," Frank greeted her pleasantly as he walked in the room, whistling long and low at the designs on the ledge. "Is this the Wilcox house?" he asked as they nodded. "Holy moly! They are gonna love this. I didn't expect this out of you, but I like the colors. Are they getting new furniture?"

"Some," she said. "These are her pieces…and these are pieces I've suggested," she added, with a sweep of her hand.

"No antiques?" Kyle asked.

"Definitely not. She likes modern, clean lines, and some rustic things, comfortable furniture, no clutter."

"Well, this is quite an accomplishment!" Frank complimented her as he prepared to leave. "Congratulations on your first assignment. Well done, Elise!" he said, patting her on the arm. Kyle had not contemplated touching Elise, but he remembered the night of the party and his hand at her back, making Lynn Schiffman's eyebrows raise, and then the time when Elise had touched his hair, making the hair on his arms stand up.

"Thank you, Frank. I'm happy about this too," she said, leading Kyle to realize they were now truly a team.

"Okay, I'll see you later. And Kyle, I'll see you sooner, right?"

"Yeah, I'm right behind you….See?" he said when Frank was gone.

"Okay," Elise said, watching Frank amble out the front door. "Thank you."

"Thank *you*," he said, referring to her good work.

"I guess I'll go call Jackie Wilcox and set up a meeting. Oh, and did I tell you that Marcus Gilmer called? I put us all on to meet with him on Tuesday at ten at his new property."

"Oh, yeah. I had almost forgotten about him," Kyle said, clicking his mouse to open up his calendar. One more project to deal with this summer, but who was complaining?

"Check your email in just a minute. I'm sending you pictures of his new purchase," Elise called from her office. "He sent these yesterday afternoon."

"Okay," he said, waiting for the email to hit his inbox, wondering what she'd do the rest of the day. "So what do you have going on today?" he asked as she appeared again in his doorway.

"Oh, I'm going shopping with Evelyn Turner for her kitchen fabrics and some decorating ideas."

"So you've made a new friend and reeled in a new client," he laughed. "Blowing Rock?"

"It's easy when you're spending other people's money. And we'll look at links I've sent her for things we can order as well. But she loves pottery, so yeah, we're hitting Main Street in Blowing Rock after lunch."

He noticed she was shifting her weight from one foot to the other.

"Can I ask you something? I need a man's opinion…which shoes?" she asked, gesturing to her feet. She wore a wedge-heeled animal print pump on one foot, from which he could see a prettily polished toenail through the peep-toe design, and on the other, a nude color sandal, also heeled, exposing toenails. He looked for a moment and she explained, "I have a date tonight, so…?"

His face burned and he tried to cover his reaction with humor, saying, "So, I'm guessing Wyatt must be secure with his height!" He thought about her neighbor, and how dwarfed he'd feel next to her in either pair of shoes.

"Well, I'm not saying it's Wyatt."

"Why not?"

"Because—I haven't done this in a while, and I don't want to jinx it, you know?" she said, and her vulnerable expression made him stop wanting to tease her. "Besides, it's not Wyatt. He has a girlfriend, I think, and he knows about Lydia."

"So?"

"So, usually when men find out I have a daughter, and that she has problems, they run for the hills. I'm pretending to be unattached, and I'm meeting him later at the restaurant. My babysitter is a girl from Lydia's day care and she's bringing Lydia home. I've never done it this way before. I feel like I'm lying, but I don't care for once. I feel so…*free!*"

Kyle racked his brain, trying to think who else she knew, imagining her on someone's arm, drinking wine, being touched, kissed….

"You're staring. You hate the shoes."

"No. I like the sandals. They make your legs go on for miles," he said, wishing he'd kept it to himself, but then, it must have been the right thing to say because she caught her breath a little and smiled.

"Okay. Thanks."

"Well, have fun. I have a date tonight, too," he said, trying not to show his concern, gathering his tube of plans and his briefcase.

"Oh, do you and Chelsea still date after ten years?"

He shook his head. "You're really making me feel old, you know?"

"I didn't mean it like that. I wouldn't have asked you about the shoes if I really thought you were old. You're *not* old. You have fun, too," she said softly, leaving his office, and looking back over her shoulder.

The sinking sun felt good on the back of his shoulders when he walked up the steps of Char later, with Chelsea on his arm. She looked more radiant than ever, in her coral sundress and sandals, hair knotted loosely at the nape of her neck. Servers dressed in black were lighting the candles as they stood at the hostess stand, where they were greeted by Sam, their favorite waiter.

"Hey!" he said, recognizing them immediately. "Just the two of you this evening?"

"Yes," Kyle said, then asked Chelsea, "Do you want to eat outside?" She nodded, and they followed Sam to a table on the porch, bathed in golden light and warmed by the setting sun. The air felt fresh and hopeful, elevating Kyle's mood.

"Is this okay?" Sam asked. They nodded, seating themselves and accepting the menus. "Can I bring you something to drink to get you started?"

"Wine, but I don't know what I'm eating yet," Chelsea replied.

"There's a shrimp and grits special tonight that's out of this world," Sam said.

"That settles it," said Chelsea, handing him the menu. Kyle did the same.

"How about a bottle of pinot grigio then?" Kyle asked her, and when she nodded, he selected one from the wine list, pointing it out for Sam.

"Coming right up," Sam smiled, giving Chelsea a little wink.

"Did he wink at you?" Kyle asked, grinning and taking her hand across the table, resting a hand under his chin to gaze at her. The sunset was magic on her face, streaking her hair with copper, and lighting her pale eyes dramatically.

"Yes, I believe he did," she giggled, fingering his wedding ring, as she often did. The intimate gesture warmed him, making him happy.

"I'm sure he would have carded you, too, if we didn't come in here all the time," he laughed, intending to make her feel as beautiful as she looked. This was shaping up to be a good night.

After Sam had opened their wine, pouring them glasses, they toasted the evening.

"Here's to a night with just the two of us!" he said, raising his glass to touch hers carefully.

"Cheers!" she said, sipping her wine, smiling at the taste. "It was nice of Mom and Dad to have the boys spend the night. They've probably picked blueberries, and right now they must be smothered in Mom's homemade biscuits with butter and honey. And Dad will probably take them out later to shoot bows and arrows, as long as the light lasts."

"Yeah, it's nice that they can go over there and run around. You can hardly throw a football in our yard."

"I know. And Stu's been bugging me again to let them play football in the fall."

"Soccer's not enough?"

"You know, they want to be like you."

"It's too dangerous," he said, recalling the accident in high school in which a boy he'd hit had died. He didn't have to remind Chelsea of that.

"I know. And I agree. I'm just letting you know they'll be asking you, too."

He sighed and looked away. "You know, I've been thinking....We're going to need more room, especially if we have another baby," he said, taking both of her hands and meeting her gaze. He felt her tremble at the words. "What would you think about building another house? We could rent the cabin to help cover the mortgage payments."

"Where?"

"Well, I've been saving this news for just the right time, and maybe this is it."

Her eyes questioned him warily. She worried too much about their finances...and she didn't like change.

"Your dad offered us a plot of land on the other side of the lake. It's just at the foot of Wayne and Becky's property. We could have a nice big yard where the boys could play, and we wouldn't have to worry about them falling in the river all the time. I could build them a basketball court, and they could have a tree house...and we'd be right there, just a stone's throw from your parents," he said, letting the idea sink in as she looked at him expectantly.

"Dad did that?"

"Yes."

She sighed and looked away. "I just always thought we'd live in Kitty's house one day. But you're right, we'd outgrow the cabin in no time with another child, and the boys need more room to play outside. Can we afford it?"

"I've actually been planning it already," he said, smiling.

She laughed. "Do I get a say in any of this?"

"Absolutely. That's why I'm mentioning it. It's in the dream stages right now...a work in progress, and it doesn't have to be anything we'd jump into right away, but it could happen when the time is right for us. What do you think?"

She looked away again, trying to picture it. "I can't imagine not being in the cabin; it's home. It's cozy. I love it there. But the boys are at the age they need more...."

He reached across the table for her hand. "I didn't bring you here so we could talk about the boys all evening," he said, a twinkle in his eye.

She smiled, lowering her eyelids, twisting his ring as she spoke. "Do you really think you could leave the river? It's always had you under its spell."

"It will still be our property. I can go there whenever I need a fix." Leaving the river was something he had certainly considered. It seemed a small sacrifice for what his family needed.

A tinkling laugh made him look into the restaurant, where he heard Shelby, another favorite waitress, addressing her table. She had that unmistakable giggle, like an unexpected glass of champagne. He looked. He blinked. Shelby was there, talking with the customers. Elise was at the table with Michael Gilmer. He watched them for a moment. Elise looked comfortable, her sandaled foot swinging slightly, her arms resting on the table in front of her. Michael sat back in his chair, holding the wine list in his lap, talking about something that was making both of the women laugh.

"What's wrong?" asked Chelsea, following his open-mouthed gaze.

"There's Elise, with Michael Gilmer," he said, trying to keep the distaste out of his tone.

"Oh! They must have hit it off at the party. I had no idea."

"Me neither. I guess they did."

"She didn't tell you?"

"No. She said she had a date tonight, but she didn't say with whom."

"Does she know about the Gilmers?"

"Do you mean, how they're all about working their way into your parents' house? No, she doesn't. It's ironic though; we have a meeting with Marcus on Tuesday to look at a new property he's bought. He wants to turn it into a bed and breakfast, and he wants us to do it. I just thought he was making a move on Elise," Kyle said.

"Well, it looks like his son has beat him to the punch on that one," Chelsea said, laughing. "What's wrong? You look like you're about to explode."

"I don't know. I just don't think he's right for her, that's all."

"Honey, it's just a date."

But she hasn't dated in seven years, he thought. *She's going to get her heart broken.* He knew his face was brooding, but he couldn't help it. His wife seemed to find his reaction amusing.

"The other thing that's ironic is that my mother has invited Elise to look at the house for some decorating ideas. Maybe she's a spy!" she laughed, eyebrows raised.

"And an unknowing one at that," he said grudgingly. He wondered whether Elise had kept this from him, thinking that dating Michael would be a conflict of interests. Maybe Michael had hinted that he wasn't on Kyle's A list. Whatever the case, their perfect evening was going to be ruined if he didn't get his mind turned around. He looked one more time at the two of them, looking over their menus and talking politely, so like a first date. He reached for Chelsea's hands again, trying to lose himself in those aquamarine eyes of hers. He would not look at them again, he told himself.

"Aren't you going to say hello?" she asked.

"Maybe in a little while. Those two are not my focus right now. I'm thinking about what we'll be doing later," he promised.

"If we can manage to stay awake, that is."

He raised his glass to her. "We have all night," he said with a wink.

The night had not been what either of them had expected, she thought, rolling over again, glancing at the clock: 3:44 a.m. She sighed, listening to Kyle's deep and rhythmic breathing. As hard as she'd tried not to let her feelings show at the restaurant, her preoccupation became clear after he'd brought her home. They'd kissed and undressed each other eagerly, but their lovemaking had been tentative at first. She'd been strangely detached, and he'd sensed it, caressing her tenderly, patiently, giving her the time she needed to relax. It had been a new feeling, being so guarded with him, until she opened herself desperately, fighting tears of frustration. He'd touched her tears with his lips, not asking why she cried, confirming her suspicions all the more. After that, he'd fallen asleep holding her, but she'd lain awake until now, regretting the way she had acted, promising herself never to speak about these feelings. But he knew. He had to know.

At the restaurant, Kyle had been so distracted, unable to hide his interest in what Elise and Michael were doing at their table, his expressions of distaste at seeing them together floating the current of her worries back to the surface. Even when she and Kyle had stopped by their table to say hello, she had pretended not to notice the tension, and made light of the situation, but something was different about Kyle around Elise, some fascination with her, some extra helping of concern for her that exceeded the usual professional relationship, which she found quite disturbing.

She awoke to the aromas of breakfast—sausage and eggs, toast and coffee. Kyle was up. She turned to the clock again, seeing 9:05 on its face.

Raking fingers through her hair, she sat up groggily and reached for her robe. The rug felt cozy beneath her feet as she stood, collecting herself, and feeling guilty that he'd started breakfast while she stayed in bed. Padding into the kitchen, she saw him at work, in a sweat-stained T-shirt and shorts, Foscoe stretched at his feet.

"Hey. You guys went for a run?"

He nodded. "Couldn't sleep." He poured her a cup of coffee as she yawned, trying to wake up.

When she went to stand beside him, he stopped what he was doing to reach out and draw her into his arms.

"Good morning," he said, kissing her, his full lips smooth against her forehead, in contrast to the scratchy stubble on his chin. "You didn't sleep either, did you?"

"No," she said, accepting the cup of coffee he offered. She held her hands around the warm mug, breathing in the rich aroma, watching him lift scrambled eggs from the pan onto the plates he'd set out. "I'm sorry it wasn't the night we had planned," she said. She might as well get it out, but she wasn't sure how much she wanted to admit to him. Still, it wasn't all her fault; he'd been as reticent as she'd been.

He carried the plates out the open door onto the porch, where a balmy breeze brought the scent of the river and warm musky earth to wake her further. She followed him, bringing forks and napkins and her coffee, wanting to enjoy this alone time with him again. He was quiet as they arranged themselves, stirring in her a sense of bittersweet emotion. She reached for his hand and he said the blessing, squeezing hers at the end, and taking another sip of coffee. Foscoe settled himself with a soft thump at their feet.

"This looks so nice. You're spoiling me," she said, hoping to draw him out.

"You deserve it. You were dead to the world when I woke up."

"I must have been. I never heard you leave, or come back in," she said, buttering her toast.

He studied her a moment before asking quietly, "So, what were those tears about last night?"

She took a bite of the toast to give herself time to think of the best way to answer this question. She watched him take a bite of his sausage. "I was just frustrated that I couldn't relax. Here we have the house to ourselves and I wanted it to be so perfect…and it wasn't," she said, meeting his eyes. Crickets sang as she glimpsed the trees moving, a fluttering of green behind him. He was painfully handsome at the moment, the breeze touching his hair, his sideburns dark with sweat, and the blue eyes burning into hers.

"I don't know what you're worried about," he said.

"What do you mean?"

"Just that. There's no pressure here. If you're not ready to have a baby, we can wait…or not. Just tell me if you don't want this."

"No. That's not it. I just felt preoccupied…and I felt like you were, too. But it's fine. I know there's nothing to worry about," she said, unable to avoid his eyes. How long would they dance around this infiltration of the enemy and not address it? But she knew she would not be the one to bring it up.

"Do you know how much I love you?" he asked quietly, making her wonder whether he said it to convince himself. She heartily wanted to believe there was nothing to his feelings for Elise, and perhaps he did, too. Still, she appreciated that he was trying. She covered his hand with hers and smiled. "This is forever," he said.

"I know. I love you, too. We can leave these dishes in the sink and try it again before we have to pick up the boys."

"I'd like nothing better."

Chapter 7

Apology

Kyle yawned as he poured his Monday morning coffee. The previous evening's picnic with Abby and Glen and their three kids had worn him out. It had not been so much the crowd of them all, meshed with his family, but the bickering between first the triplets, and then between Abby and Glen, that had all proved to be mentally tiring. *If you don't like my picnic, then maybe you should do the cooking next time*, Abby had hissed when Glen had scoffed uncharacteristically at her pasta salad. Kyle and Chelsea had driven their boys home in a stupor after they had parted ways at the park. Standing in the kitchen now, Kyle listened to Frank's tirade over the phone with the latest framing crew's foreman. Apparently at the close of Friday, Frank had driven by the Blair property, finding beer cans at the worksite, something neither of them tolerated, and now Frank was issuing the unmistakable ultimatum; clean up your act or hit the road. Chuckling, Kyle suspected he would need to make a surprise visit to the site this afternoon as well to check up on things. After this conversation, he and Elise would meet Frank in the conference room for their weekly planning meeting. Jackie and Howard Wilcox were expected around ten o'clock to see the plans for their renovation, and Kyle was anticipating a pleasant meeting, given the quality of Elise's work on top of his design and Frank's building plan.

He heard the swish of her slacks as she walked, and the click-clack of her heels crossing the worn hardwood floors as Elise entered the kitchen to fill her coffee cup. "Good morning," he said, stepping aside for her to reach the coffeepot. Her fragrance and the coffee's aroma were beginning to settle in as the morning comforts around here. She smiled at him, less guarded than usual, another good thing.

"Good morning! How was your *date* Friday night?" she asked, the smile giving her face a new glow, he thought, studying her. *Nice.*

"It was good. And yours?" he asked, leaning against the counter with a hand in his pocket, sipping his coffee.

"Oh, fine. I had a real good time.…That's okay, right?" she asked after he was silent a moment.

"Ah, I guess so," he said, rubbing his hand across his chin. "As long as Michael treated you well."

"Well, why wouldn't he?"

"Michael is just…one of those guys who's been around a lot."

"And you don't trust him?"

"Oh, I don't know…he has an awfully pointy chin on him. I don't usually trust guys with pointy chins," he said, trying to keep it light, or she would become more suspicious than he wanted her to be.

"Oh! Come on; his dad has the same chin and you're in bed with *him!*" she laughed.

"Marcus is only slightly more trustworthy. And if I'm in bed with Marcus, I'm in bed with Michael, too. So, I guess we're all in bed together."

"Uh-huh. So you're saying I shouldn't be with Michael for business reasons? Is there a conflict of interest here?"

"Maybe not…yet. I guess it depends on how heavily he'll be involved with the house we're looking at tomorrow," he said. Should he ask whether Michael had mentioned the Davenports' house? Her date was none of his business, that is, unless she was going to be a part of derailing his family's tranquility. And then, Michael's character flaws hung in the balance. He felt that surge of protectiveness toward her again.

"Actually, Kyle, you're to blame for this," she began, a playful twist to her voice.

His eyebrows shot up. "Oh really?"

"You made me come…to that party and then introduced me to him. He's an investor in your brother-in-law's winery so I had to be nice to him. So see, it's all your fault!" she said, goading him.

When his lips pressed together in frustration, she softened her tone.

"Okay, then what are you worried about?"

"Just…*you*. Michael is a player. You don't need—"

"Oh?" she snapped, turning to face Kyle directly, a hand going to her hip, fresh color blooming from the neckline of her blouse and rising quickly to her face. "Just what is it you think I *need*, Kyle?"

The tone of her question made him suck in a breath, not expecting her reaction to move him the way it did. Without thinking, his hand went to her cheek, fingertips brushing it for an instant. He wanted to press his fingers to her face and plunge them through that amazing hair. *You need to be kissed*, he thought, sure that the look on her face meant she was reading his mind. He wondered what it would feel like to kiss her right now, long and deep and hard, the way she deserved, he thought, imagining himself doing it, aware that his eyes were locked with hers, until voices screamed through his head, *What the hell are you doing?* She was riveted to him, probably imagining the same thing, he thought, realizing this had to stop, now, or there would be hell to pay. He dropped his hand, feeling his own face smoking with his thoughts. He blinked hard and swallowed, seeking composure.

"Devotion, Elise. You need devotion," he said, as calmly as he could manage. Then he heard Frank disconnect from his phone call, collecting himself to meet them in the conference room.

Elise's hand was at her cheek, as if they had actually kissed, her face in full flush now as she stared, wide-eyed at him. After a moment, she spoke. "Devotion? Well, thanks for your concern, Kyle, but I'm a big girl. I've learned my lessons the hard way, and I can take care of myself, so you don't have to worry yourself with what I need. And I'm seeing him again. Just so you know," she said, glaring at him. "If you don't mind, I'd like to keep my personal life just that—personal." Without apologizing, he glared back. She needed to know about Michael Gilmer. There would be no apology about that. But she did not need to know how he felt right now. It was unprofessional and wrong on so many levels. Still, he could not acknowledge what had just happened, or bring himself to apologize for it, even though her eyes expected it. Pressing her lips together, she dismissed him, dismissed all of it, stepping quickly away to the conference room without a word.

"*Damn,*" he muttered, following slowly. Frank was ready and waiting, drumming his fingers at the head of the table as they sat down silently on either side of him, avoiding all eye contact. Kyle slid his fingers across his computer's touch screen, watching intently as his calendar came to life. From his peripheral vision, he could tell Elise was doing the same, struggling as he was to compose herself and get on with the day. How had he let this happen? It had taken him all of five minutes and one ridiculous hormonal fantasy to obliterate totally her trust in him. They didn't need lack of trust in their professional relationship. The angry voices were back—Tyson's, Stacie's, even his father's—calling him out on his behavior. *That's why there are rules about fraternization in the workplace...and sexual harassment!* He pushed a breath out over his chin to cool himself.

"Will you?" Frank was asking.

"Sorry? What?"

"Hello? I was asking you to go over to the Blair property this afternoon and check on the crew."

"Sure, yeah, I'll be glad to. I was thinking about it when I heard you on the phone with Ray. I'll slip by there around 4:30 if you think that's a good time."

"That works. So, Elise, are you ready to make your first presentation to the Wilcoxes today?" Frank asked, covering his right hand with his left, cracking his knuckles, an old habit of his, making her wince slightly.

In place of the lovely glow and her smile from ten minutes ago, Elise wore her pleasant and professional face, with only the remnants of her previous flush on her chest, and nodded. "I'm all set. I'm looking at an email from Jackie right now, confirming that they'll be here at ten." Her voice was as smooth and composed as it always was. Most people her age didn't have that kind of self-control.

"Fabulous!" Frank exclaimed, grinning at them. "Then we're off and running. Tomorrow, we have a meeting with Marcus Gilmer at his new property. I've sent you two the address. We can meet there. I'll be at Blair in the morning."

"I'll be here, hopefully starting on getting the Wilcox building permits in order," Kyle said, taking another sip of coffee.

"I'll be here, too, going over my orders for them as well," Elise said, looking at her computer screen.

"Then we can ride together. I'll drive," Kyle offered. It was the least he could do.

"That's fine. Marcus wants to have lunch afterward."

Frank cleared his throat. "Okay, I can do that. But I won't be lallygagging around afterward. I'll be back at Blair as soon as I can," Frank said.

"Baby-sitting the framers?"

"Yup. They'll probably need me there anyway. And you'll have some designing to work on back here."

"Yes, for the Hayes cabin," Kyle said, thinking he detected the hint of a smirk on Elise's face out of the corner of his eye, leaving him to wonder how long it would take him to restore the sense of balance they needed. *Needed.* He would have to stop concerning himself with Elise Masters' needs. When Faith had been here, he had never given a second thought to thinking about what he could do to help, or cheer her up when she was down. This girl brought a whole new game to his territory.

"And so you'll know where I am, I've got a meeting with Liz Davenport this afternoon at her house," Elise said, making Kyle's brows shoot up involuntarily. Was this the beginning of Michael's coup? He narrowed his eyes at her but she ignored him. Had he judged the situation correctly? Maybe Chelsea was right; Elise was a spy. *So much for trust.*

"Well! Good for you," said Frank, grinning. "What's the nature of this business?" *Good, let him ask the questions.*

"She wants some input with designing her home office, and maybe some other decorating ideas. I don't think there will be any remodeling involved, but I'll bring you all in if it's necessary. Oh, and on Thursday, I'm having lunch with Lynn Schiffman and one of her friends who's looking at doing a kitchen redesign. I'll let you know if we need a remodel on that one, too," she murmured, scanning her screen, avoiding Kyle's glances.

"Super!" Frank commented again, looking at Kyle for the same congratulations. "I like the way you're bringing in the business. God, I love summer! It looks like you're going to have a busy one," he said to Elise, watching Kyle as he appeared to be engrossed in his screen as well.

Kyle looked up and nodded, knowing it would be suspicious not to. "Awesome," he said, sounding inadequate and ridiculous. Elise acknowledged his compliment with another ghost of a smirk.

Frank cracked his knuckles again, causing them both to look. They discussed the rest of the week, and then Frank brought up the problems at the Blair property. Elise asked to be excused, as it did not involve her, avoiding Kyle's glance again. Fine. It was going to be a rough week, he thought, noticing the tight set of her mouth as she took her iPad back to her office. He didn't relish walking on eggshells around Elise. But it wasn't his fault she'd chosen to date Michael Gilmer. And Frank was oblivious to all of it. He cracked his own knuckles, giving Frank his full attention. If he could have burped loudly, he would have, he thought, steaming.

The meeting with the Wilcoxes went even better than Kyle had anticipated. The three of them made a seamlessly fluid presentation, as if they'd worked together for years rather than weeks. And, as Kyle had expected, the Wilcoxes were thrilled with his design, Elise's interiors, and Frank's building plan. Elise had conducted herself as the top-notch professional they'd hired her to be, giving a warm touch to what he and Frank brought to the table, tantalizing Jackie Wilcox even further. In Kyle's experience, when the woman was happy, the project went much more smoothly. And Jackie was definitely happy. At the end of the meeting, the plans were approved, so Kyle could begin obtaining the building permits the next day. He would be busy for the rest of the week, probably putting in hours at home, so he could leave for vacation the following week without unfinished business hanging over his head. He would be ready to get away and see his family at the Outer Banks. Spending time with Chelsea and the boys away from here seemed all the more alluring. He sighed and shook his head, remembering his little scene with Elise earlier. What could he possibly have been thinking? This was over, he swore to himself.

He packed up and left the office about 4:30 to check on the boys at the Blair site. To his relief, the framers were coming along nicely, having almost completed the second floor, without a beer can in sight. All the men were on their best behavior, so he left as they were clearing out to head for home himself.

In the driveway, Chelsea was getting out of her car, retrieving groceries from the back when he arrived. She grinned and waved when he tooted his horn at her.

"Hey!" he said, extending a hand to take a couple of her bags.

"Hi," she said, a tired smile on her face.

"Are you okay? How was your rehearsal?" he asked, remembering she would be putting the last touches on her upcoming performance with two of her dance colleagues.

She waved a hand in the air. "I changed the whole thing, music and all, and Carmen's okay with it, but Dima's having a cow."

"He's Russian; he'll get over it."

"Right. I know, but I hate having Russians mad at me. He's so…*dark* when he's angry!"

"It's the obligatory front. He loves you. I'm sure it will be great."

"Thanks. How was your day?"

"Oh, pretty good," he said, closing her tailgate and wondering whether to tell her about Elise's visit to her mother's that was probably ending as they spoke.

They looked around, waiting for some sign of the boys as they trudged up the cabin stairs, feeling a breeze blow up from the river, heavy with the scent of water and sun-warmed foliage.

"Wonder where the guys are? They'd better not be plunked down in front of their video games on a nice day like this," Kyle muttered.

"Well, with Thomas babysitting them this week, I'll bet they're playing his guitar inside. Or maybe they're down at the river," Chelsea mused.

Kyle placed the grocery bags on the kitchen counter and called out for the boys, but he heard no answer. As Chelsea began to put things away, he walked out onto the deck to look around. Through the waving green fronds of the willow trees, he spotted the river rocks, and he could hear the clear brown water flowing over them, but still no boys in sight.

"Crap, I forgot to get milk," Chelsea said, her hand on the refrigerator door when he returned. "I ran into Glen at the store and got talking. He was telling me about the new classes he's taking for detective school, and I walked out of the store without the milk....They weren't out there?"

"No," he said, puzzled, reaching for his phone, fingering the screen for Thomas' number. After a moment, "He's not answering."

"Weird. Let's give them a minute before we call the police," she said, but neither of them laughed. They walked back out on the deck and leaned against the railing. "I talked to my mom today."

"How's she doing?" he asked, wondering whether she'd mentioned Elise's visit.

"Oh, she's okay. She and Dad are going down to South Carolina to check on Grandmother at the end of the week. You know she's not supposed to drive anymore. Well, she found the keys to her car and backed it out of the driveway. But she forgot to open the garage."

"*Yow!*" he said, regarding the concern on her face, concern that bubbled over into sudden laughter. He laughed with her, imagining the scene.

"I know it's not funny, but can't you just picture it?" she laughed again and sighed, massaging the back of her neck. "Oh, my poor mother! It's a good thing for her that Dad can handle Grandmother. I'm glad he's going down there. I guess they'll be driving her car back up here."

"It doesn't sound too good for her."

"No. They'll be talking with the resident coordinator to see about moving her to the memory care part of the facility while they're there."

"I can imagine how that will go over with your grandmother."

"I know. She usually listens to Dad and does what he says. And to think, she didn't like him when they first got married."

"That's hard to believe. Who wouldn't like Tom?"

"I know….And I forgot to ask if Jay can look out for Foscoe while they're gone and we're on vacation. I'll see Lauren when I take Thomas home, so I'll check it out with her."

Chelsea's eyes sharpened as she looked across the yard toward the river. "Here they come." She checked her watch. "It's late. Something's not right. Look at Ty."

Ty had spotted them on the deck, a look of dread on his face, and a similar look of unease on Thomas' face. Stu led the pack up the hill, the twins' jeans wet to the knees, followed by a very wet Foscoe at a trot. "Hey, Dad!" he yelled, looking exuberant as usual.

"Huh!" said Kyle, hands on his hips, taking in the variety of expressions, and giving Chelsea a questioning glance.

"Uh-oh, I have a bad feeling about this," Chelsea murmured. Ty's eyes shot up to meet hers as they disappeared under the porch to come around to the front steps. Definitely not good. Three sets of footsteps pounded across the rough boards on the porch as Chelsea and Kyle met them at the front steps, the smells of wet dog and wet boys meeting her nose head-on. Foscoe took this opportunity to shake himself one more time, showering Kyle's slacks before he could jump out of the way.

"Ugh! Get back, Foscoe! Hey, boys. What's going on?" Kyle asked, hands going back on his hips. Ty sat in the rocking chair, hands twisting in his lap, while Thomas lingered at the stairs. Stu sat on the top step with his back casually resting against the porch pillar, pulling off his wet shoes and wiping sweat off his face. His hair stood in damp points away from his head.

"Hey, Dad. Hey, Mom. You should have seen what we just saw!" he began, a grin spreading across his red face.

"Hello, Thomas. And what did you see?" Kyle's glance passed from Thomas, shifting his feet beside Stu, to Ty, and then to Chelsea, before settling on Stu again.

"Did you know there's a beaver pond not far from here? Just down that creek that starts on the other side of the river. It's so cool!"

With raised eyebrows, Kyle glanced at Chelsea again, then at Thomas. "Yeah, I've seen it. What were y'all doing way down there?"

"Following Foscoe. We were walking along the river and Foscoe took off after something. It was a beaver, Dad! It was this big!" he said, extending his hands to what looked like about three feet's breadth.

"You took them that far? To the creek and the beaver dam?" Kyle asked Thomas, who looked sheepishly back at him as Chelsea watched Ty's face, impassive, glancing at her, lips pressed together in a thin line.

"Well, like they said, they took off after Foscoe…" said Thomas.

"And…" Kyle watched Thomas. "So you all went after him?"

Thomas said nothing for a moment. "Well, they kinda got away from me, so I had to go after them."

"He found us. Dad, can we go back there? You know where it is? We can show you. It's so unbelievably cool. You should've heard them smack their tails on the water when they heard us coming! And the trees around there are all gone. They just look like little pencils sticking up out of the ground. Their pond is really big. They must've been there for years."

Kyle passed a hand over his face before answering. "Yeah, it has been there a long time. My dad took Desiree and me ice-skating there once, when we were teenagers."

Chelsea took a step closer, crossing her arms and leaning against the railing. He hadn't mentioned his father or his sister in ages.

He smiled at her. "My mom became pretty unglued about it, as I remember. That's a long way off. I guess if anything had happened to us, she wouldn't have known where to go looking," he said, his eyes clouding as he looked back at all the boys. "Which is why I'm a little disappointed about what you just did. You know that Mom and I don't like you boys going so far off that we can't see you. You're eight years old. There are snakes out in the tall grass and in the river too. Even though you were with Thomas, it wasn't the best choice," Kyle went on, his voice quiet but commanding.

"I *know*, Dad. You've taught us to look out for them and shown us where they hide in the mud in the summer," Stu said in spite of Kyle's hard stare. Kyle shifted his look to Thomas, who shifted uneasily.

"So, Thomas, where were you in all this?" Kyle asked, making the fourteen year-old's face flood with color.

He did not answer readily. Chelsea glanced again at Ty, who appeared to be wishing himself invisible.

Kyle tried again while Chelsea watched, unable to bring herself to speak.

"Thomas? Weren't you with them?"

"I was. Until Stu took off running, and then Ty followed him...."

"And you didn't?"

"I, uh, I couldn't right at first."

"Why not?" Kyle pressed.

"I would have lost reception."

"You were on the phone?" Kyle's voice was ominous, making the hairs rise on Chelsea's arms. Poor Thomas! They knew the cell phone signal gave out on the river just beyond their property line.

"Yes, sir," Thomas said, his face burning now.

"Who were you talking to?" asked Chelsea, in the ring now as well.

Thomas looked at his feet, shifting back and forth on them again. "My girlfriend."

Kyle rolled his eyes. "You do see what a problem this could have been, right? We're trusting you to keep an eye on these two, and they get away from you on the first day."

"Yes, sir. I'm sorry. It won't happen again."

"Well, you should have your phone on you whenever you're out here with them," Chelsea started, trying to take the sting out of Kyle's words, and to take advantage of a teachable moment. After all, Thomas was just a kid too, and this was new to him. "But in the future, I think you'd all be better off staying within sight of the house. Then you'll know you're safer. Being here is not quite the same as on our farm where everybody lives within a stone's throw from each other." She knew he was used to tramping around in the woods, as mountain boys did, but things were different here, and these were her children. No grandparents or aunts and uncles would be around to run to if they got into trouble.

"And you can talk to your girlfriend on your own time," said Kyle, making Thomas redden again.

"And you two," he said, pointing at Stu and Ty, "have to know what your limits are. So, no river for any of you for the rest of this week. Is that clear?"

"Yes, sir," said Ty from behind him.

"Yeah," said Stu, and then, "I mean, yes, sir," when Kyle's stare lingered on him.

"And no TV or video games tonight. Okay," said Kyle. Then turning to Chelsea, he asked, "Do you want me to take him home, or do you want to do it?"

Out of sympathy for Thomas, Chelsea thought it best to volunteer herself. "I'll go, if you'll oversee the baths. No shoes in the house and these clothes go straight to the laundry room, okay?" she said to the twins, and then glanced at Kyle. "I guess at this point we'll have hotdogs for dinner. And will you check them good for ticks?"

"I will. And I'll start the grill while you're gone. See you tomorrow, Thomas," Kyle said to his nephew, with a somber nod.

When Chelsea turned into the Davenport family driveway, her own parents' house came into view first. She glanced at Thomas, who had ridden in silence most of the way over. "I wonder who's car that is," Chelsea murmured, referring to an old model Jeep Cherokee in the semi-circular driveway in front of her house. She felt Thomas shrug beside her. Someone must be visiting her mother. She drove past the house, then the barn, and then her father's plant nursery. Turning to the right, she passed the lake, and then the winery, looking across to the land beyond the lake, the spot Kyle told her that her father was holding for them, for Kyle to build a house on someday for them. It would be beautiful, at the foot of the mountain. Looking straight up, you could see her Uncle Wayne's Christmas tree farm, dotted attractively with plots of trees, reminding her of one of her grandmother's quilt patterns. Cars were leaving the parking lot as she drove past the winery, about to close for the day. Jay and Lauren's house came into view next, a modest but attractive brick home, where Jay, her sister Charley, and she had grown up. Jay and Lauren had moved in when they got married after college, when Jay worked at the nursery with her father. It was the perfect place for boys to roam and explore. Thomas and Ethan enjoyed it as much as she had when she was a kid. She felt sorry for Thomas, on new turf at their cabin. After depositing Thomas and talking with Lauren about what had happened, she headed back to the main house to stop in to see her mother. Maybe she could even score some milk for dinner.

The navy Jeep was still there, so she stopped behind it. She spotted her mother on the front porch talking with someone, probably saying goodbye. The tall woman turned, with flowers in her hand, roses from Kitty's garden, in a mason jar. Chelsea recognized the familiar toss of hair. It was Elise Masters. She swallowed, her hand frozen on the door handle. It was too late to back up and drive away; they'd seen her. Giving a tentative wave, she pushed herself from the seat and made herself walk toward them.

"Hi, Mom!" she called out, trying to sound carefree and casual. It would have to be casual since she still wore the leotard and wrinkled cargo pants from her rehearsal, her hair probably a recovered tangle of the hot mess it had been when she left Dima and Carmen hours earlier. But Elise was as lovely and put-together looking as if she had just started her day, in slim cropped pants, silky blouse, and heels.

"Hello, Chelsea," she said, smiling that serene smile that could just as easily have said, *Kiss my ass*, as, *How nice to see you.*

"Hi, Elise. How are you? I didn't expect to see you," Chelsea said, throwing her mother an expectant glance, and wondering whether Kyle knew about this meeting.

"Hi, sweetheart! Elise has been giving me some ideas on how to redesign my office space and some general redecorating ideas for the house."

"Oh, how nice," Chelsea said, immediately imagining how Elise had probably desecrated her violet bedroom. She felt compelled to straighten her shoulders in the presence of Elise's towering height. In the late afternoon sunlight, Elise's dewy complexion glowed like pictures of women Chelsea had seen in magazines. No one looked like that, at least no one she knew. How did real people have that kind of porcelain skin? Not a pore or imperfection in sight, not to mention even a wrinkle or laugh line. That was it; the aloof expression she always wore meant she didn't smile enough. Well, Chelsea had Kyle, making her smile broadly, hoping every crease and wrinkle she had was showing. "I'll be interested to see what you're working on!" she said, dismissing this as what it was, a business meeting. *With her grandmother's flowers to take away with her.* Next, her mother would be giving Elise one of the ceramic angels she was famous for making.

"Well, thank you, Liz. I had a wonderful time, hearing all your stories and seeing everything. Your home is so lovely! I'm so impressed with your business and all you've done with it. I'll get back to you soon with some drawings and color swatches. I have all the pictures, so it should be easy to put it all together," she said, lifting her iPad in her other hand. Chelsea fumed inwardly, imagining Elise going back to Michael's place to look at the interior pictures of her family's home; just what she thought would happen after their cozy little dinner at Char the other night. But the sincerity in this woman's voice told Chelsea that she would soon become one of her mother's friends as well. Kyle had wanted her to like Elise. Why was she finding it so difficult?

"Okay! Thanks for coming out, Elise. It was good to see you again. Take care of that little cutie pie of yours!"

"I will. Nice to see you, Chelsea. Bye," said Elise, giving Chelsea and her mother a wave as she turned to walk toward her car. *Careful on that gravel with those shoes,* thought Chelsea.

As Elise's car pulled out of the drive, Chelsea turned back toward her mother. "You didn't mention she was coming out here today," she said, giving her mother a hug around the neck, trying not to sound accusatory.

"I know! I forgot all about it until ten minutes before she was supposed to be here. I was out dead-heading the roses, so I cut her some. I hope she understood why I looked so disheveled!"

"Mom, you hardly look disheveled," Chelsea laughed, thinking how her mother always seemed to wear the right thing; today, a blue blouse with white linen pants and comfortable sandals.

"But forgetting something like that…you don't think I'm starting to slip, do you?"

Like Grandmother, she meant. "Oh, no. You just have a lot on your mind," Chelsea said, swatting the air to dispel such a notion. "I forgot to buy milk at the store just an hour ago. Maybe I'm slipping too!"

Her mother laughed. "Well, you have a lot on your mind too. Come on in. I have some milk in the fridge you can take with you. And here, take these blueberries. I have some for Shelly and Stacie that you can take with you to the beach, and a cobbler for Shelly," she said, leading Chelsea to the kitchen, where the aroma of an herbed chicken in the Crockpot made her instantly hungry. Two blueberry cobblers sat waiting in pottery pie dishes on the counter. Chelsea's heart swelled with feelings only home could stir in her.

"Oh, great! They'll love it. The bushes are still coming in?"

"Like gangbusters! Oh, and I talked to Jay about taking care of Foscoe while we're gone to Greenville, so don't worry about him. Your dad is so glad he'll be here with us for a few days, at least. Foscoe is good company for him. I'll tell you though, I'm not looking forward to seeing your grandmother. The social worker called and said Mother almost burned the place down yesterday. She was baking cookies and decided to go take a nap."

"Oh, no!"

"Oh, yes. They don't take that kind of thing lightly, so thankfully, they have already started this conversation we're going to be continuing with her when we get there."

"I guess that's a good thing…I wish I could go, and help you at least."

"Well, at some point we're going to be moving her to the memory unit, so we'll have to do something with all of her furniture and her other things. I might be calling on you sooner than you think to go down there. But you need your family time, and your vacation is important. I'll bet the boys are getting excited."

"We all are. I really think we all need a break together," she said, thinking of down time with Kyle, her thoughts drifting back to Elise. "So what did Elise say about the house?"

"Oh, she gave me some great ideas about converting the front parlor into an office for myself. She gave me props for working in that dreary space of Dad's for all these years!"

Props? Her mother was becoming cool in front of her very eyes. Her teenage grandsons' slang must be rubbing off on her! "And what about my bedroom?"

"Oh! She absolutely loved it and said she wouldn't change a thing!"

Maybe Elise had some redeeming qualities after all.

"And she loved the way you've kept all of your pictures in there, the ones of Kitty, and of you and Kyle when you dated. It's nice for the boys to have those glimpses into your life before they came along."

"She said that?"

"Yes," said her mother thoughtfully, studying her daughter. "You know, I think she's a very nice person. She seems like such an old soul… to be so young, that is."

"I guess she told you about her daughter."

"Not too much. I didn't want to pry, and she didn't say a lot. It must be a difficult story to tell."

"I suppose it would be."

"And you? Any news?"

"No. You'll be the first to know, or at least the second," Chelsea said, feeling a little catch in her throat. It was disappointing not to have news to report. She thought about the boys' escapades earlier, deciding not to burden her mother with one more worry. "I guess I should scoot. Kyle's grilling hotdogs while the boys get their baths. Thanks for the goods, Mom," she said, sliding the bag of milk and blueberries off the counter and taking her mother's hand. "I hope you'll have a good trip. Tell Grandmother I said hi."

"I will. And you give all of Kyle's family a big squeeze for Dad and me. So you'll drop off Foscoe on Friday at Jay's, and then we'll see you the following Sunday night when you pick him up?"

"Absolutely. Dad really should break down and get another dog, you know?"

"I know. I don't know why he drags his feet about it."

"Maybe for his birthday," she said, breaking into a smile.

Her mother embraced her warmly. "Now there's a grand idea! Goodbye, sweetheart! Have a wonderful trip!"

Rain drummed on the cabin's metal roof; it slowed to a lull, then started again; sleep music for later when she was hoping to tumble into bed, letting slumber dissolve the day's frustrations, but she wasn't even tired. Supper had been a subdued affair, oddly, with each of them retreating inwardly into whatever trouble they'd had during the day. She stared vacantly at the socks she rolled, pulling the top of one around and over the other, wondering how many thousands of times she'd done this in her life; a mundane chore, but comforting in its routine. Ty appeared, bouncing onto their bed, clean and sweet-smelling in his pajamas, as she smiled at him and placed clothes into drawers, still warm from the laundry. Some things she placed into the waiting suitcase on the floor, aware that he was watching her, silently, with lips pressed together in a determined play at self-control; so like his father, she thought with a smile.

"What's up, Bug?" she asked, watching as he pretended to be coolly withdrawn.

"Nothing," Ty said. She could almost see the smoke coming from his ears as he hugged Kyle's pillow, stretched across the bed. Kyle and Stu could be heard in the basement, playing one last game of air hockey before bedtime. So much for the punishment of no TV or video games, she thought. Stu was milking every moment of his father's attention, which may have been the point all along, she thought, folding Kyle's favorite T-shirt and tossing it into the suitcase for the beach.

"Right," she agreed, watching Ty again out of the corner of her eye. She knew what this was; a silent plea for *her* attention, while Dad provided the distraction for his ever-present twin. After a few more pairs of socks went into Kyle's drawer, she set the laundry basket to the side of the dresser and climbed onto the bed by her son. Immediately, he thrust his head into her lap, hugging her waist, lips still pressed into the firm line. She pulled her hair loose and let herself exhale. It had been a long day for all of them, she thought, recalling Kyle's tense mood at the dinner table as well. Unusual; it didn't seem to be about what the twins had done, so what was going on with him? Absently, her fingers stroked through Ty's hair, soft, and baby-fine, making her think the twins needed haircuts—after vacation. Even after his bath, she was compelled to search for ticks. It was summer, after all.

"So…anything bothering you?"

Ty shrugged. She waited, knowing it would come pouring out of him, just like it always had with Kyle. They were like two peas in a pod. He sniffed, and then swiped at his face.

"Are you mad?"

She felt him nod.

"About what happened today?"

Another nod.

"We can talk about it some more." The conversation before dinner had not seemed finished.

"Why doesn't Daddy ever talk about Desiree?"

Her fingers paused in their slow dance through his hair. "Well…I think it's because he misses her so much. It makes him sad that she's gone. He told me one time that he wondered what she'd be like if she were still alive…you know? How would she have grown up and all. What kind of family she'd have."

"What happened to her?" he asked quietly.

Her heart raced as she thought about the best way to tell him. "She had an accident on a trip with some friends when she was in high school. She got hit by a car. I guess sometimes you and Stu think Daddy and I worry over you too much, but things like that affect people, you know?"

"That's sad," he said as she felt his hold tighten across her lap. Almost inaudibly, he spoke again. "Do you think you'd talk about me if I were dead?"

Her heart plummeted, and she felt her hand stop automatically with the thought, so unexpected, and for him, probably terrifying. "Oh, honey! Of course I would, but what would make you say that? Were you scared about what happened today at the beaver pond?"

She felt him freeze; then the slightest nod. "We shouldn't have been there. It was so far away. I told Stu to stop, but he wouldn't. I couldn't just leave him. And Thomas just sat there on the rock, talking to that dumb girl, so I had to do something."

"And you're mad at Stu?"

"I get mad at Stu a lot, Mom. Sometimes he doesn't care. He gets away with everything. He just does whatever he wants and then I end up getting in trouble 'cause he does bad things."

"Poor choices. He makes poor choices. But you're right. You shouldn't get in trouble if you're the one trying to keep him in line. I'm glad you told me."

"He told me not to tell. He said I'd be a wuss if I told."

"Did he, now? You know what that makes him, right?"

"No."

"He's being a bully, and that's not right."

"But if you tell him I told you, he'll call me a wuss. But Mom...sometimes, I get so scared. I didn't know what to do today."

"I know what you're saying, Ty. Stu doesn't have fear. Sometimes it's smart to be afraid. You were right to tell him to stop. And I'm sorry you had to go after him. And I'm sorry Thomas didn't help. So that's why Daddy said you all aren't allowed back at the river for the rest of the week. We've talked to Thomas about being more attentive. We'll talk to Stu. And we won't say you told. It doesn't take a genius to figure out what happened. You did a brave thing today. Thank you for talking about it. Do you feel better?"

"I guess...."

"Can you sleep?"

"I don't know...."

"Why don't you go get in bed and read that King Arthur book you like while Daddy and I work this out."

Gratefully, he kissed her arm before she let him go; then he slid off the bed, doing as he was told. Chelsea wandered into the kitchen and stealthily sent Kyle a text message to sit down with Stu to talk about what had happened so when she could appear, it wouldn't look like she was the one bringing it up. Thunder rumbled as the rain drummed again. After straightening up a few things in the kitchen, she trotted downstairs, noticing that Ty was in bed already with his book. She found Kyle and Stu sitting Indian-style across from each other on the bed in the guest bedroom. Kyle was listening to Stu's version of the story when she walked in.

"So why didn't you stop when you realized Thomas wasn't coming?" Kyle asked Stu, elbows resting on his knees, his hands steepled toward his son.

"He was coming. He just wasn't right there."

"But didn't you know you shouldn't be that far away, and on the other side of the river?"

When Stu didn't respond at first, Chelsea climbed onto the bed, asking, "Didn't they both tell you to stop?"

"Yeah, but—"

"*But* nothing," said Kyle firmly. "When Thomas tells you to do something, you need to obey him, just like it is with us. And if your brother comes after you, too, you know you need to listen."

Stu shut down then, looking back and forth to each parent. He knew he was being set up.

"Neither Thomas or Ty wanted to see any of you getting in trouble. You have to stick with them if they tell you something's not a good idea. This worked out badly for all of you, and it looks like you were the one who brought it on all three of you."

Stu stared at the bathroom door, fidgeting with his thumbs.

"I think you owe your brother and your cousin an apology," Kyle said, reaching out to rub Stu's knee.

"Well, Thomas could have come after me if he was really that worried!" he lashed out.

"Yes, and he should have, which is why Ty had to do it," said Chelsea as Stu narrowed his eyes at her. "And don't give him a hard time about it either, because you know it was the right thing to do to turn around and leave. Foscoe would have followed you all back home. You put your brother in danger as well as yourself. You should appreciate that he cares enough about you to have gone after you. Someone else might have just left you there, and then who knows what could have happened to you?"

"Whatever…" Stu said, rolling his eyes.

"Not *whatever*. You know what you need to do, so go talk to your brother," Kyle said, offering him a hand off the bed. "And make it good."

Stu gazed from one parent to the other. "Okay," he said solemnly.

They followed him to the bedroom door, glancing in to see the top of Ty's head over the book. Stu approached and climbed onto the bed. The boys stared at one another for a moment. Chelsea hugged Kyle around the waist and swallowed as they watched. He felt solid and warm as she pressed her cheek into his shoulder.

"Look, I'm sorry I ran off today," Stu said. "I should've come back when you called me."

Ty nodded.

"Were you scared?"

Ty shrugged.

"I'm sorry."

"Is it gonna happen again?" Ty asked.

"No. Okay then?"

"Okay."

Stu extended his hand and his brother raised his, touching their knuckles together, as they had watched men do, making Chelsea bite her lip.

"All right, guys. Good for both of you. Now get some sleep. Sweet dreams, okay?" said Kyle, tucking Ty in and then walking around to Stu's bed.

Chelsea crossed her fingers, following Kyle's lead, and kissing both their heads goodnight. "I love you," Kyle murmured to each of them as Chelsea winked at Ty. After giving Chelsea a quick hug, Stu climbed into his own bed, letting her tuck him in, a sign his anger was over. Ty set the book on the nightstand as Kyle turned out the light. They settled silently as Chelsea followed Kyle upstairs.

He waited for her at the top of the stairs. She sighed, glad the boys had made amends, and ready to move on to their evening together. She had a new nightgown he hadn't seen yet!

"So, what did you think of Stu's apology?" she asked, watching Kyle's face.

"Ah, I think he had to drag it out of himself because we were watching."

"Well, an apology is a humbling thing…especially for an eight-year-old."

"For anyone," he murmured, gazing at the floor. Then he looked at her, eyes devoid of the glow she wanted to see. "Listen, I need to sit up for a while and work on some paperwork before tomorrow. It's going to be a busy day. Do you mind?" Her spirits sank a bit, but she didn't want to appear too disappointed. If he had to work, he probably wasn't too happy about it either. He touched her hand. "I'm sorry, but if I can get most of my work done this week, I'll be a free man on vacation," he said, raising an eyebrow.

"Okay. That will be a good thing. Besides, I'm kind of tired after today anyway."

"With all the excitement, you didn't get a chance to tell me more about the dance issues."

"It can wait. I'd rather not get all stirred up again before I go to bed." She thought about Elise too, at her mother's house, and his guilty face when she'd mentioned seeing her there. It would take an effort to put it all out of her mind.

"You sure?" he asked and she nodded. "Well, I hope I won't be long, but go on to sleep if you're tired. Goodnight, baby." Feeling his arms go around her waist, she lifted her chin to kiss him goodnight, lingering at the door to their room; then she watched him pad upstairs to the loft. The new nightgown would have to wait for another night.

Chapter 8

SLEEPLESS

Rain beat down on the roof of Mountaineer Builders as Kyle listened to Elise on the phone in her office, arranging a conference with a prospective client, and Frank on his phone with the framing foreman, thankfully in check now, due to their efforts at riding ramrod over the crew last week. He drummed his fingers aimlessly over the surface of his desk, watching the rain fall in sheets out the window. The weather had prohibited yet another morning run, making him feel more restless than usual. And with this weather, it would be fine with him if Marcus Gilmer decided to cancel their meeting at his new property. Kyle did not relish the idea of being in the same room with him and Elise, wondering how Michael figured in all of this, especially since he'd messed up his working relationship with Elise yesterday morning over that same topic. At best, it was going to be awkward. Thoughts of his conversation with Stu the night before reminded him that he needed to apologize to Elise about his bad behavior, which had ruined everything. She had yet to speak to him this morning, although she was engrossed in the routine of her job, he thought, ruefully, a routine he'd always expected from Faith, but for which he had never given her the respect she deserved, quite possibly.

Sighing and drumming his fingers on the desk again, he realized that every day since they had worked together, Elise Masters' presence had consumed him, whether or not he had wanted it to do so. He yawned, regretting the sleep he'd lost the night before, worrying; worrying about her, about Chelsea and her mother, and Stu's poor judgment. The twins would need his attention more and more now, he thought, remembering his own vain attempts at that age to seek his father's notice. His sister had mastered getting her father's attention, with her wild ways, but look where it had gotten her; pregnant, and then dead. He shook his head again with a ragged sigh. Vacation could not come soon enough! He ran a hand down his face. Among the rest of his family, he would be especially glad to see Tyson, Stacie's husband, and his rock since Kyle had been seventeen and mad at the world, so long ago....

His fingers encircled the brown and green coffee mug, feeling the warmth, thinking about the colors...and the river, filling swiftly now with rain, and he imagined the sound of it, swooshing loudly tonight, when he and Chelsea would drift off to sleep. She deserved time from him, time to be held and loved and cherished the way she needed, the way *he* needed. Babies didn't get made the way they were going. He had neglected his family with his own distracted thoughts, thoughts that were wrong, and at best just a fantasy. Why was he letting this happen? *It's the seven-year itch*, Glen had said, when Kyle had questioned his distance from Abby and the triplets at one point. Could it be happening to him as well? There was nothing to get out of his system; he'd done that back in college with Emily Hayes. Why was he struggling now?

The printer stopped, signaling that his forms were ready. As the last of the proposals for the Hayes' cabin slid across the machine, Kyle made a note on his computer to give Tom Davenport a call to schedule a preliminary walk-through of the property, to delineate the traffic flow from the road, the driveway plan, and the grading necessary to prepare for the footings. Tom would come back later and design the rest of the landscape when the house plans were approved and the landscape budget was set. Kyle shook his head slightly, feeling remorseful. Tom would be livid if he knew what Kyle had been thinking about lately. More like murderous. And Tom should have been included in the meeting with Marcus Gilmer today, but Kyle had made an effort to spare his father-in-law the encounter. Lunch with Marcus would be the last thing on Tom's list of an enjoyable way to spend the day. At least, after lunch he could come back here and get in a decent afternoon of work before he went home, which would afford him more time for his family tonight.

For the next two hours, he worked on the building permits and preliminary budget worksheets for Dr. Hayes, repressing the thoughts of lonely Emily and her four children, coming up to ski in the winter and relax in the summer, without her workaholic husband. It was none of Kyle's concern, but he could have foreseen this scenario many times over, remembering ambitious Graham from their college days.

He was hardly aware that Frank had left the office when his alarm chimed on his computer, letting him know it was time to leave. He collected his camera and turned off the light in his office before stopping by Elise's door.

"You ready?" he asked, watching as she tucked her iPad and an umbrella into her large tote, and flicked off her lamp.

"Yes." Her polite face held the hint of a smile; her work face. He held the door for her as they left the building together. Thankfully, the rain had abated for the day, and sunshine fought its way from behind the clouds as they walked to Kyle's car parked in the lot around the corner. Elise held her hair in the brisk breeze that blew, promising more sunshine for later, and some drying of the saturated ground.

They drove in silence for a while, listening to the music coming from the radio, which Kyle kept at a low volume, reminding him of elevator music, hoping not to be any more offensive than necessary while he rehearsed the words for his pending apology. As usual, he had to stop at the main intersection in town, and he glanced sideways, watching Elise checking her phone messages.

"Elise, about yesterday…I didn't mean to upset you. I'm sorry if I crossed a line."

"Yeah, what *was* that?" she asked, making his feeble attempt at making amends all the more difficult.

"I shouldn't have said anything about Michael, and I'm sorry." *But not sorry for warning you.*

She looked expectantly at him, waiting for more. "That's it?"

"What?"

"There seemed to be more to it than just Michael. I understand what you meant about him. And it was actually kind of sweet that you were being protective. I totally get that. But there was something else…."

"No, there wasn't." He looked at her and she met his gaze directly.

"Yes, there was. And if you're sorry, that's fine. Whatever."

He averted his eyes from the smile he knew would start. Could this be any more awkward?

"Just…" he began, as horns honked behind him.

"You have the green light," she said. "And like I said, it's fine. I accept your apology. For whatever it was you were doing."

His face burned. He could never bring himself to put into words what he'd felt yesterday, which was probably for the best. She had just forgiven him for it anyway. She knew, obviously, so he didn't have to say it, he thought, head swimming, trying to remember where he was going in the car with her. Her fragrance was present, even stifling today. He drove forward and opened his sunroof to let in the balmy breeze, hoping it would clear his head. A frustrated sigh escaped his lips. And then, with a glance and a smile from her, he felt comfortable with her again, as she turned up the radio, and smoothed her hair behind her ear.

"Are you looking forward to your vacation?" she asked, her voice silky, absolving him of the moment. He watched as she slid the butterfly pendant back and forth, letting it drop inside the neckline of her blouse.

"Yep," he said, blowing air up into his hair. "It can't get here soon enough."

"Who's babysitting your boys this week? I tried calling Maddie the other night to babysit this weekend, but she's on vacation too."

"Thomas, our nephew. He's fourteen."

"Oh, that's nice. I'll bet your boys like having a boy to entertain them."

"Well…actually, they got in a little trouble, yesterday."

"Ooh, on the first day. That's not good. What'd they do?"

"They were down at the river and our dog ran off after a beaver, so they ran after him and ended up way off down the creek on the other side of the river. There's a beaver pond back in there and they were farther away than they should have been."

"Sounds like quite an adventure."

"Oh, it was, at least for Stu. Scared the hell out of Ty, but he felt like he had to go take care of Stu, because of course, he wouldn't come back."

"Ah, another protective Davis male. And where was your nephew in all of this?"

She caught on so quickly. "Talking to a girl on the phone."

They laughed, and she fingered the necklace again. "Of course!" she said. "No wonder you're distracted today."

He nodded, watching the road, concentrating on his driving, realizing his mood was obvious. "Do you spend a lot of time worrying about Lydia?"

She smiled sweetly at him, holding the butterfly. "Constantly."

"I guess that's parenting."

"I guess," she said, turning up the radio as an Aretha Franklin song came on. She cracked her window and sang to the music, making him grin.

She programmed her phone for directions and he followed until they arrived at a large white house with a welcoming front porch, tucked away up a side street in the next town of Blowing Rock. Surrounded by ancient trees, rhododendrons, and lilies, it had the appearance of a storybook house where he imagined children living with an estranged old aunt with stuffy furniture and lots of ornery cats. Parking behind the white Audi Quattro in the semi-circular drive, they both noticed the license plate that read SNOWMAN. *Marcus.* He snorted and turned to Elise. Her eyebrows rose as she sighed and gathered her tote bag before opening her door.

"Hey, is Michael going to be here?" he blurted, as the idea had just occurred to him.

"I have no idea. We didn't discuss business on our hot date."

Damn! Serves you right, he thought to himself, feeling hot under the collar again as she shut the door and walked up the steep stone steps to the house. The wind gusted as he held back and looked over the yard. Tom would have fun with this place. The rhododendrons and lilies bloomed freely, and oversized hostas lined the foundation, clipped off at their tops by neighboring deer. It would take a major overhaul on the shrubbery and flowers, and the trees needed pruning. The dead one near the back needed removal. But the lawn had great potential. He was inspecting the roof and the siding when Frank drove up behind him.

"Hey, buddy," Frank greeted him, adjusting his belt over his girth, as he emerged from his Suburban. "How are you?"

"Good. This is a nice old place. It'll need a new roof." Kyle snapped a picture of the house, wondering about parking for the guests if this were to be a bed and breakfast.

"Looks that way. Did you bring Elise?"

"Yeah, she just went inside. Everything okay at Blair?"

"Oh yeah. One of the crew has been replaced, but it appears everyone is carrying on as they should."

"Good for Ray for nipping trouble in the bud."

"Yeah. They should finish the roof today, now that the rain's stopped. Oh, and Faith asked about you this morning."

"Yeah? Tell her I miss her. How is she?"

"Getting antsy. She thought she'd have so much to do, but she misses working, I think."

"I tried to tell her," Kyle said, grinning, making Frank laugh. "Get her to stop by and have lunch with us sometime."

"Nah, I think she'd be afraid to step on Elise's toes right now."

"I doubt Elise would care, do you?"

"No, she seems very confident. Nothing much seems to ruffle her feathers," Frank said, and they both nodded.

At that moment, Marcus appeared at the front door. "Hello there! Come in the house!" he called, holding the door as Kyle and Frank hesitated, then wiped their shoes on the mat.

"No need to take them off. The floors are going to need work, you know."

"Nice place!" Frank commented, pressing his hand into Marcus'. Kyle followed suit, checking the doorjamb. Nice and solid, he thought, running his eyes up and down the porch, noticing the leaded glass in the oak door.

"They don't build them like this anymore," he murmured, looking at the porch swing and the solid wooden pillars in need of sanding and paint. Gingerbread accents trimmed each corner around the rafters. "What do you think Frank, 1920-something?"

"Probably. Right in the heyday when tourists started coming here."

"Well, the leaking roof has caused quite a bit of damage to the inside, but I'm sure it's what you'd expect for a house like this that's been neglected," said Marcus.

"It's a shame. How long has it sat empty?" Frank asked.

"About sixteen years, off and on, with the different family members trying to keep it up," Marcus said, leading them into the large parlor where they glimpsed Elise looking over the wallpaper and going to the fireplace, admiring the heavy, sculpted mantle that caught Kyle's eye as well. Oriental rugs and several pieces of furniture remained, shrouded in dust covers. Kyle took in the bead-board paneling, the crystal light fixtures, and the electrical outlets, thinking they'd need updating, along with all the wiring and the plumbing, most likely. Marcus and Frank discussed the former owners, a family none of them knew, as Elise cooed over the mantle, running her hand along its smooth surface, admiring the millwork.

Kyle saw stains on the ceiling in several places, along with rotting floorboards where the leakage from the ceiling had done its damage. The smell of mold hung in the air, making him sniff. Frank wrote notes on a legal pad beside him.

"Are you going to be able to salvage any of the furniture? These carpets have to go," he commented to Marcus, and lifted the camera to shoot the mantle.

"Some of these pieces have escaped the leaking ceilings, but you're right; the carpets are history," said Marcus as Elise let out a shriek.

"*Oh!* Shit!" she screamed, bolting away from the mantle, the toe of her tan wedge-heeled shoe catching on the moldy carpet, sending her sprawling toward Kyle. He put out a hand automatically to break her fall.

"What?" cried Frank.

"Holy crap!" said Kyle, as Marcus let out another expletive. They all watched, wide-eyed as a black snake oozed over the hearth and into the fireplace, disappearing into the pitch dark hole. Kyle was aware of Elise's arm around his shoulders, as she had circled him, clinging to him as if he were a shield against the unexpected reptile. The feel of her arms across his chest and shoulders brought him quickly to attention, as he tried to keep them both upright.

Marcus burst out laughing. "Bah!" he said, bending at the waist and wiping his eyes, the breath leaving him with the laughter that was consuming him. "Oh, my lord, you should see the two of you!" he cried, between bursts of laughter, and slapping his thigh as if he could not contain his mirth. "That girl is climbing you like a *tree,* son!"

Frank's chuckle erupted into a loud cackle, as he joined Marcus' amusement at the sight of his new employee wrapped around Kyle for safety.

"I'm sorry! I just can't handle snakes!" Elise said, slowly releasing her grip. "I've never had one sneak up on me like that, and in a house...*ew!* That just totally creeps me out! I should have just jumped on the couch!" she said, breathlessly, smoothing her hands over slim white pants as all the men watched, seemingly fascinated with the nutmeg color of her blouse. She looked sheepishly at Kyle, reddening from the chest up. "I'm sorry for mauling you," she murmured again. "What kind of snake *is* that?" she asked, curiosity getting the best of her.

"It looks like a rat snake," said Frank. "There are probably mice on the premises," he said, eyes dancing as Elise cringed again.

"Lovely," she muttered, looking around, as if expecting another round of snakes to appear and chase a few dozen rodents, skittering across the floor.

Kyle laughed. "So Marcus, put *'Call the exterminator'* on your list."

"Right now, please," Elise said, attempting a brave smile.

"I'm sorry, Elise! Do you have the nerve to see the rest?" asked Marcus. "I should have had the exterminator come before you all got here, but I promise I'll get on it today," he said, winking at Elise.

Kyle held the door of the Storie Street Grille for Elise. They stepped carefully inside the crowded foyer, and around the other diners who were waiting to be seated. The lunch rush was in full swing. Kyle felt her brush up against him in an attempt to avoid a man who was backing up to allow a buxom young woman with over-plucked eyebrows deliver the menus at the hostess stand. The waitress gave a practiced glance to the newcomers, her surprised looking eyes lingering on them for a moment.

"Two?" she asked Kyle, watching him steer Elise out of the other man's way, as he had failed to realize they were behind him.

"Uh, no, actually there will be four of us," he replied, catching sight of Frank waving at them from a table in the dining room.

"Oh, yes, right this way," she said, dimples appearing as she smiled at the two of them. They slid into the chairs across from Frank as the hostess handed them all menus, taking into account Kyle's wedding band. "Jessica will be right with you," she said, stretching out the word *you* to at least three vowel sounds, and looking at Elise's hands before she left them. In a moment, Marcus joined them, making the table seem crowded with his large presence.

Jessica appeared with tall glasses of water for them and quoted the daily specials. The men ordered the meatloaf special, and Elise chose the spinach salad, as Kyle would have predicted. They talked about the house and what fine shape it was in, considering its age and lack of recent attention. Marcus had plans to add two more bathrooms and do a total kitchen renovation. Elise quizzed him on his ideas for the interiors, pleased with his desire to stay with the period pieces and the whole 1920s look for the crystal chandeliers and wallpaper. The mantle and resident snake were discussed extensively. Elise promised to work the snake into the décor, possibly in a lamp or a painting somehow. They discussed the landscaping and the parking predicament, and Kyle promised to take Tom over when he was free another day. Frank made good on his plan not to stay around, thanking Marcus for the lunch and begging off to go back to the Blair site where he was to meet the electrician for the afternoon.

The mood mellowed as the dishes were cleared, and Kyle watched Marcus gaze at Elise for a moment before Marcus directed his next comment to Kyle, swirling the ice in his glass. "You know, as much as I like this place, it's not the property I really want."

Here we go, thought Kyle, wondering whether Elise would have a part in this discussion, and sliding his eyes toward her. Her impassive face showed him nothing, but her self-control did not surprise him anymore.

"Meaning?" asked Kyle.

"What's the feeling on the Davenport front about selling their house? Have they given it any more thought?"

Kyle leveled his most foreboding look at Marcus, taking a heavy moment before he responded. "Leave them alone, Marcus," he said quietly, making Elise turn her head toward him at his tone.

Marcus' eyes glinted. "So there's really no help you can give me?"

"Now why would I be your ally in this, Marcus?" Kyle said, laughing. "No one's going anywhere. Tom's family has been in that house for several generations, and just because a bunch of tourists think it's a charming place to get married, he's not going to sell it to you."

"What are Tom and Liz doing, rattling around in that big old place all by themselves anyway?"

"They're hardly by themselves," Kyle said, thinking about Chelsea and how angry this conversation would make her. "I have a big family," he said, liking the sound of the words and all they implied. "We still have a lot of living to do there." His comments registered with Marcus, who pondered them with his chin resting in his hand. Out of protectiveness for his wife, Kyle did not tell Marcus that Chelsea's dream was to return to that house to live one day. Some topics with this man were off limits. Elise was gazing at him as well. "Leave them alone," he repeated, and Marcus shifted in his seat, signaling a nuance in the conversation.

Elise's phone played its tune and she checked it, backing away from the table. "Excuse me; it's Lydia's day care. I'll take this over there," she said, getting up from the table and sliding carefully behind Kyle so she wouldn't bump the people behind him. He felt her fingers in his hair and drew in a breath with the unexpected sensation. "You have a maple seed in your hair," she said, pulling it out as Marcus saw the surprise on Kyle's face.

Watching her walk away, Marcus continued to stare with his hand cradling his chin.

"You two make a cute couple," he said, eyes twinkling mischievously.

"Huh?"

"Just that. You look like you belong together. She's a knock-out; you're a good-looking guy. Everybody here is noticing the two of you. You have an easy way about the way you interact, like you're together."

Kyle looked at him incredulously. He obviously had no idea that Elise was seeing his son. There seemed to be no attempt at any kind of a set-up here, on Elise's part, that is. Maybe he had imagined it. But what was Marcus imagining? Still, he felt defensive and didn't want to show it.

"We work well together. She's very good at her job."

"Oh, I'm sure she is. And I'm sure you don't mind working with her one little bit. *I* wouldn't."

"What are you getting at, Marcus?"

"I'm just saying I know the signs."

"The signs of what?"

"I can tell when people get in over their heads. I know because there's a reason I'm single. You know? Be careful, Kyle. As you say, you have that big family to look out for. You don't need to go messing that up."

Kyle watched the man's earnest face, surprised first at his perception, and then with his candor.

"Huh! Well, I believe you might be misreading the situation, but who she's into isn't my business anyway. And as you've mentioned, I have a wife and a family whom I'm real fond of. But thanks for the concern all the same." Marcus Gilmer was one to be reckoned with in a careful way.

Elise returned to the table as Marcus laid his credit card inside the black billfold, gesturing to their server. Kyle could feel the anxiety coming from Elise. Her fingers raked through her hair and she looked at him with urgent eyes.

"Is everything okay?" he asked, as she stood at the table's edge.

"Actually, no. Lydia got hit with a chair at the day care. They're on their way to the hospital with her. She's got a cut on her forehead, and they're sure it's going to require several stitches," she said, attempting to keep her breathing even, fidgeting with her phone.

"Oh, then let's go," Kyle said, getting to his feet in one motion.

"My car is at the office," she said, gesturing helplessly.

"I'll take you by the hospital right now. It's on the way, anyway."

Marcus stood as well, giving Kyle a nod. "You two go on. I've got this taken care of."

Kyle extended his hand, saying, "Thanks, Marcus. I'll look forward to getting back in touch with you. We'll start on a proposal and we'll meet again soon."

"Absolutely," Marcus said, turning to Elise. "Elise, it was my pleasure being with you today. I hope your little girl will be okay."

She looked touched, saying, "Thank you, Marcus. And thank you for lunch. We'll be in touch."

Kyle took her arm, guiding her to the door while Marcus sat back down, watching them leave.

Chelsea lay awake as the moonlight filtered into the room, despite the drawn curtains. Glancing over Kyle's shoulder, the clock read 3:32, *almost time for paranormal activity*, she thought crossly. She had tried to wait up for Kyle, who had spent another evening working in the loft. He'd been occupied with work he had not been able to finish at the office due to spending part of the afternoon in the emergency room with Elise Masters and her daughter. That was time he could have spent with Chelsea and the boys. But no, Elise had claimed him once again, forcing Chelsea to dream ridiculous scenarios that made her wake, fuming and irritable, in the middle of the night. In her dream, Chelsea had entered her mother's parlor, where Liz sat, chatting intimately with Kyle and Elise, who was fingering her husband's hair and laughing at a story he was telling. When Chelsea entered the room, they didn't realize she was there, despite her loud demands that they notice her. Finally when they acknowledged her, they didn't recognize her, calling her by another name, and telling her to come in so they could find her some clothes that fit her properly! It was an absurd scene, and one that mirrored the dance she had finished choreographing that day, depicting a couple struggling with their mother's dementia. She had done the piece for her mother, as a way to honor what she was dealing with, but the dream had thrown it back at her, distorted, mocking her insecurities about Elise and Kyle, even bringing her mother into the mix. She had not even had an opportunity to tell Kyle about finishing the piece because he was so preoccupied with his work and what the boys had done with Thomas all day. Chelsea sighed, rolling over, remembering Kyle slipping quietly into bed beside her hours ago, carefully taking away the book she'd been reading when she'd fallen asleep. He had kissed her shoulder, the unmistakable invitation for intimacy if she were awake, but she had resisted, pretending to be asleep, letting her resentment get the best of her. So he had left her alone, once again unaware of the new nightgown and the possibilities it held.

She regretted ignoring him now, she thought, hearing him stir, wondering whether he would wake up and want her. Being mad at him was not the way to hold him, especially if someone else were competing for his affections. He was making sounds now, groaning, and breathing hard, so she listened. A word she couldn't discern escaped his lips in a raw whisper, and then he jolted awake, freezing for a moment. She felt him move and sigh, rolling onto his back and kicking off the covers. He sat up on the side of the bed, sighing again, rubbing his hands on his face. He glanced back at her and sat a moment longer, exhaling deeply. Slowly, he stood and got his bearings, padding silently out of the room. Still, she pretended to be asleep.

He had awakened, jarred by the dream, shuddering in a sweat and unsure whether it were real. Seconds ago, they were making love on a beach, the tide washing warm over their legs. He had been lost in her. Of course, she was so different, awakening new, explosive sensations within him. It would have been the perfect dream, except for one harsh reality; the woman in the dream was not his wife.

Dazed, Kyle went to the kitchen sink, running a glass of water, and then going to the window to stand in the moonlight. He took a drink of water, hoping to clear his head of the dream. He remembered every detail, as if it had been real, and something he'd remember for a long time, maybe even the rest of his life; it was so vivid, and disturbingly pleasant. He wouldn't want this memory to last, but he knew the picture of himself with Elise would be etched in his mind, no matter how hard he tried to erase it. Shaking his head sharply, he went to the couch, sinking down into the cushions, letting the moonlight bathe his dilemma, hearing the river rushing through the open transom windows. Pushing fingers into his hair, he was still, wishing the images away, telling himself this was the end of it. The visit to the hospital with Elise and Lydia, him holding the fretful child while Elise filled out the necessary paperwork, with all the staff thinking they were an adorable little family, and Marcus' remarks from the day—they had brought his imaginings to reality, a reality he knew had no place in his life. His world would be nothing if he lost his family, and what he had been entertaining in his head lately would certainly destroy everything he had ever become. Chelsea had been the beginning for him. She had redirected him when he thought he was lost. The trust between them had only been challenged a time or two, but they had managed to rise above the doubts, deepening their resolve to be together. When they married and the boys came along, it solidified him as a member of her family, and she into his family, in a way he never thought he deserved. Nothing was more important than Chelsea and their sons. If he destroyed her trust in him, he would destroy everything they had made, and destroy *her* in the process. He couldn't hurt her like that. She was his anchor. He would not ruin their lives. But had he crossed that line already?

The feather-light sound of her footsteps startled him. He watched her step into his parcel of moonlight, becoming pale and lustrous where it illuminated her. *Damn!* He stared. This was no dream. The woman on the beach had nothing on his wife.

"I'm sorry…did I wake you?" he asked quietly, pressing his elbows on his knees, watching her reach for his glass of water, taking a sip, her hair falling over one shoulder.

"No, actually I was awake. I had the weirdest dream. I guess you had one, too?" She gazed at him, the question in her eyes.

"I guess," he said, unwilling to let her see his trouble.

"What were you dreaming about?" she pressed.

"I can't remember," he lied easily.

"It must have been pretty good from what I heard," she said, studying his reaction.

"Really? What'd I say?"

"I don't know…not any words I could make out…just a lot of moaning and groaning and heavy breathing. Are you sure you weren't dreaming about us?"

This was looking bad, he thought. From the tone of her voice, she knew, maybe. It sounded as if she were baiting him. She continued speaking, softly. "It's been a while. Maybe you want something you haven't had lately. Maybe you need something more than dreams." Her voice seduced him out of his turmoil, riveting his attention to her. She took another slow sip of his water.

"Maybe," he said, going with her train of thought, thinking how beautiful she was, the way the moonlight cast shadows around all her curves in just the right places. No woman could be more arousing to him right now. She had on some little lacy thing he'd never seen, and it looked amazing on her. His pulse quickened, imagining her without it. The image had an astonishing affect on his own body, making his eyes swim. He swallowed. She continued, absently stroking her finger around the rim of the glass. He watched, letting the erotic motion of her finger pull him under.

"Do you remember what it felt like when you fell in love with me?" she asked, the beginnings of a smile forming at her mouth.

"Which time? I fall in love with you a little more every day," he said, wanting her to understand how much he meant it.

She smiled, taking another sip of water, and then she studied the panel of moonlight. "I've missed you, you know? Even when you're here, it's like you're not here…sometimes."

"You're right. I'm sorry," he said, looking deep into her eyes, seeing hurt. He recalled seeing the disappointment in all of their faces tonight, Stu lying with his head in her lap on the couch, and Ty on the floor beside her, when he'd told them he had to go upstairs to work. It wasn't worth it, letting them down like that. Work was grossly overrated. It would be there tomorrow, and after vacation. The clients could wait. And then he thought of Elise and how he had needed to help her. She had wanted to keep her personal life personal, but he was continually getting entangled in it, whether or not he liked it. What was he trying to prove? And to whom? He shook his head, regretting all of it. There would be no more of this. "Come here," he said, standing up and removing the glass from her hand, setting it on the table. Taking her hand, he pulled her into his arms, feeling her body's warmth and breathing deeply her scent. He pressed his hand against her cheek, letting it slip to her neck, kissing her. Her mouth was as soft as butter against his, dissolving him with bittersweet kisses. Feeling her cool fingers fanning over his chest, he felt his heart pounding against them. Her touch was electrifying, turning his want of her to *need*. He felt the palm of her hand moving down across his stomach, ending inside his boxers, sending a surge of painful excitement deep within him. *Here we go*, he said to himself. Her presence moved him, creating the urgency he wanted with her, only her. *Intimacy*—it was the feeling he had with her and no one else, a warmth, a sacred thing that would only ever be between the two of them. He kissed her passionately, hard, and deep, feeling her hands in his hair, pulling him closer, wanting more. His hands moved on her body, feeling the softness of her skin, the suppleness of her shoulders. He wanted all of her.

"Show me it's me," she murmured into his mouth. It killed him to hear her say it.

His eyes opened and he sent a look burning into hers. "Of course it's you. It's always been you," he whispered raggedly, his mouth against hers. Her tongue was in his mouth as he felt her curves pressed against him. He groaned when she slipped both hands inside the band of his boxers, pushing them away. Her hands slid over his body, caressing him, stroking him, making him ache for her. Her nightgown's straps had slipped off her shoulders, and he tugged, wrestling the nightgown off of her impatiently until she was naked, her breasts soft as flowers, filling his hands. A fleeting thought of the boys, asleep downstairs, sent a rush of caution through him, making him hesitate for a moment. "What?" she breathed against his neck between kisses there.

"The boys," he murmured back, and they stifled laughter, sinking together onto the couch, both eyeing the blanket that might come in handy if they were discovered. He remembered a time before the twins, when they'd made love like this, spontaneously on the floor, and she'd complained of rug burn and bruises for days afterward! This wouldn't take long anyway, he thought, reaching for her hips to pull her on top of him. She leaned in to kiss him again, but he held her away, making her look at him, wanting her to hear her name. He held her face in his hands. "Chelsea," he said, eyes boring into hers. Holding her over his lap, he felt her, hot and wet for him, slipping over him. "*I want you,*" he whispered, filling her easily, completely, hearing her gasp, making that low sound in her throat of pain turning to pleasure. They moved together with desperation, both trying to show the other that nothing had changed, that they were still themselves without anyone coming between them. She closed her eyes, taking all of him, kissing him, giving it back. "Look at me, baby," he said, cupping a hand behind her head, and with his other hand, threading his fingers through hers. "I love you," he said, pushing himself into her harder, making her cry out softly, trying not to wake the boys.

"Don't leave me," she gasped, closing her eyes.

"Not happening," was all he could manage to say between the rushes of sensations.

"*I love you,*" she cried, shuddering with him several times until they slowly came down, settling into each others' arms in the stillness that followed. He held her tenderly, pressing his lips against the top of her head, and stroked her hair, listening to the river, *their river.* She had brought him back where he belonged.

Chapter 9

DUCK

Kyle was still floating. He fought the urge to retreat to his bedroom and crawl under the covers, as the different groups of them took their places in his mother and Mark's house, high on a knoll in Duck on Sunday night. Surfing the swells that morning with Tyson and his daughter, Abigail, Kyle's cousin, had left Kyle feeling like a wet noodle. And that was the point. It had been pleasant to the point of distraction, and he'd achieved it on the second day of vacation! Aside from Chelsea, only one person in the world could make him relax that way—Tyson Garrett. Watching the lively game of Uno at the kitchen table with Abigail, the twins, and Mark, his mother's good-natured husband, and then the trio of Chelsea, his mother, and Aunt Stacie, clustered on the floor around the coffee table, drinking wine and putting together the 1,000-piece jigsaw puzzle, he felt his head swim happily. There was no better place on the planet right now. Here was where he was meant to be, in shorts and a T-shirt, with all the people he loved most in the world. Chelsea felt his hot gaze on her and smiled coyly at him, shifting her hair to one shoulder in an absent movement that revealed her collarbone in a way that stirred him inwardly in its familiarity.

"A little help here?" Tyson asked in his quiet way, extending the bucket of recyclables and a trash bag toward Kyle. It was always Stacie's rule, even here at her sister's house, that if you didn't cook, you cleaned up. Tyson had cooked for about a thousand people last week, so placing dishes in the dishwasher and taking out the trash seemed like nothing by comparison.

"Sure," Kyle said, taking the bucket and bag, while Tyson picked up the large pot of Stacie's leftover shrimp Creole and led the way out the door. She always cooked for an army. The warm muggy air, filled with crickets and frog songs, hit them like a wet blanket as they stepped onto the porch in the dark. It was hot for the end of June on the Outer Banks. Kyle followed Tyson downstairs to the refrigerator in the garage, opening the door for him, as he went on to the trash cans in the back.

"Want a beer?" Tyson offered.

"Sure. One more…last one ever."

"Me too," said Tyson, opening two bottles and heading back up the stairs. He'd be the one driving his family home tonight. The women had been indulging themselves in their sauvignon blanc for hours. They stopped on the porch outside, listening to the laughter from the card game, and the women's raucous chatter at the table inside. The hot air felt good to Kyle, and he held his head back, gazing at the sky, milky with stars, letting the breeze whip through his hair. Tyson tipped his bottle back, and Kyle watched his friend, tanned and wiry, with the mop of dark curls and not a gray hair in sight. His green eyes crinkled as he grinned, and familiar dimples appeared at each side of his large smile. "God, it's great to see you, man!"

They tapped their bottles together in a toast. "You too," Kyle said, thinking how they could go without seeing one another for months at a time, and never miss a beat at their reunions.

The little town of Duck increased in size at each visit, but up here at his mother's house, beyond the town limits, the area seemed unchanged.

"The stars are always brighter here than anywhere else on the beach," Kyle said, and Tyson looked up, nodding his agreement. Twelve years older than Kyle, Tyson was aging well, and so was his wife, Stacie, who was nine years older than Tyson. What a strange bunch of kindred spirits they'd found themselves to be! The three of them had formed a bond when Kyle had come to stay with Stacie, the summer he was seventeen. It was the summer after his father had died, and his mother needed Kyle out of her hair to sort through the mess he'd left behind. The three of them had all been working through tough times in their lives, and that summer had been the turning point for each of them. And now, here they were with their own children, who seemed to grow and change on their own, presenting whatever challenges the three adults translated as "Payback is hell" whenever something unfortunate happened with any of them. Kyle shook his head, thinking of Tyson and Stacie's daughter, sixteen-year-old Abigail. What an enchanting girl she'd become, bearing an uncanny resemblance to his sister, Desiree.

"Surfing was great today," Tyson said, and Kyle nodded. "You brought the good waves with you. It hasn't been this good in a few weeks."

"Yeah, it was great. Just like old times. And it wouldn't be a surfing trip without breakfast at Sam and Omie's. God, I love that place. The boys will be ready to go down there with us in a couple of years....But you know, being with Abigail is just like being with my sister. It's so weird!"

"I know. That's what your mom says all the time. It must be strange."

Tyson had never known Desiree, but he had heard all of the stories. Kyle knew the resemblance had always been hard on his mother. Shelly and Stacie had mentioned it many times in the past, but as Abigail approached the age Desiree had been when she died, it made it increasingly more difficult on his mother. He knew the feeling. Naming Stu after his father had seemed to reincarnate the man with similar repercussions. They tried not to dwell on it. "Abigail is quite the surfer," he said. "She's really gotten good since last summer."

"I know," said Tyson. "I'm glad she likes surfing as much as I do." He leaned across the porch rail, pondering the stars. "It's good to have a bond like that with her. She'd be out there every day if we'd let her. If she weren't working at the Sound Side, it would be okay by me. At least she has two things to keep her out of trouble."

Kyle recalled her presence between them in Tyson's truck on the ride home from Buxton that afternoon, thinking to himself that she'd be a handful, with that long curly blond hair and smooth bronzed skin. Like most of the Davis women, she had those big baby blue eyes that would melt any guy, especially the summer boys, coming to the beach and looking for action. If she were his daughter, he'd keep her under his thumb, too. Still, it was unnerving, feeling as if he were sitting beside his sister, or even Stacie at that age, he'd thought, after seeing old pictures of her as a teenager, without so many curls.

"Has she been getting in trouble?"

"You didn't hear the latest?"

"I guess not."

"Back about a month ago, I came home from work one night and found her and her boyfriend in the outdoor shower. She was drunk and throwing up her guts."

"No way!"

"Oh, yeah! It wasn't pretty for him, let me tell you."

"What'd you do?"

"I ripped his fucking head off! Well…actually, I wanted to rip his fucking head off, but I restrained myself. Being married to Stacie has mellowed me out at least that much. But I wanted to kill the little asshole, just the same. There's only one reason you get a girl drunk and take her into the shower, you know? Needless to say, he's history."

"*Damn!* Was Abigail okay?"

"You mean, did I rip her head off too? No…but I can say I've never been that mad at her before. But yeah, she's fine. Actually, I had to protect her from Stacie. Talk about pissed off! I've never seen Stacie that angry. Abigail doesn't like the restrictions we've imposed on her, but in the long run, I think she knew he wasn't good for her. It might have been a relief in a way for her. She was in way over her head and didn't know how to get out. But I'll tell you, I never expected to be dealing with this kind of thing with her at sixteen." Tyson shook his head. "It kinda reminds me of dealing with you at that age."

"I'd gotten a lot better by the time I came here."

"Thank God. Still you were about to boil over at any moment. Stacie was fit to be tied with you that summer…all those waitresses in heat over jailbait boy! I'd sit back in the kitchen and laugh, watching her stew over what to do with you."

"Was it that entertaining?"

"Ah. You could have gone either way, you know? I guess you turned out okay."

"What about you?" Kyle asked, attempting to shift the attention from himself. "Were you the *guy in the shower* in high school?"

"Nah—however, there *was* one girl whose shower I'd like to've been invited into, but no, that wasn't me. Whatever I did, I was lucky and didn't get caught," Tyson said with a hearty laugh.

"Then she takes after Stacie. You have to expect that. She was a handful, according to my mom."

"I don't doubt that for a minute."

"*Payback is hell!*" they said in unison.

"You *did* name Abigail after a storm," Kyle pointed out.

"Good point. So who's in trouble at your house?" asked Tyson.

"Huh….Could be me," Kyle said, taking a long pull off his beer.

"Really?"

Kyle looked at the stars again over the railing, and shifted his weight from one foot to the other. "Did you ever cross a line without meaning to?"

"Probably. What'd you do?" Kyle was quiet a moment, so Tyson went on. "I'll be your priest for a day. You can confess your sins to me. What happened?"

"I don't know. I've never put words to this, and it's not something I'm proud of. But I need to tell somebody…and you're the only one who won't judge me. There's this new woman at work. She's our interior designer. We hired her in April."

Tyson let the words sink in for a moment, and then he looked over at Kyle with narrowed eyes.

"Uh-oh. What are you doing? Don't tell me you're screwing around on our girl."

"No. No, it's not like that."

"You're not sleeping with her?"

"Hell no."

"Then what? She's hitting on you? That part I'd expect."

"No."

"Are you in love with her?"

"No. I don't know what I am with her. She's young and attractive…. She has a daughter, but no husband. They need help every so often, and I've helped her out. I don't know. Ever since the first day she started, we've had this…*connection* that's more than professional. She's very direct with me, almost *brash* in the way she interacts with me," he said. *And I like it.*

"So you're attracted to her?"

"Who wouldn't be?" Kyle said, looking furtively around to see whether anyone had joined them. "You should see her. But it's more than the way she looks."

"So you *are* attracted," Tyson said, tipping his bottle back.

"I'm married, not *dead*."

Tyson hooted, "And she knows that, right?"

"Yeah, and it's not like she's asking for it. She's got her eye on another guy, one who's going to hurt her."

"Sweet, so if she hangs with you, she'll be safe. It's okay if *you're* the one who breaks her heart?"

Tyson's words cut him unexpectedly. Was he really that cocky, to assume that only *he* could provide what Elise needed? "No, I don't think that about myself," Kyle protested to Tyson's raised eyebrows. "I just think she needs protecting. But I'm supposed to be her colleague, not… whatever it is I'm doing. Hell, I don't know what I'm doing."

"Right. Okay, so I'm no priest, but hearing your confession makes me want to give you some advice. Do you want my forgiveness or my advice?"

"Both," Kyle shrugged, knowing the conversation would take this inevitable turn.

"You're not her father, or her boyfriend, so you need to drop her like a hot rock."

"I know. And I know that nothing's ever going to happen, but I just feel like I've already done something…"

Tyson rubbed the back of his neck, his green eyes glinting in the darkness. "You know, I get it. You've never been with another woman and you're curious, but look at the woman you have. Chelsea's as phenomenal as a woman gets, and you knocked the ball out of the park when you found her on the first go-round. But—you were just kids when you started. Whatever you think you're going to do with this girl is never going to be worth screwing up what you already have."

"I know that," Kyle said, twisting the bottle in his hands. "I thought I was always in control of handling myself around other women, but this...is different. I don't feel in control at all."

"Well, you know your Aunt Stacie would kill you if she ever knew you'd done something so boneheaded as hurting Chelsea. You'd wish I'd killed you first. What in the hell are you thinking?"

Kyle knew that was what Tyson would say, suddenly making him feel ashamed of bringing it up at all. "That's what I'm always asking myself. I'm fine when I'm home with Chelsea, and I can put it out of my mind... but then I get to work and there she is, and I'm gone. It's stupid. But I'd never do anything to hurt Chelsea. It's the same as it ever was with her. I'm still crazy about her. And the boys. It's just...."

"Over...is what it is. You make it *over*. You're playing with fire. And losing Chelsea is not an option for you, dude. You lose Chelsea, you lose it *all*."

Kyle looked at Tyson, an unfamiliar feeling of guilt washing over him. "You know I would never destroy my family. Believe me, my mind is on all of them right now—past, present, and future. We really needed to get away, just the four of us. This other distraction has to be over."

"What's her name?"

"Elise. Her name is Elise."

"So, I guess the important question is, does Chelsea know about this whole situation?"

"I think she does," said Kyle, causing Tyson to let out a long sigh. "We've danced around it since the first time they met, but we haven't talked about it directly. But Chelsea and I came to an understanding on our own terms the other night," he said, remembering the heat again from their tryst on the couch in the middle of the night. "I'd say we're good. She knows there's nothing to worry about. I've been trying to make that clear." With their current workload, he'd immersed himself at the office in the days before they'd left for vacation, giving Elise plenty of space, which had seemed to go unnoticed by her. The family had gotten his full attention at home every night. He had even caved on the boys' punishment and taken them fishing in the river Thursday evening when Chelsea was in rehearsal for her dance production.

"And as far as forgiveness goes...what have you done, really? Lusted after another woman in your heart?" Tyson snickered. "But still, I suppose it makes it hard when you have to work with Elise every day." Tyson turned his back to the railing and crossed his arms over his chest. "When I first went to work for Stacie, it was all I could do to keep my hands to myself, you know? And look where we ended up."

You married my aunt, Kyle thought. "It's not the same thing," he said, hoping he was right.

"Well, you're smart, so *be* smart. You know what you have to do." Tyson looked at him for a moment, and then picked at the label on his beer bottle. "Stacie said you guys're trying to get pregnant again."

"Great. That was supposed to be a secret."

Tyson shrugged. "Chelsea told Stacie and she told me. I guess she had to get hers out too."

"Nice. So does my mother know too?"

"No. It doesn't go that far." Tyson smiled. "I'm really good at keeping secrets. You tell her yourself."

"Thanks. We agreed not to tell anyone because if it doesn't happen, nobody will be disappointed."

"Except the two of you. I get it. You're crazy, but I get it." Tyson sighed and looked out over the rooftops, silvery etchings in the starlight. "Three kids...at your age...boy-oh-boy!"

They chuckled together. He'd been thirty-one and Stacie had been forty when Abigail came along. The sound of the glass door sliding open put an end to their conversation. Stacie approached, wrapping her arms around Tyson as Chelsea followed, carrying her wine glass, still half-full.

"What have you boys been cooking up out here?" Stacie asked in her sultry voice, planting a kiss on Tyson's throat.

"Nothing as wicked as you'd like to think, I'm sure," said Tyson, washing down the rest of his beer.

"How disappointing!" she laughed. "I think it's time to go home, baby. Some of us have to be at work in the morning. It's getting late and Chelsea wants Kyle all to herself, if she can keep her eyes open, that is!" she said, winking at Chelsea.

"Yep. Tomorrow morning will come bright and early for you and Abigail," Tyson reminded her.

Kyle pulled Chelsea close, letting his hand settle on the back of her neck, rubbing it the way she liked, and she closed her eyes, melting against him. "You feel so good," he murmured into her hair. Her skin felt warm, sun-kissed from her day at the beach with the boys and his family. Neither one of them would be long for this world tonight, but he'd be hers if she wanted him, he thought, stroking her hair away from her face so he could kiss her. He would make sure she knew it.

Tyson gave Kyle a meaningful look and clasped his hand in a high-five over Chelsea's shoulder.

"It's been real," he said, as he followed Stacie's lead to leave.

"You bet. We'll see you for dinner at the restaurant tomorrow night. Is shrimp and grits still on the menu?"

"Always! See you, sweetheart. Sleep tight," Tyson said, giving Chelsea a hug and a kiss on her cheek.

"'Night, guys," Chelsea said, stifling a yawn, and giving Stacie a hug.

"Goodnight, Chelsea, my darling. Sweet dreams," she said with another wink at her, leading Kyle to think a conspiracy was at hand.

"And goodnight, honey!" said Stacie, squeezing Kyle's face in her hand. "You look good with some sun! Those little boys of yours are just precious, by the way. They charmed Abigail into forgetting to bug me about going out with her friends tonight. God love them!"

More movement was heard in the house as the kids scampered toward the door at Abigail's heels, where she slipped her feet into battered flip-flops and picked up her bag. Kyle's boys certainly seemed to be enamored with their older cousin.

"Who won the card game?" Kyle asked.

"Stu!" said Mark, ruffling Stu's hair with one hand and hugging Ty around the shoulders with the other, always careful to give equal time to each of the twins. Mark and Shelly congregated at the door as well, slapping backs and saying goodnights as hugs and kisses were exchanged. The warmth of it all was the same as with Chelsea's parents, at any family gathering they had. His mother hugged him a long time, patting him on the back, the seal of family acceptance for Kyle.

"I'm not leaving," he said to her, unprepared for the catch in his voice at the words.

"I know. I just wanted to hug my son, that's all. You've made a lovely family, and I'm so glad you all are here," Shelly said, rubbing his shoulder, making him wonder whether someone had spilled the beans about the baby they wanted to make. No matter what was happening, they were his family, he thought, knowing one thing could ruin it all. But for him, it would have to be a very long fall, and one he wasn't planning to take.

"Okay, dudes, time for bed," Kyle said to Stu and Ty, his arm still around Chelsea. "Give Abigail one more hug. They have to go home now."

"I'm sorry, Abigail; you may have to pry Stu of you!" said Chelsea, giving Ty a wink. He was making a noble effort to restrain himself, Kyle thought.

"Will you come Boogie-boarding with us after work tomorrow?" Stu asked her.

"Sure! I'll meet you both at our beach at two," Abigail said. "We can make another drip castle if you want to."

"Cool," said Stu, sleepiness suddenly taking over his persona. This was the way it was with him, Kyle thought. Full steam ahead all day long, and then he would crash and burn for the night. There would be no waking up in the middle of the night for him anymore.

Chelsea's eyes sparkled at him. He felt her hands under his shirt, cool on his skin, and he tightened his arms around her. As soon as the others were out the door, the rest of them yawned, straightened up, locked doors, turned off lights, and said their goodnights before heading to their respective bedrooms.

Roll, crash, fizz…silence…roll, crash, fizz. Chelsea listened to the ocean, drowsing in her beach chair, watching the boys cast lines into the surf with Kyle at the tide. An overcast sky hung heavily, trapping the heat that wrapped her like a blanket. A soft breeze stirred her hair, tickling her cheek. It had been forever since she'd been this relaxed. The book she'd attempted to read had fallen closed across her chest. She remembered the blurring of the words on the creamy page as she had slipped delightfully away…roll, crash, fizz…silence. A squeal opened her eyes, revealing Stu jumping up and down as Ty pulled a long wriggling fish out of the surf. She heard Kyle's proud laugh and the slap of the high-five he gave Ty before clasping the fish in a towel to remove the hook from its mouth. He held it up for her to see. "A sand shark!" he shouted with a grin, and held it down for the boys to look at again. Dutifully, she sat up, collecting herself, and rose to inspect their catch. Sauntering slowly through the warm sand toward her men, she pondered how nice it would be to have a little girl's hand to hold, a little girl's hair to braid, a little girl for Kyle to adore and teach to fish and surf one day.

"Way to go, Ty!" she exclaimed, accepting his damp hug as he jumped up and down. Boys were forever jumping up and down, it seemed.

"Yeah! Look at this! This will make good bait," said Kyle. He tossed it into the five-gallon bucket where the boys watched it swim frantically around in the water.

"Whoa! Look at it!" said Ty, bending over the bucket.

Their combined exuberance made her grin. It was good to see Kyle happy like this. He'd been preoccupied lately with all the work the business was bringing in. Without the work, they wouldn't have the security they enjoyed. Still, nothing could satisfy him more than a day like this with the twins.

"Look, Mom! You missed my flounder!" Stu said, pointing into the white bucket, filled with sea water and fish.

"Yeah, and my bluefish. If we catch a couple more flounder on this shark belly, we'll have enough for dinner tomorrow night. Did you enjoy your siesta?" Kyle asked, giving her a quick kiss and grinning at her from ear-to-ear, blue eyes flashing in his tanned face. She had the feeling his smile had nothing to do with the fish, and more to do with the night before. There had been little sleep for either of them, the memory sending a current deep inside her. Chelsea glanced over her sunglasses at the twins' shoulders, which had bloomed with color since she'd napped. Their hair had dried into points sticking out every which way, making them look like elves as they hopped around in the water.

"Yes, I did," she said, stretching. "Good job, guys! All three of you need spraying down again with sunscreen. You might as well let it soak in before Abigail gets here and you start swimming again. I'll bring it down here," she said, turning and walking away, sure that none of them would follow her—not with the fish biting the way they were. She giggled, hearing Kyle's whistle as she walked, ignoring him. Boogie Boards, a kite, and their cooler filled with bottles of water, juice boxes, and sandwiches had kept them entertained for hours, and the canopy tent Stacie and Tyson kept in the garage had become their home for the day. The boys had played at being lost on a deserted island, which was a bit hard to imagine with the dozens of other people around. Even though the beach was more crowded now than she remembered the first time Kyle had brought her here, it sure was nice having relatives with beach houses, Chelsea thought contentedly. Pleasantly, the clouds began to break apart, allowing warm bits of sunshine to brighten the water to the deep greenish blue she associated with the smell of salt and wind, and Kyle.

Her step quickened, more awake now with her task at hand, returning to the water with the can of sunscreen, spraying the boys' shoulders and arms, then rubbing some of the lotion from her hand onto their faces. "Here, let me get your chest, Stu," she said. Entranced by his father's dissection of the shark on the rough wood board, he stood obediently and let her have her way. Then she started on Kyle.

"Look! There's Abigail!" Stu shouted, and the two boys were off, after the tall slim girl striding toward them in cut-off jean shorts, flip-flops in one hand, and a Boogie Board in the other. Stacie followed, waving, in a skirt and tank top, her morning restaurant wear, also carrying a pair of flip-flops.

"Abigail! I caught a shark!" Ty cried out, running to her and taking her hand. "Come see! It's so awesome! Dad's cutting it up for bait!"

"Ew! Disgusting!" she said, pushing her sunglasses on top of her head, laughing and winking at Chelsea.

"Who caught a shark?" Stacie asked, getting in the middle of the scene.

"I did!" Ty said proudly, causing his aunt to ruffle his hair.

"That's so cool! Cutting it into bait, Kyle?"

"Yep!" Kyle rose with a strip of the shark's belly. "Who's ready?"

"I want to try!" Stu said, picking his rod out of the tube stuck fast in the sand.

Everyone watched Kyle show Stu how to thread the hook through the tough, silvery skin of the shark's belly. To test it, he pulled on it and said, "That baby's not going anywhere. Okay, cast it on out there. Ty, you ready?"

"Yeah, Dad."

"Good, let's see what you can haul in this time. Get us another flounder."

"I wanna fish, too!" said Abigail, dropping her Boogie Board on the sand, instantly a kid again. Kyle handed her his rod, giving her a piece of the shark bait. Expertly, she took it and slipped it easily onto the hook and walked several paces away before casting her line into the surf.

"I have one more rod, ladies? Either of you like to give it a shot?"

Stacie wrinkled her nose. "Nah! You've got this under control. I feel like stretching my legs. Do you mind if I take your wife on a walk?"

"No, you go right ahead. Enjoy yourselves. Use your sunscreen," he said, rubbing his hand over his own chest and pointing at Chelsea's. He grinned at her again.

The women walked back to the chairs and rubbed down their arms and faces with sunscreen, and Chelsea applied it to her chest as well, giggling to herself. "Wouldn't you rather sit down? You've been at work all day."

"If I sit down, I'll get sleepy. It's best to keep moving," Stacie laughed, wrapping her blond hair into a knot and twisting a hair tie around it.

"What time do you have to be back?"

"Whenever I want. That's the nice thing about being the boss. I'm on my own time. Everyone else is running the place. I just pop in when I feel like it. But realistically, since I have to drive Abigail over, about five o'clock. So who am I kidding?"

They started strolling, taking a last look at the kids fishing with Kyle, finding the hard wet sand and falling in step. Sandpipers appeared, doing their straight-legged dance together in and out of the tide. Chelsea never got tired of watching them, or feeling the breeze, or listening to the ocean's soothing sounds. Clouds moved over the sun, causing a brief chill before they disappeared again, warming her cheeks and shoulders.

"Is this heaven or what?" Chelsea sighed, stretching her arms out to her sides and hugging herself.

"I'd say your husband thinks *you're* heaven in that bathing suit!" Stacie said, pulling her sunglasses down off the bridge of her nose so she could give Chelsea a look.

"Ha!"

"Well…how was last night?"

Chelsea smiled coyly, unsure how to answer. "Well, Kyle was pretty mad at me for sharing our little secret."

"Oh! It won't be a secret for long if you keep doing what you're *obviously* doing!"

"Yes, but he doesn't want his mother or Mark to know yet."

"Shelly's not going to know. I guess he got over it?"

"Yeah, in about three minutes."

"He can't stay mad at you. I'm sure the make-up sex was great."

Chelsea smiled again. Sex with Kyle was nothing short of intoxicating lately. And exhausting! "Being down here is so different. It's so relaxing. We needed this time for ourselves. When he took me to Martha's

Vineyard, it was like that there, too. That was when we decided we wanted another child."

"I can't remember what that's like anymore. What makes you want another baby now?" Stacie asked.

Chelsea's breath caught unexpectedly. *Because I'm trying to hold on to my husband,* she thought to herself, a thought so new it scared her. Immediately, her thoughts returned to home, and the office at Mountaineer Builders. She imagined Elise, sitting there in her office, probably working at her computer, answering the phone, thinking about Kyle. The thought made her stomach tense. There were other reasons too, that were much more valid. *Because we want a little girl. Because I'd like to stay home with my family and stop dancing…stop teaching…just be a mom.*

"There are so many reasons," she said, avoiding the topic.

"Do you want to start over again, really?"

"I asked Kyle the same thing, and he really does."

"But do you?"

"Yes. I do. I'd like to take some time off and just be our family. We might be able to swing it. Except he's talking about building another house, so I don't know if we could afford it if I stayed home."

"You'd leave that precious little cabin? Kyle loves the river as much as he loves the ocean."

"I know. We'd keep it and rent it out, of course. That way he could still go down there and fish whenever he wanted. He might just be dreaming. He's always got to be designing something. In the winter when there wasn't much work, he started working on the house. I haven't even seen it yet. I don't know that I want to, yet, at least. I don't want to be disappointed if it doesn't work out."

"How's his work now? Summer's usually better for him, right?"

Chelsea was quiet. They walked in silence for a while, the splash of their steps brushing the water and making a rhythm in her mind, helping her think. "It's good. They've been getting commissions. I never expected this much in this economy. He and Frank are some of the only builders in town that are still in business. There's still very little building going on in our area. But the renovations have kept them alive." Chelsea sighed, looking across the ocean as they walked.

"And?" Stacie probed.

Should she say it? She hadn't mentioned her innermost thoughts, even to Kyle, in so many words.

"What's on your mind, honey?"

Chelsea cleared her throat. "Oh…there's a new woman working with them. She took Faith's place, and she's beautiful. I think Kyle is struggling with it."

"Oh," Stacie said, surprised. "Why? Do you think they're involved?"

"I don't think so, but I'm sure he's tempted."

Stacie was quiet this time. "You've met her?"

"Yes, and she has him pretty spellbound from what I can see. I've stepped up my game, as Abby has advised me to," Chelsea laughed.

"Ha! From the way Kyle looks at you, I'd say you don't need to step up a *damn* thing! Nothing's changed with you two from what I can tell."

"Well, I think I might be in for the fight of my life."

Stacie was quiet a moment. "Not everyone cheats, Chelsea."

"I know. I don't think he would hurt me, not intentionally at least, and he really seems to want this baby, but it's just so…*disconcerting*. They will probably spend the next thirty years working together. You know how close he is with Frank. Frank is like a brother to him, and Faith was like a member of the family too. I love them. But I can't imagine sharing him like that with Elise. She's either going to become Kyle's best friend or my worst nightmare."

"Kyle wouldn't hurt you," Stacie said assuredly.

"I want to believe that. Have you ever wondered about Tyson? Of course not. What am I saying? Tyson is a rock."

"Yes, he is. And no, I've never worried that he would cheat on me," Stacie said quietly, folding her arms in the new chill as the sun went behind a cloud. "Cheating can cause a lot of pain, Chelsea, and I know Kyle would never inflict that on you. If he's struggling, that's why."

"Then it's going to be a long thirty years!" Chelsea said miserably.

Stacie laughed. "He'll get bored thinking about her and it will all go away; trust me."

"How do you know?"

"Because you can trust Kyle. And you'll have so much more in your life than she'll ever be able to give him."

"But what if he just kept her around on the side for years and years? Not leaving us, but not leaving her, either? People do that, you know? I wish I could be sure. I want to trust him, but then I see him around her, and it makes me want to vomit. How can you think she won't pull him away from me?"

"Because I know my nephew…and because I had an affair, and I know it will mean nothing," she said, taking off her sunglasses and meeting Chelsea's wide-eyed gaze. They stopped walking.

"You? When? When you were married to Rick?"

"No. And you probably can't understand why I would have done something like that to Ty, especially after I'd had it happen to me. I still can't believe I did it. I knew better. God, I knew better!" she said bitterly.

"How?" Chelsea asked, stunned. "How long did it last?"

"It only happened once. People say it just happens, and that's the way it was for me. Abigail went to a sailing camp one summer. Ty said he could have taught her to sail himself, but it was a fun thing for her to do. The guy that taught it was about my age, and he was living here on his sailboat, kind of a drifter. He was so kind and patient with Abigail and the other kids...and so smart and funny. One night, he took us all out on his boat. We all liked him. He was one of those people you meet whom you think you've known all your life. He came into the restaurant a lot, and I'd started to run into him all over, like at the grocery store and whatnot." She stroked her throat, recalling it all. "He'd been working on refinishing some of the teak on his sloop, and I went with him one afternoon to see the finished product. We had a couple of beers together and talked, and then...it just happened. Once. I never saw him after that. The camps were over, and he went on to the next place. I guess he came back and did the camps again, but I never saw him. I should never have set foot on that boat that day. I could have kept all of it from happening, but I didn't."

Chelsea listened in awe, letting Stacie's story sink in, memories of Kyle watching Elise sip that *Moonlight* at the winery, wrenching her stomach. After a moment, she asked, "Did Tyson find out?"

"Yes. I told him. He'd had no idea it had happened. But I couldn't keep it from him. The guilt ate me up. You can't imagine how hurt he was, and how betrayed he felt."

"Did you separate? I never had any idea this was going on."

"No. He forgave me. As hurt as he was, he forgave me. I was so ashamed. But it was a long time before we were the same again."

Chelsea sighed, pushing her hands across her forehead. "This is so confusing."

"I know; it probably doesn't reassure you much, does it? But the reason I told you is that's something that I'd do. I did it. But Kyle won't do that. Kyle has principles that I don't have. Tyson has principles that I don't have. And so do you, Chelsea. I have them now, but I didn't have them then. You keep loving him, Chelsea, even if he falls. Even if he falls, it doesn't mean he doesn't love you. I never stopped loving Ty. I *hate* what I did to him. I thank God every day that he didn't throw me out like I did Rick. But Rick and I didn't love each other. Ty loves me more than I'll ever deserve."

"But I still can't understand why you did it. I know you've always loved Tyson and he loves you too. You were my ideal of the ultimate marriage," she said, her voice breaking at the end.

Stacie floundered, seemingly at a loss for words, walking further into the tide, tucking in strands of her hair that had escaped in the breeze, staring at the water sluicing around her legs. "He needed me…" she said, so softly Chelsea had to strain to hear. "He needed someone; it could have been anybody, but I guess I was the one who'd listen to him. His wife was a lawyer and she left him when he'd lost his job. She said he'd never grow up when he started doing the sailing camps, but what else could he do? He was in his early fifties and no one would hire him. He did the camps because sailing was what he loved and he missed his children. He was lonely, Chelsea, and he needed someone to just…understand, and hold him. It wasn't love, or even sex. It was just a lifeline, in a way."

"But…you gave in to him," Chelsea said softly, making Stacie press her lips together and look away, blinking back tears. "And Elise needs Kyle. This is exactly the same thing! How is it going to be different for us?" Chelsea's question was frantic. Suddenly, the scenario was becoming all too real in her mind. "Kyle always has this…*intimacy* with the people he loves, not just anybody, but he always finds a common bond with the people who've suffered the way he has. He's found it with Elise. She got pregnant in college and now she has a seven year-old daughter who has special needs, and she's in Boone, all by herself, and struggling. She's just the kind of person he's drawn to. And she's gorgeous, and exactly his type. I don't think she flirts with him; she doesn't have to! He's already sunk."

"Chelsea," Stacie began, her hand going to Chelsea's arm. "Honey… he's not going to hurt you. Kyle is the most moral person I know. He loves you so much, and the boys…and you're going to have another baby. He's not going anywhere."

"Does Kyle know what happened with you?"

"No. No one knows, but you, me, and Tyson. He and I'd prefer to keep it that way."

"Of course," Chelsea agreed, reeling from Stacie's story, her heart aching for Tyson. The world was falling apart, she thought, pressing her fingers to her eyes, as tears flooded her face.

"Listen, I know this has all been hard to take in. I didn't tell you to make you worry. The last thing I wanted to do was upset you. Whatever happens, you guys will get through it. You're as solid as a marriage gets. But it's never perfect."

"No," Chelsea said, a sob soaking her voice, as she swiped tears off her cheeks. "It's never perfect."

"That's what makes it love."

Stacie watched her for a moment and gathered her in her arms. A couple stared at them, giving them plenty of room as they walked by from the opposite direction.

"You'll be all right; I know it. There are so many ways to feel about people, but love always wins in the end. Remember that, okay? And remember, you're married to my nephew, and he's one of the best people I know. You will both be all right."

Chapter 10

A LINE IN THE SAND

When they returned from their walk, it was easy to spot their group on the beach. Kyle and Abigail were animated, taking another fish off her hook, while the twins whooped and hollered with delight at her catch. Kyle's elation was contagious when he beckoned to Chelsea to look in the bucket. She watched him rinse fish slime off his hands in the tide, wiping them on his swim trunks.

"Four flounder and a blue!" he said proudly, hands on his hips, flicking his hair out of his eyes. "Here's tomorrow's dinner. Will you make some of your blue cheese coleslaw and cornbread?"

"Sure," she promised, glad to have something else to think about, feeling Ty's wet arms go around her waist and smiling at him, hugging him back. Stacie bent over the bucket as well, eyeing the catch, probably sharing her thoughts. They would have dinner at the Sound Side tonight. It would be slow on Monday night, giving Tyson the opportunity to visit with them in the dining room when he could escape the kitchen. Chelsea wondered whether Stacie and he would discuss the topic of her affair and Kyle's present dilemma. It was inevitable that they'd all know soon enough, making her regret ever saying a word about her situation. Hoping to find relief in sharing her problems had only reopened old wounds for Stacie, and probably for Tyson, wounds she wished she didn't know about. Stacie had risked her own trust with Chelsea by telling her story. Chelsea was still reeling from hearing it, amazed that Stacie had caved to another man's needs, not to mention those of her own. But in some small way, she felt a kinship with Stacie, an adult bond they'd never had before, and certainly a renewed faith in her husband.

Chelsea's arms circled Kyle's waist from behind, and she planted a kiss on his shoulder blade, resting her cheek there. His skin was hot from the sun that was now out in full force, and it tasted of sunscreen and salt. He leaned back to kiss her forehead in response, unaware of her previous distress. *That's what makes it love,* resonated in her heart as she held him, big and solid and strong in her arms.

"Let's go Boogie-boarding!" Stu exclaimed, remembering why Abigail had come in the first place. It took many activities to keep him occupied on any given day, so Abigail's energetic presence was welcomed by all of them.

"How much time do I have, Mom?" Abigail asked Stacie.

"Come in and shower in about an hour, okay?" Stacie told her. Abigail worked as a hostess at night after serving during the breakfast shift. It would certainly wear anyone out, thought Chelsea, knowing that Abigail was one, like Stu, who needed to be kept busy.

"I may go on up. I have some bills to pay before I take my own shower and get ready for tonight," Stacie said to Chelsea, sharing a look of understanding. She shifted a pointed stare to Kyle, regarding him in a new sober light. "Kyle, I have another cooler under the house if you want to ice those fish down for the ride back to Shelly's."

"Okay, thanks! I'll return it," he said, oblivious to her gaze.

The smile returned to her voice when she addressed the children. "Y'all have fun! Don't get sunburned!" she said, waving. "See you tonight, Chelsea," she said, giving Chelsea a hug before she sashayed across the beach to the wooden stairs that led up the boardwalk to her house.

Chelsea dreaded seeing Tyson at the Sound Side that evening. The group from the beach was subdued but happy from their day in the sun. It couldn't have been a better day for Kyle and the boys. Abigail moved about seating guests as if she were on autopilot, the pink from the sun enhancing her cheeks attractively. Chelsea watched Stacie, so glamorous in a deep turquoise dress that accentuated her big blue eyes, her blond hair curled around her shoulders, commandeering the dining room with ease, greeting people with her throaty laugh, disappearing from time to time into the kitchen and then the bar. She chatted amiably with their group at the table, as if nothing were wrong. But then, nothing *was* wrong. She was the mother of a beautiful young lady who was smitten with Chelsea's children, and she was married to Tyson, who loved her unconditionally. What woman wouldn't feel confident and carefree, having all that? One indiscretion could hardly be called an affair. It was certainly forgivable, Chelsea decided. The thought tugged at her, making her wonder whether she could forgive something like that herself. *It depends*, she thought, glancing at Kyle, who was finishing his shrimp and grits beside her at the table. But as far as Tyson and Stacie were concerned, their past was their past, and they were stronger for it.

Finally, Tyson emerged from his kitchen, wiping his hands on his apron, colliding with Chelsea full on, as she returned from the restroom, back to their table. Respectfully, they jolted apart, "Excuse me!" they said at the same time and then recognized each other.

"Oh, hey, Chels, there you are! I was hoping to see you…alone for a minute," Tyson said, taking her hand urgently, a look passing between them. *He knew about the conversation.* She drew in a deep breath, wanting to withdraw her hand, but he held it, his green eyes piercing hers to keep her attention.

"Hi," she said weakly, disappointed that she had nothing else to offer him. Embarrassment reduced her to inadequacy, as she knew much more than she wanted. She had been in this position before and had never liked keeping secrets. The thoughts of it all made her face burn.

"Hi," he said, a gentle smile building, so like him, she thought, saddened again by Stacie's story. His eyes softened, understanding her unease, and he released her hand, touching her face to cool the fire there. "It's fine, Chelsea. Stacie told me," he murmured. "Don't worry, okay? You're going to be fine," he said, walking her back to the table and giving her a hug as the others began to notice their encounter. As brief a moment as it was, it seemed sufficient for them both. "How were your scallops?"

"Oh, delicious, as usual, thank you!" she gushed, heat rushing again to her face, thankful for this opportunity to move on. He winked, avoiding any eye contact with Kyle, and hugged her again, kissing her cheek where the half-moon scar burned now. Stacie appeared with a bottle of chardonnay for the adults at the table, allowing Chelsea to take her place next to Kyle, pretending to notice nothing, and sat down beside her, filling her glass. Tyson moved on to Mark and Shelly, inquiring about their dinners.

"I hope you saved room for my key lime pie," Stacie grinned at them both.

"Mm-hmm!" Kyle nodded. "Man, it's like going to heaven every time we come here!"

"I know! I've taught you how to eat, and now you can't get enough of the good stuff," she laughed, patting his hand. "Ah! You guys are such a sight for sore eyes! I'm so, so happy you all are here. It makes my summer when you all come. Abigail can't stop talking about Stu and Ty. Would you consider renting them out to us for the rest of the summer?"

"Deal!" Kyle laughed without hesitation, giving her his widest grin. She returned his look, seemingly enamored of him, as she had always been. It made Chelsea want to cry.

"And you two, starting a new chapter in your lives!" she said, making Kyle and Chelsea both suck in a breath through frozen smiles, glancing at Shelly, who was engaged in a lively conversation with Stu and Mark about the fishing earlier. Stacie shook her head ever so slightly. "No worries!" she exclaimed, resting her chin on her hand, grinning at them again. Chelsea felt Kyle's hand stroke her back, warm and possessive, inviting, even, and she looked at him in time to see the smoldering look she needed. Stacie noticed too, and seemed delighted with the undercurrent. "*Wow!* That's what I like to see!" She gave them a poignant look and then sent Kyle a serious gaze, locking eyes with him momentarily, making Chelsea wonder whether they'd talked, but Kyle looked too contented to have had a confrontation with his aunt. "You two enjoy your evening, if I don't get a chance to tell you goodnight. Excuse me, okay?" Stacie said, standing to leave and greet some new customers who had just arrived and were speaking with Tyson.

Kyle leaned forward to whisper in Chelsea's ear. "This vacation keeps getting more and more promising," he said, moving her hair, caressing the back of her neck with a warm kiss. The feel of his breath on her neck and the conviction in his voice made her insides uncoil almost painfully in a warm pool. Her roller coaster of emotions seemed to be sliding to a stop. Maybe they were going to be fine, too. *Just fine.*

On Monday morning, laughter floated from the conference room at Mountaineer Builders. Frank and Elise were enjoying a cup of coffee together, sitting in front of their computers, ready for their Monday morning meeting and waiting on the late-comer. A plate of cinnamon pinwheels was on the table.

"Well, hey, sleepyhead! You decided to show up at last!" Frank jabbed good-naturedly at Kyle, who sauntered to the table, depositing his computer case on the table. He was never late.

"Good morning! I guess I'm still on beach time. Sorry to have kept you waiting."

Elise looked at him with amusement in her river eyes and grinned openly. This was new. Michael must still be in her picture, with that smile given so freely. She was even laughing.

"You look like the picture of R-and-R! And you're rocking that tan. Your hair is *ridiculous!*"

Kyle's eyebrows shot up with her sudden candor. "I suppose I need a haircut," he said defensively.

"I meant that as a compliment. Blond streaks become you," she said, smiling coyly, sipping her coffee.

He was unprepared for her attention and looked to Frank for a rescue.

"Get the haircut. We don't need our female clients fawning all over you."

"Okay….So what all did I miss?"

"Get some coffee and you'll see one thing," said Frank, as Kyle sauntered into the little kitchen, where he saw the results of Elise's redecoration project—a set of valances hung by black grommets and made from a fabric that looked like autumn trees in a forest, and a card table pushed to the wall with three chairs at each side, covered with a cloth of the same tree fabric. The effect warmed him, reminding him of their mountains.

"Huh! Nice! Very homey, but manly...and womanly, too," said Kyle, going to pour a cup of coffee, feeling his face burn inexplicably. The room invited cozy lunches meant for three, but Frank was seldom around for lunch. He joined them in the conference room, reaching for a napkin and a pinwheel. "Who went to Stick Boys?" he asked, referring to Frank's favorite bakery just a few blocks away.

"I did," said Elise, grinning at him again. He noticed she was tanned as well. "So, what do you think? Is it too crowded in there with the new seating?"

Not that he would be joining her for any intimate lunches, he thought, so he said, "No. It's great! I like it," making her press her lips together in satisfaction. She would be dealing with the new Kyle, the uninterested, unobsessed Kyle. But who was this new Elise?

He averted his eyes, busying himself with opening up his programs and readying himself for the meeting. The coffee was welcome to the fuzz inside his head, and he realized how relaxed he'd been all week, swimming in his wife's sensuous affections, making it all the more difficult to drag himself away from her this morning. She was killing him!

"So, you had fun?" she asked.

"Oh, yeah! It was great to get away with Chelsea and the boys," he said, purposefully including her name.

"How was the offshore fishing trip?" asked Frank.

"Great! I've never been fishing offshore when the water was that smooth. It was like glass going out. Mark's boat is very well-equipped, and we reeled in about a hundred pounds of tuna. You should come with us next time."

"Awesome! Are you planning on sharing any of that fish?" Frank asked.

"Of course! I brought back tons. I'll bring you some tomorrow."

"And you stayed at your mother's house?" Elise asked.

"Yes. Most of the time, she and Mark were all at work, so we had the house to ourselves during the day. We spent the time going back and forth from her house and my aunt's. Stacie and her family live just a short walk from the beach, so Chelsea and the boys went every day, when we weren't seeing lighthouses and the aquarium. I went with them too when I wasn't surfing or fishing. The boys are learning to surf too, so it was a great time….Mom says hi," he said to Frank. To Elise, this greeting would sound mundane, but Frank had been the one to help Shelly sort through his father's ruined business, liquidating what they had, and setting things right with the IRS. It had been a devastating period for his mother, and Frank had been kind, helping her to stay sane through it all. Whatever Kyle could do to help Frank prosper would never be enough to repay him for that.

Frank smiled and nodded, understanding. "I'm glad she's happy down there. She deserves it."

Kyle nodded as well, wanting to move on. "Where have you been, Elise? You're tan too," Kyle asked, licking cinnamon sugar off his fingers from the pinwheel.

"I took Lydia home for the weekend. We went out on my father's sailboat on Lake Norman. Lydia loves to sail, and it was a beautiful weekend."

"Yeah. You're not going home for the Fourth?"

"No. We're staying here and going to the fireworks with Michael in Banner Elk," she said, and he thought he saw the pink of her cheeks deepen. Then he realized he was staring.

"Oh. Good." He remembered that discussing Michael was off-limits for him, unless she brought it up, apparently.

"You and the family should come," Frank said, clicking the mouse until he got to the screen he wanted. "Faith and I are meeting our family at the park there around seven. There'll be music and games before the fireworks. Your little boys would have a good time. Bring a picnic and join us. Get Tom and Liz to come too."

Great. He felt his stomach tighten, trying to make it stop. He could go and check on Elise and make sure Michael was in line. He assumed

Michael had met Lydia; he wondered how it was going with her, and whether she was becoming attached to Michael. It was a hard picture to create in his mind. But then again, none of it was his business.

"Faith has been dying to see you and Chelsea," Frank added.

"Sounds like fun," he said, not committing. "I'll run it by her."

"So, getting down to business," Elise went on, "Frank and I've been over to the Wilcox house, and the renovation is coming along nicely."

"I'll be anxious to see it," Kyle said. "Maybe I'll stop by today. I'm walking Tom around the Hayes property at ten this morning. We'll go by Marcus' house too, *checking for snakes!* I'll be with him for lunch," he threw out casually.

"I'm having lunch with Jackie Wilcox today," Elise said, matching his nonchalance, eyeing him about the snake comment.

"Come by the Blair house later if you get a chance. The roofers are finished, but they have a question or two for you on those solar panels," said Frank.

"No problem," Kyle said, his head back in the game. "Did they hang the windows?"

"Yep. They look great, too. The roof looks really good."

"I've missed a lot."

Elise was giving him a wry smile. "Yes, you have. Emily Hayes was here with her mother, asking about you last week."

Kyle swallowed hard on the last bite of his second pinwheel. He took a sip of his coffee to process her assault on him. "She was in town?"

"Yes, and Sara Lynn was *so* sad we hadn't mentioned you'd be out of town!" she said, watching his face carefully, placing her chin in her hand. Bruce and Sara Lynn weren't due in for their presentation until next week.

"They're worried about the road leading up the hill past their lot," said Frank, oblivious to Elise's tone.

"Oh, yeah, where it's washing away? I think something went wrong when it was originally designed. I was planning to ask Tom about it this morning when we ride up there. If it doesn't get fixed, it will ruin their part of the road, and on down the hill as well," Kyle said, seemingly oblivious to Elise's barb. He was making an effort to conduct himself professionally. Why couldn't she? Then again, she was young…and brash, he thought. He hoped he wouldn't have to address her behavior. For now, it seemed best to ignore her. She seemed oddly fixated on him this morning.

Sweat trickled down the back of Chelsea's red, white, and blue shirt in the July heat as she tossed the last of the paper plates and cups into the trash bin. She shaded her hand from the setting sun, trying to spot Ty and Stu playing the bean bag toss game, Corn Hole, with Frank and his grandchildren in the park. The brightly colored blouse felt too hot and garish today. It had taken her three tries to find a pair of shorts that fit comfortably. A sundress would have been more comfortable, she thought, discreetly tugging at her shorts. Her knickers were definitely in a wad today! Only one thing could contribute to her bloated feeling and irritability, and she sighed, knowing it meant she still wasn't pregnant. Returning to her chair beside Kyle, she listened to her mother and Faith talking about her mother's ceramic angel enterprise as her mother packed her portion of their picnic back in the cooler, bringing out a large container of watermelon for the children. They'd be ready for a thirst-quenching treat after playing in this heat. The fireworks would start soon, as the sky was fading to dusk. Dark circles under her mother's eyes made Chelsea's heart sink, knowing her mom had been awake again as she was most nights, worrying about her own mother. Their trip to South Carolina had not gone well. Grandmother had resisted the idea of moving into the retirement center's memory care unit. At least Kyle and her father had enjoyed a fly fishing outing with the boys earlier. She worried about her father, too. Most men his age were planning their retirements, but he was still heavily involved with his landscaping business, his interest in Jay's winery, and whatever architectural work he did with Kyle and Frank. At the moment, her father and Kyle were discussing some of this business, and she overheard snippets of conversation about one of the roads they were concerned with, her father explaining that the culvert system had been poorly installed and needed rerouting before the whole road washed away. A discussion of the property owners' association followed, with Kyle promising to look into whom they should contact to put matters right. It was nice watching her two favorite men interacting the way they did, her dad stroking his mustache thoughtfully, as he listened to Kyle's take on the situation; the architects were at work, even on a holiday.

From the corner of her eye, she noticed a small group approaching, her eyes drawn to the pretty little girl with wavy brown hair and an endearing heart-shaped face. She had an odd gait as she walked, holding the woman's hand. Chelsea stifled a gasp as she realized the woman was Elise Masters with her daughter, and Michael Gilmer lagging behind, eyes roving over the crowd. The three of them were pretty together, but incongruent with Michael's detachment, obvious on first glance. *Sad.* Of course Elise would be here. Kyle hadn't mentioned it, but she should have expected her to be a part of this company outing. Chelsea braced herself for an awkward moment with Michael and her father. They had to be cordial with each other, or at least civil, with their involvement in Jay's winery, but neither her father nor Kyle had ever liked Michael personally. Kyle cleared his throat and stood, being the first to greet them. He waved them over with a less than enthusiastic look at Michael; however, Elise seemed thrilled to see Kyle, and made her way through the women first, hugging Faith and Chelsea's mother before shaking hands with Chelsea's father. A hug might have been in order for Kyle as well; instead, he gave her an awkward high-five. Elise clasped his hand for a brief moment, surprising him. *Really Kyle, the innocuous hug would have been smoother,* Chelsea thought, preparing to have to greet Elise herself. As hot, sluggish, and unattractive as Chelsea felt, Elise was supremely the opposite, standing out from the patriotic dress of most of the crowd in a silky tank top in a muted shade of lilac with short shorts—a length Chelsea had given up years ago. She looked as cool and collected as if she had just dressed for the occasion and emerged, unaffected by the heat. *So not only was she gorgeous, she didn't perspire either.*

"Hi, Chelsea," Elise said, smiling at her, presenting the little girl at her side. "This is Lydia."

"Oh! Hi, Lydia," Chelsea greeted the child, captivated instantly by her sweet and sudden smile. A fresh pink scar stretched across her forehead, reminding Chelsea of the day Kyle had taken Elise to the hospital when Lydia had gotten hit with a chair at day care. "Our boys are over there playing Corn Hole, but they'll be back in a little while," she said, wondering whether she should compare scars with Lydia, but the child's gaze was fixed on Kyle.

"Hey, Lydia!" he said, and she grinned, taking a step toward him, causing the other women to begin a chorus of "Aww!" as Lydia reached up to him. He lifted her in an easy swoop, making her giggle, and rested her on his hip where she could look him in the eye and rub her hand on his chin. He nipped at her fingertips as laughter spilled forth from her grin. Chelsea held her breath, watching them interact, as if this were a common occurrence. Her heart did a flip at the sight of him with the little girl in his arms. It even got Michael's attention momentarily, but he looked away as other people walked by, young men and women he seemed to know, waving casually. Remembering his manners, he joined their group and said hello, shaking hands with Tom and Kyle, getting reintroduced to Faith, and giving Liz a wide berth.

Finally, he spoke to Chelsea, "Hi, Chelsea. How's it going?"

"Hi, Michael. I'm doing well. How are you?"

"Great, thanks," he replied, probably wondering what Lydia's fascination with Kyle was all about, not that he seemed to want any attention from the child himself.

Chelsea ignored the scene and gestured to the cooler. "Have you all had anything to eat? We've packed everything up in the cooler, but there's plenty of food," she offered.

"Oh! No, thanks. We just finished eating at Radlers."

"Oh. That's your restaurant?" she asked. That explained the cool composure of the three of them.

"Yeah. It's more of a pub actually. You haven't been there?" he asked. Chelsea noticed Kyle listening to their conversation. When she shook her head, Michael went on, liking the attention, and a chance to plug his business. "You should get Kyle to bring you by sometime. He's been in before. We have German food, mostly, and beers. Radler is a German concoction of beer mixed with lemonade that cyclists like to drink. It's very refreshing, especially on a hot day like this." *Nice,* she thought, *he's noticed the sweat running down my chest.* "And we have a couple of Davenport wines on the menu as well!" he said, adding his attempt at kissing up.

"Well, good! Do you get a lot of cyclists?"

"Yes, we do, and our share of skiers in the wintertime. Business is booming actually."

"Good for you. It's nice to see you and Elise out together again. Are you two an item?" she couldn't help but inquire, making Kyle's head turn sharply. *Put the little girl down,* she thought.

"We've been hanging out a bit these days," he said with a stiff smile, eyes darting around the park, as if he didn't want to miss anything that might be better.

It sounded like something a sixteen year old would say. Elise, deep in conversation with Faith and Liz about the office redecoration, did not notice his comment.

"Lydia is precious. I haven't seen her until today."

"Yes, she's cute. How's it going with your work? Are you still at App?" he asked, changing the subject, surprising her. Being around children must terrify him. He must be desperate for conversational topics. At least he wasn't asking about their house.

"Uh, yes. It's good. I'm choreographing a few pieces for the summer dance programs and actually dancing in one in a couple of weeks," she said, aware that his eyes were darting again, and let her comment die. *On my birthday, in fact, and it's going to be a surprise for my mom, because it's about Alzheimer's and my grandmother is suffering with that*, she said in her head, sure that Michael Gilmer wouldn't give a damn about any of that.

"You're going to be dancing, Chelsea?" Elise asked, overhearing and coming over to find out more. "Kyle didn't mention it. I'd love to come. When is it?"

Chelsea remembered to close her mouth, shooting a look at Kyle who was still holding Lydia, nestled into his chest. *Kyle doesn't mention much.* "Uh, it's at the end of July. I'll get Kyle to give you the information," she said, loud enough for him to hear and turn toward them, and then step over to join their conversation. Michael took the opportunity to back away and take his phone from his pocket, wandering off to touch the screen and occupy himself. Chelsea looked at Kyle as Elise relieved him of Lydia; such a little family they seemed. "Elise would like to come to my dance performance, so I thought you could give her the details when you're back at the office." *And maybe all of you can sit together. Ugh!*

Kyle shrugged. "Sure. We can get you tickets. Will Michael want to come?"

Elise wrinkled her nose, "I don't think dance would be his thing, but I'd love to bring Lydia, and if my grandmother is available, I think she'd love an invitation."

Wonderful, Helen Taylor can see me fall on my face after all these years, Chelsea thought, but she smiled appreciatively just the same. "I doubt she'd remember me. It's been a while since I was with the Carolina Ballet."

"No, she remembers you very well. I just saw her last weekend when I was home with Lydia, and she said very nice things about you," Elise said with a smile, making Chelsea smolder inwardly. Why did she have to be nice? It was easier to dislike Elise when she seemed aloof and competing for her husband.

At that moment, Frank appeared with Stu and Ty, the boys looking hot and smelling sweaty. "Elise, have you met our boys? This is Ty, and this is Stu. Boys, this is Miss Masters who works with Daddy and Frank now."

The boys took turns saying hello and shaking hands with Elise, charming her into a large smile that made both Kyle and Chelsea smile as well, proud that the boys remembered their manners. They had little difficulty making conversation with adults. She introduced them to Lydia, who had now managed to stand on her own, a good head shorter than both of the boys, making Chelsea think they were giants in comparison. The child had yet to say a word, Chelsea thought with a pang of sympathy, but Elise seemed unaffected. The little girl reminded her so much of Meme Compton when they'd first met. What a transformation had occurred with Meme, Chelsea thought, thinking to tell Elise that Meme would be dancing in the show also. And maybe Lydia would like to dance in their special program in the fall. Maybe this could be their common ground.

She glanced at Chelsea and then back at the boys. "Your boys are so sweet and well-spoken for their age. Do you ever have trouble telling them apart?"

Chelsea began to feel bad, thinking Elise was trying so hard to be pleasant. Her question was a common one. Most people were intrigued with twins.

"Every once in awhile I do. Stu's face is more square-shaped, but sometimes, they play us for each other. It's maddening!"

Elise laughed, watching the children eyeing each other. Ty offered Lydia a piece of watermelon from the container Liz had produced for them. Then she looked at Kyle.

"You know, Kyle, I was thinking when I was home that it would be fun for us all to go out on my dad's sailboat. You should come…to the lake, with Chelsea and your boys and spend the weekend with us sometime," she said, tempting him with her smiling brownish green eyes. *What an interesting color.* He returned her smile guardedly and turned to Chelsea.

Forget common ground! A rendezvous on a sailboat where the two of you will discuss your problems will never happen on my watch, thought Chelsea, feeling a new heat wave take over her face, making her fan herself with her hand. Thoughts of Stacie and an unknown man in the throes of passion below the deck nauseated her as the images were replaced with the torrid faces of Kyle and Elise. Still, Elise waited for a response from him, seeming to forget that Chelsea was there. He looked away, thinking a moment.

"That's a nice offer," he said, his hand going to massage the top of Ty's head. "The boys have been sailing a time or two and really enjoyed it. Does Michael like to sail?" he asked, too innocently, and they all looked around to find Michael, who was standing several feet away, engrossed in a cell phone conversation, oblivious to them all. Kyle looked back at Elise, his penetrating blue eyes doing a number on her, but not the drowning-in-her-spell look Chelsea had seen at the winery the night of the party. This was a look of reproof, a thrown gauntlet.

"He said he does," she said quietly, her eyes falling away, her face going scarlet, understanding immediately that this would not be an outing they'd go on with Michael. And it would be too awkward without him. *So that would be that*, Chelsea thought triumphantly, putting her lips together to suppress an appreciative smile. She was sure Kyle had no knowledge about Stacie's past indiscretion, but she was glad he'd had the good sense to quell this invitation. Maybe he was more aware of what was going on than Chelsea thought. There was no mistaking he was putting some distance between Elise and him. Or, with two references to Michael, maybe he was trying to see what was going on between the two of them. It was possible that Kyle and Elise did not discuss Michael at work. He was treating her like the business associate she was. Either way, Elise was giving away nothing, now that Kyle had politely rebuffed her. Michael was on his way toward her again.

"Can I steal you and Lydia away for a while? There are some people on the other side of the park I'd like to see," he said to Elise. It was a good start, but then he'd ruined it. Not, *there are some people I'd like you to meet*, thought Chelsea. If Kyle had put it to her that way she'd have been pissed. And they had just gotten there. *How rude!*

Elise hesitated and glanced at Kyle and Frank. "Okay…will we be back?" she asked. Michael's eyes flitted about again, and he gave her a noncommittal shrug. Elise looked around, embarrassed, not knowing how to respond to his arrogance. He had probably brought them, so she had no choice but to go along. Irritation flashed across her face for a second. She took Lydia's hand, beginning to say goodbyes as they walked away. Kyle looked at the boys, who were eating watermelon out of Liz's plastic container, and reached for a piece himself, as Elise looked back over her shoulder. Chelsea waved, relieved that Kyle had not been watching after her, and that Elise had seen that he wasn't. *He had just drawn a line in the sand.*

Chapter 11

DISAPPOINTMENTS

"Whoa!" said Stu and Ty in unison. They did that a lot. Liz Cavalier and Christi were hauling a 700-pound gator over the side of their johnboat on *Swamp People*, to the guffaws and exclamations of Stu and Ty, as they sat on either side of Kyle on the sofa. He laughed in awe as well. Liz had baited the sucker, and Christi had blown him away with her .22 magnum before dragging him aboard, making Kyle shake his head in bemusement, wondering how in the hell these women did what they did. He understood why. The money must be pretty damn amazing. Still, two women and a 700-pound gator! It was getting dark and Chelsea should be home by now, he thought. When the show was over, he would get the boys in the tub, but for right now, all three of them were glued to the tube, watching the women zip back to the dock just in time to avoid the approaching storm ready to break loose any minute.

He rose, hearing Chelsea's tires crunch over the gravel in the drive. It was the night before her birthday, and tonight was the dress rehearsal for her dance production. She was not happy that Elise Masters would be sitting with one of her former benefactors in the audience. Well, she hadn't said as much, but he knew that was the case. She had ruminated about it since the Fourth of July, when Elise had invited herself to the show, and had worked herself into an absolute frenzy over it. After ten years of marriage, he had picked up a thing or two, and he sure didn't want his wife upset by the woman she considered her rival. Since their fireworks on the couch and his conversation with Tyson, he had done everything he could to reassure her about their relationship. He knew her reaction to Elise was now unfounded, but it was useless even to broach the subject with her. They didn't talk about Elise Masters anyway. Still, he thought, standing on the porch, scratching his stomach, and watching her slam the car door in the darkness, he understood what a runaway imagination could do to a person. He felt his smile build across his face as she stormed up the steps with her bag slung over her shoulder, tendrils of hair dried stiffly around her face, which was still faintly pink from dancing.

"Hey!" he greeted her, watching her face surrender into a smile. She slowed her step and met him at the porch. Her eyes were sparkling with the porch lighting, making them shine like sapphires, even though in the daylight, he knew they would be as pale as two aquamarines, rare on someone with her dark auburn hair, he thought, leaning on his elbows across the railing, letting his chin settle into the heel of his hand, watching her.

"Hey," she said, somewhat deflated, leading him to believe that something crummy must have happened tonight.

"How was dress rehearsal? You okay?" he asked, peering under her eyelashes where she appeared to be trying to hide.

"It went really well, although I've had better days," she said. "How about you?"

"Everything's fine, now that you're here."

"Hmm!" She moved closer to him, and he felt her hand slide up under his T-shirt. He closed his eyes, feeling the effects. It was a scintillating experience, and he felt her laugh gently, as he felt his skin turn to gooseflesh under her touch.

"Did you eat?" he asked, kissing her lips, then letting his mouth come to rest on her scar.

"No. I'm not hungry." She drew away and went into the cabin, eyeing the boys on the couch. Next, she looked at the counter by the sink to see whether he'd cleaned up. Good, it was dark. And she was tired. Maybe she wouldn't notice his less than spotless attempts at cleaning up supper.

"There's mac and cheese in the fridge. I can heat it up for you. Really, you should eat."

"No, thank you, though," she said, smiling at him and going to see the boys.

"Hey, Mom," they both said, and Ty came to wrap his arms around her waist, squeezing her tightly, making her press her eyelids together and bend to kiss the top of his head.

"*Swamp People?*"

"Yeah, you shoulda seen the gators Liz and Christi brought in! One of 'em was 700 pounds!" Stu exclaimed, as the credits appeared on the screen. Any diversion to avoid getting into the bathtub.

"Wow! You guys need baths," she said, sniffing Ty's hair. Her voice sounded drained.

"I was just about to get them in the tub when you drove in," Kyle said. "What is it, baby?"

She crumbled to the arm of the couch, her bag sliding off her arm onto the floor. Her cell phone was still in her hand. "I just got off the phone with Mom. Grandmother fell and broke her elbow today. She's going to have surgery tomorrow. Mom's on the way down there now."

"Clammaw's having surgery?" Stu asked, just tuning in. It was their name for Kyle's mother. They'd had a hard time pronouncing the word "Grandma" when they were little, so Mark had named Shelly "Clammaw" for them. It made Mark chuckle every time he heard them say it.

"No, honey. Clammaw's fine. It's *my* grandmother who's having surgery. Your Grandmommy has gone down to South Carolina to be with her."

"Oh," said Stu, vacantly. The boys had only a few memories of Christmases with their great-grandmother and were not personally attached to her. As charming as Chelsea's sons were, they did not seem to impress her grandmother. She admitted they were cute, but always made some dig at them, like they needed haircuts, or they shouldn't put their feet near any of the furniture, as she scraped her walker across the old hardwood floors in Chelsea's parents' house. This, coming from a woman who always managed to spill her red wine or get spaghetti on the upholstery, a woman who was having difficulty remembering whom her own daughter was. Still, she was Grandmother and needed someone. Chelsea sighed.

"But Grandmommy'll miss your birthday," said Ty, realizing what was making his mom so sad.

"And the show," murmured Kyle, wondering how she must feel. Chelsea's piece in the show was supposed to be a surprise for her mother. Her parents had just returned from Greenville where they had spent several days moving Grandmother into the memory care facility of her retirement center. They'd hired a couple of men and a truck to move her scant furniture and other personal items into a storage unit until they could decide what to do with everything. It was a heart-wrenching process to observe. He moved to stand beside her, placing his fingers at the base of her neck, massaging her in a show of empathy and support.

"Well, it will be recorded, so she can see it later," she said in a dull voice, but Kyle knew it would not be the same as having her there. The four of them sat in the dark for a moment, the TV commercial blaring too loudly to suit their mood. "Why don't you guys head down to the bathroom and get your bath water going, okay?" she asked.

"Okay," said Ty, putting his arm around her shoulder and giving her a kiss on the cheek.

"Do you need help, guys?" asked Kyle.

"Nope," said Stu, following Ty down the stairs.

Kyle held her head in his arms, holding her face to his torso. "I'm so sorry, baby," he whispered.

"It's okay. She's seen me dance a million times before."

But it's your birthday, he thought sadly. "Did Tom go with her?"

"No. He has too much going on right now. If it gets bad, he'll go. I told Mom to call us when she gets there."

"When is her surgery?" he asked gently, stroking an escaped strand of her hair behind her ear.

"First thing in the morning," she said, staring vacantly at the rip in his jeans above his knee. "I wish I could be with her."

He let out a long sigh. "The timing sucks," he said, pulling her head against his stomach again.

"Yes. It does. I think I'll go get a shower myself." She smiled up at him, handing him her phone and picking up her bag. He refused to let her go before giving her a comforting embrace, and he felt her melt despondently into his arms. After allowing him to kiss her, she pulled away and disappeared into their bedroom doorway. Standing for a moment watching the empty space, he sighed again, feeling the weight of her phone in his hand.

He pursed his lips and carried the phone to the porch, where it seemed thousands of fireflies had suddenly congregated. As if they spoke to him, he had an idea. He seated himself on the top step of the porch, running his fingertip over her phone's screen, scrolling through her contacts and placing a call.

"Hey! No, it's Kyle….How are you, man? Yeah, we're good! Listen, what would it take for you to jump on a plane and blow my wife out of the water on her birthday?"

Her heart settled finally, as she took her place in the darkness of the stage. She closed her eyes, the images of Stu and Ty's homemade birthday cards swimming in the blackness, comforting her. *Thirty-five!* A hush fell over the audience and the stage lights came up, changing slowly from a soft purple to aquamarine and then to a pale orange, the colors of dawn. Slow sweet notes of the song began. Sarah McLachlan's voice swelled into the air with the lyrics from "I Will Remember You," as Chelsea felt the warmth of orange light illuminating her face. She opened her eyes, feeling Carmen de Silva's hand on her arm, also bathed in the orange light, then felt the touch of Dima's hand on her other arm. Looking up into his eyes, she appeared to recognize him, and then Carmen, as their anguished faces melted away and they shared a happy glance. They led her into an intricate dance with them across the stage. And then she was alone again in the soft blue light, swaying back and forth, hands at her head, covering her ears. She hugged herself, crumpling to the floor. With Carmen by his side, Dima's arms enfolded Chelsea, lifting her like a child, circling them both around until his hands grasped her waist, effortlessly lifting her above his head as they drifted across the stage. Then he set her down, placing her in Carmen's arms. They embraced, smiling, and pantomiming the hand motions to a childhood game, one she had played with Grandmother, one her mother had played with her. Suddenly, the game stopped, as if the memories had ceased in midstream. Her hand went to her mouth, and she regarded Carmen as if she did not know her. She turned away as Dima came to Carmen, this time lifting her in a comforting lover's embrace as Chelsea wandered alone to the opposite corner of the stage. They were both on her again, pulling her this way and that, as Chelsea resisted the strangers' touches and the lights went to pale purple. She drew away, turning and pirouetting to her own music, it seemed, as the others watched her, a stranger to them as well. Carmen reached out desperately again as Dima held her, lifting her, carrying her toward Chelsea, who held her at arms' length, Dima holding Carmen's arms above her head, then folding them over her, across her heart and rocking her from side to side. Hands at her head, Chelsea danced away again, reaching out and pulling in, looking at her hands, filled with nothing, then grasping again. Carmen circled her, followed by Dima, both unnoticed by Chelsea. The song went on and the chorus came again. The light faded again to deep blue and almost to dark. As the couple watched her, the light changed again, brightening to a vivid orange as Chelsea raised her head, turning and gazing at Carmen, recognizing her again. Dima took a step toward them, arms waiting for Carmen to fall. Chelsea touched her face. Carmen mirrored the movement and they smiled at each other as the light slowly faded to dark.

Silence....

Someone clapped, then more applause began, erupting into thunder, as the three of them gathered for a hug and grasped warm hands, Dima and Carmen on each side of her, all breathing heavily, hearts pounding. They laughed together, as the lights came back up, shining blindingly in their smiling faces. Still holding hands, they bowed together, grinning at each other. Images of people rising to their feet as they applauded made Chelsea's heart swell with a mix of relief, gratitude, and humility. Among the other shouts, she heard her father's distinctive whistle from the middle of the crowd, making her giggle. It would do no good to search for his face in the bright lights. Dima took her hand and walked her two steps forward, gesturing to her with a flourish as she sank into a curtsy before the audience. Meme Compton was at her side then, presenting her with a bouquet of wildflowers tied with purple ribbon. They embraced, and Chelsea felt the first hot tears spring to her eyes as Meme said, "Congratulations!" in her ear and was gone in an instant.

Later, backstage, the throng of people, dance faculty, supporters, and families and friends of the dancers began to converge on them, the excited chatter overwhelming, as Chelsea was separated from Carmen and Dima. Chelsea's students crowded around her, congratulating her, and then each other. They had danced well, making her proud, and they loved her dance as well. Meme brought her family over to see Chelsea, and they embraced, once again in awe of Meme's progress, the visions of her performance still fresh and lovely in their minds. Finally, over the sea of heads, she spotted her father, tall and lanky, holding one pink rose, his eyes resting proudly on her, breaking into a slow grin as she spotted him. She glimpsed Kyle behind her dad, grinning at her as well and flanked by their boys in the line to speak to her. Meme was asking her to autograph her mother's program and she did, squeezing her flowers into her side with her left arm, laughing and asking Meme to wait around so she could autograph Kyle's.

Her father's arms were around her, lifting her off the floor and squeezing an unexpected sob from deep within her. He always brought her a pink rose. It was what Kitty would have given her, Kitty's favorite flower. She breathed in deeply of his scent, clean clothes and freshly showered for the occasion. *Don't cry*, she thought, but everyone else seemed to be. Still, she held herself together out of shame for her own selfishness. If her mother had been there to see this, it would have been perfect, but then, the separation was ironically the core of her piece, making her bittersweet feelings all the more appropriate.

Her father gazed down at her, without words, shaking his head and handing her the rose.

"I know," she said. "I wish Mom could have been here," she said, biting her lip, holding back her tears successfully.

"She'd have loved it, just like I did. That was just wonderful, Sweet Pea," he said, the endearment sending the tears falling over her lower lids like rain. He saw them and hugged her again, this time leaving her on her small parcel of the stage.

As she felt Kyle's arm go around her shoulders, she released her father, dissolving into her husband's chest, letting his arms gather her into his embrace. She gazed at him as his blue eyes glinted at her and his smile built again over his handsome face. His strength began to restore her ability to stand as he murmured into her ear. "That was amazing! I'm so proud of you! Your mother would have been, too!" He rocked her gently, kissing her again, and then said, "I love you, baby. Happy birthday!"

She felt the boys grab her around the waist and bent to receive their hugs and flowers and to kiss them both. "Happy birthday, Mom!" they said in unison.

"Thank you!"

"No, *happy birthday*, Mom!" Ty said, gesturing behind him, as if she were slow to understand. She looked in the direction he had pointed, only to see a very good-looking, muscular black man in a tight shirt and jeans grinning at her, a slight gap exposed between his front teeth. She gasped, letting some of her flowers fall to the floor.

"*Willie!*" it was more of a question, but all of them recognized her disbelief and joy at once and began to laugh as the scheme was registering on her face. Immediately, her attention shifted to Kyle. "You did this? For me? For my birthday?" *Because my mother is not here and because you love me this much?*

He continued to grin and nodded with a wink as Willie Morrison, her dance partner from high school, and now a senior member of the Ailey Two dance company in New York, stepped forward to collect his hug, swinging her around as if she weighed no more than a ragdoll.

"Happy birthday, baby! I always love watching you dance! And *that* was *ridiculous!*"

"*Get out!*" she said, quoting him. "Oh my God, I can't believe you're here! Oh, I'm so glad I didn't fall on my face. If I'd known you were going to be here, I would have been a basket case. How did you get away? Where were you?"

"I was in New York, rehearsing a new show. I'm an old guy now, you know, so they let me slip away every once in awhile."

"Well, if *you're* old, *I'm* old. I'm impressed that you'd come to see such an old woman dance in a place like this."

"I wouldn't have missed this for the world! And *girl!*" he cried, holding her out at arms' length so he could inspect her. "You still dance like you're twenty-one, full-out and giving it everything you've got! It's always from your heart. That was truly amazing. Thank you! This just makes me want to dance with you again! Ailey Two just might have to have some of your choreography. If they could see you!"

"Oh, I know, I'd fit right in!" she laughed, thinking about the company, primarily comprised of manly, muscular ethnic men like Willie.

"You're buck enough!" he said, giving her arm a little push. She pushed him back, like old times. He was so familiar, and still her dear friend, even though they rarely saw each other. She'd always been in awe of him, even long ago when he'd lifted her above his head, making her feel like royalty. He was royalty right now. And he was *here!*

Her eyes left Willie for a moment and flickered back to Kyle, who with the boys, had collected all of her flowers. "I love you!" she said, hugging her husband again, the full meaning of what he had done falling into place in her head. "You've made this the perfect birthday," she said, and then her eyes landed on Elise Masters, Lydia, and Helen Taylor, all looking lovely, their arms laden with flowers, but she was too happy to let any of this bother her. Helen was looking on and smiling, obviously recognizing Willie, which would be a good thing, a distraction from her. Today was one time when she would not mind sharing the limelight, even though she knew she had danced well, and had touched people with her choreography.

Elise glanced at Kyle, who acknowledged her accordingly, and stepped up to give Chelsea a hug. It was an odd feeling to have this woman's arm around her neck, as Kyle looked on, his expression unreadable. "Chelsea! That was so beautiful! There was not a dry eye in the house!"

"Thank you, Elise. I'm so glad you could come. I'd love for you and Lydia to meet my student, Meme," she said, looking around, but Meme was nowhere in sight. "Where is she? Anyway….Hi, Lydia, did you enjoy the show?"

Lydia gave her sudden grin, a burst of sunshine, and nodded, making them all smile at her in return.

"Helen! It's so good to see you!" she said as Helen Taylor claimed her hug, birdlike arms going around Chelsea's neck. Elise was at least a foot taller than her grandmother, who seemed tall and surprisingly fit for a woman in her eighties. But that was what dance did for a person, she thought, inspired by Helen's vitality.

"Oh, darling, what a lovely piece! I was moved to tears as well. We are certainly at a loss without you at the *Ballet!* Maybe we can arrange to collaborate with you one day. Would you consider doing such a thing, dear?"

Chelsea grinned, despite her image of the artistic director grimacing at such a thought. Instead, she said, "Absolutely! That would make me so happy! Helen, do you remember my husband, Kyle? And these are our boys, Stu and Ty," she said, as Kyle and the boys greeted her and shook her hand.

"Yes, I remember Kyle. Hello, boys! Oh, how cute!"

"And do you know Willie Morrison?" Chelsea asked, extending her arm toward Willie, who reached forward to take Helen's hand.

"Hello, Willie! Oh my, I'm a *huge* fan of yours!"

"Thank you!" he beamed at her.

"Willie, this is Helen Taylor, one of the benefactors with the Carolina Ballet," Chelsea began as Willie leaned forward to press his lips to her knuckles, causing Helen to smile and gasp.

"It's my pleasure, Ms. Taylor. We always appreciate those of you who make it all happen! I saw Chelsea dance many times with the Carolina Ballet, one of my great pleasures in life, other than dancing with her myself!" he said. Chelsea rolled her eyes while Helen continued to look starstruck. He had gotten very good at schmoozing with the right people. Elise looked on, wanting an introduction as well.

"And this is Helen's granddaughter, Elise Masters. Elise works with Kyle in their building firm," Chelsea said, eyes moving back and forth to the people she'd mentioned.

Willie reached across to shake hands with Elise, somehow unfazed by her beauty, winning Chelsea's approval, saying, "Hi, Elise; it's nice meeting you as well. What a small world it is! And who is this *breathtaking* young lady?" he asked quietly, smiling carefully at Lydia, knowing his larger-than-life-and-dark-chocolate presence often frightened young girls. In fact, Lydia's mouth was shaped in the form of an O as she observed him from the safety of Elise's skirt.

"This is Lydia," Elise began, but was interrupted by a shrill whistle and Dima's deep and commanding voice from on high. Chelsea realized that he'd climbed onto a ladder, used as a prop in one of the pieces, and was addressing the crowd. Carmen stood by, spotting him on the ladder and smiling at the effectiveness with which he'd stilled the crowd of people who were anticipating what was next. Chelsea felt Kyle's arm go around her waist and glanced questioningly at him as Dima continued.

"Thank you all for coming out tonight! What a great show, eh?" he said so enthusiastically that the large group offered up another round of applause. His Russian accent seemed to have them all captivated along with his lean, stunning presence on the ladder. He went on, an impish grin taking over his face. "We have so much to celebrate tonight with all the talent of our various dancers and choreographers on display, but let's not forget one very auspicious occasion! I'd be most remiss if I let the night slip away without singing 'Happy Birthday' to our most appreciated young faculty member, and dancer/choreographer extraordinaire, Ms. Chelsea Davis!" he cried, flinging his arm toward Chelsea, making her face blaze with surprise. The song went up all around her, with the twins jumping up and down beside her at the end, whooping and hollering. It was one thing to have a standing ovation with lights blinding you so you had no idea who was there, but quite another to be in the midst of a sea of smiling faces of so many she loved, celebrating *her*. Even Elise was smiling and singing to her, moving her strangely, making her press her arm tighter around Kyle, and holding back more tears.

The song ended and Dima spoke again from atop the ladder. "And how old *are you*?" he asked, grinning his devilish grin, a diamond stud theatrically glinting from his ear, as Carmen passed him up a bottle of champagne. He did not make an effort to come down, making Chelsea nervous.

She shook her head and sniffled, trying to compose what she hoped would be a smart-mouthed answer, when Willie's voice rang out for the crowd, "Twenty-one!" he shouted beside her, making everyone laugh as she high-fived him. More champagne bottles appeared, and after several pops were heard, she was handed a plastic flute of bubbly. Some of the dancers came around with plastic cups of sparkling white grape juice for the children.

"To Chelsea! Happy birthday, love!" Dima said, raising his glass, nodding to Kyle, who was taking a picture on his phone.

"For your mom," he mouthed.

"Happy birthday!" said the crowd, lifting their glasses to her. Chelsea raised her glass to the crowd and then to her men, her father, Willie, her sons, and Kyle, and drank to the good wishes of all of them. Her husband had done this, all of this for her. When the crowd had moved on to other conversations, she turned to Kyle. She closed her eyes, feeling him nuzzle her hair, hearing him murmur, "I love you," in her ear.

"Thank you!" she whispered, burying her face into his massive shoulder. Despite her mother's absence, Chelsea felt the birthday surprise, and Kyle's thoughtful invitation to Willie made the night turn out to be magic, exceeding all her expectations. She'd forgotten how good it felt to have created a piece, and then to have danced it, bringing the muse to the stage for her important people to appreciate. This feeling was addictive for her. It was why she danced and she would never be able to stop!

Chapter 12

AUTUMN

The four of them sat around the stone fireplace at the winery, warmed from the chill produced by getting caught in an unexpected downpour. As a result, they had the place to themselves. It had rained off and on for the past several days. The fire looked almost real, and was comforting, creating a warm ambience, along with the soothing acoustic guitar music that played quietly in the background. The smell of wet leaves on the ground and the cozy, early darkness was what Chelsea loved about October, that and wearing sweaters, she thought, watching Kyle push up the sleeves of his navy sweater, exposing his muscular forearms in the firelight. Chelsea loved this place because Kyle and Faith and Frank had created it for her brother and her father. They came here so often that it was like a second home, a respite from the chaos that autumn brought with school, the boys' sports schedules and the amount of work that consumed Kyle and her both. She sipped her wine, closing her eyes, releasing herself from those demands, thinking of fall, and her present company with her husband and good friends. Chelsea had missed spending time with Glen and Abby, and the two couples had finally been able to pin down babysitters for that rare evening out.

Kyle poured the women another glass of Snowy Ridge Rosé, a new fall bottle that had just come out. Chelsea smiled inwardly, a fleeting thought of summer entering her mind, glad that they weren't drinking *Moonlight* this evening. Bad connotations went with that one, but it was a summer wine anyway, and maybe by the next summer, she would have forgotten that particular unpleasant memory. He reached for her hand and she felt his thumb circling the back of her hand, sending her an unmistakable message as he watched her taste her wine, his blue eyes making his own seductive fire for her, instantly shattering the fleeting image. *How could it be that she was not pregnant? This man could still unravel her with a simple glance.*

Abby and Glen seemed to be back on track, at least, without barbs and insults for the past hour. They seemed to be trying harder than the last time they'd all been together. The conversation was typically about their children. Why they always succumbed to this topic every time when the point was to escape, Chelsea didn't know.

"Do you like the twins' teachers this year?" asked Abby, flipping her veil of silky dark hair over her shoulder. She had cut it to a sleek shoulder-length bob after her children were born, and the style suited her. As ever, she was attractively put together in her jeans and boots, with an orange sweater Chelsea had never seen. She had probably gotten in trouble for shopping again. "You have to tell me everything. I'm taking notes now that the kids are in kindergarten."

Chelsea thought a moment, stealing a glance at Kyle. His eyes flashed at her. Stu's teacher had brought some issues to their attention that had them considering new ideas for him. Ty couldn't be doing better, as Chelsea would expect. Still, she didn't like to compare her sons, and didn't want others doing the same thing. As if reading her mind, Kyle studied her to see how she would respond. He had many reservations about Miss Payne and what she'd had to say about Stu at the conference last week.

"Stu has Miss Payne. He loves her. She's very young, very energetic, which was what we wanted, but she challenges him. She's helping him work through some issues, like staying focused and finishing his work.

Ty, on the other hand, has Mrs. Dixon, who's been there for years. She has a passion for literature and history, so she's wonderful for Ty. He loves to read. He'd spend all day with his nose in a book if we'd let him. I lost the aluminum foil the other day, and he'd taken it down in the basement to make a suit of armor for one of the knights he was reading about. It was quite an impressive sculpture when he was finished!" she said, making Abby and Glen laugh. "But there was no more foil to line my pan!" Kyle nodded at her, squeezing her hand, approving of her story as a clever way to divert what was on their minds.

"How's kindergarten going for the triplets?" Kyle asked, handing Abby a small slice of home-baked wheat bread, smeared with goat cheese. *So adept at shifting the attention*, thought Chelsea.

"It's wonderful so far," she said, taking a bite. "The kids love school. They come home exhausted and go to bed early, so Glen and I have more time together, when he's home, that is."

"How much longer do you have in the program?" asked Kyle, referring to Glen's detective training.

"I'll be certified in January," he replied, sipping his wine, probably wishing it were beer, Chelsea thought. "I'm doing more and more with the police department now. It's a whole lot more interesting being on the investigative side of the job."

"It's more dangerous," said Abby and they exchanged a look.

"At times….But the money will be better in the long run," Glen added.

Abby sighed, fingering her goblet, letting the wine swirl around. "I really am getting tired of being at home, and now that the kids are in school, I'd like to go back to work. But finding something in my field during the school day will be hard, unless I sit behind a desk at a hotel or something. I can't imagine trying to run events and parties on the weekends with the kids at home and Glen working cases. But I want to contribute again, you know?" Glen looked pleased; maybe this compromise was the catalyst for the change in their behavior.

"You're way too independent to be sitting around," Chelsea said, grinning at her friend. *And with the two of you as independent as you both are, it's no wonder you butt heads all the time*, she thought with a smile. "Maybe something in an office?" Chelsea offered.

"Yeah…but I'd be bored out of my skull. It's worth a try, though. I have nothing to do but look, at this point."

"Check into the university or the community college. They need event planners. And most of what they do would be during the days."

"That's a good idea," Abby murmured, as Kyle's phone played a tune. He looked at the screen and rose from his place beside her on the ottoman in front of the fireplace, walking away to take the call.

Chelsea listened to him talk as she prepared the next round of bread and goat cheese. Another group of couples walked in as Bri greeted them at the door. Kyle wiped a hand behind his neck as he talked.

"Hey. What's up?" he said quietly into the phone. "Yeah…oh no, are you okay? It's okay, take a deep breath, sweetheart," he said, as if he were talking to Bri, but Bri was here. Was it Abigail from the beach? He looked concerned as he listened, then laughed gently. "So did you? Throw up, I mean? That's good. You had an adrenaline rush.…Did you call your roadside assistance? An hour and a half! That's *bullshit*.…No, I'm sure she is. So where are you exactly?" his voice was getting louder, and by now, Abby and Glen were watching him expectantly. "I know exactly where you are…You called him? Yeah, that figures…Uh, yeah," he said, this time looking back at all of them. "No, I'm sitting at the winery with Chelsea and some friends. Actually, you're kinda close. I could be there in about fifteen minutes.…No. It's all right. I'll be there.…Call me if they get to you first.…Yeah. I'll see you soon. Hey, are you wearing your seatbelts? Good. And your hazard lights are flashing? Sit tight then. Okay.… Bye."

He looked at the phone as if it bore bad news and pressed his lips together, raising his eyes to meet Chelsea's. All three faces questioned him at once when he came back and sat down next to her. Chelsea's face burned from hearing his tone with her, his concern, his *instructions. Sweetheart?* She sat stunned, knowing exactly what was going to happen next.

"That was Elise. She and Lydia got run off the road up on 105. She's stuck in the mud in front of a speed limit sign, and the mud is so deep she can't get out, even with the four wheel drive. The tow truck is an hour and a half out, and Lydia's getting cold…so she asked me to come get her."

Abby gaped at Kyle, as Glen's eyebrows shot up at him.

"Can she not call Michael?" asked Chelsea, struggling to speak through the sudden dryness of her voice. Her eyes held his, communicating her dislike of the situation. It had been months and Elise Masters had remained in the background, until now.

"She tried calling him, but he hasn't answered. They were on their way over to Radlers for dinner, so he'll be expecting them eventually." He shrugged at the women's faces. This was not what they had in mind for their evening. He spread his hands and said, "Look; I'm sorry, but she needs help, and it won't take very long. I could go and be back by the time you finish your wine…or I could meet you at the restaurant."

"Do you have a cable in your truck?" Glen asked, standing up and setting his wine glass on the table.

"No, but I've got a tow strap."

"That'll work. It'll take no time to pull her out. I can go with you and we could have her out and on her way in two shakes," he added to Abby's smoldering glare. "I wonder if she got a look at the car that ran her off the road. Probably someone texting and not paying attention. Did she call it in to the police?" he asked, the cop in him taking charge of the case.

"I don't know if she called it in. It won't be a problem, just a muddy job," said Kyle, looking uncomfortable with the situation, and glancing out the window, noticing the rain had stopped. "Look, I can do this myself. You don't have to come," he said to Glen.

"Oh, I don't mind! You're probably gonna need help," he said, making Abby roll her eyes. *So much for our dinner plans*, thought Chelsea dismally. *But please go with him! My beautiful husband needs a chaperone with that woman.*

Abby looked at her, probably wondering why she didn't protest. She gave an exasperated sigh, slapping both hands on the arms of her leather chair. "Okay then! Why don't Chelsea and I pick up a pizza and you guys can meet us later, after you've saved the damsel in distress. Sound like a plan?" she asked, trying to take charge.

"We can meet back at our house since the boys are spending the night with Mom and Dad," Chelsea offered. "Besides, it will be closer, and you're both going to be covered with mud when you're done...." *rescuing her!* It was impossible to keep the irritation out of her voice.

Kyle breathed out a long sigh, giving her an intense look of reproof, making her strangely uncomfortable. Her face began to burn under his eyes. "She's been sitting there for twenty minutes and no one's stopped. Lydia's freaking out. Wouldn't you want someone to come and help if it were you?" he said evenly.

Her face flushed and she looked away from him. Chastising her in front of their friends was embarrassing, but she could not justify defending herself.

"Yes, of course I would, and I would be forever in their debt," she said, trying not to sound annoyed and jealous, but surely he knew how she felt. What else could he do? This conundrum with her was the price he paid for being a good guy. "You should go. You're a nice man," she said softly after a moment. It was a quote that usually came from her mother when Kyle had done something to help her, which elicited a small smile from him, knowing she was trying to muster up compassion for Elise. Still, she felt ashamed of herself. Finding empathy for Elise shouldn't be so hard since she could imagine herself in her shoes, but it was. Why did he have to be *her* knight in shining armor? If it were anyone else, she would be shooing him out the door! Abby was shaking her head, glaring at Glen, who seemed eager to get the show on the road.

Kyle turned to Chelsea before they left the winery. "Will you get two pizzas?"

"And some beer?" Glen added.

She nodded. *No kiss? That's it? He's just going to pull somebody's car out of the mud,* she told herself, squeezing her eyes shut as soon as he had turned his back on her.

"Good God! We're going to have to spend the night!" said Abby, making a stab at humor. They watched the men leave the winery, and then Abby turned to Chelsea. Her doe eyes were exceptionally large. "Chelsea!"

"What?" she snapped.

"Chels…he called her *'sweetheart,'*" she said under her breath.

"There she is," Kyle said, spotting the navy Jeep in the dark with its lights flashing, snug against the pole of a speed limit sign, just off the mountain-side shoulder of highway 105. It was a long and relatively straight climb at this point in the road. He shuddered, envisaging the result if she'd been on the other side of the road and this had happened. It reminded him too well of Chelsea's accident years ago, when he'd seen her car flipped over, thinking she was dead. *Chelsea…*she was not happy about this, his rushing to Elise's aid. He'd hoped the tow truck would be there already and that he could check on them, assured they were all right, and send them on their way. But there was no tow truck in sight, and he was keenly aware of Glen's eyes on his face.

"Damn, that's a lot of mud. She's dug herself in there pretty deep. One wheel isn't even touching the road. No wonder she couldn't get out."

Kyle pulled in behind her to let the cars behind him pass. "Damn! No hitch," he said. "That means we'll have to pull it out by the axle." As soon as it was clear, he turned on his flashers and backed up, easing back out into the road, and turning the Explorer around so he could back in. "Okay, let's do this," Kyle said, opening his door and climbing down, his foot sinking into the mud, covering the lower half of his boot. There would be no way they'd be presentable for a restaurant after slopping around in this kind of mud. He walked to Elise's Jeep, his feet making loud sucking noises as he lifted them. Glen stood outside the truck, saving his steps until necessary.

Elise's window went down as he approached. He saw her face, a pinched expression there, showing her attempt at hiding her fear, for Lydia's sake as well as her own. Anyone would be rattled.

"Hey!" he said brightly, his breath condensing in the cold air. He watched as relief flooded her face, relaxing it as she allowed herself to smile, color coming back to her cheeks instantly.

"Hey! Thank you *so* much for coming, Kyle!"

"Hey, Lydia!" he said, grinning at the child whose face was white with unease. In the dark, he could see that they wore rain jackets, and Elise had tucked a blanket around Lydia in the car seat. His eyes returned to Elise's as he felt Glen step up behind him. "Elise, do you remember Glen?"

"Of course! Hi, Glen. Thanks for coming out here. I'm so sorry to have pulled you away from your plans. I hope we haven't ruined your night," she said, looking pointedly at Kyle.

"No worries!" Glen said, grinning like a fool at her. "We'll have you out in no time."

"Should we get out?"

"Absolutely, just in case we go sliding, but stand over there near the rocks so you'll be well out of the way…and the traffic," said Kyle. Elise busied herself with releasing Lydia from the seat. He heard Glen talking to her as he set about his plan.

"Did you see the car that ran you off?" Glen asked.

"I think it was a black pickup truck, but I couldn't be sure of the color. It was just getting dark when it happened."

"Did you see the make?"

"Uh…no."

"Did you call the police?"

"No," she answered sheepishly.

"It's understandable. I can't believe no one stopped to help you," he said earnestly. He waved inside the Jeep to Lydia, who regarded him curiously.

Kyle went to the back of his SUV, rummaging around inside the tailgate, looking for a flashlight, the tow strap, and a large piece of plastic he kept on hand for lining the cargo area when bringing plants home from the nursery. It would come in handy when he'd lie down on the ground to secure the strap around her axle. As Elise and Lydia watched from the shoulder where Glen had directed them to stand, Glen held the flashlight and watched for traffic. Kyle slid under the Jeep on the plastic sheet to loop one end of the strap around the rear axle. Glen checked the road again as Kyle slid back out and stood to pull the strap's other end into position to loop it onto his trailer hitch.

Glen went back to the Jeep and climbed into the passenger seat, starting the motor and adjusting the gear shifter to neutral. Kyle pulled the plastic off the ground and folded it, placing it across the floor of his Explorer, stepping into the driver's seat with his boots, now caked thoroughly with mud. He put the truck in drive and stepped on the gas, noticing the tow truck approaching from the direction they'd just come.

Nice timing! He felt his truck pull slowly, getting some purchase on the Jeep, and pushed down slightly harder on the gas pedal as the Jeep rolled slowly forward and free of the ruts that had trapped it. The driver of the tow truck pulled over, allowing them plenty of room, and watched as Kyle parked his truck and jumped out with the plastic again, helping Glen unhook the strap. With the back of his arm, he wiped his nose, running now from the damp cold air. As he folded and stowed the tow strap in his tailgate, the driver of the tow truck pulled forward, calling out, "Need any more help?"

Kyle responded coolly, "Nope. I think we have it under control. Busy night?"

"Towing some folks from the parking lot at the mall. Students, you know? Thinkin' they can park there all week for free."

Kyle responded with an icy look, grabbing a towel from the back of his truck.

Elise stepped forward with Lydia on her hip. "I tried to call and cancel, but I couldn't get through."

"Not a problem, ma'am," said the man, around the plug of tobacco in his cheek. He spat neatly to the side, avoiding both Kyle and Elise. "I was probably in that low pocket down there when you called. It happens in several places around here. Sorry I didn't make it in time to spare you the trouble, sir," he said to Kyle.

"*Not a problem,*" Kyle said, mirroring the man's words, closing the tailgate with a thud, and wiping his hands with a towel.

"All right. You folks have a good evening," he said, waving and checking the traffic behind him.

Kyle waved him on. Glen appeared and Kyle handed him the towel.

"My knight in shining armor," murmured Elise, teeth grazing her bottom lip as she looked up at him, and then at Glen. "Both of you," she added. Then, glancing back at Kyle she said, "This is twice you've gotten to me first."

He looked puzzled a moment and then it dawned on him that she was referring to Wyatt's late arrival when she wanted her dresser removed from the back of her Jeep.

"Well, I'm glad we could help. I guess you can get on your way now. Lydia looks cold."

Elise looked at Lydia. "Tell Kyle thank you, Lydia," she urged gently.

"Thank you," Lydia said, quite clearly, but the shyness in her voice made it difficult to hear. Her lips curled into a reluctant smile as she nestled her head into Elise's neck.

Kyle's solemn face broke into a grin. "You're welcome! You all have a nice evening," he said, turning, but not before Elise's arm was around his neck in a sweet-smelling hug. He felt her lips brush the side of his neck as she released him, dazing him for an instant, her river eyes melting into his. Then she turned to Glen.

"Thank you, Glen!" she grinned, reaching for Glen as he eagerly accepted her one-armed embrace.

"Mm, my pleasure entirely!" he said, winking at Kyle. "You ladies have a fun evening." He ushered them to the car where Elise lifted Lydia into the backseat, strapping her in securely. Kyle helped her climb into the driver's seat and closed her door, patting the window ledge as she buckled herself in.

"Sorry about the mud," he said, knowing she'd be cleaning out her car tomorrow.

"Oh. Not a problem," she said, staring, as if she had more to say.

"See you Monday, then. Drive carefully," he said, smiling at her. He refused to mention Michael. *Tell Michael I said to go fuck himself. Bastard.*

She brushed her hair back and smiled gratefully again. "Okay. See you Monday. Have a nice weekend."

"You too, Elise."

She looked back, giving him a wan smile before checking the traffic and pulling out into the road.

He stewed for a moment, looking around on the ground for a stick to wipe off some of the mud.

Glen guffawed by his side, watching him, as if in awe. "Holy *shit!* That is one *fine* looking woman!"

Kyle said nothing as he leaned against the truck, scraping mud off his hiking boot. "Wipe off your boots, would you? I don't want you messing up my floor."

"Right!" Glen laughed, finding another small stick and going to work on his shoes. They settled back into the truck and Kyle proceeded out into the road.

"Why don't you call the girls and let them know we're on the way?"

"Roger that," Glen said, fingering his phone. "Man, no wonder Chelsea looked so pissed off. That girl's got it going on. And for you, too."

"What do you mean?" Kyle asked, lips pressed in a firm line.

"She's into you!"

"Uh, I doubt it. She's on her way to see Michael Gilmer right now. They date, you know."

"Whatever…" said Glen, listening to Abby answering the call. "Hey, baby! Yeah, we're on our way in twenty…Yeah, everybody's fine. We're a little muddy. Did you get beer? Okay, meet you there in a few. Bye." He rolled his head to watch Kyle. "I don't care who she's going out with, I think she's got it bad for you, man."

"Don't start this," Kyle warned. "It's nothing. Don't make this into a big scene at home for us. Okay?"

Glen grinned, shaking his head. "Whatever you say, boss."

Kyle drove in silence for a while.

"How do you do it?" Glen asked.

"What?"

"Work with her and keep it in your pants?"

Good that you didn't ask me this last summer, Kyle thought ruefully. Instead, he said, "You're depraved."

"Yeah, depraved, deprived, all of that. Chelsea's Vesuvius, getting ready to erupt, if you haven't noticed," Glen said studying him in the darkness, the occasional flash of oncoming headlights illuminating the two of them inside the Explorer.

"You know about women *erupting*, do you?" Amusement crept into Kyle's voice. It was unusual to have a serious discussion like this with Glen. And amazingly, his take on the situation was spot on.

"Yes, I do. You need to get a handle on this. Trust me."

Kyle came back in the house from emptying the trash, with Foscoe at his heels, and locked up for the night. He stepped across to the fireplace and shoveled through the dying embers, smothering what was left of the red coals. Flipping off the track lighting, Chelsea made one last sweep through the kitchen, wiping down the counters and the sink, depositing beer bottles in the recycling bucket below the sink. Foscoe wandered around as if lost without his boys tonight. Kyle leaned over to stroke his ears to comfort him. With a loud yawn, the dog finally settled in a soft thump at the end of the rug, right in front of the fireplace, where he usually kept them company on long autumn evenings. Chelsea was glad Abby and Glen had not stayed long, and had left soon after most of the pizza was consumed. Kyle had sent them on their way with the remainder of the beer and pizza, and the tension that was omnipresent in the room after the rescue.

No, the tension was still there, Chelsea thought reluctantly. She busied herself with taking inventory of the fridge for the grocery list and then checked the calendar on the refrigerator door. From the corner of her eye, she noticed Kyle had returned and was watching her as he leaned the small of his back into the kitchen counter by the sink, arms crossed, making his shoulders look enormous.

"Remember, the boys' soccer game is at nine in the morning," she said, referring to the calendar.

"I know," he said softly, watching her rake her fingers through her hair. She met his scorching blue eyes, knowing what would happen next, and felt her insides release, painfully, wanting him. "Come here a minute," he said. He took a step toward her, reaching for her hand and pulling her to his chest. Or so she thought.

"Let's talk, okay?" he said, pulling her behind him to the large chair beside the picture window they called the Christmas card window. In an instant, she was in his lap, engulfed in his sweatered arms, feeling his soft lips caressing her hair and then coming to rest on the scar on her cheekbone. *I like kissing it*, he'd said once before when she was healing from the accident. "Talk to me, baby. What's on your mind?"

There was no hiding from him now. She swallowed, collecting her thoughts, which had all been brought into the spotlight from the last few hours spent talking with Abby and Glen. She was unprepared for this invasion from him. Why was he asking now? They'd avoided the subject of Elise for months. She pulled her teeth across her bottom lip, looking up at him, and saw his eyes constrict with concern. "So much…" she said, and it was true. Her heart was pounding with all that had gone unsaid, tonight, at the beach, every day….She was still reeling from his rebuke about Elise at the winery, but there was more on her mind as well. *Stu might have ADHD and you don't agree. My mother is still worrying about Grandmother. Elise Masters drinking Moonlight with you and your dazzling smile. There is no baby. Maybe it's for the best. I love my job.* He held her face away from him so he could study her eyes in the lamplight.

"Then talk to me. You're angry...."

"Yes," she whispered, looking away from his penetrating blue eyes.

"Why? Is it because we didn't go to the restaurant, or because I went to help Elise?"

She made an indignant sound. Put that way, both choices sounded childish.

"It's certainly not about missing dinner out somewhere. And yes, it is about Elise. I don't know why she gets to me," she said, but she knew very well why Elise got to her. And she loathed being the jealous wife. She had been down this road before with Kyle. It seemed there would always be women falling all over her husband, with good reason, and she was going to have to learn to deal with it. After ten years, she'd hoped to be a bit farther along than she was.

"You shouldn't be angry," he said, stroking her hair and holding her face tenderly, his touch creating more painful arousal within her. She imagined what he had done tonight to comfort Elise. It would only take a look, his smile, a touch on her hand....

You can't tell me how to feel, she thought. "But she's beautiful and polished and provocative. I can't help it. You have to *look* at her...every day."

He looked surprised, and traced her lips with his thumb. "But she's not *you*, is she? I'm here with you now, tonight, and every night, wanting *you*. Flowers are beautiful, all of them, but I prefer pink roses by far over the rest. And you do, too, for the same sentimental reasons. You're my pink rose, Chelsea. Does that help you to put this all into perspective?" *Could he say anything sweeter?* His handsome face, framed by the tousled mass of sun-streaked hair, never failed to melt her at times like these, when he was so endearing.

Her lips lifted one corner at a time into a smile. She giggled, loving his metaphor.

"See, there's nothing to worry about," he said, giving her a pointed gaze.

"You always say that."

"I know. And it's always true. You should trust me. Do you? Trust me?"

"I…do."

"That's hardly convincing. What a hard sell you are. What do I have to do to show you?" he asked, trailing his fingers across her lips, her throat, ending inside her blouse where they rested on the swell of her chest. He pressed his forehead against hers, then kissed her with promise of more to come.

"I wish I could let you show me. I want you to show me, but it won't happen tonight," she said, sadness creeping into her voice.

"*Oh*," he said, understanding at once.

"I'm not pregnant…again."

He thought a moment, seeing the letdown in her eyes. He ran his fingers through her hair, pushing it back from her face. "Hmm! I can't imagine what we're doing wrong; can you?" he asked, kissing her scar again, then her lips with such tenderness it drew hot tears to her eyes. "Back to the drawing board, then, Mrs. Davis. In a few more days, that is. I was really looking forward to seducing you tonight." A grin began on one side of his face that did nothing to quell the desire building inside her.

He was so good at hiding his disappointment. It made her heart ache. "Then I guess we'll have to settle for a really hot make-out session and some serious cuddling," she said, trying to sound unaffected.

"Then I'll warn you, I might not be able to contain myself," he threatened, with a dark smile, scooping her up and carrying her into the bedroom.

Chapter 13

GOOD KNIGHT

Elise's usual Monday morning glow was not there; nor was the telltale laughter that assured Kyle that Michael Gilmer was doing things right. After their usual planning meeting, Frank had left for the Hayes property to supervise the pouring of the footings. After a long and arduous debate with Bruce and Sara Lynn Hayes, the building of their secondary residence had finally gotten underway. Sometimes, the most difficult clients were the ones they knew personally. Bruce and Sara Lynn just needed to learn to trust him. His patience had been tested to the limit with the two of them, but of course, he'd won, in the long run. His arsenal of charm, competence, and good sense had finally made them see things his way.

Kyle studied Elise as she began to close her iPad into its case. She was unusually pale this morning, and he was sure it had to do with her off-roading experience on Friday night. He was curious, but wary of her mandate to let her keep her personal life to herself. *Oh hell, why not just come out with it!* After all, he had rescued her. It would be impolite not to inquire whether she had made it home all right.

"So…did you make it to Radlers after all on Friday night?" There, he had avoided the use of Michael's name.

Looking surprised, she raked her fingers through her hair, noticing that her coffee cup was empty. Avoiding his eyes, she said, "Uh…no. I thought Lydia'd had enough drama for one night, so we drove through Wendy's and went home to get warm."

"Drama?" he let his question hang while she wondered how to respond.

"As you might imagine, Michael is not so much into children."

"Oh. But he hasn't run for the hills?"

She smirked, tucking a strand of hair behind her ear. "Oh, well, I don't think it will be long. At least I got a few nice dinners out of it." *And more, maybe, if the guy had a pulse, he thought.*

He raised an eyebrow and followed her into the kitchen, going for a coffee refill himself.

"Don't say it, okay?" she said, giving him a wild-eyed look. Here was vulnerability again, he thought, averting his eyes out of respect for her privacy.

"Say what? *I told you so?*"

"Yes!" she snapped.

"Okay," he said, amused this time, hoping she'd soon relax. He restrained himself from asking whatever it was that she saw in Michael Gilmer. Now was definitely not the time. They hadn't had a conversation like this in a long time, and he knew he would need to cut it off soon. At least he could take the attention off her. "How is Lydia doing? Hopefully not too traumatized by the whole incident," he said, sauntering into his office and taking a seat at his desk.

She leaned in the doorway, warming her hands with the cup, seemingly unaffected by his comment. "She's doing okay."

"How's school going for her?"

"It's…okay. That same little boy who threw the chair at her over the summer is in her class."

"No! They should have put him in the juvie jail for that!"

She laughed. *Finally!* "He's only seven years old!"

"Exactly my point. If he's this bad now, just think what he'll be like at eighteen!" He grinned at her, eliciting a slow, reluctant smile.

"Oh, he's a piece of work! He calls his teachers bitches."

"What?"

"Yes. They have a code name for it. His mother makes excuses for him and says he's really calling them birds because they call each other 'birds' when one of them gets testy."

He nodded. "I like it."

"He has ADHD, so it's something they have to work on constantly."

"Hmm. Stu might have that as well," he admitted, thinking Chelsea probably wouldn't like him discussing it with Elise. She tended to agree with Miss Payne, but he still wasn't convinced.

"How do you think that?" she asked, taking a step into the office and sitting in the chair across from his desk.

"He has trouble staying organized and finishing his work. Sometimes he can be very stubborn. He has difficulty dealing with things that have lots of steps."

"Sequential memory."

"Yeah," he said, this time the vulnerable one.

She tilted her head to one side, regarding him with knitted brows. "Has he thrown any chairs lately?"

He laughed, completely disarmed. "No. He has not thrown a chair. And I don't believe he's called his teacher a *bird* either."

"Well, if he has ADHD, I've never seen it. He seems very well-mannered and delightful. You've done a great job raising him, and Ty."

"Chelsea can take more than half the credit for that. She's a wonderful mother," he said, watching Elise's face bloom with color. She cast her eyes around and stood with her coffee, smoothing her skirt.

"I'll let you get to work. Way to go on getting the Hayes show on the road, by the way. Do you always get what you want?" she asked, lingering in the doorway.

He met her look straight on, rubbing the pen he held across his lower lip. "Yes."

She flushed under his look. "Then I'm glad you're the boss," she said, smiling at him. "I'm meeting Sara Lynn for lunch today, so we can go over a few more of the changes I've made."

"Excellent," he said, relieved that he'd have the kitchen table to himself for lunch. He was getting tired of eating at his desk in a pretended show of over-focused behavior. Then it dawned on him. *He was back in control.*

Kyle sat at the kitchen table with Chelsea and Stu, going over Stu's math assignment that had been due on Friday. He'd slipped up and forgotten about it, so they were going over the word problems before bedtime on a Sunday night. Kyle had an assignment as well, looking down at the form in front of him, and glancing enviously at Ty on the sofa by the fire, who was reading his latest library book. Thanksgiving was next week, so Chelsea had arranged to take a couple of days off to accompany her mother to South Carolina for some moral support while bringing her grandmother back home for the holiday. Plans to move her closer to home were in the works, so Liz and Tom had been combing through the local facilities.

Chelsea looked at the work sheet over Stu's shoulder, twirling a strand of hair around her finger, distracting Kyle from his task. "So, what operation are they asking for here? Look at your key words that you've underlined," Chelsea coached Stu, watching him as he read back over his work.

"*They have four baseball cards each,*" he read. "That means multiply."

"Exactly!" she said, looking at Kyle with a victorious smile. She watched Stu write out the problem on the paper, nodding as he had lined up the numbers correctly in the proper columns. "See, you really don't need my help at all, do you?" she said, but they both knew he'd be far from finished without her presence to encourage him and keep him on track. Kyle noticed the puffiness around her eyes from lack of sleep. The combination of the boys' soccer games, school, her work, her mother's state of mind, and running the household had begun to take its toll. It would be nice for her to have a break over the holiday.

He finished, looking over the form, and slid it across the table to her. She had filled out a behavior rating scale on Stu for his teacher, and Kyle had checked over it to see whether he agreed with her responses. She looked up in anticipation of his reaction. He tipped his head in the direction of the stairs.

"Boys, why don't you get your book bags together and head downstairs to get ready for bed," she said, glancing over Stu's math sheet. "Looks good, sweetie," she said with a wink. He took the paper and went to put it in his book bag. "Put it in your red folder, so you'll be sure Miss Payne gets it. I have some more things to put in there for her, too. Just leave your book bag right there."

"Okay," he said, following Ty downstairs.

"We'll be down in a bit, guys. Go ahead and start your showers," Kyle added.

"So what do you think?" Chelsea asked, picking up the form.

He shrugged. "I agree with most of the things you circled. I don't know how it will make him look. What does this mean, a pill, or something?"

"That would be up to the doctor. The information they're collecting is for us to take to Dr. Lucas, and then she can make a diagnosis. Even if Stu has ADHD, we don't have to medicate him. He's not even below grade level yet, but I don't want to see him struggle any more than he has to. He's starting to think of himself as a bad boy."

Kyle's eyes narrowed. "Who's telling him that? It's not us."

"No. It's not Miss Payne either. He just sees himself struggling to keep it together, and he notices that she has to redirect him all the time. And you know he compares himself to Ty. He may be better at sports, but he wants to be a good student like Ty. Miss Payne feels bad for him."

"Maybe she's not firm enough. He should have had Mrs. Dixon."

"Oh, honey, you know they couldn't both be in the same class. And Miss Payne *is* a good teacher. She really is doing all kinds of things to help him stay on task."

Kyle's phone vibrated in his pocket and he answered. "Hey, Glen. What's up?" He listened for a moment and she saw his eyes flash before he shot up from the table. "Shit! When did this happen? No…are they okay? Yeah…yeah, I can come over there. Is anyone else around? What about Michael; has he been contacted?" His voice was urgent, frightened almost as he paced the kitchen floor.

Chelsea's heart sank. *Here we go again.* Something was going on with Elise and he was frantic.

"Okay. I'm on my way," he said, ending the call.

"What happened?"

"Elise surprised an intruder at her apartment tonight when she got home from a movie with Lydia."

"Oh, no! Is she all right? What about Lydia?"

"Whoever it was punched Elise in the face and knocked her down on the sidewalk when he was coming out the door. She's okay, just shaken up. Lydia saw the whole thing and is scared. The door was kicked in so they can't stay there tonight." He looked at her briefly, not asking the obvious question. "I'm going over there. Glen's there, working the case."

Her voice shook when she asked, "Did she ask for you?"

He looked pained. "No. But Glen thinks I should come. He has some questions."

They looked at each other for several moments.

"*Go then,*" she said. He looked torn. "No, it's fine. I'll get the boys in the bathtub and put them to bed."

"I won't be long."

A smile began at the corners of her mouth. "That's starting to be a refrain. Look...if she needs a place to stay, they can come here. She and Lydia can stay here," she felt herself saying.

"I'm sure that won't be necessary," he said, looking anything but sure.

"I'll wait up," she said, standing and giving a little shrug.

"Okay. I'll call you." He took her in his arms and kissed her forehead before walking out the door.

Blue lights swirled in the darkness as he pulled up in front of Elise's apartment. Two patrol cars and an unmarked car were parked in front. He leapt from his Explorer and bounded up over the curb. Living on the first floor had been necessary for Lydia's impairments, but certainly not the safest place to live. An officer walked back inside, as Kyle stepped through the door. Another officer stopped him, asking, "Can I help you?"

"I'm Kyle Davis. I was called here by Glen Dunham," he said as Glen appeared at the door.

"Yes," the officer said, looking for Glen.

"Dougherty, this is Ms. Masters' employer, and a friend," Glen said, giving Kyle entrance to the apartment. "This is Detective Browning." He nodded to the detective, who was making notes on a pad in a chair across the room. It was cold inside with all the police's comings and goings, plus the door having been kicked open at the deadbolt so it wouldn't stay closed. Kyle looked beyond Glen to see Elise sitting on the sofa's edge, holding an ice pack to her face, with Lydia in her lap, answering questions. Her mouth dropped open when she saw Kyle, and then she glared at Glen.

"Did you call him?" she asked, her voice sharp but still shaky.

"Yeah, he did," said Kyle, beside her on the sofa in two or three steps. Seeing the ugly red blotch on her face undid him. "You were *hit*?" he asked, his voice registering the shock of what he already knew had happened to her. His hand instinctively went to hers, but he withdrew it quickly under the detective's scrutiny. She didn't seem to notice, her attention divided between the detective and Lydia, who was clutching Pink Bunny in her right arm, and holding fast to Elise with her left.

"Yes. The asshole hit me and knocked me to the ground on his way out my front door," she said vehemently, unconcerned with Lydia's presence at the moment. He looked at Lydia, who wasn't budging from her mother's arms. She looked at him with eyes as wide as dinner plates.

"Hi, Lydia. Are you okay?" he asked her, trying to keep a soothing tone to his voice. She looked scared to death, but she watched him intently, talking to her mother.

"Did you hit your head?" he asked Elise, eyes roving over her, noticing a bandage on her arm above her elbow, remembering not to touch her again.

"No, but I can say I saw plenty of stars. I wanted to throw up again, too. This is starting to become habit-forming," she muttered, her knees jiggling Lydia nervously.

"Where do you hurt? Is Lydia okay?"

"Other than being wrenched around from getting thrown on the ground, I'm fine; we're both fine," she said, moving her head and shoulders. "Thank God, Lydia wasn't hurt. He took my *TV*. You've seen it. Isn't that ridiculous? He was an idiot, Kyle. Do you know how much most of these antiques are worth? And that painting? He took my stupid TV!" she said, trying to keep her voice from breaking, and scaring Lydia. He noticed the detective sitting in the chair across from Elise, writing notes as he studied Kyle, and waiting patiently for them to conclude their conversation.

"You have renters' insurance?" Kyle asked quickly, and she nodded.

"Ms. Masters, I have a few more questions. Uh, Mr. Davis, where were you this evening?" the detective asked.

"Really? I was at home with my family. You can call my wife. 828-509-8998," Kyle said, his eyes going a stormy blue.

"Just ruling you out, sir. Is that your vehicle outside, the black Explorer?"

"Yes, and my wife drives a white Subaru," he responded coolly, making the detective return an indulgent look, accompanied by one cocked eyebrow.

"Ms. Masters, they're calling your property management company right now to see when they'll have someone out here to repair your door. Hopefully, it will be tomorrow, but I'd suggest you spend the night somewhere else. We'll place one of our officers here tonight to watch your apartment, but it's your call, whether or not you're up to staying here."

"Oh, of course," Elise said softly, her face as pale as Kyle had ever seen it.

"You can come home with me. Stay at our house," he said quietly, aware that the detective was listening.

Elise looked up at him, eyes searching his, her lips parting in surprise. "Oh. No, I couldn't do that. Not a good idea...."

"There's plenty of room, and Chelsea and I want you and Lydia to come. For the night. Until your door gets fixed," he said, but she regarded him warily.

"There's a Hampton Inn a few blocks from here. It will do just fine," she said, as if holding herself together, some color returning to her face, and returning her attention to the detective.

Glen motioned to Kyle to come outside. When they were clear of the others, he raised his notepad and spoke in a low voice. "Elise didn't recognize the man who hit her, but she got a look at the vehicle he left in. It was an older model black pickup truck."

Kyle stared at Glen, feeling his eyes grow cold. "The same truck that ran her off the road?"

"That's what we're thinking, but we don't know that for sure. She said she saw some kind of pirate decal on the rear window before she hit the ground. This may not be a coincidence. Detective Browning knows all this, but I wanted to get your take on it. There's an APB out for a black pickup as we speak."

"Jeez, no wonder she's so rattled."

"You got that right. Who would want to do this to her?"

"I can't imagine anyone wanting to hurt her."

"Does she have anybody—old boyfriends—anybody you think would be looking for her for some weird reason? Anybody she's mentioned she might be afraid of?"

"No. Nobody like that."

"Has she mentioned being in any kind of financial trouble?"

"Who isn't these days? But no, she hasn't said anything."

"Has she gotten any strange calls at work, or anything out of the ordinary?"

"Not that I know of. Were you able to contact Michael?" Kyle asked, watching Glen scribble in the notepad. He must be moving up in the process, Kyle thought.

"Yeah. He said he would come over as soon as he could get away from the pub. What does he drive?"

"Surely you don't think he'd show up here in the getaway car, do you? I mean, I'm no detective, but shit!"

Glen shrugged. "*Just ruling him out, sir.* What does he normally drive?"

"I've seen him in a silver Porsche—an old Boxster."

"Hmm, nice," Glen said, making a note. "So are you and Michael going to fight over who gets to take her home?"

Kyle regarded him with narrowed eyes. "Is that why you called me? To make us all feel uncomfortable?"

"Nah, I thought you'd want to be here. And after the last incident, what if Michael didn't show his sorry ass? She needs somebody."

"Fine, but does it seem to you like *she* doesn't want me here?"

"Yeah, maybe, but I thought you'd like to know about the black pickup. Besides, you'd have been mad if I hadn't called. And I had questions for you."

"My *alibi*? Are you fucking kidding me? Maybe you should follow up on Frank too while you're at it," Kyle scoffed.

"Hey, *easy!* That was Browning's question, not mine. Look; everyone's on edge. It's not surprising after what's happened. I wanted to know if she's scared of someone. You'd be the one to know."

Kyle studied him a moment, feeling his jaw muscle tensing, and ran a hand through his hair. He went back in the room where he found Lydia standing beside Elise as she talked on the phone. "Hey, Lydia," he whispered, squatting down and smiling at her, making her offer up her shy smile. She took his offered hand and he squeezed hers, so tiny in his. "Don't be scared. Mommy's safe. You're safe."

"All right, that's done," said Elise, hanging up the phone. "I'm checking into the Hampton as soon as they're done with me here. I'm going to pack some clothes for us."

"Wha—*okay*. At least take tomorrow off," Kyle said, striding after her into her bedroom.

"Why, so I can sit around and stew about all this? About how somebody in a black truck is out to get me? I'd so much rather come to work and do something productive," she muttered out of Lydia's hearing. The red mark on her face was larger than he'd thought, and it was swelling without the ice pack.

"Well, see how you feel. Don't push it, okay?" he said, watching her toss a nightgown, bra, and lacy panties into a small suitcase that lay open on her bed. She rummaged through her closet, taking out a pair of pants and a sweater and throwing them over her arm, picking up the tan wedge heels and tossing it all into the bag.

"We'll see. Lydia should go to school anyway. It will be much more stimulating for her there than sitting around in some boring old hotel room."

"Have you called your parents? Jeez, have you guys even eaten anything?" he asked, raking a hand through his hair.

"Kyle! Stop fussing over me like a mother hen," she said, moving on to Lydia's room, and pulling clothes from her drawers. "We are fine," she laughed apologetically, folding Lydia's clothing over her arm. A quick stop in the bathroom to collect a bag of toiletries and several pull-up diapers finished her packing, and she zipped the suitcase with a flourish.

He went into her bathroom, noticing a bottle of pain reliever on the counter. "Have you taken anything for your face?" She shook her head. He opened the bottle and handed her two pills, with a glass of water. He watched her swallow the pills and took back the empty glass.

"Thank you," she said with a sigh, looking at him resignedly, wiping water from her mouth with the back of her hand.

"Look, if you're scared, come home with me," he said softly. She gazed up at him, silent. "Don't spend the money," he added with a shrug.

A new voice came through the door. Kyle recognized Michael's voice instantly. Rolling his eyes, he watched as she waited for him to pass through the police barricade and the questions. She dragged the suitcase off her bed and proceeded to the living room. "Are we done, Lieutenant? I'd like to head on out if that's okay," she said, picking up the ice pack and placing it against her face again.

Detective Browning nodded. "Sure, you can leave. Can we reach you on your cell in case we have news?"

"Yeah, that's fine. I have my charger. Thanks."

Michael walked up to her and wrapped her in a careful hug, looking surprised to see Kyle. "*Elise!* Oh, my God! Are you all right, baby? God, what *happened to you?*" he asked as she pulled away from him, allowing him to inspect her bruised face and the bandage on her arm. An intimate look passed between them, and then her irritation returned.

"I'm fine. Look; I've been robbed, knocked on my ass; I'm tired and pissed off, so I'm taking Lydia to the Hampton Inn right now, okay, guys?" she said, taking Lydia's hand and rubbing her shoulders.

"No, stay with me," Michael insisted, taking her in his arms again, glancing at Lydia, whose face was set in a grim line, *trying to be brave*, Kyle thought.

"I don't think so, Michael. Lydia's tired. *I'm* tired," she said convincingly, pushing her hair back from her face, watching him, truly crestfallen at her refusal. "But thanks just the same. You didn't have to come by."

"You didn't think I'd come?" he said incredulously. "Seriously? I came as soon as I could get away. Anyway, it's *Sunday*," he said, stroking her hair, a hint of passion in his voice, as he glanced at Kyle. "Do they know who did it? What'd they take?"

She sighed. "I need to wear a frickin' sign around my neck. He took my TV, but I arrived before anything else was taken. Lucky for me, I guess. Now…I'm sorry if this sounds impolite, but it's been a *really* long day, so Lydia and I are going," she said, getting her purse and fishing out her keys.

"Let me walk you to your car, at least," Michael protested, looking hurt, and taking her suitcase. Kyle glared at him.

"Shouldn't you at least follow her over there and make sure she gets settled in properly?" he said icily.

"*Obviously*," Michael growled back, making Elise shake her head, impatient with their pissing match.

"Okay. Thanks for everything, Glen," she said with a tight smile. "I guess your friends here will be keeping an eye on the place?"

Glen nodded. "One of us will call you as soon as your door is fixed and we think it's safe for you to come back."

"Okay. Bye, Kyle. And thanks for coming over to check on us. That was really sweet. I'll see you in the morning," she said, the sincerity in her voice making Michael cut a sharp glance toward Kyle. She took Lydia's hand and followed Michael out the front door. She glanced back at him once more.

"Sleep well," he said, watching Michael follow her out the door. He pulled his phone from his pocket to tell Chelsea there would be no house guests tonight.

He found her standing in the bedroom in her camisole and panties, brushing her hair, and watching the ten o'clock news.

"Oh! You scared me!" she cried, jumping, as he took off his jacket and laid it across the bench at the end of their bed.

"I'm sorry. You didn't hear me drive up and unlock the door?"

"I guess not. I was brushing my teeth. How's Elise?"

"Jumpy, like you…and really pissed off. She went to the Hampton Inn to spend the night."

"Don't tell me Michael didn't show up again."

"Oh, he was there all right," he said, going to her, and pulling her into his arms; he breathed deeply into her hair, and gave her lips a light kiss. "He was pretty upset, but she didn't want anything to do with him, or me for that matter. He wanted them to go home with him, but she'd already booked a room and wanted to get out of her apartment. I can't say I blame her."

"Me neither. So do you think he really has feelings for her?"

"It appears that way. I don't think she knows where she stands with him, though."

"Because of Lydia?"

"Yeah. He's not into children."

"No, he's not," she said. Kyle watched her click off the TV and rub lotion into her hands. She pulled down the covers and slipped into the bed, resting her head on her hands as she watched him move about their bedroom.

"How was Glen? Working his first case as a detective...."

"Actually, he was pretty fucking annoying." From his tone, she let it go.

"There was nothing on the news about what happened."

"Hmm. Maybe it will hit tomorrow." Slowly he peeled off his clothes, down to his boxers, leisurely folding his jeans and sweater, and tossing his shirt into the hamper, well aware of her eyes on him. He hung his jacket in the closet and went into the bathroom to brush his teeth. She continued to watch him as he walked to the bed and turned off the lamp, leaving him lit only in moonlight. Slowly, he dropped his boxers to the floor, then picked them up and sling-shot them into the closet.

"So, what do you want to do now, Mrs. Davis?" he asked, trying to give her his most smoldering look.

"Be seduced," she tried to say seriously, unable to suppress the grin spreading across her face.

He tipped his head to the side, a lopsided smile beginning, and then climbed in beside her, taking her hungrily into his arms. "I think that can be arranged!"

Chapter 14

DECEIT

Kyle stared at the basket. Twice now he'd lied. He'd mentioned to Frank that Chelsea was out of town tonight and would be bringing her grandmother back from South Carolina with Liz tomorrow, the day before Thanksgiving. Elise had jumped on the opportunity to invite him and the twins out for pizza with her and Lydia. So he'd lied. Suddenly, they were batching it with Tom, but he knew full well that Tom would be eating dinner with Jay and Lauren. He knew Chelsea wouldn't like the idea of him hanging with Elise while she was gone. Hell, she wouldn't like the basket either, but it was a really sweet gesture on Elise's part. Maybe he and the boys could devour the bear claws and he could give the wine away. Moonlight was no longer a favorite of Chelsea's, as he so clearly remembered. He put the bottle in the refrigerator, thinking he'd handle it later.

He looked at the card again. She'd made it by printing and cutting out a picture of a suit of armor off the Internet and gluing it onto a blank card. The handwritten message on the inside had read simply, *Thanks yet again for your kindness, Elise.* She'd said the basket was for Chelsea and him, but he couldn't imagine showing his wife this card. Still, it was a very thoughtful gesture, and he'd remembered the endearing expression on her face that even Frank had noticed. So many dilemmas. *And this is how you stay in control?* He sighed as the boys clunked through the front door with Foscoe.

"Go wash your hands, guys, and we'll eat," he said as they deposited their book bags at the top of the stairs. Homework would be next after dinner at the kitchen table. He emptied the bag of hamburgers and fries he'd picked up on the way home from school.

"Last night of homework ever! Woo-hoo!" said Stu, grinning, his dimples appearing in his cheeks, making Kyle laugh.

"Well, for five days—but I'll take it," laughed Ty.

"Ooh! Are these *bear claws*?" asked Stu, supporting himself on his elbows and looking into the basket.

"Yep. We can have them for breakfast in the morning."

"Cool! Who's this card for?" Ty asked, pulling the card from the envelope.

"That's for Mommy and me, from Ms. Masters," said Kyle, wishing he had put it somewhere else.

"Thanks for what?" Ty asked, his big blue eyes questioning.

"You remember; the other night when I went over there to check on them after someone broke into their apartment."

"Oh, yeah. Did the cops catch those guys?"

"No, they didn't," said Kyle, thinking the guy in the black pickup was probably long gone. Elise was resigned to the idea the black trucks had just been a coincidence. She had been much happier after coming to that conclusion and even contrite after her post-robbery jitters had caused her to be so rude that night. He wondered how she had made it up to Michael.

"Hey, Daddy, can I have this card?" Ty asked, his eyes lighting up at the picture of the knight's armor.

"Sure—"

"*Foscoe, no!*" Stu yelled, and they turned their attention to the dog, who had snagged a glove and was chewing on it by the fireplace.

"Get that from him, would you? And you guys go wash up for dinner," Kyle reminded them, moving the basket of bear claws to the counter. Elise had remembered those from the first day they'd interviewed her in the office. She'd watched him eyeing them as she'd answered Frank's questions. The girl didn't forget anything. *Behave yourself!* Stacie had warned him the last time he saw her before they'd left the beach last summer. She always said stuff like that to him, but that time had seemed different. It was the way she'd squeezed his chin in her hand like a vice. He'd guessed the girls had been talking. He was trying desperately to behave. But he wasn't the one doing anything, not now at least. He had made good on his promise to himself to turn off his feelings toward Elise, but she was bringing unexpected nuances to the table. He sighed again as the twins appeared, wiping their hands on their pants as he poured three glasses of milk.

"Can we shoot pool after supper, Daddy?" asked Stu.

"Yeah, after you finish your homework," Kyle reminded him.

"I did most of it at ACES," Stu said, referring to their afterschool program.

"Good. We'll check over it, then," he said, knowing that Ty's would be finished already, and gave him a subtle wink. He thought about the behavior rating scale and whatever Miss Payne had been doing for Stu. He seemed to like school more than ever this year, ironically. Maybe Miss Payne wasn't so bad.

"How do you like Miss Payne, Stu?"

"She rocks!" he said, grinning, his mouth full of hamburger. Ty looked at him and laughed. It was not lost on him either that Stu liked school this year, except for doing homework. "She loves me," Stu said earnestly, making Kyle's heart feel heavy at once.

"I love you, too," he said. "Both of you." It was something he told them a lot. Something he hadn't heard from his father when he was a kid. That wouldn't do for his family. Things would be different. He would make sure they knew it.

"I *know*," Stu said impatiently. Good. He knew. Mission accomplished, Kyle thought, squashing his hamburger wrapper. Ty smiled quietly.

"You up for pool too, Ty?" he asked, eating his last French fry.

"Sure," he said, draining his glass of milk.

"Then let's clean this up and check that homework."

He was in deep doo-doo now, he thought, aware of Chelsea seething beside him at the Thanksgiving table as Liz poured them glasses of the forgotten bottle of Moonlight after Tom had said the blessing. Chelsea had discovered not only the basket and bottle of wine, but the card in Ty's room, so Kyle had come clean and offered her the bear claw he'd saved for her. At first, she had seemed conflicted, touched by Elise's offering of thanks, directed toward both of them, then ashamed for the unmistakable jealousy that had reared its ugly head after seeing the card. There was anger at him as well, for forgetting to mention it, as if he'd been hiding it. As usual, she had kept her feelings inside, but there was no getting around it. His wife was *pissed*.

On cue, Grandmother was offering up one of her distractions; it made him cringe that he welcomed what was coming out of her mouth, directed at Chelsea this time.

"Elizabeth, when are you ever going to cut your hair? You look like a teenager still!"

The heat that radiated off his wife was about to blister him. "I'm *Chelsea*, Grandmother," she said evenly as everyone at the table made a face. Grandmother blinked several times, waiting for an answer.

"She'll never cut it on my watch. Her husband loves her long hair!" he said to Grandmother, giving her his most beguiling grin, holding her eyes until she shrugged, disarmed. He wanted to go on, telling her how he loved the way Chelsea's hair hung over his face when she made love on top of him, but he kept the words to himself. He had confused Grandmother just the same.

"Who's her husband? Oh. Well, whatever…" she said, tucking into the turkey that Tom had cut up for her.

Chelsea blinked and shot him an appreciative glance, blushing at the look he returned. He placed his hand on her leg under the table and skimmed it up her thigh, making her squirm and smile. *Whatever it takes to make you see, baby*, he thought. Eyes rolled and throats were cleared as the awkward Grandmother moment passed. Conversation went on around them, and Kyle could hear the kids talking and laughing from where they ate in the kitchen, safe for now from Grandmother's comments.

On his right, Charley, Chelsea's sister, sent furtive glances around the table, irritated at their grandmother's behavior as well. "As if *her* hair has *ever been coiffed!*" she muttered under her breath, knowing Grandmother wouldn't hear since she refused to wear her hearing aids. If the woman started on the children, it would be all out war, he thought, remembering previous holiday dinners. Jay would keep her in line, if the girls didn't pounce on her first. "Let's set her out on the front porch with a cocktail for the rest of the mountain to see. Knock her right on her ass!" Charley whispered viciously, making him almost choke on his turkey and dressing. "And you two *are* behaving like teenagers, by the way," she hissed, grinning, knowing what his hand was doing, forever fascinated by watching Kyle and Chelsea interact. Kyle glanced over in time to see Steve, Charley's husband, grinning like a Cheshire cat and shaking his head.

"Kyle, Charley really liked what Elise did to my office and the front parlor," Liz said pointedly, to admonish her oldest child.

"Oh, good!" said Kyle, glad the conversation was shifting, yet aware that Chelsea might not like the topic.

"It's beautiful! I love the light blues and yellows. It's so you. When did you have that done?" asked Charley, ignoring Chelsea's raised eyebrows.

"Elise helped me with the ideas. I just got it all together last month. I've really enjoyed giving your father's office back to him," Liz said, trying to include Grandmother, and smiled at Tom. Kyle glanced at Chelsea again as the reference to Elise made her simmer.

"What day is it we're supposed to go over and christen the new B and B?" asked Tom, a wary expression on his face.

"Tuesday at five," Kyle responded, feeling his wife bubble over beside him. He reached for her leg again, soothing her so she could eat.

"What B and B?" asked Charley.

"Marcus Gilmer is opening a new place in Blowing Rock," Jay began. "Dad and Kyle have been renovating it."

"Oh," said Charley, looking around the table for reaction. She'd heard the stories about Marcus and Michael. "Those guys haven't been bugging you all about buying our house lately, have they?"

"No," said Tom. "Kyle's been keeping them in check for us," he said, winking at Kyle from the head of the table.

"I'd like to see what Elise has done with the interior design in there," said Liz. "She's very talented."

"What happened to Faith?" Charley asked, wiping her mouth with her napkin.

"She left us for her grandchildren," said Kyle.

"Oh! I bet you miss her," Charley said, looking around again.

"Yeah. I really do," Kyle replied, giving her a long earnest look that made her nod and return to her sweet potatoes.

"I can hardly hear what you all are saying with the children making all that *racket* in there!" Grandmother complained. "Is that Stu or Ty making all that noise?" she asked, as they listened to the laughter coming from the kids' table in the kitchen. *How did she remember their names and not know Chelsea?* Chelsea was ready for spontaneous combustion at this comment.

"I think it's a combination of all of them, Mother. It's nice to hear them enjoying themselves. They rarely get together like this," said Liz.

"Well, then the rest of you should speak up. People don't *enunciate* the way they used to. I find it very annoying!" she said, taking a sip of her wine.

"Oh. My. God," said Charley under her breath. Kyle could feel her foot tapping under the table. Several of them were laughing. Lauren, Jay's wife, had yet to say a word, staying purposefully out of the line of fire.

"Liz, may I have some more of your delicious dressing and gravy?" Kyle asked. Liz picked up the bowl and passed it to Chelsea. "Is this your recipe, Grandmother?" he asked to keep the conversation on something civil until it was time for the pumpkin pie. He'd be glad to carry her out to the porch and give her a cocktail! *A double*, he thought, giving Chelsea a wink and offering her the bowl before he helped himself. She shook her head, eyes locking with his.

"Oh, lord, no, honey. I always made my dressing with oysters. This must be what's her name's recipe." *Meaning Kitty.* The table went silent.

"Well, Mom, it sure is good! Pass that over here, will you?" Jay said, looking from Liz, whose eyes were lowered, to Kyle. He noticed that most of the family's plates were cleaned, and it was almost time to farm Grandmother out to the porch, or more realistically, in front of the fireplace where she'd be subjected to the series of football games they were set to watch. The men would clean up, except for the china and crystal that Charley and Chelsea would handle.

"Yes," Tom said, looking evenly at Grandmother. "I've always loved Elizabeth's cooking. You can tell," he said, patting his stomach. Then to Liz, he smiled broadly and said, "And sugar, you've outdone yourself once again. This is quite a feast!"

"Here, here!" said Steve, leading the charge to raise their glasses and toast his mother-in-law.

"Yes, thank you, Liz, for a wonderful dinner. Happy Thanksgiving," Kyle said, beaming at Liz, and tightening his hold on Chelsea's thigh.

For an afternoon in November, the sky was a brilliant shade of blue. *Cerulean*, Chelsea thought, as she and Kyle walked up the steps to the Snow Drop Inn Bed and Breakfast. The air was crisp and cold with the promise of winter around the corner. Chelsea felt him sweep her hand into his. She'd dressed up a bit more than usual that day, with slim black pants and boots, a feminine blouse and scarf underneath her coat.

"Cold?" he asked, tucking her hand under his arm, and pulling her a little closer as she nodded, enjoying his warmth. "You're going to love it, Chels. Look at the landscaping before we go in. Your dad's handiwork, finished just in time for the winter." His excitement was contagious, the way it usually was when he took her to see the completion of his projects. Feeling a little burst of pride already, she took in the newly refurbished stone walkway and steps, as well as the manicured shrubbery around the front of the house, and the neat parking lot to the side where they had parked their car. They entered the doorway, greeted first by the smell of new wood, paint, carpet, and fabrics, all the smells of a new house, blended with a vintage charm that was immediately appealing. They stepped inside, onto a lush patterned carpet. Kyle took her coat and hung it with his on a coat tree in the foyer. Her parents were already there, chatting amiably with Marcus Gilmer by the gas logs in the fireplace. The mantle was stunning, and decorated with candles and swags of lighted greenery. Chelsea's eyes took in the décor. Subtle hues of deep reds and greens, in patterns of berries and foliage on cream and warmed with accents of pale yellows, lent a Christmassy feel, but could also work as a cooling palette for the summertime. Antique brass and painted black fixtures and frames added an elegant touch, she thought, as her eyes flickered over the furnishings and accents. *Was that a snake lamp? How odd.* A Christmas tree stood decorated in the corner, lit with large vintage colored lights, where it could be seen by passersby.

"Well, hello! Welcome to the *Snow Drop!*" Marcus said, extending his arm to wrap Chelsea into a large bear hug. "Chelsea, you look lovely as always! Hi, Kyle," he said warmly, grasping Kyle's hand in a firm shake. "You done good!" he exclaimed, slapping Kyle on the back.

"Hi, Marcus," Kyle said, grinning, pleased and proud of their latest project. They went to Liz and Tom to give them hugs as Elise entered from the kitchen, elegant in a taupe sweater and a long black skirt. She carried a tray of appetizers that she placed on the sideboard, where a bucket of champagne sat with glasses waiting. Pink Depression glass champagne glasses and dessert plates glistened in the lamp light on a tatted dresser scarf covering the sideboard, reminding Chelsea of Kitty's treasures at home.

"Oh, Marcus, I'm so impressed!" Chelsea said, almost liking the man who was grinning at her from ear-to-ear.

"Your husband did all this. And Frank and Elise, of course," he said, gesturing behind her. "And then I guess you saw what your daddy did outside. The whole thing is outstanding and has exceeded my expectations."

"Chelsea, hello!" Elise said, her usual aloof expression gone at once, embracing Chelsea. "Hi, Kyle," she said to him from across the room.

"Hi, Elise. This is beautiful! It's so warm and inviting," said Chelsea, a twinge of envy tugging at her, knowing that her husband and this woman had put their heart and souls into transforming this lovely home from what it was.

"Thank you! Come and look at the before-and-after pictures," she said, leading Chelsea to the dining room where a display of pictures was attractively set on the round mahogany tabletop. Chelsea felt Elise's eyes on her as she studied the pictures Kyle had taken, suddenly wondering whether Michael would be joining them.

"Chelsea, I wanted to thank you personally for offering to let Lydia and me stay with you the night of the robbery. I was so agitated I couldn't even think straight. I thought it would just be best if Lydia and I had some time to ourselves...."

As Elise spoke, Chelsea noticed the slight discoloration on her left cheek that she'd covered as best she could with makeup. Her stomach lurched, imagining what they'd been through.

"Oh. Of course! I'm glad you're okay, Elise. I understand completely. And thank you for the gift basket. That was very sweet of you," Chelsea said, thinking of the card and what it implied about Kyle, her knight in shining armor. *Please!* "Will Michael be joining us tonight?"

Elise's eyes froze for a split second and she looked away, saying, "No. He's working tonight. He's not an investor in this business anyway," she said, offering the impassive face again. "Oh, here's Frank and Faith." The two entered, loudly and enthusiastically greeting everyone.

"Champagne, everyone!" Marcus commanded and began pouring as Elise handed around the glasses. "I'd like to say I've never had such pleasure developing a property as I've had working with all of you on this one. You are a wonderful team, and I hope we'll work together again. To the Snow Drop!" Marcus said, lifting his glass as the others toasted with him. "Let us give you the tour, and then come and have a little snack before you go. And don't forget to take a peek at the before-and-after pictures so you can fully appreciate what you've all accomplished. We have our first guests arriving in two weeks—my sister and her family for a sort of *soft opening*," he laughed.

"You've been busy then, getting your licenses together," Faith commented.

Marcus winked at her. "You just gotta know the right people, honey."

"Oh, I'm sure you do!" she said, making Tom and Kyle share raised eyebrows over their champagne.

"Who's your chef?" Faith went on, and they continued their discussion as he led the group into the kitchen. Chelsea followed, listening to Kyle and Elise's quiet conversation behind her.

"Where's Michael?" he asked, his voice low.

"He's not coming," she replied, her voice trembling slightly. "No, it's okay. I'll tell you later."

Chelsea turned, seeing Kyle looking inquisitively at Elise, his hand in his slacks pocket.

"Oh, I just *love* what you've done in this kitchen, Elise! Was all the vintage hardware here already?" exclaimed Faith.

"Some of the pieces were here. But I shopped for a lot of it, mostly the accessories," she said. Chelsea noticed a small chandelier with knobby glass globes and different sizes of glass apothecary jars on the counters along with a variety of old aluminum serving trays and more Depression glass showing through the cabinet doors.

"She's been on the hunt for months, since we started this project," Kyle said.

"This reminds me of an old French kitchen with the white marble and antique white finish on these cabinets. And look at this leaded glass in the doors! Oh! I could just move right in!" Faith gushed, giving Elise's arm a squeeze. "What a team you all have made!" The four of them beamed with pleasure as Chelsea watched Elise shoot Kyle a glance of admiration he didn't see.

"Oh! And honey, Frank told me about your *robbery*!" Faith continued as Elise's face fell. "I'm so sorry! Are you and Lydia okay?" *Not the best time or place,* Chelsea thought, feeling sorry for Elise.

Chelsea held Kyle back as the rest of the group went upstairs.

"What's going on with Elise?"

"I'm not sure," he said. "The police detective on her case called today and said they have no leads, which kinda shook her up. That and the fact that Michael was supposed to be here tonight and he hasn't shown up yet."

"*Oh!* She told me he was working."

"I know," he said uneasily, his hand at the small of her back, guiding her through the dining room until they caught up with the group at the top of the carpeted stairs, where Frank was showing off the new en suite bathrooms, making the place a bona fide B and B. Each bedroom was painted a different color, using the same hues of red, green, and yellow, and was named after a different flower: Amaryllis, Laurel, Jonquil, and muted purple for the Iris room. As they passed the others, now descending from the third floor, Chelsea gasped when she saw that the entire floor was comprised of the honeymoon suite. The Snow Drop suite was lovely, decorated in varying textures and shades of cream, white and taupe. Chelsea lingered in the intimate suite, gazing at the small marble fireplace in the corner, the antique dresser, and a comfy overstuffed loveseat and chairs with a coffee table made from an old window, topped with paper whites. The large bed was particularly inviting.

"This room was designed at my request. Maybe we'll come and stay here for our next celebration, Mrs. Davis. Would you like that?" he whispered suggestively in her ear, making her shiver. She nodded and swallowed, unable to speak. Faith could never have envisioned all these details, without having the eye for the eclectic mix of antiques and modern pieces that Elise obviously had. The art alone was mesmerizing. Kyle's eyes were shining. This house had truly been a labor of love between the two of them. *How could she be in this room with him, knowing they'd discussed their passions and turned their fantasies into reality together?* The boudoir collaboration's intimacy took her breath away. But the look he was sending her meant that he'd done it for her.

He continued to seek her approval with his eyes, waiting for her to speak. "Do you want to see the bathroom? The shower is big enough for two, and there's an old claw-footed bathtub that's surprisingly large," he explained, an alluring smile beginning on his lips. Realizing she was still unsure, he continued, "This was supposed to be a surprise for you. I hope you like it." *Was he holding his breath?* She smiled up at him, understanding what all of his pent up excitement had been about on the drive over. This was for *her*, not Elise, even though Elise had had a hand in the creation of this lovely house, and particularly this room, but it was Kyle's tongue-in-cheek way of turning Marcus Gilmer's project into something they could treasure privately. It warmed her heart to think her husband was so delightfully devious! A laugh bubbled over as she allowed him to lead her by the hand into the bathroom.

"See?" he asked, standing behind her and circling an arm around her waist. "Part of the deal is that I get to use this room with you whenever we want, when it's not booked, that is. So, what do you think?" he asked, nuzzling into her neck and breathing deeply.

"I think it's perfect. You're amazing. Let's come on a special night."

"We'll do it soon then," he said, kissing the nape of her neck.

It was an unmistakable sound, sniffling, a small gasp, and then sniffling again. Elise Masters was *crying*, Kyle thought, sitting at his computer and turning down his music so he could hear. Frank was gone for the day, and she was packing up to go home, but she was definitely crying, something he had never witnessed. He stood slowly and waited at his doorway, hoping he was wrong, but the sniffling went on as he heard her putting on her coat. He walked through the gathering room to her office and poked his head in the doorway.

"You okay?"

She jumped. "Oh! I thought you were still working," she said, quickly wiping her tears and reaching for her bag.

"What's wrong, Elise?" he asked as the dam broke and her tears turned to sobs. Her face began to crumble and she raised her hands to hide her meltdown.

Shit! He took an awkward step forward and reached out his arm. It was what he would do if one of the boys were upset, or Faith, or anyone for that matter. When people were in pain, you hugged them. After a moment of hesitation, she was in his arms, and he felt wet tears on the side of his neck as her arms wrapped around his back, her hands clutching his shoulders. She had been quiet all day, not forthcoming about Michael's absence at the Snow Drop last night. All she had asked him was whether Chelsea had liked the boudoir, and she'd been pleased when he'd replied that she had. She had withdrawn to her office and immersed herself in her work, so he hadn't pressed. It was part of the deal. Still, right now she was losing it and nowhere near ready to release him so he could go home. *Damn!* He placed a hand on her back and rubbed it to try to calm her down.

"What happened?" he asked inadequately.

He felt her lips on his neck as she began talking. She was much taller than Chelsea so this felt odd to him. Hell, the whole situation felt odd!

"I went by Michael's last night after we left the Snow Drop…" she said, a sob interfering with her story.

"Does Marcus know you guys are dating?"

"No, we've never told him. I didn't want a conflict of interests, if you remember," she said, beginning to recover her composure. She drew away, suddenly embarrassed by her closeness with him, and apparently angered by what she remembered from last night.

"So, I get over to his house and he's there, right?" she said, heaving and reaching for a tissue on her desk. "But he wasn't alone. Some blond woman named Elle was there, snuggled up on his couch, drinking ice water in her yoga pants and some skimpy little tank top. You could tell they'd been doing it, too. And she was *old*, too! *Ugh!*"

Kyle sucked in a deep breath. "*Badass Barbie!*" he mumbled, leaning against her office door and shoving his hands in his pockets.

"You *know* her?" she cried, eyes wide, looking at him with renewed interest…and shock.

He nodded. "That was what Glen and I used to call her back in high school. She was a major mean girl, and I guess she never grew out of it. I'm sorry, Elise," he said, shaking his head, thinking that Michael had it coming, and now he was about to get it if he were hanging out with Elle McClarin. He covered his mouth so she wouldn't see the smirk he couldn't suppress.

"What?"

"I'm sorry. How does he know her?"

"I think she works at the restaurant across the street, that Italian place."

"Oh, yeah. So…what happened? I'm sure it was awkward."

"*Oh!* Awkward doesn't come *near* describing it. For me at least. He introduced us and acted like they were just friends, but I could tell from the way she was acting that they were way more than that, at least last night they were. He didn't even explain why he didn't show up at the Snow Drop."

"What'd you do?"

"I didn't stay more than a couple of minutes."

"Did he at least walk you to your car?"

"Hell, no. He opened the door for me, and I went on my way. I'm *so* done with him!"

Kyle didn't know what to say. He could only shake his head and let his anger at Michael boil inside him. "I'm sorry."

"I know. You're always so nice to me. Why can't I find someone nice?" she asked, looking at him.

He gave a slight shrug and hugged her again. "There's someone out there for you," he said, not knowing what else to say, and believing it was true as well.

She released him, this time grazing the side of his face with her lips. "Okay, thanks for the pep talk. I'm sorry for dumping my personal life in your lap again. I promise, no more of this," she laughed, picking up her purse and her tote bag to leave.

"Wait, I'll walk out with you," he said, going to his office and shutting down his laptop, collecting his work, and stuffing it all in its case. His face felt hot from where she had kissed him. She watched as he slipped on his coat and slung the bag over his shoulder. She started to speak but then stopped.

"What?"

"Nothing. Nothing."

A little snow was falling when he pulled into Radlers. It was nowhere near on Kyle's way home, but after telling Chelsea on the phone that he'd needed to run a quick errand and be home a little late, he pulled into the parking lot and parked the Explorer. The pretty dark-haired bartender greeted him enthusiastically and he ordered a Hefeweizen. She had the biggest brown eyes he'd ever seen.

"Whatever's the coldest you have," he said, giving her his most disarming smile and holding her gaze. "*Sarah*," he added, reading her nametag, "is Michael Gilmer in tonight?"

"Yeah, do you want to see him?"

"I do. Please. Will you tell him Kyle is here?" He didn't bother to sit down, but leaned in toward Sarah.

"*Kyle*," she said, letting his name register. "Sure." She left the bar and went through the kitchen doors. He looked around. Nice place, nothing so unusual; just a bar with plenty of German beers. The food smelled good.

Sarah was back, pouring his beer into a frosted glass from the tap. "He'll be right out," she said, giving him a pretty smile as she set down his beer on a small mat. Kyle drank and nodded to her, nice and cold. She clung to the bar, wiping the counter, asking whether he'd be dining with her tonight. He shook his head sadly. Depending on how things went with Michael, a little flirting with the bartender might work to his advantage.

In less than a minute, Michael appeared, a smug expression on his face when he saw Kyle was alone.

"What's up, Kyle?" he asked, stepping behind the bar and glancing at Sarah, who made a hasty retreat to the bar's opposite end where she checked on her other customers.

Kyle got right to the point. "What are you doing, Michael?"

"What do you mean?" Kyle took a long pull off his beer, making Michael wonder a little longer.

"What kind of *sick game* are you playing with Elise Masters?"

"That's none of your business," he said bristling.

"It is *my* business. It's my business when she comes to work upset with the company you're keeping."

Michael rolled his eyes. He studied Kyle for several moments and smirked. "You know, you *really* don't know what you're talking about. Elise and I don't have an exclusive relationship. She knew that going into this, so…end of story."

"Good idea, Michael," he said, placing a hand on the bar. "You should end it."

"Oh, I think that's up to her."

"That's what I'd expect from you. And I'd say she's finished with you. Don't bother her again."

"Are you threatening me?" Michael said, glaring at Kyle.

"Maybe. If you keep messing with her, you can call it what you want."

"I don't think you're in a position to be calling the shots, pal." Of course, he meant the winery, but if Marcus weren't aware of what his son was doing, Kyle might well have some leverage on all counts. He took another swig of his beer and considered Michael.

"We'll see," said Kyle, tossing a ten on the bar. "And you might want to think about getting tested," he said as Michael's face clouded over with a look of alarm and suspicion. "Thanks, Sarah!" he called down the bar, turned, and walked out the door, as he heard Michael slam through the kitchen door.

As Kyle got in his car and buckled his seatbelt, he wondered whether he'd made the right call, coming here and confronting Michael. Was what he had done merely a vain attempt at trading testosterone with Michael, or would his actions actually help Elise? Here he was again, in her business when he should have been minding his own. He backed out and noticed two cars blocking the driveway, their drivers having a mid-parking lot chat, requiring him to drive around the back of the building to get out. He saw Michael's Porsche in its own special parking place, but as he crept around the corner, avoiding the cars by the dumpster, he felt a lurch in the pit of his stomach. A black pickup truck was parked beside it. On the back window, he noticed a red and white decal depicting a skull and crossbones. He read the caption under his breath, "Surrender the Booty."

Chapter 15

INTERFERENCE

"It's a black Mitsubishi…early 2000 model, NC license ABX-7885…. Yeah, and I just called Elise, and she says the decal is the same one she saw. Right. Okay, I'll talk to you later," Kyle said to Glen on his cell phone, and after a brief hesitation, pulled into another parking spot and turned off the motor. *Why not?*

He pocketed his keys and strode back to the pub and in the front door. He stood a moment, assessing the crowd at the bar, and made his move. Good, no sign of Michael.

"Hey, Sarah," he said, giving her his most dazzling smile.

"Oh! You're back!" she said, smoothing her bangs away from her big eyes and blinking them twice.

"Yeah. Listen, do you know who owns the black pickup in the parking lot?"

"Yeah, it's Randy's."

He looked bemused. "Randy Maynard?" he tossed out Frank's name to see whether she'd correct him.

"No, Randy Conley, the dishwasher. He's here. Do you want to see him?"

"No, but he might want to check his bumper. Someone hit it backing out a few minutes ago and didn't stop. It didn't look like too much to me, but just in case, you know?"

"Okay. I'll tell him."

"Okay. See you. Have a good night."

"You, too. Come back and see us, Kyle," she grinned.

"You bet."

He left quickly, and once back in the Explorer, placed another call to Glen. "Yeah. I went back in there and chatted up the bartender. The truck belongs to Randy Conley, their dishwasher. He and his truck are still there. I just thought you'd like to know, in case the truck isn't registered in his name."

"Whoa, nice work, Detective Davis!"

"No problem. What's next?"

"I'll get Browning on the phone. If we can bring him in, we may be getting together a line-up. You think Elise would be up for it?"

"Maybe. She's freaking out, wondering what's going to happen. I didn't tell her I saw the truck here."

"Jeez. Are you still there?"

"Yep. Waiting to see what Randy Conley looks like. Oh, yeah…and here he comes now," Kyle said low into the phone, watching in the rear-view mirror a man in his early twenties emerge from the kitchen with a red bandana tied around his head, similar to the way Kyle had worn his at the Sound Side when he washed dishes as a teenager. It was hard to tell in the dark, but Randy appeared to have dark hair and be about six feet tall, and well-built, meaning he had probably packed a tough punch for Elise to take. He considered the bruise that still colored her face and shook his head in disgust. Watching Randy bend over to inspect his rear bumper, Kyle didn't feel bad at all anymore for coming over here. Any guy who would hit a girl like that was fucked up or something.

"You still there?" asked Glen.

"Yeah, I'm here. Tell me to leave so I don't nail this guy."

"Go home, Kyle. Chelsea's probably wondering where you are. Let us take it from here."

"Okay. See you," he said, ending the call, watching Randy stand away from the bumper and walk back and forth, looking for the dent he expected to see. He gave up and went back inside the service entrance. Kyle went on his way as well, placing a call to Chelsea, letting her know he was on his way. He had some explaining to do.

The next day, Elise met him at the coffeepot with steam coming out of her ears.

"What the hell did you do?" she demanded as he reached for his favorite cup on the countertop.

"What do you mean?"

"I got a very nasty call from Michael last night after you and I hung up. I want to know what you were doing snooping around over at Radlers, and why you felt you had to go in there and bust his chops about me."

Kyle stepped back and ran a hand through his hair, unprepared for this kind of reaction.

"Well, I was trying to help you out," he began, noticing the dark circles under her eyes.

"Great. Thanks. I had to drag Lydia out of bed last night and meet Detective Browning over at the *police station* and sit through a *line-up*! Can you imagine…putting a *child* through that?"

"Did you identify the guy?"

"*No!*" she shouted, making him look toward Frank's office, where Frank was talking on the phone as usual. She looked at Kyle with wild eyes and raked fingers through her hair. "Look, I know you think you're trying to help, but…things are worse than ever, right now."

"What did Michael say to you?" Kyle asked, eyes narrowing, wondering whether he had turned the tables and was threatening Elise. How could all of this have backfired?

"He said you came in there warning him to stay away from me, and then you told him to get *tested!* And then the cops come and drag his dishwasher down to the police station? What in the hell, Kyle?"

"Yeah, I said that. And if he's been sleeping with Elle McClarin, he *needs* to take an STD test for sure. I was just busting his balls…" he said, knowing it sounded ridiculous.

She gaped at him for several moments and then began laughing, covering her face with both hands. "You should see your face! You're adorable when you're humble, you know?" she said, her face softening, making his own face burn. "I'm sorry," she went on. "I didn't mean to embarrass you. I'm touched that you would stand up for my honor; I really am," she said, biting her lip to keep from laughing again.

"Okay. So what happened at the police station? You couldn't identify the guy, so did they let him go?"

"Yeah. He wasn't talking and Michael told Browning that Randy was at work both nights, the night I got run off the road, and the night of the robbery. They couldn't charge Randy with anything so they let him go."

"*Shit*," he muttered. "So now we're back to square one. If that's the truck, Michael's covering for him."

"Why would he do that, Kyle? And what if it's not the right truck? Do you know how many black pickups I've spotted in this area?"

"But how many have that decal on them? So you're letting this go?"

"What else can I do, Kyle? It was a four hundred dollar TV. The cops aren't going to keep looking. I can't keep living in fear that some moron is out there watching me and waiting to do something else," she said, turning away from him so she could pour her coffee. *That's exactly what she's doing*, he thought, *living in fear.*

"Who would do this to you, Elise?" he asked. A cheap TV was one thing, but assault was different.

"I don't know. Maybe you're overthinking it. I think it's all a coincidence, you know? And I'm done worrying about it. I'm done worrying about Michael too, just so you know. Last night's conversation is the last one I'll ever have with him…unless you're intent on bullying him further," she said, a lopsided smile starting on her face.

"No. I promise," he said, raising his hands in surrender. "I'll stay out of it all from now on. I'm sorry I caused you any unnecessary trouble, Elise."

She put out her hand, "Truce?"

"Truce," he said, shaking her hand. "But I'm still watching your back, just so you know."

She smiled, looking down into her coffee cup. "Thanks. May I go to work now?"

He made a flourish with his hand to allow her out of the kitchen ahead of him. "By all means, Ms. Masters. Let's go kick some ass."

Chicken pot pie was Kyle's favorite. Chelsea smiled, watching him devour the last of it on his plate, and grinning playfully at her, going back for seconds. After the last couple of nights' drama, she was looking forward to an easy night. She had hidden away her current batch of Christmas presents, and the boys had little homework, so her plan was to park them in front of *How the Grinch Stole Christmas* for a couple of hours of alone time with her husband. Snow had been falling sideways out the window for the past few hours, and she was hoping to see the school closings streaming across the bottom of the TV screen before the twins had to go to bed. The laundry could wait another day…or two.

This November was the coldest they'd had in sixty-some years. Appalachian State University had not canceled classes in ten years, but tomorrow, the first day of December, might be a first for her. She snuggled contentedly into Kyle's arms on the sofa in the sunroom, covered up with a blanket as they listened to the snow tinkling on the windows like thousands of pins being thrown against glass. It was a hopeful sound, she thought, remembering many nights like this as a child, nestled warm in her bed, dreaming of Christmas, or days off from school, and the promise of sledding and hot chocolate, and her father making crackling fires in the fireplace. They heard the boys giggling from the den with their own hot chocolate. Jim Carrey always made her laugh, too. Kyle kissed her forehead and stroked her hair. She let herself relax, feeling the comforting rise and fall of his chest under her cheek.

"How's your mother?" he asked, referring to their visit earlier in the afternoon.

"She's better. After she was wrestling with the idea of bringing Grandmother home, Dad had the good sense to convince her that they can't take care of her there. Not with her dementia as advanced as it is. It wouldn't be safe. She needs someone to watch her around the clock. That and the fact that she's not nice."

"Well, she hasn't been *nice* for a long time, even before the dementia started."

"I know. I just feel bad for Mom. She's always beating herself up, wondering why she couldn't get along with her own mother. I didn't know everything she was going through until recently. So much *guilt*, you know, because she took care of Kitty."

"I'm sorry she's had to deal with a relationship like that. You know it will never be like that between you and your mother," he said, continuing to stroke her hair.

"I guess you never really know what people are dealing with," she said, her thoughts going back to the summer and her walk on the beach with Stacie.

Kyle seemed lost in his own thoughts as well. She felt his chin rubbing back and forth on her hair.

"How was Elise today?" she asked.

"Mad as hell. She wants me to stay out of her dealings with Michael and all this other mess, so I told her I'm done interfering."

Chelsea sighed silently, relieved that he'd come to this conclusion. She was through being mad at him for going to Radlers and confronting Michael. After all, his protectiveness was one of the things she loved about him. He would go to the wall for anyone. "What happened at the police station? Did they arrest the guy from Radlers?"

"No. They didn't have the evidence to hold him. Glen called me later and told me I'd probably screwed everything up by going in there and talking to that bartender, trying to get the name of the person who owned the truck. Michael found out, so that was probably why he vouched for Randy. If Randy really did rob Elise, Michael could be protecting him to get back at me."

"Aren't the police doing anything else about this? Can't they get a search warrant?"

"I don't know. I'm off the case, remember? But Michael still pisses me off."

"He's so twisted," she said, looking up at him.

"Well, look who we're talking about. Is your dad alarmed about any of this? Or Jay? I'd think they'd be pissed that Michael could be involved."

"Dad wasn't there when I stopped by. I didn't tell Mom. She has enough on her plate right now. Michael was the last person I wanted to talk about. But I've got to say, I'm starting to like Marcus, the more I get to know him."

"So am I," Kyle said. "He was great to work with on the Snow Drop project. I'm sure he'll do well with the place. He's a genius at marketing."

"What does he think of Elise dating Michael?"

"He doesn't know. And anyway, she says it's over with Michael, so it's a moot point."

"It's all weird to me." Chelsea stroked his forearm, which lay across her chest, and thought about Elise; *single*, vulnerable, unprotected, and talented Elise. She closed her eyes to dispel the unwelcome thoughts. He'd opened up more and more about Elise since the summer, since the beach trip, making Chelsea think that somehow he'd made a passage back to her, where he belonged. Part of her wished he would keep his thoughts to himself, but part of her yearned to hear it all. Here, lying in his arms, his fingers stroking the back of her neck with their boys in the next room, she thought their lives looked so perfect. *Do you ever really know about people?* The snow continued to fall, beckoning her into its fairy-like spell, where she could sink into the moment, forgetting her troubles, and be happy. As if reading her mind, he whispered into her hair.

"I'm so happy this way," he said, his fingers continuing their caress on her skin. "I have everything I've always wanted." At that moment, they heard a loud whoop from both of the boys, who had leapt off the couch and bounded into the sunroom.

"No school tomorrow! It was just on TV!" Ty exclaimed while Stu jumped up and down, pumping his fist in the air.

"*Yesss!*" he shouted. "Does that mean we can stay up later tonight?"

"No," Kyle laughed. "It means off to bed after the movie, and you can sleep in tomorrow."

As the twins trailed back into the den to finish watching their show, Kyle turned Chelsea's face to his and kissed her tenderly. "You and I are sleeping in too, love," he said.

∞

Two days later, Kyle sat in the gathering room at Mountaineer Builders, his feet propped up on the coffee table, talking with Frank on the phone as Elise busied herself in her office, arranging her current treasures with fabric samples for one of their clients. He could hear Adele on the radio, singing about setting fire to the rain, a sentiment he was sure Elise was personifying in her own mind.

"No, this is why they should have made their decision to go along with our plan months ago….I know; at this rate, it will be June before they get in, especially as cold as it's been. If this is any indication of the winter we're going to have, we're in for a deep freeze….I know, I don't remember a winter like this since I was a little kid. And it's not even officially winter yet."

Elise took a break and sauntered into the room, stretching, and seated herself opposite Kyle, watching him talk to Frank. "Yeah, well, you tell Sara Lynn I told her this would happen…I know, I know. Well, have fun. You coming back today? Okay, then we'll see you tomorrow."

He ended the call and looked at Elise, sprawled across her chair, legs hanging over the arm, like he had never seen her before. In her jeans and a heavy pullover sweater, she looked like a college girl, as opposed to the professional he was used to seeing every day. The filtered morning sunlight bathed her face from the window, making her appear younger as well.

"What?" she asked, her fingers stroking absently through a strand of her hair.

"Nothing. You just look more relaxed than I've seen you in a while," he said, noticing her look soften as she gazed at him for a moment. "Your bruise is almost gone."

"Yeah. No makeup today, either."

He smiled. "Who's keeping Lydia?"

"Maddie walked over from campus. She was bored since classes were cancelled. She really wants the money, too," she laughed. "What did you and the boys do yesterday when school was out?"

He smiled. "Chelsea and I took them to her parents' place and went sledding."

She looked away and sighed. "That's so nice. I want that for Lydia someday. I mean, she can go sledding, and she'd stay out all day, but I'd like us to be a family with someone."

He nodded. Of course she would. Who wouldn't want what he had?

"Do you ever wonder what it would have been like if you'd never gotten married?" she asked.

He looked up at her, questions in his eyes. He'd never considered that.

"You know, if you'd been the young, ambitious architect who could have gone anywhere and done anything? What would you have done?"

"You mean, do I regret not designing some incredible skyscraper in a big city, or an art museum somewhere?"

"Yeah," she said, her fist going under her chin as she scrutinized him, so much possibility in her eyes, making him slightly uncomfortable, as though she were asking him to run away with her. He did not avoid her gaze.

"I don't know. I've never really thought about it. Museums and skyscrapers would have been nice. I guess I was always focused on one thing, and I went after it. I wanted to be with Chelsea. My job was just a means to an end."

She smiled wistfully and looked away.

"What about you? What did you dream about doing?" he asked, knowing it couldn't be what she had ended up with.

She snickered. "I wanted to design the interiors of yachts. I wanted a glamorous life. I wanted to live in big cities and travel all over the world.

I guess being in New York so much made me think I could really have that kind of life, and then…it just wasn't meant to be."

They were silent a moment, letting their thoughts settle, and his mind drifted to Chelsea and the boys again. They were probably back at her parents' house right now, getting ready for round two of sledding with Thomas and Ethan, and bugging Tom about when the lake would be frozen enough for ice-skating. It was so simple. He was happy. Elise was not. It would always be difficult to have these kinds of discussions. It was the same feeling he'd gotten from her when they'd designed the Snow Drop honeymoon suite, the yearning for what he had with his wife, the envy, the ache for more. He remembered feeling the same way when he'd worked for the firm in Alexandria, and how life with Chelsea had seemed to be just an unattainable dream. But now, he had it all, and he realized, watching her now, his life from her point of view was torture.

The front door chimed and they rose, wondering who would be coming to their office unannounced in the snow and ice. Glen and Detective Browning appeared through the doorway, making an effort to stamp the bits of snow off their feet as they entered.

"Hello! Detective, Glen," Kyle said, shaking hands with the men, as they looked at Elise and greeted her as well. "What can we do for you?"

"We're here to see you, Elise," said Browning. "Is there somewhere we could talk privately?"

Elise looked at Kyle with worry on her brow.

"Use the conference room," he said, leading the way and flipping on the light switch.

"Would you stay?" she asked as he backed out of the doorway.

Kyle looked at Glen and Browning, who shrugged, so he walked back in the room and they sat down around the table.

"Do you have news, detective?" she asked, making her voice steady, and assuming her impassive facial expression, something Kyle realized he had watched her do many times in the past. *She had covered up so much.*

Glen and Browning shared a look and Browning began. "Yes, Elise, we've had a break in your case," he said, the first hint of kindness on his face Kyle had seen. "Someone came forward and we now know quite a bit about what's been going on."

"Who?" she asked.

"Sarah Proctor from Radlers came into the station late yesterday afternoon with your TV."

"Sarah, the bartender?" asked Kyle.

"Yes. She overheard Randy Conley talking to Michael Gilmer about what to do with the TV. You see, the two of them, Randy and Sarah, live together. She'd seen the TV in their closet, covered with a blanket, and when she heard the conversation, it was enough to make her wonder what was going on. She'd gotten more curious when you showed up at the bar, Kyle. She overheard your conversation with Gilmer, and then when we went in to pick up Conley that night for questioning, she started putting two and two together."

"Why would she turn Randy in if they lived together?"

"Apparently, he's not the best boyfriend," Glen said, taking up the story. "He's hit her before, and she'd been thinking about getting out, but after what she heard, she thought it might be the best revenge to turn him in."

"She heard Michael talking to Randy about making sure he had a lawyer and never to tell his part in any of this. Michael paid Randy to rob your apartment while you and your daughter were at the movies," Browning said.

Elise's mouth fell open. "He knew we'd be there. I told him." She looked at Kyle, her face ashen.

"Why would he do that to her?" asked Kyle.

"That's the part we don't know. He was trying to scare you, Elise, but we don't know why. We do know that it wasn't his truck that ran you off the road. That might just have been a coincidence. Sarah vouched for him that night too. Said he was at work. But Michael knew the incident had you rattled, so he came up with the other things to freak you out," said Glen.

Elise sat frozen with wide eyes.

Kyle looked from her to Glen to Browning. "Apparently, Michael was trying to scare you. He wanted you to get so upset you'd leave town," Browning said, but his words hung like a question.

"That's why he had Elle at the house the night I went by."

Kyle nodded. Glen raised his eyebrows, familiar with the incident from Kyle. "That, by the way, was brilliant on his part. Badass Barbie would scare anyone off, Elise," Glen said with a smirk. He and Kyle laughed, but cut it off at Elise's expression.

"Why would Gilmer want you out of town, Elise?" Browning asked, leaning in across the table so her eyes were unable to avoid his.

"I don't know," she said. "It's not like I'm cramping his style," she said bitterly. "For the record, I've had nothing to do with Michael Gilmer since last Tuesday night. Can I take out a restraining order on him?"

"Yes, you can. He's facing some charges as well as his friend Randy. Randy was quite talkative after we got the TV and the story from Sarah. We have plenty of evidence, so there's nothing more you have to worry about. They were both arrested last night. Out on bail this morning, but we have charged them."

Elise looked relieved. "So the truck that ran me off the road?"

"Probably just another dark pickup truck. Probably coincidence, but if we find out anything more, we'll let you know," said Browning, watching her. "If you can think of anything else that might be important, you'll call us?" he asked Elise, sliding another card across the table to her.

"Yes. I will. Thanks."

"And what about Sarah?" Kyle asked.

"She's moved out, bunking with some girlfriends. She's quit her job at Radlers and is looking for work as we speak. She took out a restraining order on Conley, too."

Kyle scraped his thumb across his lower lip as a thought came to mind. "How does Elise take out a restraining order on Michael as well?"

"Come by the station and we'll fill it out there and file it. Michael will be informed through his attorney," Browning said, directing his comments to Elise and watching her reaction. "Are you all right, Elise?"

"Yes," she said, but it was barely audible. "Who is his attorney?"

"I'll get you that information when you stop by the station. Would you like to go down there with us now?"

"Not yet. I'd like a little time to take all this in. I'll come down later." Glen looked at Kyle, raising an eyebrow.

"Okay. I wouldn't wait, though. I don't think Michael will do anything irrational, but it's better to be safe than sorry. Oh, and you can claim your TV," said Browning kindly.

"Sure," she said softly. The men looked at Kyle, stood, and walked toward the door.

After shaking hands with them, Kyle returned to Elise, who sat like a stone in the conference room.

"Elise…you must be so shocked. I know I am."

"Yes," she said again, her voice a thin whisper.

He leaned his head to the side and tried to catch her eye. "Are you okay?"

"Do you know a good lawyer, Kyle?"

"Yeah. Frank and I have used Mac McCloskey for all kinds of things over the years. Why? What's going on?"

She looked at him as if she might implode at any moment.

"Michael is Lydia's father."

Chapter 16

Transparency

Kyle's face went slack with surprise. He stared at Elise as she sat in the chair, seemingly smaller and more wide-eyed than he'd ever seen her. She was motionless, apart from her thumb and forefinger, which she rubbed together compulsively as she gazed at him. Suddenly, the room was too bright, and he noticed the buzzing of the fluorescent lights.

"Say something," she said at last.

He closed his mouth and continued to study her, eyes narrowing, trying to assess her condition. She was past the point of crying. "How long have you known this?"

"Since the night of Faith's party at the winery. He recognized me first and came over to introduce himself."

Of course. *Elise, what an unforgettable name.* It all made sense now; Lydia's heart-shaped face and her impossibly red lips, the curly brown hair, all mirrored in the person of Michael Gilmer. No wonder Lydia had seemed so familiar when Kyle had first seen her. Still, his mind raced back to that night when he'd been so protective of Elise and watched her shake hands with Michael. She had the impassive expression down to an art. What self-control this woman possessed!

"How?" was all he could manage to ask.

She sighed, a ragged weary sound, and pushed herself to standing with her hands on her knees. He followed her into the gathering room where she collapsed onto the sofa, plunging her fingers into her hair and closing her eyes. He expected a meltdown of catastrophic proportions; instead, she collected herself and met his stare as she began to explain.

"I had no idea Michael was here, if that's what you're wondering. As I told you in my first day confession, I hadn't seen him since the night we'd spent together, and I still did not remember his last name. So you can imagine the shock and awe I felt upon seeing him that night."

"You covered it well."

"Thanks."

"Why didn't you say anything?"

"Are you kidding? I hoped I could close my eyes and he would just disappear, but he was all over me to go out with him. Then I found out he was in business with your family…and I knew you didn't like him. I thought you'd be so disappointed in me."

"Elise…there's no judgment here. It doesn't matter," he said, shaking his head, but she shook hers in disagreement.

"Yes, it does matter, Kyle. It matters a great deal what you think. I love working here, and I really need this job, and the respect you and Frank have shown me."

"So, when did you tell him? He knows, right?"

"Oh, yes. He knows. I went on two dates with him before he met Lydia. I told him I had a daughter, but he never suspected she was his. We got along well and I wanted to see what he was like before I introduced him to her. Well, of course, it only took one look at her for him to know he was hers. He was *livid!* First, because I had kept it from him, and then I just knew he didn't want anything to do with us. He kept up the relationship out of guilt, maybe. Or just that he couldn't figure out what to do about us. I should have cut it off immediately. I don't know why I thought he would want us, or why I wanted anything to do with him. I just had to know how it would all play out."

"But…he must realize he has obligations," Kyle said, thinking of precious Lydia, and wondering how anyone could not fall in love with her.

"Of course he does. When you went over there the other night and told him he needed to get tested, he thought you were talking about a *paternity test!*" she laughed.

Kyle blinked at her and threw back his head, roaring with laughter. "No wonder he was so pissed off! I guess he thought you'd told me everything."

She smiled and rose from the sofa, walked into her office and unlocked her top desk drawer. She came back with an envelope in her hand. "This is his response to his obligations," she said, handing him two checks, made out to her, each with five figures in the amount block. He looked away, not wanting to know.

"You haven't cashed them."

"I don't want his money. I only wanted his decency, but he has none of that. And, by the way, *devotion* would have been nice, too, but, it's Michael, so…."

"We need to call Mac McCloskey. If you want, I'll call him and see when we can set up a meeting."

"Thank you. That would be great."

They looked at each other, realizing one more elephant remained in the room.

"And then there's Marcus," he said, watching her nod. "Oh, I'm sure he'll react in a much more favorable way, Elise. I don't think Michael and he are as similar as I thought. Besides, I know Marcus has made his own mistakes, and he's probably much more human than Michael. Knowing that he has a *grandchild....*"

She stared out the window, a finger tracing her lip as she thought. Finally she said, "What do you think will happen to Michael?"

"Oh, I think his lawyer will drag this thing out as long as he can and try to make it disappear, but the word will eventually get out. Around here, trying to scare off your baby mama doesn't sit well with folks, so eventually he will probably have to sell his business. Can you really see a guy like Michael sticking around in our mountains?"

She smiled ruefully. "No, I guess not." Her voice softened beyond what he expected, and she looked at him, hanging onto whatever support he could give her.

"So, promise me one thing. Don't let him run you off, Elise. You're going to be way more successful here than he will be."

"I wasn't planning on running."

"Good. You have guts; I'll give you that."

"Well, about seven years ago, I gave up thinking that my life would be easy," she said, smiling, some color returning to her face. She tapped the checks on her hand.

Kyle had a sudden thought. "Can I ask you one thing? Out of curiosity…did Michael ever talk to you about the Davenports' house? He and Marcus have been all over it for the past couple of years, wanting to turn it into a bed and breakfast."

She rolled her eyes. "Oh, I know all about it. He knew I'd been to see Liz and that I was working on redecorating her office. He was dying to get an in, but I had no intention of ever helping him, especially after you'd made it clear to Marcus that the family wasn't interested. I mean, how pushy can you be?"

Kyle smiled, satisfied with her answer. "Would you like to go down to the police station now and take care of business? I'll drive."

"Sure. Do you mind making that call first?"

"Not at all."

The cabin felt blessedly warm as Chelsea hurried through the door on Sunday evening, pleased and proud that Kyle was cooking, and that someone had set the table for dinner already. An open bottle of pinot noir sat on the table with two waiting glasses. This dinner and the wine was certainly over-payment for what she'd done, but she felt happy; happier than she'd been in months. Aromas from the Bolognese sauce and garlic bread from the oven smelled divine, reminding Chelsea that she was hungry. Pulling her fingers out of her gloves, she took off her coat and scarf and hung them on a hook by the front door.

"Hey!" Kyle said, going to her and giving her a swift kiss and a hug, pulling her in with the dish towel he held in each hand. "Damn, baby, you're freezing!" he said, throwing the towel over his shoulder and taking her face in his hands, then clasping her hands in his.

"I know. It's eighteen degrees outside."

"So...how was it?"

"It was...*great* actually. I had a really good time, and I think they did, too. Elise and I had a wonderful time talking, and Lydia is so darling," she said, referring to the performance of *The Nutcracker* Chelsea had taken them to in Boone. "I think Lydia might want to do our *Setting the Barre* program next fall," she said, rubbing her cold hands together and stepping out of her black pumps, but Kyle frowned.

"Leave those on," he commanded. "And take off that dress," he added with a lopsided smile.

She laughed, her face going warm. "This is my favorite black dress."

"I like it too. It's slinky and sexy, and it looks amazing on you, but you know what I like best on you?"

"What?"

"*Me*," he said, engulfing her in his arms and kissing her deeply as she squealed with laughter against his mouth.

"Where are the boys?"

"Downstairs, playing pool," he said, giving the sauce a stir and going to pour her a glass of wine.

"Here, taste this," he said, holding the wooden spoon out for her to sample his labors.

"Mmm! Delicious! They didn't snoop around looking for their Christmas presents while I was gone, did they?"

"No, they didn't."

"I don't want them finding their ice skates," she said, glancing around to see whether they'd arisen from the basement, unheard.

"And speaking of presents, guess who called me today and gave me the best present ever?"

"Who?" she asked, taking a sip of her wine and stepping back into her shoes, struggling for balance, making him ogle her playfully.

He raised his glass to hers for effect and said, "Lynn Schiffman. She's been spying on our website since Elise came on board and she has a new project for us."

"Oh! That sounds nice."

"More than nice. She wants to build a hotel here. After the first of the year, she's planning to move here. I imagine she'll keep a winter place in Florida, and she has that loft in New York. But she sold her holdings in the hotels in South Beach, and she's bought property up here already."

"A hotel? That sounds very rewarding."

"It will be. She wants Mountaineer Builders to do the whole thing. She's coming up in a few weeks to talk more about it; isn't that great?"

"Wow! That is great. Merry Christmas! And congratulations!"

"Thanks. It will be a nice present for Frank and Elise too. It's about this time of year when we start worrying that we won't have the business to sustain ourselves."

"Well, that should tell you how highly she thinks of you, calling you first with the news." Chelsea thought fondly of Lynn and how she'd treated Kyle as her favorite architect over the years, after he had built her condos ten years ago, continually sending other business his way.

Kyle studied her a moment and stroked her face. "So, today was okay?"

"Yes."

"Are you and Elise going to be friends?" he asked, searching her eyes for the truth, but without any hint of chastisement, merely hope.

Yes, like you wanted. He had been thrilled that she had come up with the idea of inviting them to the ballet on her own. And once she had gotten away with Elise without *him*, she had not regretted having a change of heart, allowing herself to open up to this enigmatic young woman. Chelsea watched him stare at her, waiting for her answer. *Oh, he was so hot when he was vulnerable!*

"I think so. She's really not what I thought at all. She seemed so relieved, now that everything with Michael is out in the open. Although, Lydia won't know anything about him until Elise is ready to tell her. Honestly, I can't imagine what that was like, finding him here, and having him treat her the way he did. I know she's ready to get past all of that and move on."

"She's been through a lot."

"When will Marcus find out that he's Lydia's grandfather?"

"I don't know. She's waiting to see if Michael will tell him. I'm glad you invited them to the ballet. She needs friends."

"I know. I introduced her to a ton of people. She met Meme and her family. There was another little girl from Lydia's class and her mother at the ballet, so they talked. I heard them making plans for a play date."

"That's good." He smiled and went to the refrigerator for the salad he'd made. She felt a pang of love for him in that moment, love and relief that all her weird imaginings were over and things between them felt normal again. The awkward moments had vanished. Not only had she stepped up her game, but it seemed that he had tried to do the same thing for her. He'd impressed her in a major way when he had surprised her with the Snow Drop honeymoon suite. He had made a reservation there after the New Year, and just thinking about it, her insides unfurled with anticipation. *Just the effect he had in mind*, she thought.

"Is there anything I can do?" she offered, stealing a cucumber from the salad bowl.

"Nope. If you want to change, there's time. But leave those shoes on, okay?"

"How about I put them on later, after I give my feet a break?"

"Promise me you will, *without the dress*," he whispered, winking as the boys thumped up the stairs like a herd of elephants.

The Bistro Roca was one of Lynn Schiffman's favorite places for lunch. Kyle had been disappointed that Elise had already had plans, but once she divulged that she'd be meeting Marcus at the Snow Drop Inn for a private luncheon, he was glad to take up for her, knowing he would arrive there later with Lynn, to see the latest in their collaboration. Lynn had taken a risk last summer, recommending Elise to her friend, Justine, for her kitchen remodel. The success of Justine's project had solidified Lynn's opinion of her as a designer, and one who'd be worthy of a hotel build to take place in the coming months. Elise had no idea of the coup she'd scored with Lynn.

They entered the dimly lit dining room, decorated with large Christmas ornaments and white lights, and scoured the menu for their favorite dishes, making it easy to order when the server presented himself at their table: water with lemon and a Tomato Melon Prosciutto salad for Lynn, and a Carolina Bison Burger and iced tea for Kyle.

"Oh, it feels so good to be back here!" said Lynn. "I'm so sick of Florida! The mountains have been calling me for a long time, and I'm finally succumbing to the inevitable. And I *love* cold weather!" she laughed, raising her glass of ice water to Kyle's iced tea. "Merry Christmas, Kyle!"

"Merry Christmas to you, too!" he said, touching his glass to hers. "Is this the first Christmas you'll have spent in the mountains?" he asked, cocking his head to the side and regarding her curiously, knowing she was Jewish.

"Yes. Although we do a Christmakkah kind of thing, you know? My daughter, Rachel, married a Gentile, and then there's my son, Ben, who's always wanted a Christmas tree, so, I guess the mountains will fulfill their fantasies much more so than anything I could do for them in Miami. They've never spent any time at my house up here in the winter, and what better time to do it than at Christmas?"

"Gotcha. It might snow too, as it has every other day, so it will be especially charming for them. Just make sure you've stocked your pantry in case you get snowed in. It can be pretty ghastly."

"I will. It's certainly cold enough. I'm really looking forward to seeing the Snow Drop. I'm glad Elise will be able to meet us there after lunch," she commented, taking a bite of her salad, as he chewed his bison burger contentedly.

"You couldn't have sent us better news than entrusting all of us to build your hotel."

"There's no one else I'd even consider. And I chose the location primarily because of you," Lynn said, watching Kyle carefully. "You and Frank did a good thing, bringing Elise on board. I've been checking out her work. She's very talented. I think she makes you shine even more as an architect. Do you know what a fine combination the two of you make? You know, I could have done this anywhere, but I had to choose the mountains, and Mountaineer Builders. It just feels right. I think your economy here is about to turn the corner, with the university and all it brings to the table, so this endeavor will be a win-win for all of us."

"I hope you're right. Lots of folks around here have lost their shirts."

"Except for you and Frank and your father-in-law and the ones who've played it smart. How's the winery doing?" she asked, wiping her mouth.

"They're hanging in there. Nothing spectacular, but their wines are winning awards and attracting attention in the magazines, so people are coming. And Marcus has that knack for attracting crowds."

They ate in companionable silence for a while. Then she asked, "How's Chelsea?"

"Chelsea is excellent," he said, a feeling of pride surging forth. She was still disappointed that they hadn't conceived yet, but he knew it was only a matter of time. It certainly wasn't from lack of effort! "Still dancing and teaching at App."

"And your boys?"

"They're doing well. We're always trying to pay them the same amount of attention, and they have their unique gifts, but everything's great. We live tired, but we're doing well."

"I'm so happy for you, Kyle. I knew you'd have nothing but success if the gods were smiling on you, and it looks like they are." He knew she'd always been in his corner, after her personal relationship with his father, who had built her house. She had known the best of his father, Kyle thought, and he found it moving the way she had taken up his cause.

"We've been blessed, that's for sure. And you are a part of the grand scheme, you know. Your business couldn't have come at a better time for all of us."

"Well, seeing Elise's creativity and knowing what you and Frank can do has gotten me pretty excited. I think the university will be glad I'm doing this project, especially since they're turning their flagship hotel into dorm space in the next year. It seems to be the prime time to take advantage of this opportunity."

An hour later, they were hurrying into the warm lobby of the Snow Drop Inn. Kyle took a deep breath, realizing that this meeting could be complicated with all the nuances they would need to keep from Lynn. He took her wrap and hung their coats on the coat tree in the foyer. The fireplace generated a cozy feel, as Kyle listened to Elise and Marcus quietly wrapping up their conversation inside the dining room, where they'd had a one-on-one lunch. They had cleared any sign of their lunch as they emerged to welcome Lynn and Kyle, Elise straightening her leather skirt, the color of cinnamon, and brushing crumbs off her black turtleneck sweater. Discreetly, she wiped a tear from the corner of her eye, making it look as if an errant eyelash were in her way, and set her face to impassive mode, as she reached forward to shake Lynn's hand. Kyle peered into her gaze, trying to assess her condition after the difficult conversation; she rewarded him with a smile of relief.

Marcus intervened kindly, welcoming them with his booming voice and characteristic good cheer, understanding his part in the mechanics of this kind of business meeting, making himself that much more like-able to Kyle at the moment. They regarded each other cautiously since

Kyle knew Marcus and Tom had been on the phone, agreeing to sever Michael's ties from the winery. Marcus clasped his hands and rubbed them together, as though ready to display the latest decadent chocolate dessert, asking, "Are you ready to take a tour of the Snow Drop, Lynn? I can guarantee that you'll be amazed by what these two young people have done with the place. You'll have to take a look at the before-and-after photos to see just how well they did. If you want them to design your hotel, this couldn't be a better example of their work."

Kyle's eyebrows cocked in surprise. He had not expected such a glowing endorsement.

"Thank you, Marcus!" Possibly after his conversation with Elise over the disappointing revelations about his son, and the new knowledge that Elise was the mother of his granddaughter, Marcus was more invested than Kyle had ever imagined he'd be. Elise gave Kyle a small smile, face flushing with relief, or something—gratitude that she was appreciated, perhaps. He acknowledged her with a smile of his own, conveying his appreciation of her, and that everything would be all right. The thought of designing a hotel had flipped her world upside down. This was the big time.

"Well, I was certainly pleased with my condominiums, and Kyle's winery is just lovely as well!" Lynn said, grinning at him, as though he were her firstborn son.

The Christmas tree lights winked cheerfully at them from the parlor as they began the tour, with Lynn noticing the snake lamp immediately and asking for the story. Next she crooned appropriately over the selection of mixed antiques and modern pieces, along with the artwork, the color scheme, newly appointed bathrooms, and state of the art kitchen.

"It's so beautiful; it makes me want to live here. I never thought I'd find another place I liked more than my own house, but I just love the honeymoon suite," Lynn said, patting Kyle on the back as they returned to the parlor where Elise narrated the before-and-after pictures.

"Well, if your children start to get on your nerves over the holidays, you can just send them over here. They won't even think they're in trouble!" Kyle said to Lynn, making her giggle.

"Oh! I can't wait to take you on a tour of my new property. And I have some preliminary ideas for the hotel, with some examples of other places I've visited to give you an idea of what I'd like to build here. Something low-key that fits with the landscape and the feel of the mountains."

"Sounds great! We'll do it, right after the holidays when Frank is back in town," Kyle said, catching a glimpse of Elise's face, blanching at the thought of the challenge's magnitude. He'd had a shiver or two of his own as the reality of the project set in, but with the team of them and their best commercial construction crews, he knew it could be done. Perspective was something he'd gleaned over his last twelve years as an architect, and something Elise would become acquainted with soon enough as well, he thought, studying her, as she answered Lynn's questions about the kitchen renovation. Still with what she'd been through the last few weeks, and especially today, she had to be struggling just to tread water at the moment. If anything should make her feel better, it was that everything was out in the open and she could relax and be herself with all the players. He gave her another encouraging smile, trying to infuse some confidence into her, and she responded with a distracted smile of her own, making her face light up, *finally*. At least she appeared to be breathing!

As Marcus and Lynn chatted about the inn, Kyle motioned to Elise to walk with him into the kitchen. He'd never seen her as nervous as she appeared at the moment, raking her hands through her hair when she was out of Lynn's view.

"So, how'd it go with Marcus? Are you okay?" he asked gently, watching her hands tremble.

"It went fine, much better than I'd expected. Michael told him all about it last night, and he called this morning to ask if I'd like to meet him for lunch to discuss some things. I'm sorry I was so cryptic with you this morning. I just didn't know what to expect since I'd hidden all of this from Marcus."

"Well, I'm sure he understood why you couldn't talk about it?"

"Oh, yeah, he's been very understanding and kind. He'd like to be the go-between with Michael and me, knowing that I don't want anything to do with him anymore. Marcus wants Michael to be held accountable, and he wants to help me and Lydia. He really wants me to accept Michael's money. I told him I only want what would be normal child support, not some kind of pay-off to make me disappear."

"Absolutely. But this could all be retroactive, you know? And run all of this by Mac the next time you talk to him."

"Of course. I don't want any friction between Marcus and the company because of us."

"No. There won't be. I've filled Frank in and he's completely cool with whatever you need from us. We're a team, remember?" he said, watching her eyes fall to the wood flooring, the color rising again to her cheeks. "Don't be upset about this, from our end, okay? We just want the best for you."

"I know…thank you. I don't know why I'm being so…freaked out about all of this."

"It's a lot to digest. You'll be fine. When are you and Lydia going home for Christmas?" he asked. She needed her family more than ever now. His question made her take a deep cleansing breath.

"We're leaving tomorrow morning. My parents are so anxious to see us. After all of this, I'm going to be really glad to see them, too!"

He resisted the urge to give her a comforting hug as Lynn and Marcus entered the kitchen.

"Thank you for the tour, Marcus," said Lynn. "Your place is exquisite. It's quite a transformation from what it was. Now I have even more to think about for my hotel. And I'd like you to be thinking about a name over the holidays. I still haven't come up with anything."

"We will," Kyle said for them both. "Maybe when we see the site, we'll have a better feel for it."

They moved into the foyer and began wrapping themselves for the cold as Marcus turned off the gas logs and helped Elise into her coat. It seemed to be, for Marcus, a touching gesture, thought Kyle; just the thing a man would do for his daughter-in-law. There had definitely been a change in Marcus since the last time Kyle had seen him. He winked at Kyle, making him realize it was an apology for his comments during that day at lunch, after they'd seen the property for the first time and Elise had been spooked by the snake. His assumptions about Kyle and Elise had been false, and he was making amends, and a lot more, given what Michael had done.

After hugs and handshakes, they bid one another a Merry Christmas as they headed out into the cold, gray afternoon. Snow began to swirl lightly in fat flakes around their heads, making them all smile, wishing for a white Christmas. It was the best of omens.

Chapter 17

A New Year

It was indeed a white Christmas. The break from work and the subsequent time off with Kyle and the boys was just what Chelsea had needed to focus on her family. She had been happy to move from house to house, sharing the celebrations first with her family, and then going to Kyle's grandparents' home in Charlotte, where Shelly and Mark joined them, along with Stacie, Tyson, and Abigail. There was little time to relax and reflect until they'd returned home several days after Christmas for some real down time with Kyle and the twins. The boys had been overwhelmed with so many gifts from all the doting relatives, but she was glad that their favorite gifts had been the ice skates Kyle and she had placed under the tree from Santa: new hockey skates for each of them, not the usual hand-me-downs from their cousins, which they were accustomed to wearing. Normally, they'd have to wait until January or February to skate, but it had been colder than usual, and her dad had told the boys it was safe to skate on the lake, showing with his hands the expected six inches of ice they'd need to skate there.

A full moon was just beginning to wane as they headed for her parents' house on New Year's Eve. Sounds floated around the snowy landscape as if each one were close by. Moonlight on the ice transformed the lake into a large flat pearl set at the foot of lacy grape arbors. It was tradition in the Davenport family to meet at the lake for a bonfire on New Year's Eve, for the purpose of burning the Christmas trees and roasting marshmallows. It was an event Chelsea had always looked forward to; the going out of one year and the coming in of another, with all the promise and mystery it held. The entire Davenport clan would be there; her Uncle Wayne and his wife Becky, and their older children, Bri and Brett, along with Jay and Lauren with Thomas and Ethan. Tonight, there was a new addition, Bri's new boyfriend, who seemed to fit in comfortably with the family. Even Foscoe's presence was expected for the festivities. It was like having a family hockey team, with all those men and boys on the ice. Liz, Becky, and Lauren insisted on time-outs at intervals so they could skate in peace. Chelsea and Bri had taught the twins to skate almost as soon as they could walk. As cold as it had been, the ice was thick across the lake, so they all had room to do as they pleased.

Ty gazed at the moon as he waited for Chelsea to finish tying her laces around Foscoe's exploring nose. The smell of new leather was his addiction. "Look at the moon, Mom. It looks like a flashlight, shining down on the lake like that," he said, tapping her on the arm, making her smile at him. "Will you skate with me tonight?" Chelsea wondered whether that was a hint that he might not be up for the rough hockey game he anticipated with his dad, Jay, and his cousins.

"I was hoping you'd ask me," she told him, listening to Ethan describing the play by play of their hockey game from the afternoon for entranced Stu. She felt Kyle's eyes on her from across the fire, as if no one else were there. Seated on his log next to Stu, Kyle watched their interaction, blue eyes glinting at her, as if filled with desire, making her quiver inwardly. He looked so hot in his gray hooded sweatshirt that peeked out of his windbreaker, and his old jeans, the crease appearing at the side of his mouth as his slow smile formed. His windswept hair was darker now, with sideburns that accentuated his cheekbones. He was still hers, every bit of him, and he'd been making a point of showing her in his actions and attentions over the last few months. She had never seen him so tuned in to the boys.

He handed Stu his hockey stick and winked at Ty. "Do I get a chance to skate with Mommy too?"

Ty thought a moment and played along. "Maybe," he said. "Aren't you going to play hockey?"

"Probably not. Hard to see the puck at night. But I'll give you plenty of time with Mom."

"Why did we bring the sticks then?" Stu asked.

"You always bring the sticks."

"We can see just fine, Dad." Stu gestured to the four lanterns mounted on boat cushions at designated corners of the lake.

"It's your puck," Kyle shrugged. "If you lose it, it's gone, so you might think about saving it for daylight," he told Stu as Ty stood and made his way to the ice, stepping on with Thomas to try out his new skates. In an instant, Stu was zooming out ahead of them, circling around them with his stick, making believe he was pushing his puck toward the goal.

He gave the imaginary puck a slap and yelled, "*And he scores! The crowd goes wild!*" He made a static sound, deep in his throat, to mimic the roar of the crowd as he pumped his fists and thrust the stick into the air.

Kyle laughed, taking Chelsea's hand as they skated around the kids, giving them a wide berth for good reason. She watched her father and Uncle Wayne tossing Christmas tree branches onto the fire. It would be a nice hot fire when they were ready for a warm up. Kyle put his arm behind her and rubbed her shoulders, sensing she was cold. From across the fire, her mother smiled at them, keeping her place on the log, wrapped in her favorite woolen blanket.

"What do you think of Bri's boyfriend?" Chelsea asked, watching the two holding hands and skating in a circle together.

"Jonathan, he seems nice. He really seems to like her. What do you think?"

"She likes him, too. She's never brought anyone home before. After that last guy, it must be pretty serious."

"She's old enough to know what she wants."

"How old were you when you knew?" she asked, half-kidding him with her voice and sparkling eyes.

"I was seventeen, and *very* sure of myself. I think I made the right call; don't you?" he asked, low in her ear and pulling her a little tighter. "Still, it's different for other people."

"How?"

"I'd found *you*. There aren't many people out there like you. I'd have been pretty thick to have passed you by. I was no fool then, and I'm certainly not one now," he said, sending her a message with his eyes. He'd told her things like this for months, making her feel secure, erasing all her doubts once more. Was her life about to return to normal with the new year arriving in a few more hours? It couldn't be more perfect, she thought, gliding across the ice with him, feeling his competent hand at the small of her back. She let herself snuggle into him, and even in the cold, she could indulge herself in the smell of wind on him, reminding her of safety.

He passed her hand to Ty, who'd skated up beside her, making her giggle in surprise.

"Hey, sweetie!" she said, letting him pull her along around the space's perimeter. "Do you like your skates?"

"Yesss! They're the bomb, Mom. *Bomb, Mom,*" he laughed at the rhyme. "You have to pay attention 'cause they're really fast, but it's like *flying!* Watch this!" he said, suddenly releasing her hand and charging forward, making an arc around her, and coming up with a whoosh beside her as he came to an abrupt halt. "Did you hear that? *Crrrsshh!*"

Stu was there next. "Mom! Can we sign up for hockey? Kevin and Brandon play on a team. Ty and I could too! Now that we have our own skates, we could really show 'em our stuff."

"We'll see," she said, adding, "Do we really need one more thing to do?" to herself, as the boys were off and skating across the lake again, catching up with Ethan and Thomas on the other side. She took the opportunity to slip off the ice and sit with her mother and Becky, who were discussing the background facts on Jonathan. They were already referring to him as Jon-o, and commenting that Brett was competing with Bri for his attentions. When a brother liked the boyfriend, it was a sure sign of acceptance. She let their conversation lull her into peacefulness as she warmed her hands by the fire.

An hour later, it was time to round up the troops and head home for the night. Kyle winked at her as they gathered their blankets and discarded hats, placing them into the large tote they'd brought. It was unlikely they'd be awake at midnight, and hopefully, the boys would be out for the count as well, after all this exercise. The fire had been reduced to embers as Kyle called for the boys to come off the ice. Ty and Thomas were there, wiping their noses on the backs of their sleeves and removing their skates. Foscoe watched as the skates disappeared into another bag.

"Got everything?" Chelsea asked.

"Except Stu," Kyle said, turning to see Stu and Ethan grappling with their hockey sticks on the lake while Jay and Lauren were bringing in the lanterns and boat cushions. "Stu! Come on! It's time to go!" he called, helping Jay carry the lanterns to his Jeep. Chelsea helped stack the cushions in the back as her mother loaded her little sled with the accoutrements from the s'mores—marshmallows, chocolate bars, and graham crackers. It would be easy to pull it back to the house, and Kyle could pick her up on the way out of the property. Her father took the rope from her and said, "I've got this, Sweet Pea. You go on with Kyle."

At that moment, they heard a creaking sound, a snap, and a splash. A scream went up next, and Chelsea swung her eyes around to the lake. Kyle did the same and turned to meet her frantic eyes.

"No! Not Stu!" he shouted, scrambling to reach for a hockey stick, and then running through the few feet of snow to the lake. Chelsea watched in horror as the hole in the ice gaped black and open, like a wound where her son had disappeared. Then in another second, his head appeared again and the sputtering desperate scream sounded, as Kyle was sliding prone across the ice, with Jay, Brett, and Jonathan behind him on their stomachs, making their way to the black hole.

"I've got you, Stu! Grab the stick!" Kyle yelled, but Stu's head was gone again.

The voices of the men were deep and urgent.

"Where is he?" Jay shouted.

"I don't know! I can't see him!" Kyle shouted back, reaching into the frigid water, the hockey stick in his other hand. "Where is he? *Damn it!*"

"It's not that deep. He should be right there," said Jay, sending Kyle a look of despair.

"I'm going in," Kyle said, slipping into the hole and disappearing in blackness. For a moment, they were all frozen in fear. Chelsea clutched Ty's shoulder as they watched the scene, helpless and alarmed. Then Kyle's head came back up. His arms thrust the top half of Stu onto the ice; then pushed him the rest of the way out. "Turn him over on his side!" he shouted, breathless from the frigid water, as Jay did as he was told.

There was no sound from Stu, who looked as blue and lifeless as the snow in shadows underneath the trees. Jay helped Kyle the rest of the way out of the hole and Kyle threw Stu back over onto his back and straddled him, pushing on his chest with the heels of his hands. On the second thrust, water gushed forth from Stu's mouth and Kyle turned him on his side quickly, letting the lake spew out of his son. Stu gasped and choked after what seemed to Chelsea like an eternity. Tom stepped past her with Liz's blanket, as Kyle slid the boy to the lake's edge and lifted him to his chest, wrapping arms around him as the child coughed and looked about, seeming disoriented.

"I'm so cold," he said, shuddering, as Chelsea was there, hands going to his back, feeling him to reassure herself he was truly alive.

"Stu!" she gasped, fear exploding from her eyes. She watched as Kyle carried their son, dazed and frozen. "Oh, my God! *Kyle!*" she cried. Kyle's arms were clamped around him as he tried to surge toward the house, her parents' house, toward warmth, toward safety. Her father's towering presence stood in his way, putting a halt to everything, as he held up a hand to Kyle.

"Give him to me, son," he said calmly, holding out the thick blanket to accept Stu. Kyle obeyed him immediately, helping to wrap the blanket around him, as they all processed quickly to the house.

Chelsea was vaguely aware of her brother and uncle saying, "We'll take care of this," meaning the fire and the other things they'd been putting away when Stu fell in. On the way to the house, she felt herself trembling, trying to imagine what Kyle must feel, and watching the chill rack his body with shaking. A wave of nausea threatened to overtake her on the way up the hill to her father's house, but she followed, as if flying along, never feeling her feet touching the ground. *This wasn't happening!*

Her mother's voice was in her ear as they entered the kitchen, which felt unbelievably warm. "Let's get hot baths going for them, honey. You go upstairs and start one for Kyle, and I'll let Stu get in our tub down here. We'll throw their clothes in the dryer while they're soaking."

Chelsea nodded, making herself put one foot in front of the other, noticing it was strange that her mother wasn't wincing with all the water all over the floors. Her eyes never left Stu and Kyle. Stu was literally blue and Kyle was heaving, trying to fill his lungs with warm air while he untied and removed Stu's skates. Chelsea was frozen in place, eyes riveted to her son, knowing she was expected to go upstairs and start Kyle's bath.

"*Go!*" her mother commanded, taking Stu's jacket off, and working on his pants as the water poured into the tub in her bathroom.

"Okay," she said, breathlessly, draping a towel around Stu, still unable to tear herself away from him as her mother sighed and followed Kyle out of the bathroom. Chelsea poured a capful of bubble bath into the water and checked the temperature before helping Stu into the tub. She took his clothes from the floor and looked at him one more time before exiting the bathroom. "Are you okay?" she asked her shivering boy, who could only nod as he sank down in the water. She leaned over and laid her fingers across his head, still cold to her touch.

On her way through her parents' bedroom, she stopped, caught by surprise as her mother knelt down beside Kyle next to her bed. He was on his knees, head pressed to his hands, which were clasped together on the bed as his body shook, with cold and with sobbing. Her mother stroked her hand across his wet back as water dripped in pools off his clothes onto the flowers of her hooked rug. Her eyes went to Chelsea's.

"I'll go up and start his bath," she murmured as Chelsea took her place on the floor. "Dad's getting some hot chocolate going in the kitchen."

Chelsea hit her knees beside her husband. What could she say? There were no words to express what they felt. "Thank you, God!" she whispered breathlessly, watching Kyle. He continued to shake, making her wonder whether he could be in a physical state of shock. "Okay, you need to get warm. Come on," she said, pulling his arm to help him stand. She pushed him up the stairs where the water was tumbling into the claw footed tub, the one in which she'd bathed everyday during her last two years of high school.

"Take off your clothes," she said, searching his eyes, red-rimmed now, from the tears he'd shed downstairs.

"I'm sorry," he whispered, pulling the soaked sweatshirt over his head with her help.

"For saving Stu?" she questioned, confused. She helped him drag the jeans and boxers down to the floor and helped him steady himself as he climbed in the tub and sank to his neck in the hot water. Her mother had added bubbles to his bath as well. On another day, she would have smiled, wondering when was the last time this big man had taken a bubble bath. But right now, she felt only relief and inadequacy at what could have happened. She dipped a washcloth in the water and wrung it out, pressing it to his forehead, as he closed his eyes and let the heat restore life to his frozen limbs. She scooped up his clothes and started for the door. She looked back, feeling a pang of emotion, the fear she'd felt when Stu disappeared into the hole, and which had increased when she'd watched him disappear momentarily. "I'll be back," she said, the cold from the wet clothes making her shiver. He would have to borrow a pair of her father's shoes to make it home tonight. His were soaked.

After starting the dryer with all the wet clothes, she returned to check on Stu in her mother's bathroom downstairs where she heard laughter and splashing. Peeking around the door, she saw that Ty had stripped and joined Stu in the tub, and was currently amusing him with their old wind-up ducks and boats, the toys from their babyhood that Liz still kept in a basket by the tub. One never knew when toddlers might come to stay. Stu looked considerably brighter, warmer, and contented, now that his brother was there to entertain him. A heavy sigh of relief escaped her lips.

Ty. Darling Ty. Chelsea had all but forgotten about Ty. How terrified he must have been to have witnessed his twin disappearing into the gash in the ice. It had all happened so quickly and they had acted with such speed and effectiveness that there had not been time to acknowledge him. But what does a twin endure when a thing such as this occurs? When something of this magnitude happens to a very part of his own soul, yet he remains unacknowledged during the entire event? Her heart ached for Ty, and shame washed over her; shame for ignoring his feelings, his very existence during the whole ordeal. He was watching her now, the duck in mid-wind as he sat among the bubbles with his identical brother, trying to make him laugh.

She went to him, squatting at the side of the tub. "Are you all right, Ty?"

He nodded, searching her face for…*what*? A sign of resentment that she'd forgotten him? She deserved that, at least.

"That was so scary, wasn't it?"

He nodded again, his vast blue eyes assessing her, the smile vanishing for an instant. His attention turned to Stu again, letting go of the spring on the duck, as its webbed orange feet spun ridiculously fast, propelling it through the bubbles, making Stu laugh. It seemed to erase everything for Ty, as he smiled and laughed with Stu, lifting the duck to do it again.

"Stu, are you getting warm?"

"Yeah!" he giggled, reaching for the duck, as Ty made himself a bubble-beard, both turning their attention away from their mother.

She watched a moment longer and turned to find her mother coming through the doorway with fresh towels. Her mother handed her a mug of hot chocolate and gestured for Chelsea to take one of the towels. "Maybe this will help Kyle warm up on the inside. Go. Be with him, honey. He needs you," she said, her brown eyes filled with compassion. "I'll sit with the boys. They're fine."

Chelsea took the towel and the mug and dutifully went back upstairs. Kyle had submerged and risen, his hair slicked back, and the washcloth pressed around his neck as he lay still in the bubbles. His eyebrow arced when he saw her.

"How are the boys?"

"Ty is in the tub with Stu. They're revisiting the days of rubber duckies and motorboats. They'll be totally waterlogged when they're through. Mom is sitting with them."

"Join me," he said softly, making her insides surge. She gazed at him a moment; the look on his face gave her no choice but to twist the lock on the door, and lift her sweater over her head. Her jeans, panties, and socks joined the sweater in a pile on the floor, as she let her bra fall on top of the heap. He watched as she twisted her hair into a knot, securing it with a hair tie she found next to the sink, and climbed in the tub, sitting down opposite him. She picked up her feet and placed them on either side of his hips, sinking to her chest in the bubbles.

He sighed contentedly, reaching for her hands. "You're so warm. Come closer," he whispered, pulling her forward until her chest was against his, feeling the delight of skin-to-skin contact with him. His hands slipped along her back, coming to rest on the curves of her hips. She felt his lips plant a slow kiss in her hair.

"You do know that not everyone can do this, right?" she asked, referring to her posture.

"Yes, I do, and I thank God everyday for your amazing flexibility, among other things."

She snickered, kissing his chest, feeling warmth returning to his body. "What other things?"

"Your wisdom, for one. I wish I'd listened to you when we'd talked about Stu's impulsiveness before. It seems that you and Miss Payne may have been onto something that I couldn't bring myself to admit…until tonight, that is." She was silent and let him continue when he was ready. "Maybe there is more to his difficulty than being just 'all boy.' Ty doesn't do the things he does. Fearlessness is not necessarily a virtue….Tonight I was so scared to think that we'd lost him. I can't deal with the thought of losing any of you."

"But you saved him, Kyle. You went in after him and you saved him." She looked into his face and saw the doubt in his eyes.

"What if it hadn't gone that way? What if I'd failed?" He sighed, and pulled her closer.

"It wasn't supposed to happen like that," she said, hoping her words would convince herself as well as him.

"There's nothing…nothing more important than you and the boys, Chels. If we need to take him to the doctor and get him checked out, then let's do it. Make the appointment, okay? I'm with you one hundred percent on this, all right?"

"Okay," she said, stroking his chest as he lifted her chin to kiss her. "I love you," she said, allowing him to engulf her in his arms, burying his face in the curve of her neck.

The boys decided to sleep together in the guest bedroom at home, with Foscoe on the floor beside the bed. By eleven o'clock, Chelsea had fallen asleep between them, so Kyle padded quietly upstairs to call his mother and Stacie and Tyson to wish them a Happy New Year. He wanted to give them the accident report firsthand. His mother would be freaking out when she heard, so she might as well hear it from him. Bed and sleep could not come quickly enough tonight, but he wondered whether he'd actually sleep with all that had happened. After ending his call with Tyson, he set the phone on the coffee table, staring at it, listening to Foscoe's soft snoring from downstairs. His gaze drifted to the fireplace, and the mantle, where four ceramic angels stood in the center. The one that resembled Chelsea was the first one he'd had; a handcrafted gift from her mother on their first Christmas together back in high school. She'd made the one of him for their wedding, and the ones of the twins when they were born. He'd often wondered how long they'd all live together as the four of them. Death was what he knew, but he'd tried to dispel the notion that death was what you expected. Life was what he expected; life together for all four of them for a very long time. And how close they'd come tonight to meeting his old expectations. He sighed and ran both hands through his hair, saying one more silent prayer of thanks. Soft footsteps sounded on the steps, too small for Chelsea's, and when he turned, it was Ty's head that appeared silhouetted in the lamplight beside him on the sofa.

"Hey, buddy. Can't sleep?"

Ty shook his head with that look of his; the look that meant they were about to have a profound conversation. "Is it New Year's yet?"

"Not for another hour. What's on your mind? You must've been plenty scared tonight. I know I was," he said, reaching out to let Ty snuggle next to him on the sofa.

Ty nodded. "Stu and I used to dream about stuff like that happening all the time. It's weird. We used to have the same dreams at the same time. You and Mom dying and all." Kyle understood that. He'd remembered dreaming those kinds of dreams himself when he was a kid. Just when you realized that people wouldn't live forever....But for his twins, how odd it would be to be on the same wavelength all the time that way. Ty was quiet a moment, as Kyle massaged his head. Then he said, "What did you mean tonight when Stu fell through the ice?"

"What?"

"You said, *no, not Stu*....Why did you say that?" Ty asked quietly, his eyes holding Kyle's with reservation.

Kyle exhaled slowly, letting his fingers rest on Ty's head, as he searched for the words to explain the most complex feelings he'd ever had. How was an eight-year-old supposed to understand? Kyle rubbed his hand across his chin and sighed again. How could he promise his son that none of them would ever die? He looked straight at Ty.

"You know that your grandfather, my father, was named Stuart. After he died, it took me a very long time to understand what he was like, and why he did some of the things he did."

"Did he do bad things?"

"He made some bad choices. Choices he couldn't live with."

"Like Stu does."

"Yeah. You could say that. Stu's hardheaded just like my dad was. It took me a long time after he'd died to love him…like the way I love you and your mom, and Stu. My dad and I didn't know each other very well, but I think he loved me too; he just wasn't good at saying it, so I wasn't sure for a long time. Anyway, when you boys were born, Mommy and I wanted to name you after Tyson, because we love him so much, and we wanted to name Stu after my dad…."

"Because you loved him, too?"

"Yes. But we worried about it because he had died."

"But people name their kids after people who have died all the time," Ty said, making Kyle feel as though he were talking to another adult.

"You're right, but with my father it was different."

"Why?"

Kyle hesitated. They'd never told the boys about his father's suicide. They'd struggled with how to tell them, wondering how old they'd need to be so they could understand.

"Your grandfather took his own life...so we thought it might be a bad thing to do, to name Stu after him, but then we decided it was a way to make the best part of him live on, you know?"

"So, now you think it was bad karma, after all?"

"You know about *karma*?"

"Dad, I wasn't born yesterday," Ty said indulgently. No, he wasn't. And he was one who read everything he could get his hands on, so why did his knowledge continue to surprise Kyle? And he didn't seem surprised to hear this story.

"Did you know about my father, taking his life?"

"Yeah. I've heard Clammaw talking about it when she thought I didn't hear. And how freaked out she is that Abigail is just like Desiree."

The boy had missed nothing. How had he dealt with all of this in his young life?

"Does Stu know, too?"

"I don't know. I didn't tell him what I'd heard. I thought it would hurt his feelings. It is kinda bad karma, especially now. That makes me feel better though. That wasn't what I thought you meant."

It dawned on Kyle like a slap in the face what Ty must have thought. "Come here," he said. He pulled him close and hugged his son, kissing the top of his head. Ty must have thought Kyle meant that he wished it had been *him* and not Stu who had fallen in tonight. That's what was bothering him. As hard as they tried not to favor one son over the other one, Ty had worried that he wasn't the favorite. It was the same thing Kyle had done with his own father, without the competition of an identical twin. *How had he let this happen?*

"Did you think I'd have preferred it if *you'd* been the one to fall in and not Stu?" Ty shrugged almost imperceptibly, but Kyle felt his arms tighten around his torso. "That wasn't what I meant at all. Your mom and I have tried so hard not to let bad things happen to either of you. You seem to make the best choices and you're more like your Uncle Ty. Stu has been more reckless, like my father, but we never intended to curse him because of the name we gave him. That's all I meant tonight, Ty. That's all it was. We love you and Stu the same. And you know I would have jumped in after you too, boy. Sweet boy," he said, stroking his hair. "I love you, son."

"I love you, too, Dad."

Kyle sighed, letting his hand rest on Ty's hair. "It's time for bed, okay?" He lifted him off the sofa, as if to carry him, but Ty wriggled his way to a standing position and hugged him before walking down the stairs on his own volition, with Kyle following him. Chelsea lay asleep beside Stu, her hands folded across her chest.

"Mom looks like a princess, doesn't she? You should carry her upstairs," he whispered, grinning at Kyle, as he pulled the covers off of his mother and let Kyle scoop her up out of their bed. She woke, protesting, and made him put her down. Stu did not move. They tucked Ty in the bed with him and kissed him good night.

"Happy New Year, buddy," Kyle whispered to Ty, giving him a wink and one more kiss.

Chapter 18

LEAVING

In the weeks to come, Kyle concentrated on his family. Chelsea and he called each other daily at work to check in, something they hadn't often done before, but he felt solidified talking to her in the middle of the day that way. She was still his touchstone. He spent a couple of evenings each week going to the gym, while she took the time on Thursday evenings to hold dance rehearsals when he stayed home with the boys. They'd taken on homework with a new resolve, and with the help Stu was getting at school, paired with the new medicine the doctor had prescribed, his attitude and work had improved remarkably.

The office was his place of work only until the day was done when he could bolt and head for the next part of the day. Meetings with Lynn Schiffman and Frank and Elise were going well, but the requirements of commercial property development were slow and tedious, making the building process creep along without his usual control. The hotel Lynn had envisioned would be a green, sustainable project, state of the art in every way. The Foxfire Inn would offer first class accommodations as well as a five star restaurant, spa, and conference center, which would appeal to the university and the hospital, both of which were growing rapidly. It was the first project in a long time in which Kyle had been able to lose himself creatively, and he continued to enjoy working with Lynn, who trusted his advice implicitly. She had amazing ideas of her own, and having spent her career in the hotel business, her perspective was invaluable. They would have a screaming success on their hands, which would do wonders for Mountaineer Builders' reputation.

Elise set a cup of coffee on his desk. He was so wrapped up in his current drawing that he hardly noticed until she cleared her throat.

"Oh…hey! Thanks. I didn't hear you come in. You don't have to bring me coffee."

"I know. It was the end of the pot, and I didn't want it to turn to mud. Besides, you should take a break." As she turned to leave, he tried to think of something to say to her. At this point in the project, she had little to do and was probably getting bored furniture shopping online without the specs for the rooms she'd be designing. He'd broken his concentration anyway, so he sat back and took the cup of coffee. His eyes were dry from staring at the drafting table.

"Thanks. I should take a break. I'm getting stiff sitting here."

She smiled, the river eyes lighting up at the chance of adult interaction. "Gym night?" she asked, noticing his bag on the floor.

"Yeah. Glen and I are going to work out if he doesn't get called in."

"So, he's a full-fledged detective now, right?"

"Yes, he is." The silent space was devoted to Michael, whom they no longer discussed, and Kyle wondered whether Marcus was still keeping in touch with Elise, but it was not his business. Elise had heard about the accident with Stu and had avoided asking him much about it, realizing how upset he'd been, and how he'd tucked inside himself, burying himself in work. He figured that this was the way they were supposed to interact, finally, as professionals in an office, nothing more. He was glad that Chelsea and Elise were on good terms.

"What have you been working on today?" he asked.

"Light and bathroom fixtures for Sara Lynn Hayes. This is the second go-around on her kitchen lighting, so hopefully this will be it." He nodded, thinking that Frank was at the Hayes property right now, overseeing the electricians today for the initial wiring.

"Sara Lynn turned out to be very hard to please, didn't she?"

"Yes, she did. I'm glad the roads thawed so we can get inside and get going on their house. I'll be glad to be done with this one."

"Me too. As long as the trucks can get up their road, let's keep it moving."

"Amen." She peeked over his shoulder at the table to see what he was working on.

"Take a look," he said, backing his chair away so she could see.

"Nice," she murmured.

He took another sip of his coffee and stood up. She watched him stretch, and went back to her office as he emptied his cup, washing it out at the sink, where she'd cleaned out the pot. He heard her singing along to her music, this time, a spunky country ballad, called "Post Cards From Paris," about a woman falling for a man she shouldn't. He laughed to himself. At least Elise's music was brightening up. Chelsea liked that song, too. He had listened to his share of country music lately, thanks to both of them, and his boys. Was liking old rock 'n roll dating him that much? *Such an old man*, he thought glumly. He caught her staring, making him wonder whether she was dating anyone, and then let the thought go. Surely, there were plenty of young men in the mountains who would clamber for her attentions.

As cold as November and December had been, February was proving to be warmer than usual. It had not snowed since early January, which was excellent for their business. Bruce and Sara Lynn might get into their cabin early if all went as scheduled. Frank was in the office on a Thursday morning, as the three of them arrived at once and began getting down to work. Kyle sat at his computer, checking emails and planning his day when Frank came in and closed the door. Kyle looked up as Frank sat down in one of the chairs across from his desk, sliding a piece of paper toward him.

"What do you know about this?" Frank asked, his voice low, the seriousness in his eyes unmistakable.

Kyle glanced down and took the letter, reading to himself.

Dear Frank and Kyle,

It is with much regret that I offer my resignation from Mountaineer Builders, effective one month from today.

He looked up at Frank with brows cocked in surprise. Frank's fingers drummed the chair's arm as he sat with his jaw clamped in his other hand.

After much careful consideration, I have decided to accept an offer from my previous employer in Charlotte, Tarleton Designs. The close proximity with my parents will be helpful to me in the care of my daughter, and the offer Tarleton has presented is too lucrative for me to ignore. I believe, based on working there before, that the Charlotte area may be more productive over the long term, and I must go where there is more work in my future.

I appreciate everything both of you have done for me during my time at Mountaineer Builders. I believe we made an excellent team on the projects we have done together, and I have grown professionally as a result. I will continue to work with you on the Foxfire project until its completion, if that is what you desire. Mr. Tarleton was specific in allowing me to take the time necessary to fulfill my obligations to you in that regard.

Respectfully,

Elise Masters

Kyle stared at Frank, stunned at the words he'd just read. He shook his head.

"This is news to me. You didn't know either?"

"*Hell*, no. Do you have anything to do with this?" Frank asked, eyes measuring Kyle's reaction.

Kyle was immediately defensive and blown away that Frank would ask this kind of a question.

"*Hell, no*," he answered. "What are you asking me?"

"You two are tight," he said, leveling his gaze at Kyle. "Have you talked to her?"

"No. And we're not that tight. Have you…talked to her?"

"Nope. This was on my desk this morning. I'm assuming she left it here before she left last night."

This was typical Frank; avoid the people conflicts at all costs and dump it in Kyle's lap. But still, he implied there was a personal nature to this problem, and Kyle didn't like it. Kyle backed his chair away from the desk, but stopped. "I know we get slow in the winter, but the hotel is a huge deal. I can't believe she'd just…walk away in the middle of this."

"She says in the letter that she'll finish it, but that will be pretty inconvenient, and it could drag on forever."

Kyle popped a sigh from his lips, feeling hot air on his chin. He raised his hands and let them fall.

"Okay, I'll go see what's going on," he said, standing and leaving his office as Frank went into his and closed the door.

Soft lamplight fell from Elise's office door, a warm glow, greeting whoever came inside, making the ambience noticeable before even entering her space; so like her to contrive such a feeling. He heard Adele singing softly in the background while Elise typed away on her computer.

Depressing. Eventually, he brought his hand up to knock on her door, the letter still in his other hand.

"Come on in," she said, meeting his eyes as he entered. She turned down the music, took a deep breath, and said, "Sit down," gesturing to a chair, but he took a seat on the edge of her desk instead.

He shook his head. "You're really doing this?" he asked, incredulously, holding up her letter, seeing the unease on her face at once.

"Yes. I'm sorry this is coming as a shock, but I've been thinking about it for a while."

He stared at her, knowing she was uncomfortable, but trying to find some shred of understanding in her expression.

"Shock doesn't quite cover it." They were silent a moment. Then he spoke. "Does this have anything to do with Michael Gilmer?"

"No."

"Because you said you wouldn't let him run you off. You promised me that."

She closed her eyes and turned away. "Yes. I know I did. And it has nothing to do with Michael or Marcus or any of that."

"So, is this about money? Did Tarleton come to you with more money? Elise, you're the best designer we've had. We can give you whatever you want."

"No, you can't."

"Then tell me what it's about."

"If I did, you'd have to fire me," she said, leveling her river eyes at him and leaning across the desk onto her elbows.

"For…?"

"Oh, God, Kyle…" she said, shoving her fingers into her hair. And then he got it. *Sexual harassment.*

"What are you saying?"

"You can't give me what I need, Kyle. I didn't want this to happen, but I won't let myself be another Emily Hayes," she said, her face burning.

"What?"

"You're so confused. I knew it would be this way."

"You went to Tarleton."

"Yes. I've been keeping in touch with my friend there. She said another one of the designers is moving. Her husband got a job in Texas and they're leaving in a month. So I called Ed…" she said, lifting her hand.

"We can make this work out."

"No, we can't, Kyle. I can't do this anymore. I can't work with you. I'll finish the Foxfire, but I can't be around you. I'm so sorry."

He searched for what to say. "No. I'm sorry. Did I do anything…?"

She laughed, "*Yes*. You did everything….You were just being *you* and you're just…everything I want. But I can't have you."

"Elise…"

"Don't say it. I've been wrong to let myself get so tangled up in you. It was *so* wrong. I didn't plan on needing you, but you let me. You told me one time that I deserved devotion. I want devotion from someone like you. I want a forever man, like the song you're always playing, but it can't be you. You belong to Chelsea and you always will. So I have to leave."

They stared at each other.

"I don't know what to say."

"*I know*. It couldn't be any more awkward, but at least now you know."

"When…?"

"That day in the kitchen. I mean, the first day I walked in here, I was so floored and intimidated by you. But that day in the kitchen, when I thought you were going to kiss me, that totally did me in." She looked distraught. It was all his fault. He had started it.

He shook his head. "I'm sorry. This was my fault. I was wrong. Yeah, that day, I was way out of line."

"No, I was in it, too. Something about you has always compelled me to spill everything. That day though, it just happened."

"Yeah. No. It didn't happen. I mean…."

"What? You felt it, too. I know you did."

"Yes. There was a time when I was caught up in you, too, I have to admit. It was wrong, and I knew it, and I backed off. But now…what are we supposed to do? We work so well together. Frank is so pissed right now. Can we not just…move on?"

"*No.* Do you know how hard it is for me to come in here every day and be near you? You've ruined me. I can't even…be here." Her hands were shaking. *Was she drunk? Was he drunk?* How could they even say all this?

He sighed and ran a hand through his hair, placing his hands on his hips. "How are we going to finish the hotel then?"

"We can work online. I'll come up here when I need to. It can be done. It will be better this way."

He looked at her, watching her raise her chin, pulling together all the poise she could muster.

"Don't tell Frank all about this, please. It's bad enough that you know. Just say that Ed Tarleton offered me tons of money and I took it."

"Did he? Can you live off of what he'll pay you in Charlotte?"

She stiffened. "I can, in Elizabeth. Lydia and I will be fine. I've already looked into a place for us there. And my parents are thrilled to have us close by again." He knew the neighborhood she'd referred to. At least she wasn't moving back in with her parents. She'd need privacy whenever it was time to date again. "This is all going to be for the best, Kyle. Please don't be angry. Just let me go. I'll make this work. I promise. I won't let you down."

He collected his words, then said, "You'll find your forever man, Elise. You and Lydia deserve it. It will happen. But promise me, you'll put yourself out there. Stop hiding behind Lydia."

Tears welled in her eyes. "How am I supposed to do that?"

"You did it with me. Find him, Elise. You can make it happen. You can do anything. I want you to be happy."

"I didn't want this, Kyle. I'm so sorry," she whispered, searching his eyes for forgiveness.

"Me too, Elise. Me too."

It was after nine o'clock when they got home from the science fair that night. Chelsea had met them at the school gymnasium after her dance rehearsal. Ty had won an honorable mention from the judges, and Stu's project had earned several favorable comments from the spectators, especially from a girl in his class named Amber, who'd written *two* comments. Ty had razzed him about it on the way home in Kyle's car, and Stu had taken it proudly.

The boys had skipped baths and gone directly to bed. Chelsea was leaving again for another long weekend. The previous weekend she had gone with her parents to South Carolina to move Grandmother into a new retirement center in their area, putting her much closer to home. Liz would have easier access and could spend more time with her mother. Their situation had improved. It seemed the less Grandmother remembered, the more civil she'd become, creating more conflicting feelings for Liz, but it did make it easier to care for her that way. Now, Chelsea was repacking her suitcase for the following day when she'd leave for Charley's house in Wilmington. Kitty, her fifteen-year-old niece, was dancing in *Giselle*, and Chelsea was honored that her presence had been requested. The weather forecast was clear with temperatures in the low forties, so Kyle had relaxed about her traveling. February weather in

North Carolina could mean anything. The evening had been so hectic they hadn't had a chance to talk. So far she hadn't noticed his distraction.

After he'd locked up for the night and brushed his teeth, he sat at the foot of their bed watching her pack. She seemed so happy. Tired but happy. And he was about to ruin it.

"Which dress, the black or the red one?" she asked, holding up two dresses on hangers for him to choose from.

"Definitely the black," he said, forcing a smile. She noticed.

"What's wrong? I haven't even asked about your day," she said.

He sighed, "Elise is leaving. She resigned today."

"*What?*" she looked perplexed, tossing the dresses aside and tightening her robe. She closed and zipped the suitcase.

He cast his eyes about the room, searching for the right words. "She's going back to Charlotte, to her old job," he said, picking at the rip in the knee of his jeans.

"*Why?*"

"Her old company decided to rehire her. She's been keeping in touch with them. Someone was leaving and…."

She studied his face. "But right in the middle of Lynn's hotel build? Are you kidding me? Why would she leave you and Frank now?"

"The timing was right…for her," he said, but she'd picked up on something. "She'll be here for another month."

"No, please don't do this to me now," she murmured, closing her eyes, a hand going to her head.

"What?"

"She's in love with you, isn't she?" Chelsea said, her eyes squinting with sudden realization.

"Chelsea....She's leaving to be closer to her parents. They can help her with Lydia. She'll make good money, and there will be more business in Charlotte."

They locked eyes for several moments before she spoke. "I thought we were past all of this."

"We *are*. There's nothing...."

"I know. But, she has feelings for you?"

He shrugged. "She's ready to move on, Chels. I can't speak for her."

She gazed at him, knowing there was more, knowing he wouldn't tell her.

"You *know* I love you," he said firmly, reaching for her hand, making her look at him. "You *know* it's us and the boys. This will all be for the best."

She sighed, crumpling onto the bed, folding the black dress over her arm.

"I'm sorry, Kyle. I didn't think Elise would let her feelings interfere with her work. She was strong that way."

"You knew?"

A slow smile formed on her mouth as she looked at him with a sparkle he did not expect to see. "Of course I knew. She couldn't hide the way she felt from me. I'm used to looking for this sort of thing, you know? But I thought she could handle it. *You* were handling it."

"You knew that, too?"

"Yes, I did. But Elise was good for the company. What's going to happen now, with the hotel?"

"Tarleton has given her permission to continue the project with us until it's completed. We'll work online, and she'll come up here when she needs to. Lynn's doing a lot of it, commissioning some local artists and that sort of thing. It will be all right."

She inhaled, glancing at their hands. He stroked his thumb in a circle around the back of her hand.

"What will you and Frank do in the meantime?"

"Faith wants to come back. She's going crazy with nothing to do. Retirement was *not* agreeing with her after all." They laughed. He gazed at her, feeling the bond they'd always had growing a little stronger. There was certainly something to be said for women's intuition. His wife was amazing.

She looked away and took the black dress to the closet, slipping it into a garment bag.

"Would you mind taking my suitcase out to the kitchen?" she asked, and followed him out of the bedroom. She hung the dress on a hook beside their jackets.

He turned and caught her in the moonlight filtering through the door's window. "Damn, you're beautiful!" he whispered. "I'm going to miss you." He slid his hand across her cheek, his fingers ending in her hair. He pulled her close and breathed in her sweet scent—the scent of home. He kissed her tenderly and wrapped his arms around her. "I love you so much."

He felt her hands on his back as she allowed him to hold her for several moments, but then she drew away, searching his face with those incredible aquamarine eyes. They filled with tears and his heart sank, wondering what was wrong. And then she smiled up at him.

"That night in the bathtub, after Stu fell through the ice?"

"Yes…?"

"I'm pregnant."

Chapter 19

THREE YEARS LATER

Chelsea stood on the stone terrace of her parents' house, letting the warm sunshine bathe her face. What a perfect day for a wedding. Bri and Jon-o couldn't have placed a better order, her mother had said over their morning coffee. A slight breeze stirred the scent of Kitty's heirloom roses, making Chelsea smile. Even Kitty couldn't stay away today. Walking to the terrace's edge, she could see the house. Nestled at the foot of the Christmas trees and across the lake from the vineyard, her father had picked the most beautiful of locations for their home. It still smelled new and would smell that way for a long time, Kyle said. She'd never lived in a new house that she could remember.

"There you are!" Abby's voice came from behind her, the familiar sound of the screen door banging shut.

"Hey! I was just enjoying the view."

"I know, what a great day, right? You know, this house would be a great place for a wedding!"

"Oh, don't start!"

Abby laughed. "One day I know you're going to turn this place into a bed and breakfast, but it will be on your own terms and in your own time. And I want to run it, of course."

"Yeah. Maybe when Elizabeth goes off to college and I have loads of free time. But you have the winery now that Bri is gone, so I'll have the B and B all to myself."

"You'll be retired by then and I'll still be plugging away, still trying to pay for three kids in college!" she laughed. "But we could work the venues together."

"That would be fun. I don't know when we'll ever convince Mom and Dad to leave this place, but their new home is ready and waiting," Chelsea said, thinking about the downstairs in-law suite in their new house, complete with a private entrance and an elevator. Kyle had thought of everything.

"What time is Kyle bringing Elizabeth over? The bridesmaids' luncheon is going to start in almost an hour."

"I'm looking for him now. I just talked to him on the phone and he was going to wake her from her nap. I don't know how she could possibly sleep over there with all those men in the house." The men in the wedding party were being housed at their place, while all the girls had bunked at Liz and Tom's for the night. Becky had a houseful of her own relatives and was grateful to have the rest of them out of her hair. The brunch was being set up in the sun room, and after they had all dressed, the parties would converge for the wedding at the winery, a fitting place, considering Bri had been the original manager years ago. Abby had done a wonderful job coordinating the whole affair, and the weather was cooperating beautifully.

"Does he miss the cabin?" Abby asked wistfully.

"No," she smiled. "He likes to go fishing with the boys, but he seems happier to be away. Once Elizabeth came, he wanted us to have a place we could call our own. I think I miss it more than he does though."

Abby looked out across the lake. "Oh! There they are now. Oh…look at them. He's so cute with her! What are they doing?"

Chelsea shaded her eyes with her hand so she could see. Kyle walked slowly down the drive and into the road leading up to the house as their daughter toddled along beside him. He stopped and held two-year-old Elizabeth's tiny hand in his, with her dress for the wedding in a plastic bag draped over his shoulder. They were looking at something on the ground, and she was bent over at the waist, her gingery curls moving softly in the breeze. Her hand was like a tiny star as she held it out and pointed at the ground. He looked too, rearranging the dress so he could squat and watch as a turtle made its way across the road in front of them. She could hear Elizabeth's giggle across the lake and Kyle's laughter in return. They watched until the turtle had made it safely into the grass, and then he scooped her up in his arm and looked up, waving at them.

"He has his hands full. Can you believe I forgot to bring her dress this morning?"

"I'm surprised you didn't bring *her*."

"Kyle wouldn't let me. He's very attached, you know. He didn't want her to be too much out of her element. I had no idea how much he really wanted a little girl until she was finally here. And the twins dote on her like she's a little princess."

"Well, she *is* a princess!"

"No. I don't ever want anyone saying that about her."

"Honey, as beautiful as she is, you won't be able to control any of that. Men will be lying down at her feet and throwing money at her!"

"Oh, God! Stop. You're killing my Mommy buzz, right now. I just want a few innocent years with her when I can dress her in lavender smocked dresses and let her play with mud pies. I don't want her to be spoiled."

"Spoiling her definitely won't be your job."

Chelsea shook her head, resigned, knowing her friend was probably right. "I'll go get her and be right back."

"Okay. Kyle's not allowed anywhere near this house. Tell him the wedding planner said so."

"Yes, ma'am!" She laughed and started down the gravel road to meet her family.

"Good morning…again," Kyle said, grinning at her, the lines she loved creasing the edges of his smile.

"Mommy!" Elizabeth cried, hopping into Chelsea's arms when she reached down for her daughter. She smelled sweet, fresh from her bath, her curls still damp at the ends.

"Hi, sweetie-pie! You bathed her?"

He shrugged. "What else was I going to do down there? All those guys in the house sitting around the TV watching fishing shows. It's boring as hell. No, seriously, your dad's rustling up a big breakfast and everybody's just getting up. I promise, we'll get it all cleaned up before you come home."

She narrowed her eyes at him as Elizabeth's chubby little arms circled her neck. The little girl planted a wet kiss on her mother's cheek with a pop that made her laugh. Chelsea reached for the dress, a creamy chiffon sleeveless frock with a salmon colored sash that looked lovely on her daughter, but Kyle held out an envelope.

"Here, before you take the dress, I want you to see this. It came in the mail this morning," he said, a reserved expression on his face.

She looked at the strong and loopy script on the envelope, addressed to both of them, and noted the postmark. "Who do we know in Spain?" She did not recognize the name on the return address.

"Open it," he urged.

As she removed the card depicting Picasso's *Hand with Flowers*, a photograph slipped out. In the picture were four people, a man and woman and two girls, dressed in wedding attire, posing on a beach. She peered at the bride.

"Elise?"

He nodded. "Yes. She married the doctor from Duke in Costa Brava."

"*Oh!* Yes, she did! What a nice picture. He was the one they met in the pediatric unit when she took Lydia there for her orthopedic check-up a couple of years ago? We ran into them at the restaurant that time we were in Charlotte with your grandparents."

"That's right. His wife had died and he had a little girl, too. She wrote a note."

Chelsea opened the card and read aloud:

Dear Kyle and Chelsea,

Adam and I tied the knot two weeks ago in Costa Brava. Lydia and Sophie are almost like sisters. Thanks for your support and friendship over the years. Come and visit us if you're ever in Durham.

Best wishes,

Elise

"That's really sweet. I'll bet she didn't send out many of these. Hmm. I guess when you know, you know, right?"

"That's what I think," he said, circling his arm around her and kissing her soundly on the lips.

"It's ironic that her card came today, on Bri's wedding day."

"It's a big day; that's for sure. And this little lady has a *very* important job to do today," he said, giving Elizabeth a tickle on her tummy, sending her into a fit of giggles.

"That's right. Not just *anyone* gets to lay the pink rose on Kitty's chair, Elizabeth."

Elizabeth's aquamarine eyes were bright with laughter as Chelsea tucked a curl behind her ear. *Oh, to have that baby skin again!*

"Kitty, Kitty!" she squealed and Kyle grinned at her.

"Yes, Kitty, Kitty," said Chelsea, thinking of the picture of her grandmother that her mother had shown the boys and Elizabeth the night before.

"I'm the flower girl!" she said with perfect diction, making her parents laugh.

"Yes, you are!" murmured Chelsea, nuzzling her daughter's soft cheek.

"Well, I guess I'd better get back to the dude ranch. I heard I'm not wanted here until we meet at the winery," Kyle said, reluctantly turning to go after giving Elizabeth's fingers a kiss. "I'll see you lovely ladies later." She smiled, suddenly remembering her conversation with Stacie on the beach three years ago. *He's one of the best people I know.* He handed her the dress and started to walk away, hands shoved in the back pockets of his jeans. Another thought tugged at her as she arranged the card with the hanger so she could carry it all.

"Hey…are you happy for her?" Chelsea asked, shifting Elizabeth to a more comfortable position on her hip.

He stopped and turned. "Yeah, I am. She deserves it. But I'm happier for us." He looked away for a moment and then tilted his head, returning his gaze to linger on her and Elizabeth as her tiny fingers entwined in Chelsea's hair. His eyes met hers tentatively, the breeze stirring his hair. He looked so young then; the boy she'd fallen in love with half a lifetime ago. "It's as perfect as it gets, isn't it?"

She smiled at him, not wanting him to leave, feeling her own stirring inside. "Yes, it is." She sighed contentedly, and watched her forever man turn and walk down the road toward home.

Three Gifts - Book Three

"There is a Celtic saying that heaven and earth are only three feet apart, but in the thin places, the distance is even smaller."

"Throughout *Three Gifts*, you will be rooting for Chelsea and Kyle, young marrieds so appealing, yet real that you'll wish you could clone them. They settle in the mountains, near Boone, North Carolina, and when they are faced with tragedies, they handle them with courage and grace. Even those oh-so-human doubts and fears that threaten occasionally to swamp them are banished through humor and the abiding love that sustains them. This is a journey of hope, faith, and love that you'll want to share with them."

**~Nancy Gotter Gates, author of
the *Tommi Poag* and *Emma Daniel* mysteries,
and women's fiction *Sand Castles* and *Life Studies***

Introducing a new, stand-alone novel, apart from the Kyle and Chelsea series, The Nest...

"Mary Flinn realistically captures the ideals of an empty nest filled with rekindling passions of soon-to-retire Cherie and her rock-and-roll-loving husband Dave—then flips it all over when Hope, the jilted daughter, returns to the nest to heal her broken heart. Between her mother's comical hot flashes that only women of a certain age could appreciate, the loss of her laid-back father's sales job, and the good news-bad news of other family members' lives, can Hope find the courage to spread her wings and leave the nest again? Flinn's deft handling of story-telling through both Cherie and Hope's voices will send readers on a tremendously satisfying and wild flight back to *The Nest*."

**~Laura S. Wharton, author of the award-winning novels
Leaving Lukens, The Pirate's Bastard, and others**

About the Author

A native of North Carolina, award-winning author Mary Flinn long ago fell in love with her state's mountains and its coast, creating the backdrops for her series of novels, *The One*, *Second Time's a Charm*, *Three Gifts*, and *A Forever Man*. With degrees from both the University of North Carolina at Greensboro and East Carolina University, Flinn has retired from her first career as a speech pathologist in the NC public schools that began in 1981. Writing a novel had always been a dream for Flinn, who began crafting the pages of *The One*, when her younger daughter left for college at Appalachian State University in 2009. The characters in this book continued to call to her, wanting more of their story told, which bred the next three books in the series.

Flinn has recently been the recipient of the Reader Views Literary Awards 2012 Reviewers' Choice honorable mention in the romance category for *A Forever Man*. First Place Award for Romance Novel in the Reader Views 2011 Literary Book Awards, as well as the Pacific Book Review Best Romance Novel of 2011 went to *Three Gifts*. *Second Time's a Charm*, also released in 2011, won an Honorable Mention in the Reader Views Literary Awards.

Mary Flinn lives in Summerfield, North Carolina with her husband, and near her two adult daughters.

The Nest is her fifth novel.

www.TheOneNovel.com